D1505417

Bing Crosby's Last Song

ALSO BY LESTER GORAN

NOVELS

The Paratrooper of Mechanic Avenue
Maria Light
The Candy Butcher's Farewell
The Stranger in the Snow
The Demon in the Sun Parlor
The Keeper of Secrets
Mrs. Beautiful

SHORT-STORY COLLECTIONS

Tales from the Irish Club
She Loved Me Once and Other Stories

MEMOIR

The Bright Streets of Surfside:
The Memoir of a Friendship with Isaac Bashevis Singer

Bing Crosby's Last Song

LESTER GORAN

PICADOR USA ❧ NEW YORK

BING CROSBY'S LAST SONG. Copyright © 1998 by
Lester Goran. All rights reserved. Printed in the
United States of America. No part of this book may
be used or reproduced in any manner whatsoever
without written permission except in the case of brief
quotations embodied in critical articles or reviews. For
information, address Picador USA, 175 Fifth Avenue,
New York, N.Y. 10010.

Picador® is a registered trademark and is used by St.
Martin's Press under license from Pan Books Limited.

Design by Nancy Resnick

Library of Congress Cataloging-in-Publication Data

Goran, Lester.
    Bing Crosby's last song / Lester Goran. — 1st ed.
        p.   cm.
    ISBN 0-312-19540-0
    I. Title.
    PS3557.063B56   1998
    813'.54—dc21   98-19394
                                              CIP

First Picador USA Edition: October 1998

10   9   8   7   6   5   4   3   2   1

For Deedee

In "The Parochial Story of Ireland"
(1814) it is recorded how the storytellers used to gather together on a
wild evening and tell their tales. And
if any had a different version from
the others, they would all recite theirs
and vote and the man who had varied
would have to abide by their verdict.
In this way stories have been handed
down with great accuracy.

W. B. YEATS

PART ONE

Revelations, 1968

One

On a fine spring day in 1968, Daly Racklin, six months short of fifty, was told by a doctor at the Montefiore Hospital in Pittsburgh that he had less than a year to live. He had come to be reassured that the occasional ringing in his ears, the tightness in his chest, and the shortness of breath was an occasion of vodka and tonic and a lack of exercise. Instead, he was solemnly informed that the arteries leading to his heart were shot and his heart itself beat irregularly. As it happened, the doctor explained, in a few years' time, given the research of a certain physician in South Africa, the probability was there might be something done to save him, but for now it was put your feet up and wait for the second stage of eternity.

Daly shook hands with the physician, his grip firm, but his heart, true to itself, signaling to the world his blind panic in his dangerously racing pulse.

Described frequently as a lawyer of eloquent speech and subtle thought, Daly remarked to himself for the record, alone on the elevator down: "Casey Jones, mounted to the cabin, took the farewell journey to the promised land."

He called from the telephone in the hospital lobby first Jessie O'Brien, the one person who might tell him best how to pull himself together around the news, neither awkwardly joking nor crushing him with the seriousness of his situation. Her gift for saying things truthfully and well was what kept him attached to her, no matter his doubts on where they were going as man and woman.

Her phone rang ten times, and there was no answer.

He sought a second opinion on the all-too-soon prospects for his last rites, and that took him to Coyne's Bar and Grill, on Oakland Avenue, where his physician of faith and incidental healing, Richard I. Pierce, M.D., known widely as R.I.P., usually sat in a back booth from three in the afternoon until eleven at night.

Doc Rest in Peace did not officially practice medicine. He had not for more than twenty years. But he showed up responsibly at any of the neighborhood's hospitals at the first announcement of an old friend's illness, to provide comfort in words of one syllable, or two at most. If all went well in his diagnosis, he said, "Have a drink, you'll be fine." In situations more precarious, he said, "Have a drink, on me, Senator, do you no harm at this point." He dispensed advice on medicine and interpretations of the verities from the oval bar at Lasek's, and the dark corners of Coyne's, Edward's, the University Grill, or Frankie Gustine's, wherever the day's winds took him.

On thinking it over, Daly had been surprised he had lived as long as he had. If the X rays had been read correctly, from the moment the doctor at the Montefiore Hospital had shrugged, turned his eyes to the ceiling for prophecy, and asked, "Do you have a history of heart disease in your family?" he knew he would be buried for eternity before the gentle rains of the next springtime.

"No, no heart disease in our family that I know."

"How old was your father when he died?"

"My father died in his early forties."

"Well, you've done better than your father already."

"Lived longer, not done better," Daly said.

Doc Pierce was not at Coyne's, where Daly found Vanish Hagen and asked him to please ask Doc to call. At the Atwood Cafe, Daly left word with the bartender that should Doc arrive, tell him to call the Right Racklin. And at Edward's Bar and Grill, he left the same message with Paul Flynn, who occupied a bar stool eight hours a day there, no less. At Lasek's, Daly wrote Doc a note asking him to call when he could and wishing him good health and a long life.

The long walks between bars tired Daly. "Casey Jones," he sang softly to himself, "orders in his hand, took the farewell journey to the promised land." He was not counting, but he had more than four vodkas. And they worked as well as a kind word from Doc Pierce. His problems seemed less pressing. He hoped Doc, who had been under a death watch for decades, would not die that day.

DOUBLE TRAGEDY ON FORBES: TWO OAKLAND MEN
DIE DRUNK IN SEPARATE BARROOMS

Friends for Forty Years Expire Five Minutes Apart

The world along Forbes did need Doc desperately and the granite solidity of things in place, Daly thought, promise that there was something brighter than the gathering gloom of the streets in 1968. Today, it was rioting in Pittsburgh, buildings set afire at rage over the assassination of Martin Luther King last month, and snipers shooting the firemen who came to put out the blazes. People shaking their fists into television cameras and other people in the streets with weapons and flames in Detroit, Chicago, and Washington, firing on policemen and one another.

There were now costumes on the sidewalks in Oakland that made every block a branch of the Barnum and Bailey Circus. Drug addicts stumbled into telephone poles on the streets. The University of Pittsburgh, whose marriage with its neighbors had always been shaky to disloyal, gobbled up hillsides, parts of Schenley Park, streets and parts of streets, and changed the patterns of traffic. The university bought hospitals and lots where there had been restaurants and shoemaker shops on Forbes and reached everywhere into parking meters and homes. They maintained their own police force to roam Oakland, as if one more was needed. Parking lots stood where once one knew the names of everyone in a certain house: uncles, cousins, and cats and dogs. Gone. Brushed aside by an idea going somewhere: The university would expand, tentacled and grasping at ground as if it needed the oxygen of places to keep a large land beast from suffocating by being confined. Revelations of change everywhere.

Before Daly went home to look for sleep against the unwelcome news that had crept into things, he strolled the few blocks to Robinson Street, where he had been born. There the world had once promised order and, if not kindness, cruelty elsewhere. At the top of the hill he could see the street below in afternoon shadows. It lay as undisturbed as it had been when he was a boy.

If ever a street slept, this one did, for years, decades. He had wandered among his people on their porches and the narrow walkways between their houses like the wind down Robinson. He had loved their suspenders and shawls, and their hand-me-down visions, their unchanging ways. Nights held a glow from their pipes in the dark. He wished on an anxious afternoon like this one that he could be down there as he once had been, healthy and dumb and happy and complete.

As he walked back down the hill to his house off Forbes, on Coltart, he hoped, as he strolled slowly past St. Agnes, the church where he had been baptized and would soon be eulogized, on the corner of Robinson and Fifth, that his heart would go now. He stopped, catching his breath. Now, he thought, here.

Lately Daly had been visiting in the hospital his last reminder of his late father, the first Right Racklin, an uncle named Finnerty. The old man lay in tubes and hoses and cold, mechanical sounds, swathed in the unnatural quiet of the intensive care unit and dying in inches of mute humiliation: no way to go.

At the corner, turning onto Fifth, he stopped, thinking he had heard his name in a pronouncement, not called out, but simply stated. He looked up Fifth and down—no one there to say his name. He waited. There was no sound except traffic.

Daly went home and worked on his will, nothing much to attend to there. He made a note to look into the matter of the portion of his father's inheritance to come to him on his fiftieth birthday. That was in November. Would he be around to collect it personally?

When his mother died, she left nothing except the family lamps dating from biblical times, old mirrors stained enough to have been conceived to conceal rather than reveal a person's face, and carpets ruined and discolored with the years. At the time, Daly was in the process of breaking up his own housekeeping. He had little to divide in his divorce; his wife left Pittsburgh with a suitcase and, under the circumstances, the best wishes possible for him. Daly gave away everything that once was in the home of the first Right Racklin and his wife and three children, a brother, Al, and his sister, Ruth Marie.

By the terms of his queer will, Boyce Racklin, his father, left everything to his wife and son Daly. Daly was to receive the money partially when he was thirty, the rest when he was fifty.

With his mother dead, Daly received on his thirtieth birthday what there was of the inheritance to that point: the less than grand sum of four hundred and seventeen dollars. He assumed it was not entirely a serious sum from his father, who as often as not saw himself and his comings and goings as lessons for other people. There was no message with the sum. It was handled by an attorney in the Grant Building downtown, but the trustee of the will was a once well-known politician and philanthopist to Catholic charities, an old friend of Boyce Racklin's, but probably now, having had a stroke, not fully capable of handling his own affairs. Daly had not thought of the inheritance for more than a half hour a year in the two decades since his thirtieth birthday.

His uncle Finnerty treated the will as a joke. Serious enough on Boyce's part, but it was a laughing matter to sensible people.

"It's his last statement to the world," he said when he heard the sum left Daly. "He's going to strengthen you morally, Daly, by showing you there's nothing but hard work going to make you rich. Don't expect something for nothing."

"And when I'm fifty?"

"You'll get a torn pair of pants he used to wear when he was pretending to be doing work around the house. The man never lifted a finger under his own roof, for any of you."

"Uncle Finnerty, you're no man to talk."

"I'm not the subject under discussion, only the lessons taught by my revered brother."

But confusing the two of them was easy, the one abstemious and never touching anything stronger than iced tea and the other, Finnerty, delighted to never have the sensation of his feet touching solid ground. By whatever door a Racklin entered the world's stage, he or she left it in a dance part Charleston, a lot of waltz, jitterbugging to beat the band, and inventing queer somersaults and flips to add to the fantastic element in their characters.

It was on the program till the end. Two days before Boyce Racklin's death on the river, Uncle Finnerty brought to the Racklin home a big chandelier he wanted to install in the apartment where the family lived for a year after moving from Robinson Street. The building had a supervisor, too nosy for the taste of both Racklin brothers. Uncle Finnerty assaulted the housing manager when he demanded that the chandelier be taken down. And his father, the rationalist Boyce Racklin, almost lost his license to practice law, defending Finnerty when the police came.

And it was all junk glass, held together by frayed wires and string. Finnerty had found it in the alley behind Frank and Seder, an old broken window display and useless except to provoke apartment managers, as it hung perilously by a thread in their living room. The police threatened Finnerty. Finnerty shoved a policeman. Boyce went to his aid.

Daly's mother stood between all of them, calming the storm.

The chandelier was removed and then immediately replaced when the police left, only to come crashing down that night, never to be installed again.

"It was a lovely gesture, but we were almost evicted," Daly's mother said whenever the chandelier was discussed.

Daly was amused at the idea he would not be alive anyhow to collect a nonexistent legacy strengthening his character. A lesson there, too: Be sure, Father, the audience for your sermon is not dead. He fell asleep.

When the telephone rang, there was daylight, pale with no sun yet, under his window blinds. "Yes," he said, burdened. "Daly Racklin here."

"Racklin," a young man's voice said, not at all encouraging in its hoarse alarm. "Thank God, you're there. I'm in trouble, Mr. Racklin, it's serious, it's deep. I'm minutes from going under."

Daly thought for a few seconds, then said, "May I ask: Who the hell is this?"

"Tom."

"Tom who? Try to get ahold of yourself, Tom."

"Tom Guignan, Tommy Guignan's son."

"Tommy Guignan's son? Yes, Tommy Guignan's son."

Daly's mind turned to a boy not altogether the quickest youth he had known—slow was the charitable word, stupid even, within the range of kindness.

"I think I may have just killed a man."

"You're not sure of that, Tom? There's a dead man somewhere and you think you have some connection to him, sort of—that you may have recently killed him. Where does the doubt in your mind come in? Is there a body, something solid—maybe not living—but a body to establish there's been a murder or a death by misadventure?"

"Sure, there's a body. I can see it from here at the telephone. I'm not seeing things!"

"Now, Tom, I know this is a bad time for you, but I must ask you not to get angry with me, or I'll hang up and you'll go to the electric chair if the murder was premeditated and the police decide you did it."

"I'm sorry, Mr. Racklin, but I'm standing here with an ax in my hand and there's a man on the floor, maybe been chopped up, and I'm wondering did I do it."

"Why the doubt?"

"I'm real drunk, Mr. Racklin. And I'm not a murderer is why I think I didn't do it."

"Tom, why did you call me instead of the police? I have to call the police now, you know."

"My father before he died, he said, 'Real trouble, boys'—he was talking to my brother and me—'you call Right Racklin, you understand?' This looks like real trouble to me."

"Yes, it does to me, too. Give me the address where you are, and I'll try to get there the same time as the police. I'll call them as soon as I hang up. Say as little as possible, admit nothing."

"Like what?"

"That you killed a man with the ax you're carrying."

"The more I think about it, the more I think it wasn't me. I wouldn't do nothing like this, Mr. Racklin, and, furthermore, there's no damned blood on the ax. How'd I chop up somebody without there being blood on the ax? And . . . Mr. Racklin, there's someone banging at the door."

"Tom, put down the ax, put it where you won't be tempted not to kill another person, and go sit by yourself."

"Mr. Racklin, whoever it is is going to break down the door."

After considerable thought, the young man gave Daly the address, and Daly dialed the Number Four Police Station on Forbes. The crime scene was ten minutes away from the station, twenty at most from Daly. "May I speak to Captain Carr?" he asked pleasantly, in his manner the matter of arranging for lunch.

"Jimmy! Right Racklin here."

"Racklin, I'm leaving for the morning. On my way to Mass. I came on at midnight. If this is about the Pirates, call me later—anything else don't talk to me about it, not now. Second thought, not ever. We're not a charitable organization, if you follow me?"

"I follow you, Jimmy. But this is Tommy Guignan's son, young Tom. Do you know the boy?"

"Habitual. I know him as a habitual. Him and his twin brother, Louis."

"Twin brother?"

"Young Tom is the simple son, the other, Louis, is the smart one. Carnegie Tech. Engineering. The way it goes."

"Jimmy, one question? Are these identical twins?"

"Can't tell one from the other. Except the habitual is always drunk, almost always—I saw him what could have been sober one night about two years ago—and the other is always walking with a book."

"Jimmy, the one, Tom, may have killed somebody."

"You ain't sure."

Right Racklin gave him the address. "He's there now," Daly said.

"So are we. We had a call about twenty minutes ago. Someone was screaming like murder was being done. We're on the scene."

"Good. That's why I called. I'm going over there now."

"Right, how'd you know about this?"

"The boy called me from the scene."

"You and not the police? Not Father Farrell? Not J. Edgar Hoover or Bishop Wright?"

"Well, his father told him to call me if he was ever in serious trouble."

"It's not a confusion between you and the bishop?"

"No, it's me been delegated."

"That's one good dutiful boy. What did his father tell him about murdering another person do you suppose? We'll handle it, Right, there's no need for you to come to the scene. You're a good man, Daly. A little push here, a tug there."

"Not even a very good person when it comes to that," Daly said. "I rearrange other people's furniture because I know what it's like to live in a disorderly house of my own. Ordinary at best, Jimmy. Tomorrow's the anniversary of my old man's death. There was a man, Jimmy. I'm not in the same book."

"No, better than that. You're in the book. Four stars with the rest of your kind."

* * *

The phone rang again later that morning, and Daly was suddenly elated. He knew from the ring it was about Right Racklin; his father was remembered somewhere other than his one son's failing heart. "Right Racklin," he said proudly.

"Daly, it's Jimmy Carr. It's about that ax murderer you called me about."

"Not proven in a court of law," Daly said, covering his disappointment.

"There was no blood on the ax."

"The boy told me that."

"And the victim was not chopped up."

"You think then there wasn't a murder."

"Hold on. That's what we give the coroner money to decide."

"What do you think personally?"

"You ought to find another line of work."

"Jimmy, I haven't taken the boy as a client. He just called me."

"He said you're his counsel."

"Well, I'm not."

Carr was silent on the other end, then he said, "This is one kid who needs you."

"Why don't you represent him?"

"I'm not a lawyer. And he's got a bond hearing coming up. If we do let him out, someone has to be responsible he shows up for court."

"Why didn't he call me himself, Jimmy?"

"He lost your number and then his hands were shaking too bad to dial you. So I done it for him."

"You know, Jimmy, I always thought you'd make a better priest than a cop."

"No, they don't get laid, Daly, but then, thinking it over, I don't much either. Maybe I'll join up after all."

Daly laughed. "Okay, Jimmy. I'm your man, the kid's top on my list."

Daly was called Right Racklin even as a boy. His father, famous for representing the cast-low and anonymous, had died without funds to be buried, leaving money to lepers and shelters for people who had no consistent champion except the first Right Racklin. A union attorney for the United Mine Workers when he managed to hold a steady account, he had gone to court for old men who had no teeth and rescued babies from foster homes without indoor plumbing. He had carried a picket sign in the lobby of the Federal Building in downtown Pittsburgh until he was reminded he was an officer of the court.

On his first outing as an attorney after graduating from Duquesne, Boyce Daly had gone to volunteer in West Virginia for a small, bitter coal strike that poisoned the atmosphere in the hollow where the strikers and operators fought to a standstill. Shots were exchanged, the miners armed, the company hiring strike police; and Boyce Racklin had gone to file briefs and petitions in support of their futile cause. He stayed to carry blankets and food he had collected in Pittsburgh—shoes, cans of tuna, old clothing, milk for babies—and worked himself into despair and exhaustion, there being no end to what the miners and their families needed. "It was an empty sack with a hole in the bottom," he told his son. "You couldn't pour enough in, it came out the other side. But more and more, it was more of everything they needed, and all of it was the things people in caves had in some fashion."

He was arrested in a small town, Beckley or Chambers, Daly didn't remember, on a felony charge for leaning on a pole or throwing a candy wrapper into a public garbage can. That can was brought into evidence, it and the wrapper to demonstrate contempt for the law by a big-city attorney with no respect for small-town morals. "It was scary," Boyce said. "Those local judges down there were handing out hard-labor sentences for wrongful breathing in those years."

When the courtroom had been called to order, the judge said, "Boyce Racklin."

Three miners stood up and two of their wives with them.

The judge said, "Just a minute, this is Boyce Racklin I'm calling to trial—public intoxication, littering, vagrancy, incitement to riot, and resisting arrest without violence."

"It's me, I'm Boyce Racklin," one of the miners said.

"Don't be ridiculous, I know you," the judge said. "Your name is Amos Starberry. I know you."

"I'm changing my name this minute to Boyce Racklin. Legally this afternoon."

The other miners nodded.

The judge in a fury banged his gavel and shouted the words that rang down like legend: "I want the Right Racklin. Give me the Right Racklin!"

The case evaporated of its own accord, Boyce Racklin convicted but given probation as long as he desisted from breathing in West Virginia; and, as the strike was over, the poverty continuing unabated, the wretched no happier, no sadder either, Racklin took his solo bus ride back to Pittsburgh, an apparent loser in his first case.

But the trial and the judge's demand preceded him. Wherever he went in Pittsburgh, particularly in the bars in Oakland, there would come a low chant, so soft as almost not to be heard distinctly, as men and women gently tapped their glasses on the bar or on tabletops when he entered a room: "Right Racklin, Right Racklin, I want the Right Racklin."

After a while, the soft chant stopped on his every appearance, but the name and its distinguished pedigree clung to Boyce and trailed him where he stood and sat and was transferred like a royal title to his son Daly, a burden, an obligation, a warning, and a fate. In that grand moment of love and testimony in West Virginia there fell a spiritual legacy on the Racklins: The name followed all the days of his short life the father in all his decency, a generosity as wide as it was long, an inheritance to his son.

His father's death was judged an accident, drowning in pursuit once more of saving someone else. A man on the wharf at the Allegheny River on Water Street swore he heard someone, a woman, call for help just before the first Right Racklin, who could not swim, leaped into the black river.

Daly carried the name with pride. The sequence of events on the banks of the Allegheny River and in the water itself was dim; the newspapers had run Right Racklin's picture at the time of his death and pronounced him a hero, but his last hours were not talked about much, and for that Daly, who planned to die unmissed and in retreat from the human race, was thankful.

It is a heavy millstone, Daly sometimes thought, to be the son of a good father. Living in the same house since adolescence, seldom traveling, Daly worried little about money, and took only clients now who had no one else. "Pay me with a chicken," was his favorite joke, knowing that between ingratitude and penury a literal chicken mostly would be more than he could expect in payment.

Now fully awake, Daly remembered with a rush: He was condemned tonight to take to dinner the Carneys and their visiting aunt Brigid, from Detroit. He had been seduced into serving as watchdog for the family, a dissolute and shiftless bunch: two daughters, a mother and son. He had known their father and husband, Mark, a man deserving better than to have this herd disgracing his good name after he died.

Daly knew the Carney women and the young man man by intention were dishonest, crooked, narrow, and deceiving, prone to lie even when there was little advantage in it. He had never met Aunt Brigid from Detroit, so he could not denounce her from personal acquaintance, but he knew his odds. Aunt Brigid was ten to one to be the worst woman in her congregation where she worshiped in Detroit, a trial to her parish priest and neighbors. But Mark Carney had been an easy touch in his time, a companion for long hours of dreams and talk with Daly, and after Mark's death Daly, starting with an occasional visit to their apartment, had gone from looking in on the family, checking locks on their windows or studying pipes for a gas leak, to contributing monthly to their rent and food bills. It was, he realized, a strange twist to his life: Daly Racklin, eluding for almost fifty years the burdens of domesticity, now found himself the chief support of two young women, near prostitutes in looseness of comings and goings, and a mother alternately screaming or silent as a bedpost and morose. The boy was a wrap-up of the mother and daughters, loud or mum, and, as people used to say of a certain type, a born thief.

Daly lectured the girls, drove the mother to a mental health clinic once a week, taking calls from her the other six days, and periodically bailed out the boy from reform school. Mark Carney would have committed suicide rather than let pneumonia blessedly take him had he foreseen the fate of his immediate descendants. Mark had been an honest pharmacist, never owning his own shop, traveling vast distances to work in hospitals on the other side of the county. He drank next to nothing with alcohol in it, and held as his highest promise of a life well lived the prospect of getting his son one day into law school or at a point of settlement the Pittsburgh Fire Department and the daughters safely and securely married. As he brushed his white hair, each in place, and dressed in a suit and tie, Daly thought he would rather clean out a hundred stables than try to meet even Mark Carney's modest dreams with that impossible clan.

There was a bar near the Carney family apartment where Daly occasionally stopped, and he hurried toward it. Two glasses of wine before the fray.

The bartender there was a man named O'Malley, and O'Malley spoke often of Daly's father, seeming to have noted every good deed forgotten by the world. O'Malley had worked in any number of saloons in Oakland in his time, and from one or another he came to know everyone. Daly wanted to hear about his father tonight; he wanted to feel like a good man's son—that things that his father represented, no need for fine words on the subject, were not buried with old-fashioned popes or the Latin Mass. But O'Malley was busy with a baseball crowd in the bar and could only wave to Daly as he mixed drinks. Daly saluted him and went to the door, not ordering anything.

He stood pensive on the sidewalk, then walked on. Climbing

the steps to Mark Carney's old apartment, he had in mind a festive dinner. Feeling forlorn, he would raise the spirits of his woeful charges. Who else would serve them anything but dog food? And that is where kindness must begin: where it is least expected and unwarranted. No one holds back charity and love from the beautiful and graceful and bright. Only the lost Carney types are told, Don't-let-the-door-hit-you-in-the-ass-on-the-way-out. Truculent and sullen, doomed to be themselves cast forever in stone, none of the Carneys were eager when Daly arrived; none of them were prepared to leave, nor did they seem as if they would ever depart. They stared at him like people suspicious of his motivations: He had been their caretaker for two years and they waited to hear the catch. He wanted to say: You ain't dogs, you know, come around without the bark, the growl, and the bite.

Aunt Brigid was a short, old, angry woman with a cane, a recent widow, who said, "Where're we going?" as if Daly had put a gun to her head with a peculiar demand.

Daly replied, "I'd like to show you all a good time tonight, Poli's in Squirrel Hill, a little treat for your visit, Aunt Brigid."

Heather Rose, the younger daughter, said, "Uncle Daly, Aunt Brigid says she has allergies."

Heather Rose was sixteen, and Daly supposed she was already notorious on Forbes, where certain records on sexual misconduct were collected. Daly said, "We'll watch out for this good woman's allergies," and he called for a cab. He had decided to leave his car at home: This might be an evening where an automobile would be a liability to a man seeking to run at breakneck speed from a terrible situation. Trapped in his own car with the Carneys might well be the scene of his final adventure. Fleeing a cab or bundling them into one as he did something else was a jolly prospect even in the anticipation of the freedom it would give him.

The sisters claimed they cleaned Daly's apartment in small payment for his kindness to the family but stole his shirts and socks for their boyfriends and younger brother, Terrence. Daly could not swear to it, but he thought that on an occasional rainy afternoon they brought men there. He had nothing of great value in the place; he considered his lost shirts, cuff links, and socks part of his contribution to the memory of the late pharmacist.

At Poli's there was a crowd and people almost on the sidewalk, and the restaurant took no reservations: a very bad beginning.

"All my kids had allergies," Aunt Brigid shouted over the conversation of the people waiting for tables in the foyer.

Daly sat alone at the bar. He abandoned the idea of two glasses of white wine and instead drank three vodka and tonics. Old times and dead, invisible friends hovered close to him tonight. He courted his memories, the dead people; he thought deeply about them, pressing to remember specific smiles and faces touched by sunlight. The sisters and the boy Terrence sprawled about on upholstered benches, and Aunt Brigid stormed around the restaurant thumping her cane, bending to look at what people were eating. Terrence had said to Daly that he must talk about an emergency, whispering into Daly's ear in the taxicab, and in that direction, Daly knew, there lay trouble later. But it was the mother Daly periodically left the bar to observe. If she became enraged—at a slight or a look from a stranger or friend—she would throw things.

"My husband died a year ago," Aunt Brigid said as they were finally seated, and Daly asked, "Was he sick long?"

"Why do you ask?" Aunt Brigid shouted.

"Just a question," Daly said, with a smile broad on his pink face. He often wondered if it was that frank, open look about him, often feigned in terror, that had saved him over the years from being punched. Tonight, he was not sure his record would survive.

"See here, Racklin," Aunt Brigid said, "I'm not up to putting together medical histories for strangers."

She had several prominent warts on her chin and Daly did not look there.

"Uncle Daly's not a stranger," Eileen, the elder daughter, said.

"He's a stranger to me," Aunt Brigid said. "Let him go somewhere else he wants to be a detective."

"Let's order," Daly said, wallowing in false joviality, thinking it was some sort of penance he paid tonight.

"It's too late at night to be ordering food," Aunt Brigid said. "Even if they served us this minute, I'm going to have to sleep sitting up. I have an esophageal hernia. Food can come up on me and choke me to death. I'm sure Mr. Racklin wouldn't care, but I'm not out to injure myself. I'm not eating tonight, thank you."

But she read the menu aloud, pointing out what was acceptable to her there among the food, the items on the list dangerous to her allergies or esophagus. Daly ordered a coffee milk shake, not hungry, while everyone else except Aunt Brigid ordered large dishes of fried shrimp and crab cakes and potatoes. Watching each order, Aunt Brigid silently shook her head at each request. When Daly's milk shake came, Aunt Brigid took a sudden gulp from his glass, paused, and said, "I'll have the same. If we get out of this trap soon enough, I'll take a pill for the damage. I'm allergic to milk, you know."

Snatching food from others' plates, she ate french-fried potatoes, a hush puppy, four shrimp, and half a crab cake. Her mouth filled with food, she said, "I envy you all eating here like farm animals. I eat like you do and it's curtains. But enjoy yourselves; life is short enough, ask me. Eating like this, devil take the hindmost, was what led to my hemorrhoids in the first place, and then the operation, and then the prayers of the whole congregation that brought me back from death's doorstep."

Daly said, "The human spirit is dauntless. Aunt Brigid, as you can attest, it can overcome the worst of physical adversity. We all respect you, dear woman, for your suffering."

"I went to doctors," Aunt Brigid said, "who told me the excruciating pain in my spine was imaginary. I spent two thousand dollars for X rays."

"Maybe," Terrence said, "losing your husband caused it. A psychologist told me I had headaches because our father died young."

"This talk is giving me a headache," his mother said, alarming Daly. Mrs. Carney had been unnaturally quiet; she was either not listening or waiting for the right moment to shout that the waiter was giving other people at the table larger portions.

"I'll tell you something, Terrence," Aunt Brigid said, "my pain wasn't imaginary. It was real."

Daly remembered now the tie Terrence had on. It once was a favorite of his. He spoke quickly. "Imaginary pains!" he said. "Doctors talk a lot of mumbo jumbo. You're quite right, Aunt Brigid."

Mrs. Carney then threw the flowers on the table at Aunt Brigid, followed by the ice in a glass of Coca-Cola she had been drinking. "I never liked you!" she cried. "Now you're insulting Mark's memory. Terrence gets headaches because Mark died young and so do I. Mark caused all our problems, and you're adding to them."

It was the moment Daly had dreaded and it called for all the shamelessness and artifice he had learned in his years of successful mediation. He leapt to dust and wipe at Aunt Brigid, one hand flailing behind him to restrain Mrs. Carney in her indignation. He whispered to Aunt Brigid, "Grief has unhinged the good soul; stronger people than this poor woman have cracked under less. Forgive her. Call up mercy, Aunt Brigid. Mercy here, mercy for a grief-stricken widow." And he turned to Mrs. Carney as the others helped Aunt Brigid, smoothing her clothing, wiping at the ice. "Alice," he murmured to Mrs. Carney, "the old woman is off her senses, she hardly knows what an insult she's presented to poor Mark. But think of him now—he'd find forgiveness here. Forgiveness is the word. Don't let the old rat bring you down to her level. Forgiveness, think of Mark, your beloved husband and my best friend."

He smiled, he nodded. He waved away waiters, no trouble, no trouble, an accident with the flowers and the ice. The moment passed, apologies. "She's sorry for the misunderstanding," Daly said to Aunt Brigid. Then to Mrs. Carney: "A regrettable turn of phrase with no malice behind it."

Daly briefly retreated to thoughts of Ireland now, the green fields, the fine stallions, the stalls with produce on corners, Dublin with its laughter in the streets, as a place he would never leave—

though he had never been there. Eventually everyone at the table found someone to whom they could apologize. Daly loudly ordered dessert. The mood became expansive. Everyone demanded exotic cakes and pastries. Mrs. Carney said once, "No one can tell me about my headaches," and Aunt Brigid said, "Eating chocolate pie at this hour of the night is like taking poison."

Daly said to the restaurant at large: "You're right, that's right," agreeing, accepting everyone at the table for what the evening, a catastrophe, had really meant. His record was intact. He had lived forty-nine years and never been punched by man or woman in the pursuit of peace. But while Daly tried to bundle the troop of hapless remnants of a family in mock civility into a taxicab, young Terrence reminded Daly he had business with him.

"I had a lovely evening," Aunt Brigid said, shaking Daly's hand before the cab departed. "It was a pleasure to meet you. When you're in Detroit you know where to come for an evening of family."

"I do, I do, yes, I do."

Daly waved at the cab as it pulled into traffic on Murray Avenue.

He turned to the boy. "I have some things to see to," he said. "Is this something we can discuss briefly?"

"Well, discuss, yes, briefly. Short and sweet. There's a fellow going to kill me I don't give him six hundred dollars."

"Six hundred dollars! You're saying 'Six hundred dollars'?"

"Six hundred dollars."

"This is a bank you robbed making a settlement?"

"No, nothing illegal. Not like a bank, more personal."

Daly restrained himself: There was nothing about this miserable boy that did not shout between-the-cracks, square peg, life-in-the-ash-can. He would not state the obvious to the boy about himself. A judge at Juvenile Hall had called Daly aside after he once came in to represent the boy, then thirteen, for burning down a tree on the campus of the University of Pittsburgh. "Mr. Racklin," the judge said in the privacy of his chambers, "this is a losing cause. He's going to be serving time and soon. The boy's got to be removed from that environment, it's unwholesome. You're only postponing the inevitable." And Daly nodded. "No doubt there's great truth in what you say, Judge. Great wisdom."

Then, foxy, appraising, the judge asked, "What's your interest in these people?"

Preparing to tell the truth—it was an old pal, one of the best, the man's memory deserved better—he stumbled into silence. It was not the whole truth, and he would not lie.

"Mr. Racklin?"

No way to say it. But words came anyhow. "There's no one else, your honor, and I guess I've been elected."

"Uncle Daly," the boy pleaded now, "I'm going to get killed for that six hundred dollars."

"Tell me," Daly said. The sky overhead, dark and filled with stars, was shining with the face of the first Right Racklin. He heard his father in the grind of a distant streetcar. If he put his hands out to his sides, Daly thought, somewhere close he would touch him. He breathed deeply; his father was on the air tonight, making himself known to his son.

"I borrowed a ring from a guy, intending to give it back, and someone stole it and the guy who owned the ring said it was six hundred dollars, give back the ring, or go swimming in the Monongahela River."

"Do you swim, Terrence?"

"I don't, Uncle Daly."

"Then you shouldn't steal rings. How much did you get for the ring?"

The boy was almost eighteen now. He searched desperately for an adequate evasion.

"How much?" the boy asked. "For the ring?"

"Never mind."

"It was stolen from me."

"I said, 'Never mind.' "

"What am I going to do?"

"Call the guy and tell him you'll get him a hundred and fifty."

"No, he ain't going to go for it. I can't do that."

"He'll go for it."

"No, he ain't. What do I say if he says, 'You're chop suey, Terrence'?"

"Tell him you'll get him another fifty."

Daly took a hundred and fifty dollars from his pocket and handed it to Terrence. "Now, son," he said, "your first thought is you are going to take this money and go to Boston. Or somewhere. Don't. If there's really a guy going to kill you, think to yourself your life is worth a hundred and fifty at least. If there's no guy, no ring, nothing, take the money as a gift. But don't leave town. Your mother and your sisters need you. They need all the help they can get. Don't desert them, it's not what your father would want."

The boy put the money into his pocket quickly. "The bastard will have to take the hundred and fifty," he said. "There ain't no more coming to that bastard." He was thinking quickly. He settled on what to say. "Uncle Daly, I got a girl pregnant."

Daly said, "Terrence, can we stick to one story at a time? Have I stirred you with the possibility of getting another hundred and fifty from me? Relax, deal with the guy and the ring. Save the pregnancy for another time."

The boy laughed. "Another guy is blamed for it anyhow," Terrence said. "I'm sure it was me, not the other guy. But, like you say, Uncle Daly, another day, another story."

"That's the spirit."

Daly was relieved. The boy's pleasure with the money was apparent. He had outwitted someone in a life of being a goat; the sum was small for the elevation Daly had witnessed. Can a million dollars buy such joy, given to the wrong person at the wrong time? Daly felt himself fortunate. At small price he had liberated the neat, constrained part of himself that yearned to see the helpless know small pleasures, what the rest of the world comes to by birth. He shook hands with the boy and began the long walk back down

Forbes to Oakland. He rejoiced in the memory of his father, tried to think of details, his hands and the lines on his face. In the soft June night, strolling down Forbes, he felt his father at his side, heard his footsteps, and knew that the first Right Racklin accepted the tribute in being remembered kindly.

He drank alone at the bar at the Metropole. O'Malley was busy cleaning up. The white wine, delayed, was good and cold. He tried to hold on to his father. Memory, he thought, is a broom with straws missing.

"Sit awhile, Right," O'Malley said. "I've still a few glasses to wash, and I'll have one with you." As a sophomore at Pitt, O'Malley, a halfback, had once scored two touchdowns against Maryland. He broke his knee the next week, and it was the end of his career.

"I'm thinking tonight of my father," Daly said. "It's twenty-five years since he died, tonight."

O'Malley's nose was broken in two places. His brow was heavy with thick eyebrows.

"When I look at you now," O'Malley said, "sitting there, I see your father. You could be him. Same color in his face, hair white as yours. You're the picture of him, big shoulders, just a prince."

He and the bartender had talked about his father for years. The bartender had made him a saint, a man who walked on water, a friend to the poor, lighting up rooms when he appeared at the door. But the man O'Malley described tonight was not his father. It was another saint of the streets around Forbes Field, the Carnegie Museum, and the Oakland of thousands of Irishmen peering around corners to discover if what's true lay there. Daly's father, the real man, was nothing like his son. The first Right Racklin was short, no pink face there, no white hair, mostly bald with a few dark strands. All these years and O'Malley had another person in mind. Annoyed, Daly started to explain, to admonish O'Malley on the treacherousness of his memory. But he stopped. He gazed around the empty bar and felt a sudden comfort. The sense of his father, close on the streets, had not left him.

He was in the long, vertical light falling from the neon signs in the windows down the whiskey and wine bottles behind the bar. O'Malley's broken nose held him, and the familiar man wiping at glasses spoke to Daly of an old cause, revived with each twist of the bartender's wrist as he swiped clean another shot glass. Daly held close the warmth of a well-loved face, and he wanted to buy O'Malley drinks until dawn lit up the streets outside and car bumpers reflected the sun in its new day. Why, the two of us are celebrating goodness that doesn't need a man attached, goodness so pure in the air that it inhabits one man or another, no matter. My old man was fine as they come, but there was another somewhere just as good, and who would want there to be less good when there's so little of it on the sidewalk. Daly waved his hand for another wine. He sat, enthralled, a willing captive of the present comfort in the Metropole. Outside the night wore shoes of iron, but in here there were good men to spare.

Two

At ten the next night Doc Pierce was at his usual booth at Coyne's, lost in thought. He himself had been given a death notice some twenty years earlier: a matter of failing lungs, kidneys, bladder, and liver. He had closed his two offices and abandoned his practice, packed his bags for the long, last trip. His wife headed for the door (she never married again, good Catholic in intention), and his children ignored him while he sat drinking away what he thought would be the last hours of his life. But his last hours stretched to months, then years, and the old kidneys, liver, and bladder held on, through surgery, a transplant, periods of remission—he had not been able to drink himself to death in twenty years and more, altogether exactly the man to see after the mortality mirror had been held up before poor Daly Racklin.

"I tried to call you," Doc said. "I got your messages. Paul Flynn said you looked bad—and coming from him, bad as he looks on a good day, I suspected you were terminal. But here you are, ready to outlive us all."

"Doc," Daly said, "it's good to see you."

Walking into the familiar bar, Daly felt like the same boy who had thrived in Oakland what seemed like centuries ago, death in the air as it was in his own body now, but not his permanent demise: Forever a kid inside, he still could not believe boys died.

Although then he knew, from doleful experience, that not to be the case: In the war in France and Germany he had seen boys and girls die before their time, undignified death coming to them when they and their families sometimes were about ordinary business. He had seen them lying like castaway rags, an entire family in a kitchen in London one morning, dead from bombs dropped on their heads the night before. In Saarlautern later, a city of the dead, American troops trod gingerly not to step on someone's son or grandmother in the dark and frost.

Still, death then was somewhere else than in him, not at his elbow, not in his mind, not in his heart gasping along inside his chest.

"Doc, you're looking exceptional."

"My back hurts, Daly," Doc said. "I think I'll stroll down to the Atwood Cafe and try a booth there for medical purposes."

Daly set down his vodka and a beer he had brought for Doc. Doc did not accept drinks from everyone. Well set up, he liked to do the buying, but he knew Daly was solvent, and he poured the beer. On fine nights Dr. Pierce walked home carefully the twenty minutes up Oakland Avenue and then down Fifth. On nights when the weather was inclement or he had too much to drink— or a little hit him wrong—he called a cab. He was known as a careful, precise man.

"It can't be another one of those widows and orphans, son?" Doc asked. "Need for blankets in the winter, electric fans in the summer, kids without shoes, you have that look. Lady need a bus ticket back to Connellsville, the pressure of big-city life too much for her?"

"No, it's me, I have a heart that might stop any minute."

Doc said, "That'll kill you, Daly."

"I know. It's what I wanted to ask you about. Dr. Cobble up at the Montefiore the day before yesterday showed me the calendar of my future, Doc, and, give or take a month, the days left are already being X-ed in red."

"The answer is, before you ask: I don't know, twenty dollars, please. Could be a year, could be fifty, depends on how you respond to treatment. There's medicines. He give you some tablets to carry with you?"

"Yes, right here in my pocket. But I'm not sure I'm not ready to go."

"I know you, Daly. Whatever the length of time it is that's the longest on record for your type of heart problem, you're going to break it and then some. If I may say so, Right, yours is the usual line certain rugged individuals say to get themselves ready for the ruts in the road. You guys sing to me all this darkness in the world, and then hit the ball over the center-field wall, four hundred and eighty feet every time. Please, Daly, for my sake, save the I-think-it's-my-time for someone doesn't know you. O woe!"

"I feel I wasted my life."

"Compared to who else? Vanish Hagen there on the bar, he doesn't think he spent ten minutes in his life on nothing but the highest pursuits. Ask him, he'll tell you he wishes he could have learned real estate sales, but the fine print was too much for a guy with a fifth-grade education. Said an hour ago he had something urgent he wanted to discuss with me and then there's a Pirate rally in the fifth against Los Angeles and he can't tear himself from the television for the last forty minutes."

Vanish came to the table and stood looking from one man to the other. He was very thin with a long nose, and, even though the day was warm, the collar of his shirt was buttoned. He could have been forty or sixty, but he was, as he proudly told one person or another, enhancing some point he made, fifty-four. "Two of the brightest lights in Oakland," he said, "assembled at one table within reach of the common man. It makes my heart jump with joy like a little red tomato in a can on television to think what a wonderful world this is, and a great country. It's a great country, ain't it? Him getting out of the way, the president stepping down and throwing the door open for Bobby to pick up where his dear brother left off."

"You like the turn things took?" Doc asked. "Bobby Kennedy picking up the torch?"

"I did not say that," Vanish said. "Neither of them Irishmen, Mr. Eugene McCarthy or Bobby, gets my endorsement until I hear their line on some subjects close to me."

"Vanish, they will not talk about the University of Pittsburgh, and neither will Nixon. It's not of major concern, your subjects."

"Doc, none of it is going to do anything for me. That's not the point. The point is the atmosphere, the atmosphere, all the way to the air we breathe. That's the point. The subjects close to me don't have to affect me personally. I think Mr. Robert Kennedy is going to create a better atmosphere, and that's better for the country."

"I think he's a good man, too," Doc said.

"You, Doc," Daly said. "You have a good word for a politician?"

"Bobby, yes, I do."

"But what if the war goes on," Vanish asked, "and the people says, 'The Micks done us in. Micks like wars because it means people have to have more children to replace all the ones killed by the Viet Cong'?"

"Why don't we just wait?" Daly asked. "How much worse can he do than what's been done?"

Vanish said, "I'm leaning strong to Nixon. Let be what'll be. Let the country go to hell and it's Mr. Nixon done it."

"Vanish, you have my vote," Doc said. "It's the atmosphere every time. You for president, Nixon the vice-president."

"You're kidding me," Vanish said.

"It's not much more than atmosphere," Daly said. "All's said and done."

Vanish said, "It's that, but a lot of sadness, too, on the local level, down on the streets where decent people are putting together their beer and pretzels, and regrets and recriminations from high to low. And that's what I want to talk to you about, Doc, not that the Right Racklin can't listen—without hearing all the specifics."

Daly started to stand. "Vanish, I heard enough specifics for one day," he said.

"No, stay," Doc said. "This is probably more in the legal line than the medical. Vanish, am I correct you consulted with Daly on your sister, same as me?"

"You're correct. This ain't about her. I give up on her for the time being."

"Good, neither Daly or I can have a person committed because they say the Lord rose on the third day, do you understand? It's in the Bible that way. You can't lock up two billion people who might believe that."

"It's the way she says she believes it that's the bone of contention—sometimes she says she was an eyewitness to the spectacle, and she knows He'll be back in time to keep Pitt from bulldozing our house—but that's not the cause of my grief today. Today I have the saddest task a man can be asked to bear. Today I have to place a man in the middle of a great tragedy like Bette Davis in *A Double Life*."

"Not *Shane*, where Alan Ladd rides off at the end, and you know the kid's never going to see him again?" Doc asked. "You told me last week that was the story of your life."

"Like that, like that, tragic like that. Well, a certain man the three of us know, the three of us respect, in fact, the three of us think of as a younger brother is about to see Shane ride off across the prairie, never to return, you hit it, family about to go up in smoke, reputation ruined. And it's all information I searched out and got to deliver to him. He asked me to look around for him. I did. And now I cause his house to come crumbling down with the news I carry."

Daly slid out of the booth quickly. "Gentlemen, I have only enough time to sleep my allotted hours before church tomorrow. I'll hear of this historical calamity another time."

Doc leaned over and took his arm. "You know," Doc said, "I think you ought to listen carefully to what you've been saying, Daly. You'll hear a different tune than the one you think you're singing. It's not time yet to turn out the lights."

Vanish said, "Fuck me, I interrupted an important conversation."

"No, no," Daly said, "no more important than any other. If Doc can't help you with the man riding off across the prairie, call me, okay?"

"I know I can count on my friends—ain't it a world!"

"Thanks, Doc," Daly said.

Vanish caught Daly around the middle and jogged-danced a few steps with him, and said, "I never went past the fifth grade and look at me now."

Among other occupations that Vanish held was that of a self-styled private investigator. By temperament an elusive man, he followed people at the request of other people, men wanting information on their wives, fathers on their children, occasionally employers on cashiers they considered as dividing up too ungraciously the profits of a business. He was as unobtrusive as the gray area outside the boundaries of where lamps cast rooms into illumination or exact shadows. He seldom spoke of his assignments, never gave names. Calling him Vanish was coming as close to describing him as it was possible, Daly thought, for a word to convey a human quality. He was not as darkly present or as invisible as a shadow, he was there for a certainty, twitching, looking off into a distance, reading a newspaper when it was necessary, there, but not there. He had been that way from a child. "No nun ever called on me," he used to say as one of his credentials for discreet investigation. "Never saw me, in classes, mathematics, reading and writing, there wasn't but one or two of them holy women ever even knew my name was Hubert."

Daly called Jessie but was unable to talk about his heart: Her high spirits about their going to Mass the next day stopped all his claims to find composure in her words of comfort. Sundays were a day they thought of as particularly belonging to their whimsicalities and simple delights. His heart was too final a matter for Daly at this point; he wanted far horizons. "I feel it will be a beautiful day tomorrow," Jessie said. "Come early."

Then he had to tell Ruth Marie, his unhappy sister, about his dilemma.

Given the terrors that lay in the last suffocating moments he would experience when his heart failed and an eternity that might not be all that he wished, Daly thought he'd settle that moment for a quick heart attack rather than a conversation with his sister. He called her, by the calendar, once every six weeks; she, in turn, called him every six hours when the mood was on her to lecture him on morals and the perils of a wasted life.

She reminded him of the worst in himself. We left our wings, the two of us, in the cloakroom. Daly thought that it was enough that he had one living self-anointed guardian of morals in the family, his sister, older by five years. She did not, of course, announce it to the world, but waited for the world to catch up to her virtue, the Vatican and all its machinery for ascribing worth. She beat around the bush, saintlike.

"Ruth Marie," he said to her on the phone, thinking he would tell her about his heart quickly and get it over with, "I've heard a few things that are bothering me. I don't want you to be upset. It's nothing that's not manageable."

"It's that woman you're seeing, isn't it? You can tell me."

Ruth Marie had been born on November 11, later famous as Armistice Day, the day celebrating the end of the First World War in Europe, a time for oneness and eternal peace, a significant birthday for a woman who tried, she said, to bring harmony wherever she went.

"Daly," Ruth Marie said, passion in her voice almost strangling off the words, "I'm ready to stand with you against her," when he was silent. "Only tell me what we must do, I'll do it. It's her, I'm not upset. I'm proud you came to your only sister."

She believed there had always been about her a quality that drew people to her, caused them to want to confide, to share their innermost secrets with her. As a child, with her father and Daly standing before the old J. P. Harris Theater downtown, there emerged from a large, black car, Rudolph Valentino; and he stopped to wave at people on the sidewalk waiting to see him, smiling, but for all his good looks, notoriously shy. He came to where the velvet rope separated him from his eager admirers and stooped to meet her eyes, crouched down and distinctly said, "Hey, little girl, you're some kind of little girl." A star come to earth, he had been stopped in his great movements when he saw her, obeying the net of love she cast before her.

"Daly!" Ruth Marie shouted into the phone. "Are you crying? I hear you crying?"

"I'm not crying, I'm not anything. I'm waiting for my turn to talk."

It was the love for everything inside her that sensitive people like Valentino could see, she insisted to Daly, goodness written like a sign of welcome in her eyes, the tilt of her head when she listened. Born with love running in her veins—not there in Daly or their brother Al, and not passed on to her son, a solitary sort of miracle that could never be explained, just known and witnessed by Ruth Marie—she admired it in its beauty as if it were something possessed by a stranger. She saw in a particular continuous holy vision skies, water, beasts, and existence itself, and shared her sacred connection with others less fortunate, never letting on directly what they missed, being subtle and kind. But Daly could see it in her eyes, the hunger for sanctity when she looked at him. About twelve years of age she started it: There, did you just see what I saw?

"It's her—it's that horrible woman," she said.

"No," Daly said to her, the phone unnaturally quiet, "it's not Jessie. I don't want to discuss Jessie with you."

"We must talk about her. Where are you now? I'll come to you. Together we can get you out of whatever trouble you're in with her. Daly, I'm proud you called me: I knew this day would come."

"No, no, it's nothing. A passing thought, no more, nothing to do with Jessie."

She was still talking when he hung up.

Her closest circle was made up of women, although sometimes a man appeared on the periphery, lingered a few months, a year or two, died significantly and dramatically mostly, left town or simply became an alcoholic or a drug addict and was lost forever. But Inez, Irene, Belle, and Caitlin stayed over the years through disasters and their recounting of the catastrophes each to each and all to Ruth Marie, and she gave their various enterprises a quality of centrality and importance as each new turn in their lives was discussed, rehashed, and made larger.

As Daly renounced sainthood for the third time that day, thinking it could put him into bad company, the phone rang again two minutes later, and Daly did not answer. It was Ruth Marie's habit to call several times after every conversation, thinking of a last word.

After Mass, Daly and Jessie walked to the Webster Hall and had coffee, and Jessie said she had to tell Daly about something that was troubling her. His sister, Ruth Marie, had called a week ago and asked Jessie if it were possible the two women might meet after Mass. Jessie said she told her she'd probably be attending Mass at St. Paul's, the cathedral, with Daly, and asked was it important.

"She said, 'Important enough, I don't get the picture with you and Daly.' "

Daly forced himself to laugh, softly, not too heartily. "She said that?" he asked.

"Yes, what picture?"

"I've told you about Ruth Marie."

"What picture?"

"How can I know what's on the mind of a person chosen to bear the trials of the world?"

Jessie laughed openly. She sipped her coffee and said, "I think she's meddlesome."

"I think I agree," Daly said, and then he suggested that they take his old Chevy and drive down to the Montefiore Hospital, where his uncle Finnerty lay. "You'll wait downstairs in the lobby while I look in on him. Just a quick look. I'll feel better for it, and then we'll do our Sunday usual."

"Sounds fine."

Uncle Finnerty was exactly as he had left him two days earlier, but for the fact he now had a nephew about to join him a lot sooner in eternity than he'd expected. He took his uncle's hand. "You and the old man, you lived lives beyond me, Uncle Finnerty," he whispered to him. "There's things I want you to tell me about how you lived your life so happily. What am I to do now that I know what will kill me and damned near when? Don't die."

Uncle Finnerty in his web of tubes and wires gave no sign he heard.

Later, as Daly and Jessie sat in Schenley Park talking, Jessie leaned forward on the park bench, looking up at Daly. She moved her head rhythmically to the sound of his voice as if he were singing and she kept time.

"I'm sure I told you about it," Daly said.

This is hard, Daly thought. This is very hard, the goodness of it, and he knowing it was evaporating around them and she sensing nothing.

"Well," Daly said, "a long time ago, it was shortly after my brother Al was born in the middle thirties. My uncle Finnerty took me, in the absence of the old man, who was re-creating the world in a manner God would have chosen had He known as much as the old man did, on the only trip the two of us ever took together, a long bus ride down to East Liverpool, Ohio, where he used to work. He claimed there were famous gunmen and lawbreakers on every corner of the town, himself included.

"Our mother had said, 'Finnerty, you're crazy; you were born crazy like your brother, you'll die crazy.'

" 'I am the Wrong Racklin,' Finnerty said mysteriously. 'I hold the sacred obligation to be a trial to my brother and all his kind. It's my calling, wine, women, and a dirty song, a clean one if need be. I'm working at finding an eighth deadly sin. I'm conspiring by the hour to be a disgrace to my memory when I go.' "

"Oh, you do him beautifully, Daly," Jessie said. "I can see him."

A bundled and gloved Daly Racklin, trussed in long underwear and galoshes and scarf, wearing sweaters taken from his elder brother, had sat on the overheated bus with his uncle for three hours going somewhere beyond the powers of words to describe.

"He was in a rare mood, not even a little drunk, like the time he told me he'd been brought back from the dead," Daly said. "Same staring at me, taking off his glasses to wipe them. Looking up at the sky and sighing for all that he'd been through."

"Wait!" Jessie said. "You never told me your uncle had been dead and came back."

"I'm sure I did."

"No, you said once an angel in the men's room of a saloon in East Liverpool told him he was going to live to a hundred if he never drank one more glass of white wine."

"I guess he'll make a hundred yet," Daly said. "It wasn't one glass he drank since then."

"You said he told you once he looked down an elevator and saw John the Baptist standing there with a bucket of water to purify him, and he ran because he thought it was the devil disguised, trying to convert him to being a Protestant. You never told me he died and came back."

"Please, no digressions, I'm on the bus with him for East Liverpool," Daly said.

"No, I must hear about the resurrection first. Daly, don't joke with me about serious matters."

"Okay, serious," Daly said. "It was about twenty-six years ago, just after the Japanese bombed Pearl Harbor. I asked did he think the souls of men killed a thousand miles from home somehow get together with those who died in the old neighborhood. He says, 'Daly, better than speculation about the nature of the afterlife, there's the matter of how to live this one right, and you happen to be talking to someone who can give you knowledge of both places, here and the beyond. I've been both places.' Being more inclined to public skepticism then than now, I stuck to my guns and said, 'Since the people there don't have bodies, do they carry tags for the newcomers so they can tell which soldier or sailor is theirs?' "

" 'Daly,' Uncle Finnerty says, 'my message is not a preparation for heaven. Once you're there, things take care of themselves, you know, work out. My story is how I was buried in a tomb for three days, only it was more like three hours, but it was a tomb and I was dead, without sight or sound but one.' "

"You do him wonderfully," Jessie said. "I hear him, he's one of your best. Do you suppose he was really dead?"

"He says he was."

"Yes, go on."

" 'It was like this,' " Daly said, taking on his uncle's voice again. " 'There was nothing but blackness all around. No angels. And being dead, I wasn't reciting the holy Rosary, no good at that point, just dead, annihilation. But first there was sparks to send me on my way, big flashes of light, electric, you know, night lit up overhead and through the windows of the trolley, the 67 Swissvale, I believe, taking me out Forbes to Oakland.' "

"He died on a streetcar, how remarkable."

"I said, 'Uncle Finnerty, are you sure you were dead and not in a coma?' He turned to look at me, Jessie, took off his glasses, and says, 'Do you think I'm a goddamned fool and don't know the difference between being dead and in a coma?' "

"That's exactly what he should have said, you were impudent," Jessie said.

" 'You're here now,' I says, 'so something must have come between you and eternity—unless we're both dead, Uncle Finnerty.' "

" 'Of course something intervened! I told you I was resurrected, didn't I? I didn't say I'd died for eternity. I'm not a ghost, Daly. The streetcar stopped in a flood in downtown Pittsburgh, August 20, 1937, look it up. I was electrocuted—another man on the streetcar was, too, and he's not here to relate my message. Dead with a grieving widow while I was given a second chance.' "

Daly stood and took Jessie's hand. She pulled back.

"Daly Racklin, this minute, the resurrection."

He sat down, holding her hand.

"He told me he lay dead for maybe a year, or five minutes, all time gone from his mind, and then he heard a voice. And the voice said from the dark, 'The good in us comes from what we're not as much as what the world tells us to be.' "

"Daly, that's a strange thing for the voice to say."

"He took it to mean he should quit his job at Broad and Lovener down on Fifth and be something better. He used to work at one place or another in jobs like unwrapping packages all his life. He said when the Democrats came in he was going to manage a huge hotel down in Uniontown, but the Democrats came in and he was still unwrapping packages down on Fifth."

They stood and the walk to his car was warm and Jessie nodded as he talked, holding him by his arm. She had been blind since twenty-two days before her fifteenth birthday, first a fuzziness and a burning in her eyes and then things vanishing from the peripheries and finally darkness, a matter of less than four months. She always seemed to know where his arm was when she took it again each time. "I'm sure you're handsomer than either of my husbands," she said when Daly told her he was nothing special to see, just tall.

Jessie lived outside Oakland. It was on a street off Center, a business district. When he walked home from her house, on fine days not caring to be burdened with his loud, generally useless Chevy, he walked up Center, past Pitt medical buildings, and descended home from a hill past an old cemetery.

At her house, Daly said he'd be off, unhappy with the spell in the ordinary beauty of another Sunday.

"You'll be fine while I'm gone," he said.

As she sometimes did, she tried to hold on to the moment, his voice, the thrill of the stories, and the sun priceless and too soon gone for the day for the both of them. But he knew it was final days: The air held other currents for him.

"Did your uncle Finnerty say what he died of on the trolley?" Jessie asked.

"Yes, a combination of drowning and electricity," Daly said. "Electrocuted by the trolley's currents and what was left of him mortally succumbed to water in his lungs."

"I always marvel that those voices speaking to the dead don't have more to say of some use."

"Our uses. Who knows their uses? They may be joking, knowing the human race."

Jessie alone in the world caused Daly considerable uneasiness, often moments of panic when he would run to a phone to call her, sometimes almost at a jog, dashing the two miles from where he lived to her house to observe her situation for himself. She was frequently amused at his concern, contrasting him to her husbands, who had abandoned her. Beyond occasionally holding her close and brushing back her hair, kissing her hard on certain holidays, particularly one New Year's Eve, they had gone no further. Sometimes she clung to him, and he wondered if the moment had come for the two of them; but its postponement over the years had given sex between them an importance Daly felt too weighty. He wanted her exactly as she was to him, as much promise as physical woman. Now he questioned even his reliance in her, given the hallucinatory transformations in society.

"Jessie, be careful," he said, not able to say the rest, but having to say something.

"Daly, I told you I'm over twenty-one, I don't need your supervision."

She took his arm and walked with him out to the doorstep, the day not lost yet, the sun in the trees in front of the house, falling on the doorway and the small wooden porch where they stood. He kissed her gently on the forehead and turned to go, and she said, "Wait, you haven't told me what you were going to do in East Liverpool that day on the bus."

"He wanted to show me the cornfield where Pretty Boy Floyd was shot and killed three years earlier, that very October day."

* * *

When Ruth Marie's son was discharged from the coast guard he never wrote her. Nebraska, Wyoming, he could have been anywhere. He called sometimes at Christmas, but she said she always said something wrong and they closed with him angry.

It was one of the large sorrows of her life: She had a son and a brother who lived mere blocks away and didn't love her, but perhaps that was in the religious nature of things, first a husband, then a son, and now a brother. Daly decided that left only the rest of the human race to acclaim her. One had only to observe her own cheerful nature, she said, what she concealed behind her smiles and merry laugh, to see how well her sense of humor worked. "I never complain, even though there's enough here to fill a cave with the unfairness I've been handed." Not that her friends, Irene, Belle, Caitlin, and Inez, followed her advice. She had been left a good sum on her husband's passing, those investments growing from the initial amount, and increasing in value over the years as the money grew for her, through no great inspiration—and her friends, it was apparent to Daly, resented it. He knew by their glances that they said among themselves that she knew nothing of making a living; and, a widow with good memories, at least of her husband, she had had all that marriage seemed to offer, and now seemed content without the struggle for money or the love of men. Meanwhile, Inez, Irene, Belle, and Caitlin thrashed with plumbing that devoured their bathroom floors and electrical outlets that threatened to set their modest residences ablaze, occasional men who beat them, bosses who terrified them, and problems of complexions and weight and sickness and faithless children.

She sighed at each tale brought her, held her breath, even moaned slightly, then like a loyal, ever true fountain poured forth her sympathy. As her savings accumulated, she remained in the house on Ward where she had lived with her husband, six blocks from where she been born on Robinson, never elevating herself above her friends, she told Daly. She had her roses and lilacs, a thousand familiar scents on the air, old faces she had known a lifetime.

"This has to stop," Daly told her when she admitted him to the house.

"What?" she asked. "Daly, you're flustered."

"You called Jessie. Do not save me!"

"I wanted to know the woman. You introduced us. Please have a lemonade. I have lemonade made. The lemonade will calm you down. Perhaps you'll have a Pepsi."

"No, I'm not staying, I'm not calming down."

"Daly, has Jessie told you something about me?"

"Only that you called."

"If it bothers you I'll never talk to her again. You two are free to marry, do as you please. I'll be mum as a doorstop. I have one brother in Pittsburgh, and if you want me out of your life I'll follow your wishes."

"Stop meddling."

"You should know that marrying a blind woman has its penalties."

"Ruth Marie!"

"Daly, you're almost fifty now. If you had listened to me the first time you married I could have saved you the grief and sorrow. You should grow up. You're going to get Father's inheritance soon. You must learn how to manage money."

"Ruth Marie, Boyce Racklin left no money. There is no money. Our father owned two pairs of shoes between the time he was eighteen and when he died."

"God put me on this earth to protect you from yourself."

"God put you on earth to drive me crazy."

"Daly, I can take it. Throw your spears."

He stormed from the house; it was either that or let his heart whirl and thunder and close what remained of his arteries. "Daly," she called after him, "this isn't at all like you," rewarding him instantly by placing him with the other troubled spirits she counseled into the cosmos among the stars she loved and the silver moon, the fish in the sea.

He walked up to the Number Four Police Station, but Captain

Carr was not there. Breathing hard from his recent confrontation with holiness, he left his telephone number for Jimmy and went home and pulled the shades and closed his eyes, trying to forget the Racklin contamination.

Captain Carr called him about Tom Guignan an hour later.

"You got to put an oar in," he said to Daly. "Otherwise, the boy's leaky rowboat sinks."

"You were going to call me about bond."

"No bond. He didn't kill anybody. Natural causes, the man died of a heart attack, history of problems. There were witnesses saw Tom up in Oakland at the time the man probably died."

"Saw him where?"

"Wandering near the park, drunk."

"What'd he do with the ax? Trim the bushes in Schenley Park?"

"I have to see you, Daly."

"Jimmy, to tell you the truth, I have a little more going on in my life than I can handle. I'd just as soon pass on Tommy's son, even if he's not a murderer."

"Can you see me in a half hour? Make it Gustine's. Come on, Daly, the boy needs a hand."

The bar was quiet and Jimmy sat there over coffee, every hair flat on his head, spruce in his uniform. He shook hands with Daly. "I'm glad you could come," he said. "This boy has a problem."

"Jimmy, like I said, I'm going in two directions at once. I heard some medical information that set me thinking—but I was thinking too much before that."

"You were thinking and reading books without pictures in them when we were kids. It's your big flaw."

Daly ordered coffee, and Captain Carr said, "That's the kid sitting there in the booth."

The boy did not look up from the pie he was eating.

"He looks normal enough. I remember him."

"He's just fine when he's not drinking. Then he starts to ramble out of his head. He walked into that guy's house, saw the dead guy, picked this up, and decided he committed murder."

Jimmy took from inside his tunic a twenty-four-inch children's rubber ax.

"That's the ax," Daly said sadly.

"That's the ax."

Daly took it and said, "Where'd he find it?"

"I don't know. It's always a mystery the things you find in a murder investigation that make no sense. There's a shoe missing and we never get an explanation of where it went. Three witnesses swear they heard a cat meowing, and there's no cat; nobody ever saw a cat in the house. Once I found seven hundred, give or take, packs of Doublemint chewing gum in a murdered lady's house, most of it impossible to chew, like shoe leather. Poor woman, nothing to steal, except there it was, chewing gum."

"I guess all that's different is that there's cops there to investigate a crime. Aside from that, there's hundreds of packs of chewing gum in people's houses, missing shoes, life goes on like normal."

"No word like that in a cop's vocabulary. I don't know how young Guignan found his way into the old man's house any more than I know where he got the toy ax. Nobody in the house can claim it. He brought it with him from somewhere."

"Jimmy, I can't handle the boy."

"It's just to look in on him, I can get him a room, the state to pay, and someone official there to check him once a week. But I need you to check him. See he doesn't drink. The alternative is he spends the next two years in mental evaluations, psychological counseling under lockup until he's twenty-one, and then we find him frozen dead in a doorway or jumping off a tall building. This way, you interested, he gets a two-year start on not touching alcohol—maybe he'll go off that same building, but there's a three-percent chance he doesn't go to hell."

"I'm not up to it."

"Sure, you are. Look at him and think Tommy Guignan."

"Where's his brother? The brainy twin from Tech."

"Won't talk to him in the street. Nobody else will either. And, you know, he's a nice-looking kid, reminds me even a little of his father. You remember Tommy always looked good."

"Where's he been living?"

"His mother's sister. She's old, real old, she locks him out and there he is wandering around the north side, a candidate for getting himself murdered for his socks."

The boy came over to the men and shook hands with Daly. "Mr. Racklin," he said, "I don't mean to be a bother to nobody. They tell me I called you, well, I'm sorry. But it was my father said to do it, and, you see, man, everything turned out for the good. It was good advice."

"Jimmy," Daly said, "give me the address when you have Tom set up. I'll look in now and then, okay, Tom?"

"Okay with me, Mr. Racklin, I just don't want to cause anybody any trouble."

In the bright sunlight outside, Daly blinked his eyes against the brightness, and there stood in a vision of lost youth and wasted possibilities Ruth Marie's great friend Inez, a sight on an ordinary day to send Daly scurrying in retreat between parked cars and risking death under the wheels of passing trolleys. Sometimes, he thought, that would be a kinder fate than listening to Inez. He had over the years attended to legal matters for numerous people Ruth Marie announced were her friends. They ran together into one floating school of tiny fish escaping a yawning sea creature with huge jaws in pursuit of them. He could not remember after decades: Was she the one men beat or did she thrash sleeping men in bed who had betrayed her? Like all Ruth Marie's friends, they opened conversations with him by saying, "Daly, I'm glad to see you. I'm worried about Ruth Marie."

This afternoon, she said: "Daly, I'm worried about Ruth Marie."

"I'm fine," Daly said, "just fine, little neuralgia, it's good of you to ask. I've had the limp for years, nothing to worry about, but kind of you to notice. This is just a bad cold, I haven't had the mysterious symptoms come back for two days in a row, no falling down or walking into walls—no problems, no problems at all. Except for the old left leg going dead about three every afternoon, but, you know, you get used to it."

"Don't kid, Daly, your sister is suffering the agonies of St. Anthony."

"Sounds serious. St. Anthony, this is serious."

"I called her last night and she was weeping, crying like a baby, said it was for all of us and her roses and her garden and a turtle she seen in the garden and she says, 'What is it we can know of the dreams and desires of that little turtle?' And I says, 'Personally, nothing, I ain't thought of it, my own dreams and desires are a mystery to me.' She's inconsolable, thinking about snails and butterflies and such. I hung up and says to myself, 'Great hearts are made only to be broken.' She says the same thing to me many a time herself, letting me in on one of her secrets, the great heart she knows is beating in her bosom."

Daly knew from experience that Ruth Marie started out at night with a solitary bottle of red wine to overcome the pain the suffering world caused her, and made wild telephone calls at midnight to doctors with sudden ailments she had decided could kill her that night and to lawyers denouncing accountants who were cheating her—but by morning pretended to keep her private turmoil from her friends, martyred and content that no one knew or would ever know how the world treated her. She was here for others, say no more, I won't discuss it, she told Daly as she unveiled hints to her ascension.

Daly decided to speak the truth to poor Inez, melting on the hot sidewalk like a frozen Klondike tossed away by a willful child. "This ain't no world for saints," he said, preoccupied by the thin line between comedy and sobriety in such matters. "Saints freeze in the winter same as the rest of us and bake in the summer, Inez."

"I wouldn't know, Daly, I'm not in your family."

At the Montefiore Hospital, Uncle Finnerty slept, and Daly knew nothing he said or did, tears or shouts or news of disaster, could wake him.

Three

The next morning the world continued its downhill slide.

The television reported at seven that the night before in California Bobby Kennedy had been assassinated. Daly turned down the sound, silently weeping at the pictures of the living Kennedy and his family. Given the missing shoes in an inexplicable life and the stale boxes of chewing gum, he supposed his heart had spared him to know this grief, too: Now he could go with a fitting last straw.

He knew the old boys: There would be no festive trip to Ireland in celebration of the four getting, more or less, up there in years and still soldiering on. Instead, it was to be, whatever else life held, the burden for the rest of their years of living with Bobby's death and none of them sure a far better man hadn't died with, loosely speaking, half their time on the planet.

Daly was the youngest of the friends. The others were in their sixties and seventies. They were once, being older, heroic to Daly; now he was a hero to them, a lawyer. The friends had come a long way from their youth in Oakland. They were, Racklin thought, still hardy, resilient, brave, no complaints, as if they still were boys with great prospects ahead. He did not know what he would say when the phone call came.

They had descended, all four of them, into a profound depression, still not lifted, when John Kennedy was shot five years ago, and now what? Was this a cosmic test for the race itself, and each individual in it? There's never a time to take death as a private insult, to intrude on a time of tragedy with a look-what-this-has-done-to-me. A wilderness howls across the world and it is death and there's no pain in its arrival unless one chooses to invent sense around it.

The telephone rang.

"Daly." It was Owney O'Doherty. "I guess you know. We're not going to Ireland. I canceled for all of us."

"That's the right thing."

"I'm not going to make it through the day sane. Half crazy now. You seen it all on television; it's set to test our reason. I failed. I'm crazy. I'm going to kill a stranger who looks wrong at me."

"No you won't."

"And why's that?"

"You're asking me? That's the way things are, that's all. You're not going to kill anybody."

"I can't get drunk," Owney said. "I already had four vodkas this morning, and I'm sober as the day I was born."

He began to cry audibly on the phone, and Daly joined him, but more quietly. "Oh, fuck," Owney finally said, "double fuck, triple."

They agreed that they'd invite Silk Brogan and Sydney Mahon to go with them to New York for Bobby's funeral, and if Brogan and Mahon did not care to attend, they'd drive, the two of them, to New York in Owney's new Cadillac.

When Daly called them, Silk said he was too broken up to go to New York, and Sydney said it might as well be New York, since Ireland was out forever in this lifetime. He said don't expect too much—these aren't days for doing anything but digging a hole in the ground and climbing in. "If I wasn't a Catholic, I'd find a tree and hang myself," Sydney said. "There's not much good going to come of anything."

"Well, I figure it's all not going to be left to us to decide anyhow," Daly said to each of them. "Don't hurry it, it'll come." And he thought when he hung up each time of that cold, solar wind that blew out from space and carried before it all human dreams and probably made a noise like planets crashing into stars, so awful was the heart stopping blood to the brain and a soul left without a body, but fortunately humans couldn't hear the shriek across the heavens. They just called it death and let it go at that.

He called Captain Carr, and Jimmy cursed like the others. Daly said, after a while, "What I'm calling about is that I'm going up for the funeral in New York. You're welcome, of course."

"No, no," Jimmy said, "there's no time off for me. But it's the boy, right?"

"Yes, I'll be gone a few days."

"I'll have it all worked out when you get back."

"Well, I didn't want you to think I forgot what we agreed on the boy."

"Daly, you ain't forgot a thing we talked about in fifty years."

Daly then called Jessie.

"I can't believe it," she said, "Daly, I can't believe it."

Bare-armed giants had once wrestled in the sky, and high grasses parted to disclose the silken wings of seraphs when Daly and Jessie talked. She had traveled in England and Spain and described castles to him and herds of sheep in gray grass and low stone walls a thousand years old she had touched, things he had never felt himself.

"Well, I'm going up to New York for the funeral, with Owney and Syd."

"Of course," she said. "I knew you would. I'll manage."

"But I'll be back in a few days."

"Just knowing that makes it easier. It's not something that's going to go away in a day."

"I'll call you the minute I get back."

"Be careful."

"Now, you be careful," he said and then, "You know I love you."

"Good-bye, Right Racklin."

And as he had never said that to her, Daly wondered at what strange paths he took to break off with a woman. *I love you* was signing on for life.

Later that morning it was good to see Owney, brisk and sure of himself. He wore leather driving gloves. He had done well in scrap steel, real estate, investments, and every year he bought a new Cadillac. Sometimes it was gold, sometimes bright red. He wore a little driver's cap and he looked official behind the wheel. The cap gave him a sobriety as if it certified what he was, a fairly short man, legally entitled to drive the long, gold boat. He picked up Daly at eight and they drove to Sydney's house, where he lived with his sister. A widower, he had not been married to anyone for at least twenty years. Owney, on the other hand, had been married three times, one marriage lasting less than a year, a much younger woman, and ending in divorce, the other two wives dying young.

"It was Silk Brogan's wife kept him here," Sydney said. "I hear he has a lot of problems, lots of problems with her."

"What the hell?" Owney asked. "He married rich. Anybody knows it has its price. His wife has demands. His father-in-law has demands. You pay and pay, see what happens to a guy from Robinson took the easy road."

Daly said, "He was the best fighter to come out of Oakland, excluding street types. He could beat light heavies. Nobody would fight him. He knocked out the middleweight champ of Pennsylvania when he was nineteen."

"This marriage ain't like knocking out anybody," Sydney said. "What's he going to do? T.K.O. his wife and father-in-law? Silk barely made it out of Central Catholic. His wife went to Vassar and then some. He was overmatched by two hundred pounds at least."

Sydney brought three flasks and they nipped at each down the Pennsylvania Turnpike. Vodka and gin, and good feelings toward each other; they planned to walk around in New York, then the next day attend services for Bobby at St. Patrick's.

At each rest stop on the turnpike, amid the clutter of dirty dishes on the tables and sweaty people in lines for food, the talk was of nothing but the death. People's eyes were swollen from crying. Occasionally, someone sat by himself on a curb.

Still, what Daly sensed in himself and his friends was an abandonment, a curious loneliness; it was as if they all had had an appointment somewhere with Bobby Kennedy and the man was not there now to keep it. We've lost another one! Was that it?

They checked into the Taft Hotel at Fifty-second and Eighth, a woolly part of midtown, holding memories of the old days when they had gone to fights at the gardens across the street and walked Manhattan in amazement at a city of Irishmen: a city of Jews, too, and Italians and blacks and people who were unidentifiable to them, slender-armed women and men in seersuckers and straw hats with bright bands: hicks from Pittsburgh lost in the wonder of the New Ireland, Daly thought. In Pittsburgh there were plenty of types, too, but you had to pick your spots. Here everyone seemed Irish, even the men in high-fashioned shoes and the women in stylish haircuts. "I never seen anything like it!" Daly told his uncle Finnerty after his first visit to New York, when he was sixteen.

"Not like on the farm, right, son?"

"What a world?" Daly asked seriously. "Is the answer always fuzzy at the edges, Uncle Finnerty?"

"For all except your father," Uncle Finnerty said. "He believes he's descended from chimpanzees, you know. And for my part, the chimps got the worst of the bargain."

The friends had all been to New York on numerous occasions since those heady days when they had plunged ashore like Columbus, water to their knees, onto the soil of the new land, where behind every bush and hailing cabs like he owned the streets was a man probably named O'Connor or Shaughnessy.

They drank in a bar called the Shamrock Cafe. But in the sorrow and uncertainty in the room there were too many noisy arguments. Men shouted at each other and took easy offense.

"Goddamned Irish," Sydney said, "they're going to battle each other at the throne of God."

"If He's Irish, He'll have a stout stick to keep them in order," Daly said. "And then they'll make music."

At the next place, a quiet bar, Owney began to cry. "It's not him dying," he said. "It's him dying wrong. He was too young. I'd give him anything I have left of years on earth, him alive and me gone."

"That's not it," Daly said as Owney wiped away his tears. "It's death that's as common as rain, it comes young, it comes old. But what it comes on when it lands is what its meaning for good or bad is. Coming on Bobby like it did, well, it came right. Age means nothing, good or bad. He did plenty and I'm saying there was a lot more possible, but since the end has to come—and that's the way it is—it came right. Died with a good life left to be judged. Take my uncle Finnerty, he's eighty-three and I love the man, but it's not a life I'd want to be judged for."

"I would," Sydney said. "I know Finnerty Racklin and all the whoring and drinking and not working and loud talk and up all night with whiskey and when that runs out, wine, and when there's no more of that, beer, and never lost a night's sleep for the bad condition of the world. I wish it was all on my record and not his."

Sydney began to sing "Take, O Take These Lips of Mine," and did a good enough job of it that when he finished the few other patrons of the bar applauded. He was slender and wore a thin pencil mustache in white and had bushy white eyebrows. He stepped off the stool where the three men sat at a counter and bowed in various directions.

"I always said the world lost a tenor," Owney said, "when you turned to selling printing supplies."

Sydney asked in general, "Do you remember when it was time for the Irish Club to close, the bartenders wanting to go home, and there was a few of us still ready to hear another story? We used to say to Paul Kerry, the bartender, 'Hold on, Paul, we just put on a Bing Crosby record, it would be disrespect to leave in the middle of "Don't Fence Me In," ' and Paul, like the rest of us, loved the man—and we'd sit for another two hours, playing the jukebox, showing respect by drinking until five in the morning."

We became even younger, Daly thought, than our bright, young years in the tapestry of our adventures. Believing in lives that weren't ever going to be altered, we would always be where the best friendship was, where Bing Crosby sang only for us on the haunted sidewalks of our youth.

"Sometimes, it was Eddy Howard, or Vaughn Monroe," Sydney said. "We said it was disrespect to Eddy Howard, too, to turn out the lights while the man was singing his heart out for us."

"Eddie Fisher, Paul liked him, too. There was a lot of good voices then. Perry Como."

"It was Bing Crosby was the best," Owney said, his voice thick with emotion. "I remember Joe Toomey saying to me when we were having a drink, the night before he was swore into the marines, 'You know, Owney, it comes to me this might be the last song I hear Bing Crosby sing. I might never be sitting here again like tonight hearing him sing like this.' It broke my heart every time I heard the man sing after, they never found Joe's body wherever in hell it was he died in the Pacific."

"I'm not saying Bing Crosby wasn't the best," Sydney said. "I remember the man: 'White Christmas,' 'Silent Night.' I'm just saying there was others, too, that's all. When it comes to that, you ask me to make my choice and I'll make it Bing I hear sing the last song for me, last voice I hear. 'Moonlight Becomes You.' "

" 'I'll Be Seeing You,' classic. 'Be Careful, It's My Heart,' the man was a genius."

"He's still alive, you know, Christmas shows once a year, but I'll bet there's not a jukebox in the country carries a record of his," Daly said. "I'll bet there's months go by you don't hear him on the radio. The man already sang his last song for himself."

"It doesn't matter to me," Owney said, "he sings in my heart off and on all day long. The man's voice is an inspiration to me."

"God-given."

"Speaking of singing, do you remember Elwin the singer, younger kid back then," Daly asked, "and Chickie Muldoon? They stood up at the Irish Club and sang away and the hell with who was listening and didn't like it?"

"Chickie Muldoon? His late mother didn't remember him. Think of it, you bringing his name up tonight, Daly. He didn't mind nothing, him, well, he wasn't no great friend of yours—I remember that."

"No, it wasn't me, it was lawyers he didn't like. He never, in a manner of speaking, laid eyes on me personally. We didn't talk, that's all. It wasn't personal with him, it wasn't personal with me. It was his getting up and singing I meant I admired. It wasn't even his voice, you know, he wasn't that good at it. It was getting up in front of everyone and singing Frankie Laine songs, 'That's My Desire', 'Shine,' putting on a voice like a Negro."

"Elwin McCord could sing, that was a singer. John McCormack."

"It was Chickie Muldoon I admired," Daly said. "He got up and he was no singer and he was no Negro and he threw his arms out and lifted his eyes to heaven six times a song. He would have been making a fool of himself if he had the sense to know it. I had the sense to know it and I sat fast in my seat and I regret it today."

"Daly, you're the damnedest guy, regretting twenty years later you didn't make a fool of yourself."

"Well, I do, I do regret not making a fool of myself a thousand times I had the opportunity. Too much good sense is like a noose around your neck."

"You're young," Owney said. "You have plenty of time, Daly. You can be a world-champion fool you try hard enough. You remember poor Chickie. He died when that woman wasn't even his wife scalded him to death with a pot of boiling spaghetti over he left her with three kids for a girl danced in a bar on tabletops. He never amounted to nothing is the truth, terrible end, but the truth is the truth."

Daly was silent, hardly thinking of the late Muldoon, larger issues intruding: He wanted to die with a bullet in his brain, like Bobby, young, dead for having done right for all that was in every blood cell, nerve, and muscle in his too-soon-gone body.

On Fifth Avenue the barricades were up keeping people on the sidewalk, but starting at the entrance to St. Patrick's the line waiting to enter the cathedral stretched up Fifth toward the park. Quietly, Sydney, Owney, and Daly walked in the street toward the end of the line. As they walked they looked up occasionally, and the people in the line looked at them: There was not the curiosity or the distance of strangers about the appraisal. The people in the line looked directly into Daly's eyes and he looked at them and then he looked down at the hot pavement. No impatience there. They knew in even the long line of the living that what they waited for was permanently up the cathedral steps, the entrance to a time of judgment, another hour, two, Bobby's body would still be inside, the symbols of the Trinity would stand, if not here, somewhere in the future of the people in the line. Only their faces in repose, swollen, hot, disheveled, lost and bewildered, spoke of their left-behind fates: Their eyes were level. He could say, Daly thought, It's a hot day, isn't it, and that would be right. Or he could say, We stand every second on the edge of eternity, dumb to even who we are at our final time, and they would find that appropriate to the vacancy in their eyes. Nothing human was wrong today, a June afternoon of grief and confusion, blankness and bottomlessness.

The line did end in Central Park. They joined it and stood for a half hour, moving slowly forward, sometimes four abreast. Without language Daly felt himself in mourning connected to the other men, their histories as binding as the time now where they moved more or less forward in unison, but Daly felt the shuffle forward oppressive after a while. Their common pasts became lost. There was only the heat of the day, the death of Bobby Kennedy, all the people they had known together, dead, many deaths that united them, but irretrievable now in sunlit moments that became unreal.

"I'm a little light-headed," Owney said.

They're old, Daly thought, this isn't for their arteries and heart and tired brains. He did not feel the wait physically himself, but he realized his friends did.

"Boys," he said, "there'll be sure as the sun rises in the east another Irishman killed tomorrow. Let's go back to the hotel and drink to him."

Sydney was horrified. "Not see Bobby's coffin?" he asked.

"I'm feeling my years," Daly said, and nodded to emphasize the grave condition of his physical bearing.

"You look fine," Owney said. "You know, I'm a little tired myself. It's the vodka and wine combination. It gets me every time."

"Do you remember, Silk Brogan used to say he could drink for a week hand running except it was the Irish Club hard-boiled eggs used to do him in?" Daly asked.

"I heard Cavanaugh say one time," Owney said, "that his father drank three fifths of rum one day, a quart of Scotch, and a fifth of gin and choked to death that night eating a pretzel at the Knights of Columbus Hall, caught in his throat and caused him to cough to death."

"And do you remember the point of the story?" Daly asked. "Italian pretzels have an ingredient in them dangerous to Irish types."

Sydney laughed and said, "Well, it's not a crusade out here with me. I'd rather fight the infidels than wait in this line another two hours. I hadn't counted on the heat. So if it's getting to you, Right, I'll give up my place in line to one of these priests or nuns."

"Do you notice," Owney asked, "they don't have that impatient look you see here or there?"

"They could make it forward for six hours in this line on their knees," Daly said. "And I say that in all respect." He sighed. "I guess living on the lip of the volcano, so to speak, a little rumble down in the valley doesn't set them off with somewhere better to go."

The friends left the line and, feeling among themselves they had betrayed a cause, did not walk past the line back to the hotel down Fifth. "Moving about," Owney said, "I'm feeling that damned combination. It's been doing it to me since I was seventeen—I never learn."

They circled down Central Park South and stopped in Trader Vic's and felt refreshed drinking daiquiris heavy with ice. By the time they strolled back to Eighth, their spirits had revived; and they all sat in Owney's room and watched the funeral on television.

It was Owney who first made the suggestion and it fell on ears not altogether unreceptive to breaking the cycle of gloom and worse that had fallen on all of them. The trees on Fifth Avenue mocked them with the ripeness of the season, and the drinking brought no talk or ease, only numbness; the blue sky over the buildings was empty for all its spring beauty. "We ought to get some women," he said. "We aren't going to Ireland, we ain't going to see Bobby president, or even the poor man alive to raise his children. We ought to do something aside from bear witness to death—it's not like tragedy is a surprise to the three of us, maybe some women for a last tune before we go under."

Whatever uncertainty there was at the proposal, no one spoke. Owney himself broke the silence: "Of course," he said, "I can see the bad manners in it or the unfortunate timing, but there's nobody can say that the situation with us isn't that we're three breathing souls who haven't been through such adventures in our time. Maybe that's the way to honor things, go on about our business, big things in life, and death only interrupting now and again the daily go-round."

"St. Thomas would have given you the twisted-logic award on that one, Owney," Daly said.

"Better twisted than no logic at all."

It was done then with a word to the bellman and a tip too big for the occasion, Owney putting two fifties into his jacket pocket, the man nodding, and a half hour later, as the three men sat in Owney's room, a knock came at the door and the women began arriving. Owney, looking at the other men, said, "Maybe this is not the way Bobby would have pictured us at his funeral, but no one here can say the man could have disagreed with us. All bachelor boys, all young and in our prime, and all that's missing is a couple of women to tea."

Daly, who was uneasy, either from the drinking or the inappropriateness of the gathering, still could not focus on what bothered him. What earthly reason was there to question hiring three women? Bobby would be just as dead if they entertained prostitutes or not. The grief would be the same, perhaps alleviated for an hour; and then, rationally now, no one could say that high jinks on a double bed was not an affirmation of life. Wasn't there enough death in the air to last people a lifetime? He could find no reason not to stand when the third woman arrived and he smiled at her.

The bellman had said the women were models working for an escort service, but, as Daly studied the young woman who walked with him to his room, he knew she was not a model. And she did not work for an escort service—none that could brag of her sophistication or elegant clothes. She was a kid.

"Hi, my name is Rosa," she said when the door closed behind them.

"How old are you?"

"Well, I'm not a virgin."

He said nothing, observing her, the two of them standing six feet apart.

"Twenty-nine," she said.

"You're not eighteen," he said.

"Come on, cut the compliments. You don't look like you're eighteen either."

"No, I'll be fifty soon."

"What's the difference how old I am? I'm ready to learn."

"No, I probably need to be taught," Daly said.

"Why don't you come over here and take hold. Why are you staring at me?"

"It's the cross on your neck. I'm looking at it. It's pretty."

"Does it bother you? I wear it for luck. It was a gift."

"May I ask who gave you the cross?"

"Sure you may. My father."

"Is he alive?"

"Jesus Christ! Are you going to try to save my soul, too? I had one of them once. Don't save my soul, my soul is my own matter."

"Do you know Bobby Kennedy was killed a couple of days ago?"

"Yeah, it's a bitch! But what—hey, do you think I'm stupid? Everybody knows Bobby was killed. I liked him. Why are you staring?"

"When did you get the cross?"

"Okay," she said, sitting on the bed. "You can ask all the questions you want. But I get a hundred a half hour, I'm plenty good. If you want to talk, nothing more, I'll stay forty-five minutes for the hundred."

He looked at her, the brown drapes, the carpets, and the bed. The walls had brown flecks in them from some previous disaster, water, maybe a fire.

He said, "Yes, we'll talk."

He gave her two fifties and sat in the room's one chair.

"Do you want me to tell you how I got into the life?"

"No, I want you to tell me when your father gave you the crucifix."

"Well, it wasn't going to be a true story. It wasn't my father who gave me the cross. It was a man named Benny. He said since I was a Catholic it would bring me luck. Benny's not had good luck lately."

"Not the country either, I think."

"I wouldn't know about that."

"Who's Benny?"

"A man I do business with."

"I see."

"Benny brings me good luck. This cross will be with me no matter what happens. There could be a fire or a flood, anything. I'd run back for it. I'd jump out of a window holding it. He gave it to me two weeks ago, and my luck has been okay, okay for me, not so good for Bobby Kennedy."

"Do you believe in heaven or hell?"

"That's personal."

"God?"

"That's personal, too."

"Do you think there's a devil?"

She hesitated, and said, "Yes." Then she asked, "Can you keep a secret?"

"Sure."

"Benny says he's the devil. He can look in a person's eyes and tell you the country they come from, I mean their families if they were born in America."

"I don't see the usefulness of Benny's gift."

"He says it gives him an edge. He says the devil gave him a way to look into people's souls. He gets information there. Having information about things gives him an edge. He told me things about myself I almost dropped dead when I heard he knew them."

"Like what?"

"Personal."

"Okay."

"Can I show you something?"

She pulled up her dress to her thigh and there was a tattoo of a grinning devil with a pitchfork. "You see," she said, "I'm covered in every direction. I got this cross Benny gave me knowing I'm a religious person—then he told me how to put the tattoo on my leg to make sure I got everything covered. Benny thinks of everything!"

"What else does Benny do with his information except keep away bad luck?"

"To tell you the truth, he doesn't do so good with bad luck personally. It only works for other people when he helps them."

"How so?"

"He thinks he has cancer of the bladder, and he's going to die soon. I'd say that's bad luck."

"I'd say so, too."

"Can I tell you another secret, something you'll keep to yourself?"

"I promise."

"Swear it."

"I swear it."

"Benny says he's twenty-two, but I know somebody knows him from his neighborhood in the Bronx. The son of a bitch, excuse me, is seventeen years old. Ain't that something! A guy seventeen years old seen and done all he's seen and done. I know for a fact he was born while his mother was in jail. Something, ain't he?"

In the morning, after the three friends repacked for their trip back to Pittsburgh, Sydney and Daly were to meet Owney with his Cadillac in front of the hotel on Eighth for the trip back to Pittsburgh.

"The town's a jinx to me," Owney told Sydney on the phone. "Let's go home fast. I never closed my eyes last night."

Owney hung up the phone and said to Daly, "Sydney says I had too much good times with the escort lady last night."

"You don't look the worse for it."

Owney left the room with his cap at a rakish angle, and Daly and Sydney a few minutes later took the elevator down together. The lobby was crowded, more like a train station than a hotel, cabbies running with suitcases, bellhops charging through groups, knocking aside baggage.

Checked out, at the front entrance outside in the street they saw Owney in his car, little cap in place, driving gloves on the steering wheel, sitting there upright as always and commanding the view out the windshield, the same old Owney, but dead as a doornail.

Taking his stiffening fingers from the wheel, easing the body out of the driver's seat, Daly thought, And what a story this would make one day after the grief stops washing over me like acid poured down from the sky. But he remembered that sagas stayed alive only so long as the storytellers and the old bastards are around to tell them or to hear them. Owney O'Doherty died: period. There would be no song to accompany his legend, no one to sing it, no one to applaud it. A man of seventy-four who did well with his investments, and not a word of the scrappy kid who could climb fences and let the others in to ballparks or drive down the Pennsylvania Turnpike like Dynamite Dunn on a speedway in one fire engine red Caddy or went to heaven in another one gold in color.

At Owney's funeral at St. Agnes it seemed to Daly that scarred old troopers from unremembered wars were gathering for a reunion: The lined faces, some bearing the obvious wounds of too many years, were there, but the absences were marked, too. He found himself judging who was ailing and present or sick and missing and who dead as he looked over the crowd. Owney was being buried out of a funeral home in Greentree, in the western part of the county where he had purchased a large home, when the bargains were there. His house sat on the boundary with Mt. Lebanon, a good address for a boy from Ward Street who shared with two brothers one pair of dress shoes.

Owney's family was mostly gone, so Daly made a few of the arrangements for the wake—Owney had left instructions—and after the funeral the old boys gathered again at Owney's house in Greentree to talk.

Silk Brogan was there, and he said, "I keep having this feeling if I had come with the three of you to New York, somehow I'd have caught something in his eye or his mouth to know something was wrong."

Silk himself was the same age as Daly, but he looked as if he could still go an easy ten rounds with some kid anxious to knock his head from his shoulders. He had aged like movie actors on the screen did, a little white to his hair at the temples, mostly the coal-black shine still there. When he left for war at eighteen, the nuns at St. Agnes at the foot of the hill gave him little cards, and one offered a precious family crucifix. They loved us all, Daly thought, but him the most. "Daly, I have to talk to you," Silk said. "Not here. I have a little thing bothering me, just a discussion. I don't need a lawyer." He laughed. "I mean, not that I know I need a lawyer, you know what I mean?"

"You got my number."

"Any bar in Oakland, any night of the week. I envy you, soak."

After an hour, Daly had exhausted himself in the language of farewells; on a bright spring day it was Owney O'Doherty's turn to provide opportunity for past memories and the look of grass and trees on other spring afternoons when everything was younger and less stale. Daly could not shake the feeling that a wake should be held in crowded rooms and grandmothers in black should be sipping a small glass of sherry and a priest should be in the parlor having one drink too many and children should be underfoot. In bright sunlight on a lawn of smooth grass with trimmed bushes and bright flowers everywhere it seemed to Daly it was a wake staged by someone born thirty years too late, and, leaving things to an unschooled imagination, had modeled the moment after a plumbing advertisement in a magazine or a commercial for margarine on television. There was too much cheer of the high school graduation to it.

He turned abruptly at the hand on his sleeve. "You're Daly Racklin."

He said yes to the woman before he was completely aware of her, handsome, as tall as he was, groomed and unlike everyone else there, seemingly not hot in the late sunlight. Her makeup was fresh, her eyes were bright.

"I'm Gloria, Owney's second wife, Mrs. Scone now, but a widow."

"Excuse me," Daly said.

"No, we've never met."

"I would have remembered."

"I've heard you described so many times I was sure it was you."

"How's that, barely standing, reaching for another vodka from under the table?"

"No, a man of integrity, honest."

"What's that look like? John Dillinger had a good look to me, honest, man of integrity."

"Prematurely white hair, smooth, fresh complexion, smiling, looking people in the eye."

"Lawyer's tricks."

"You look like a person someone could be friends with."

"Well, you have something there. I have more friends than I know what to do with."

"Do many women love you?"

"Gloria, Mrs. Scone, please. You're moving too fast for me."

"You never heard of what a man-trap I was? Owney divorced me in less than a year."

"No, I never heard that you were a man-trap."

"I was thirty years younger than Owney, that was the truth of the matter."

"I didn't know the difference was that great. I knew you were younger."

"No, it was the age difference that came between us. But he was fun."

"Well, he never married again."

"Neither did you after you and your wife broke up."

"No, I didn't. She called me Mr. Fix-it. If it's the truth, it's a terrible indictment."

She wrote on a cocktail napkin her name and address and phone number. "I live in Connecticut now. Mr. Scone was rich. Call me if you're in Connecticut."

"Thanks," he said, putting the napkin into a shirt pocket.

"No, I mean, 'Come to Connecticut, and call me from Pittsburgh before you leave.' I have plenty of room for you at my place."

She was full figured and her neck was long. She wore black and had a tiny veil on her hat covering up part of her forehead. But mostly it was her eyes, rich, filled with amusement at their conversation, his obvious uncertainty with her boldness. And her smile: large mouth and white teeth. He watched her as she walked across the grass, went into the house by a patio, and he knew she had left the wake altogether. She had put a finality to an afternoon of being at an unlikely place to mourn and celebrate a boy of smoky rooms and old wallpaper: There would be no confusion of purposes with Gloria Scone.

"Whew!" he said aloud, and went for a vodka, the afternoon ripe with cross-currents, but try as he might, he could not see this sunlight and death as appropriate.

Outdoors in heat and eating small cookies with goose pâté and reaching for a glass of champagne from waiters circulating with trays was no place for a people who came from narrow cottages, rooms filled with too many people, to commemorate the time of someone's passing. The crowds are what we are, Daly thought sadly, rubbing shoulders, feeling each other's breath, privacy of sea and fields and solitary horsemen on night paths, but birth and death not barbered and with too much space separating us. It's the distance that's pulling us into ourselves and away from the hints of poetry in each other, incomplete unless it's tossed in the air between us. And never in sunny, golden air, or places neat and cut to specific measurements. Daly felt like an intruder in this sumptuousness. He rode home with Quinn Toomey and Eddie Flannery, not talking, and they spoke little, too. He understood the sullenness. Owney deserved a more serious wake.

Four

*L*ater that night, thinking he heard his name called, Daly turned to look up Oakland Avenue. There was no one there on the empty street, but the moment of searching for the source was enough to condemn him. Coming out of Gustine's, signaling him on Forbes like a ship going down, there stood Belle, Ruth Marie's oldest friend, who suffered terribly with the others for all the agony his sister felt for an erring world.

He remembered with a clarity too sharp for the occasion exactly now which friend of Ruth Marie's this was.

"Daly Racklin!" she said. "Daly, I had a glass of wine just now, but I couldn't finish it for worrying about our blessed Ruth Marie."

"I'm fine," he said. "Occasional headache, but it goes away before morning, the old knee too, you know, but no denying age, it's the one headache won't depart with morning. But good of you to ask."

"Daly, you're going to joke at your funeral, sit up in the coffin and try to be funny. You may be then, but you ain't now. It's your sister, Ruth Marie."

"Ain't it always?" he asked, wondering if clapping his hand to his forehead, mysteriously saying, "Oh, my God!" and breaking into a run toward home might not be all that was necessary to elude poor Belle. Like the other friends of his sister's, she was a discarded unwrapped package with an unwelcome gift that no one wanted any holiday of the year.

Belle, who seemed to attract such men, was beaten up regularly by her fiancé, Daly remembered now, an inspector at the post office; and Ruth Marie had had Daly bring the brute to court years ago, and she saw Belle through counseling, and eventually persuaded her to separate from him.

Belle, a large woman, did, but not before she broke up a birthday party in the man's honor—she had been expressly asked not to come—by kicking to pieces a huge cake with white icing, a very bad moment for Belle, a woman quiet beyond the normal. "He brought you to this, sweetheart," Ruth Marie told her. "This isn't in your nature, it isn't like you at all, and I know you better than anyone on earth. He's lucky this time it was his birthday cake and not his head you bashed, considering what he did to you. Right, Daly?"

Belle said, "But I felt so dirty doing it, throwing that cake in people's faces, screaming—there was his little girl there—and smearing cake on the walls."

Daly had been called to Ruth Marie's living room to listen to the details, for fear there might be as a result of the shattered birthday cake a lawsuit pending against Belle. Assault on a birthday cake, Daly thought, no icing for twenty years.

"Well, it's cake and that's what's done to cake when it's not properly eaten with a scoop of vanilla ice cream," Ruth Marie said. "Right, Daly? Don't give it another thought, see your frame of mind at the time—you will someday and how it could have been worse. It wasn't a fire you set, only sent flying a cake with no ice cream."

"There was ice cream, Ruth Marie, and I wiped it on the drapes before I pulled them down."

"He brought you to it. I know the man."

Unhappily, somewhat later, after she had slashed the tires on his car, Belle did try to set fire to the man's house where he had set up housekeeping with a new wife, and nothing Ruth Marie could do could save her: Daly had gone to the judge with her, but she was given a sixty-day jail sentence. Ruth Marie visited her twice a week and sent her at the Allegheny County Jail comical, cheerful cards three times a week. "Without you steering my path," Belle said on her release to Ruth Marie, as Daly picked her up downtown at the courthouse in his clattering Impala, "I would have hung myself four times what that man brought me to."

"And he'd have been the final winner!" Ruth Marie said, exalted. Daly could see she felt a profound victory over something sinister and dark. "You didn't let him cause you to descend to his level more than an incident or two. And you're not hurt and neither is anyone else and that's what counts. It was God put out that fire, and He's watching over you—I know He is."

"The prison psychologist said I wasn't really trying to set a fire; I did it to get caught. The fire was a symbol."

Even though Belle was required to attend counseling sessions for six months as part of her condition of parole and Ruth Marie always in her advice cooperated with the authorities, she could not sit silent for that one. "Well, don't ask the know-it-all to his face," Ruth Marie said, "but keep it in your mind—if it was a symbolic fire you were setting, why did you use real matches and gasoline and not rub two sticks together and douse the place with lemonade?"

Daly had gone with the two women to the Brass Rail downtown, and all had had a celebratory white wine. Looking at Belle now by the neon on Forbes, burdened by thoughts of that oceanic depth to which people passed from human memory once gone, Daly felt a great sorrow for her. She was not thought of at this moment. She was alive, but a ghost on Forbes before her time.

And in the neon light of these bars themselves were visible ghost saloons, beneath the University of Pittsburgh's plan for paving, purchase, and oblivion, the street a phantom thoroughfare already buried by some master plan.

Belle began to cry. She said, "Last time you spoke to Inez you said this was no world for saints. I've been puzzling it and I'm coming to think you're right. But it's no world for anyone else. I'm sixty-two and living in a sister's house. Shouldn't there be some feeling for me same as there is for people God loves like Ruth Marie and you?"

Daly assured her that he at least loved her as strongly as he did his sister, and that it was only a peculiarly gloomy night that stirred such thoughts in her. He led her back into Gustine's, ordered two wines, drank his quickly, and left money from a ten-dollar bill on the table. He kissed her cheek as he fled, knowing there were at least three more wines in the bar change to help her find clarity in her ruminations about injustice visited on the good.

He turned right on Forbes, toward home.

In the doorway of Lee's Fine Men's Clothing, hurrying, tired now of the night, he observed a boy in a top hat curled up, head down, sprawled lifelessly. It was the last of Forbes as he knew it in such scenes. He moved closer. Seeing people asleep in doorways had always been a cause for alarm to him, but while it was harmless enough in the days in Oakland when it was most likely a drunk, these days it could be a dead person. There had been murders in Oakland, on the streets, drugs, strangers, brutal robberies.

Daly bent over the boy. "Are you okay, kid?" he asked.

"Spare change, mister?" the boy mumbled, and from his deep state between waking and coma, he reached out his hand, palm up.

"Write your father," Daly said, but pressed a quarter into the boy's hand.

"Fuck you."

Daly tried to help the boy to his feet, but the boy wrestled with him. "You can't just lie in doorways in this day and age," Daly said. "Here's a dollar, will you stand?"

The boy stood and reached for the dollar. Holding it before him, Daly backed away. "Come on," he said, "you're doing great, son. This is real good, dark streets and doorways aren't for fine boys like you this time of night."

Finally, after the boy had walked a few feet after the dollar, Daly handed it to him.

"See how easy it was?"

The boy swayed uncertainly, perhaps no more than sixteen.

"Now get yourself a bowl of soup."

The boy turned and walked across Forbes but did not go into the diner across the way. He walked away into the darkness of Bouquet Street toward where Forbes Field had once stood, his top hat and stagger a notice to the world: I don't know the odds. He paused to lean on a wall, straightened himself, lurched down the street.

Maybe what brought us to this, Daly thought, was angels swooping low, scattering celestial dust to repair humankind for the better—always with free will, of course. But wherever one looked, the dust of restoration had been misappropriated by the people who misunderstood. Before self always came kindness. Still, hidden in the seeming changes on the streets was the ripe, perennial carnival of colors and trumpets of the music in symphonies and even merry-go-rounds. It was a continuous uproar, all of it, till the endmost song was over.

Daly was moved by the excitement and noise and promise of more turmoil in the times: Sleeper, awake!, it said to him, like a pamphlet for a health food. Who was to say no good would come of any of it, given human history as one great comedy of mistaken identities?

Soon I'll wear a top hat and sleep in doorways. Imagine the release of it, the simplemindedness, a call to freedom and brotherhood in the expectation that an outstretched palm would bring it. He laughed. Well, they won't tell me to write my father.

At Edward's Bar and Grill, he found sitting at a table two younger men he knew. They both leaped up when they saw him. "It's the Right Racklin," the man called Billy said. "Chomp, it's Right himself."

Chomp, a sturdy man in his late thirties or early forties, an occasional bouncer at downtown bars, once in jail for six months for public intoxication, sometimes a maintenance man at the Montefiore Hospital, said, "Right, Billy had used your name not a half hour ago."

Billy ran to the bar and brought back glasses of beer. "There's a problem I've had thrust at me, Daly," he said, "but it's more along your lines, and that's where your name came up."

Billy's nose was long and his chin was small. He had once been a bartender and had his own place until illness had forced him to quit the struggle and drink to forget his fine past. He had developed a twitch in his cheek, and he said he couldn't find a job because of it. He lived with his wife of twenty-odd years and three children. His wife had her own dressmaking shop and did well, and many people said, all in all, Billy did well, too.

"I went to Owney O'Doherty's funeral today," Daly said, "and I've been thinking of the big problem, the one really big problem, gentlemen, all day. If what's on your mind isn't death itself, let's leave it for another time."

"Worse than death, the soul."

Daly stood. "Billy, Chomp, I've had a long, long day. A long day." He walked steadily toward the door.

"Owney's gone, he was something to all of us," Chomp called. "I'm sure he'd appreciate your thinking of him."

"This is serious," Billy called. "Right, this is very serious. When do you want to talk?"

"Soon," Racklin said, "soon. Not just this minute."

He walked slowly up Forbes, the night clear and warm, and he finally felt tired enough for sleep. He placed the cocktail napkin with the name Gloria Scone and her address and telephone number on the night table near his bed and looked at it with rapt attention. He brushed his teeth and hoped his night would be dreamless and for several hours it was.

At three-twenty his phone woke him from a sleep as deep as a well beyond sound or measurement.

Daly thought that he would not answer, taken by the whimsy that whoever called with their troubles, by his putting a pillow to his ears, would dissipate on the night air with the last vibrations in the phone's shrill signals of need.

He picked up the phone. "Mr. Daly Racklin, attorney-at-law, here, twenty-four hours on call."

"Daly!" Billy said. "What's up?"

"Billy, how do I know what's up, you called me—it's after three in the morning. I saw you just tonight!"

"You said to call soon; it's not too soon, is it? It's a favor someone asked my aunt Elizabeth," Billy said.

"Why couldn't they ask me themselves at noon? I'm not a boy anymore, Billy, I'm in bed at this hour. I am a very old man for my age, getting older the longer we talk."

"It's a lady who doesn't know you personally, my aunt Elizabeth's friend from bingo in Wilkinsburg," Billy said. "I wanted to talk to you earlier, but I respected your wishes. This lady has a granddaughter, and the granddaughter is a mental case, you know what I mean? She's not shaking like she has to be locked up full time and restrained for her own good, but she's screaming and shouting at the slightest provocation. But not bad enough to be put into a straitjacket except once in a while, you understand?"

"I understand more with each passing minute."

"This lady," Billy said, "told my aunt Elizabeth her granddaughter comes down to Oakland once a week, you know, for outpatient therapy at Western Psychiatric and there she runs into an undesirable element hanging around the door where the mentals come, young hoodlums, maybe not so young, thirty-like, the Little Sport and Fingers Malloy, guys from down on Bates and Semple. They take this mental and her girlfriend, a bird of a feather in the insane lunatic catagory, out to Schenley Park or over to the Little Sport's house—when the family isn't there. The Little Sport is a married man. And I think Fingers is in the same situation. They invite all their low friends, you know, and they acquaint the girls with bad habits. You know the guys for years, the element, so you know the unnatural things. The lady thinks this is defeating the purpose she's sending her granddaughter down to Western on Saturdays."

"Where's the granddaughter's mother?"

"Locked up somewhere for her own good?"

"A mental case, too?"

"No, shoplifting."

"Why doesn't the lady who is the grandmother go with the granddaughter?" Daly asked, and then he listened carefully to the phone receiver near his ear. "I hear breathing, Billy," he said, "you there with a dog gasping in the phone? What are you doing?"

"Chomp Farnsworth," Chomp, on the other end, shouted into the phone. "I'm waiting here patiently for my turn to ask you about a personal matter."

"Where are you gentlemen phoning me from?" Daly asked. "I don't hear a sound except you two sniffling and moaning."

"Still Edward's Famous Bar and Grill, Mixed Drinks a Specialty," Billy said. "Arthur, the cleaning man, let us in, so we come in and we're going to move some tables for the use of the phone, help him out. You know, where you saw us earlier when you asked me to call you on this matter."

"Chomp, is what you want to talk to me about related to the subject of Billy's call?"

"No, man, this is personal—I told Billy—I ain't interested in nothing having to do with degenerate guys, the Big Sport, Markie, or Fingers. It's a personal question."

"Can I finish, please, one thing a time. Why doesn't the lady go with her granddaughter?"

"She says the girl starts to scream and shout and act hysterical when she mentions it. And anyhow she has to mostly go visit a cousin who's turning to stone."

"Billy, I'm not asking one word about the cousin turning to stone. You start to tell me a thing on the subject and I hang up, okay? The granddaughter! Okay? Not a word about another member of the family, not the one in jail for shoplifting, not the one turning to stone."

"Sure, Daly, don't get mad at me. It's a condition sounds weird to me, too."

"It sounds like the granddaughter doesn't mind Fingers and the Little Sport teaching them unnatural things."

Daly held his hand over the phone. He could not control his sudden laughter.

"Yes and no I see it. The lady says the granddaughter is sixteen and too crazy to know what she wants. But, Daly, I don't think you ought to be laughing. This is a serious conversation."

"What does the lady want of me? Where'd she ever connect me with Fingers and the undesirable element?"

"She knows the respect guys of all types have for you. You're the Right Racklin coast to coast. But she don't know you laugh at misfortune. She knows you're from around. She says you talk to them they'll leave her granddaughter to recover her mental condition."

Daly looked at the phone. He knew himself to have more than a toe in the water with Fingers Malloy, the Little Sport, and for that matter the mad granddaughter—and maybe the cousin turning to stone.

"She's got the wrong party," Daly said, tired, too much out there for one person to comprehend, much less change. At the rate we're going, we'll all turn to seaweed or stone or blow away like ashes before we take on our universal forms, he thought.

"Would you do it," Billy asked slyly, "if you could save a poor girl and her upset and hysterical friend from going to hell? Would you, Daly? It's not a chance comes along more than once a lifetime. Maybe not in a regular person's lifetime and a half. We were in the choir at St. Agnes together and we know we each have mutual faults, things in our characters we're working to straighten out, but I don't think you're the kind of guy sends young girls off to hell if by a word to a couple of hoodlums a whole change in a person's life could occur. Maybe I'm wrong. Maybe I don't know my Daly Racklin."

"Okay, drop it, please. Listening to you sing me holy songs makes me want to buy Markie and Fingers cigars. I'm saying,

Quiet, because I'm tired of listening. Okay? I'll maybe see you both at the Edward's Bar at two, tomorrow afternoon. I'm not promising anything, even that I'll be there—and never again a call after ten at night! Are we clear on that?"

"Daly, I told you many times straight to your face. You have feelings of superiority to other people, even your best friends, but I told my aunt Elizabeth you'd come through," Billy said, "you always do," and hung up.

He dodged Chomp and Billy for three days. He visited Uncle Finnerty and Jessie daily. Visiting Uncle Finnerty had become something of a religious devotion: Always he came into the small, sterile room, sat before the oxygen tent, nodded at a doctor, and pictured his uncle somewhere here, near heaven or purgatory, no word anywhere even now of his final place in eternity.

There were no words to be said, but occasionally he whispered, "I remember you the way you were."

Not answering his phone, unable to sleep for other people's problems, Daly thought at midnight he'd slip up to the University Grill, where mostly college youth drank. Walking on Forbes, he was stopped by Doc Pierce in a taxicab.

Doc had the cab pull over to a curb as he beckoned Daly.

"Doc, it's good to see you."

"Something bad to tell you. Get him to tell you himself. Silk Brogan."

"Is it a legal problem?"

"It's everything, if you know what I mean? A question for Father Farrell, too. Grave, Daly, serious. Call him tonight, tomorrow early."

In the University Grill at the bar twenty minutes later sat Billy Curran himself, a man who loathed a college atmosphere. He waved Daly onto a bar stool next to him and said it had been only an hour since he had called Daly and received no answer, and here he appeared like a vision at Lourdes. "And people say the age of miracles is over," he said. "Let them try this one on for size. I've not set foot in this place in six years, and I was drawn here like a magnet tonight." He had been calling Daly all week, he said. "Zero hour approaching. The young hoodlums is on the march tomorrow."

"Hello, Billy, good to see you."

"The woman is going to throw herself off the Homestead High Level Bridge," Billy said. "The granddaughter's going to be put away for life if Fingers and them don't start acting responsible. And you're the man can save them all, excepting the parties with no scruples, hopeless in the sight of God. I'd go down there myself to Western Psychiatric Saturday morning, but the hoodlums would laugh at me. You know. 'Billy, a little piece wouldn't hurt nothing for you, either. This ain't your brother the priest, this is low-class *Billy* Curran, not Father Curran from over at St. Ignatius.' "

One of Billy's ordeals, and occasional glories, was that brother Frank who was a priest, Billy generally falling wide of the mark.

"I'll be there," Daly said.

"The lady said she called your house and she didn't get no answer, either. She hung up and called me to tell me she's going off the bridge noon tomorrow you don't help her."

"I'll be there. Now, tell me about the girl turning to stone."

"I thought you didn't want to hear it."

"I want to hear it now."

"It's more a woman than a girl, it's a woman the top of Robinson Street, your old neighborhood. But I'm not speaking of it if you're going to start to laugh again at more unfortunates than yourself. You know I think you're laughing at me some times. And I ain't turning to stone. It happens to be a disease known to doctors all over the world, like it could happen to everyone. Like your water shuts off and you can't pee for six days. Why you laughing?"

"I don't know. Something funny hit me."

"What I said? Racklin, the woman's leg is stone; you can chip it with a hammer and chisel and pieces go flying you'd need welder's glasses a rock don't take your eye out. Man, you're fucking laughing at the eighth, maybe the ninth, wonder of the world!"

Five

Daly called Silk Brogan's apartment and left his number with a maid. It was eight in the morning. Checking the Pirates scores in the paper, he saw in the local section that a young man had been murdered in Oakland. The young man's name was David Brill, but he was known as Top Hat for the hat he wore night and day, summer and winter. He had no home address but seemed to be a person who lived on the streets. He had been crudely choked to death on Oakland Avenue and his shoes were missing, and, the story was vague, apparently someone had cut off at least three toes from each of his feet. Daly put away the paper: The Pirates seemed far away this morning in the new land where baseball was from another time. Perhaps, as the Pirates came to bat in the ninth, hopes for a rally evaporating with each pitch, the boy's soul left his body in the darkness and his top hat tumbled into the gutter as he died, obviously no connection between any of it.

A half hour later, he strolled up the hill to the out-patient entrance at Western Psychiatric. He saw no one there. It was ten to nine. No Fingers, Markie, or the Little Sport and their friends assembled for a festive morning. He saw no young girls at all there, deranged or sensible. Only two nurses. He nodded and they returned his greeting with slight smiles.

He saw a familiar woman walking down the hill toward him, as quickly as her stiff legs could carry her, a former neighbor.

"Mrs. Grain," he said, genuinely pleased the woman still lived.

"It's the Right Racklin," she said. "But, excuse me, sweetheart, I'm late, real late for work. Bradley took sick this morning, same as always, but a little later than usual. And now I'm late, and jobs aren't growing on trees at my age."

"You look wonderful, you're a sight."

"The Sun Drug," she said, "cashier there. Promise you'll come see me."

"I will."

"A promise is a promise."

"Never broke one in my life."

She hobbled along faster. "First it's the ankles," she said, "then it's the knees, and next the hips." She called back: "I don't know which hurts worse. I make myself a bet which it'll be at the end of the shift. Good-bye, sweetheart, you promised."

"Good-bye, Mrs. Grain," he called, and thought, There ought to be a kind building like Western Psychiatric to house us all, but it would span continents, bridge oceans for all that's crazy and we take for normal. Poor Mrs. Grain, betting with herself what part of her body will double-cross her most!

Western Psychiatric Hospital stood formidable over him, solid and stable, like a place that could take a person by the collar and shake sanity into him if all else failed. Daly had grown up within ten minutes of the place, passed it in boyhood twenty times a week, had it connected in memory with the great Pitt and Notre Dame football games played not five minutes away in the Pitt Stadium, dreaded the building with its beyond-the-mirror threat to the reasonable and the odd thought that all things that concerned people walking on the streets of Oakland were nothing to the patients inside the building.

Madness held its charms: It could be the peace that passeth understanding. But why, then, the tears and the anguish Daly occasionally saw on the faces of the people on the streets, the obvious patients, near the building? Was there no comfort in lunacy either? There was certainly none in too much lucidity.

Two girls, about sixteen, walked toward where he stood on the path. They stared straight ahead, but Daly could see they were observing, walking slowly, allowing someone hidden to see them.

"Ladies," he said, smiling broadly, clownlike in his simplicity. "My name is Daly Racklin, here's my card."

The one girl looked at the card and said, "I heard of you, my cousin Michelle."

"I'm a lawyer, and I'm representing you today."

"About what?"

"No crime yet—but this is between us. There are unsavory street characters hang around this hospital. The police watch for them. They lie, the truth isn't in them. I'm here, as a matter of fact, to warn one of them that his conduct could get him twenty years in a state prison."

The girls were uneasy. Both wore makeup arranged as if in a dark room. Their cheeks were painted near their chins; their lipstick was crooked. Both wore a greenish mascara. Daly thought if they broke into a run the heavy makeup would, like a suit of armor, stay in place while the girls dashed away from their coating of powder and perfumes. Both very thin, they seemed unlikely candidates for rendezvous with local hawks—but it was 1968, Daly thought, and a person needed to give anyone under eighteen a drug test to affirm whether a specific conversation was making sense.

"What's your meaning?" one of the girls asked.

"My meaning is that you can be in a lot of trouble. I'm here to talk to certain guys, not the two of you. But you'll be implicated, of course."

"What's 'implicated'?"

"Involved."

"Involved how? Are you a cop?"

"No, a friend, honestly, a friend—I'm telling you choose your company wiser."

"Well, thanks, I have to see the doctor. Thanks for the advice."

"We don't know what you're talking about," the girl who had been silent said.

"Then no harm done," Daly said, looking down the hill for the street boys.

"My cousin is Michelle Shortall," the girl who did most of the talking said. "Michelle Shortall?"

"Yes, I know her. I haven't seen her in years."

"She's a mess," the girl said, "like something out of a comic book," and the two of them turned and walked down the driveway to the outpatient clinic.

Two uniformed policemen pulled into the driveway where Daly stood watching the girls.

One of the policemen leaned out of the car window and asked, "Daly Racklin? Daly, are you planning confinement, son? I'll testify you belong in there with the other baskets."

"I'm waiting for someone."

"Not one of them sick-minded girls? Daly, you must be ready for the head doctor. The locals gather outside here on Saturday mornings like flies on an old man's beard. You ain't young enough, Daly, go take a cold shower."

"Marty, it's me, the Right Racklin."

The policeman asked, "Then what are you doing here?"

The other policeman who had not spoken opened the car door and came around to where Daly stood. Daly recognized him as a mean old-timer from Number Four. He was red from a deep sunburn and drinking.

Daly said, "The truth is I'm here waiting for a friend of mine."

"What's his name? Was you talking to two girls just now?"

"Well, it's a lady I'm here for, she wants me to see a certain man and talk to him."

"Edward Malloy? Fingers?" the policeman standing over Daly asked.

"He's known by that name."

The cop named Marty took Daly's elbow. "Daly, St. Augustine

couldn't work this out: I know you mean well, I know you do. But this is law-breaking. We catch them hoodlums at it, they go to jail. If you're a friend of law and order, advise them to run when I apprehend them. Tell me you will so I can plan to shoot them someplace up close it won't kill them, just maim them for life, in the knee or the shin maybe. And if I was you I wouldn't be talking to young girls on their way to the head doctor either."

Daly climbed into the front seat with the mean officer. "You ever have nightmares about these loony girls Fingers and the rest molest?" he asked.

"One of their grandmothers asked me to come over to the hospital and talk to Fingers about things. I said hello to those two girls while I was waiting. There was a rumor Fingers was going to be here—I don't know any more about it than that."

"You never been here before today."

"Never, except to walk past the place on my way home."

"Where do you live now, Daly, it's not the same no more?" Marty asked.

"Same place. Coltart. Not Robinson, not for years."

"It used to be people like your people and my people in Oakland," Marty said. "Now it's junkies and communists."

The cop driving said, "I knew your father. I just made the connection, funny ideas, but a great man."

Marty said, "The first Right Racklin."

"That's my father."

Both policemen were quiet, and one said, "You know them girls are innocent. They're carrying the burden of being crazy."

"That's why I'm here," Daly said. "No other reason."

They drove down to Number Four on Forbes and the policeman stopped the car.

"Okay, good Samaritan, take a walk," the cop at the wheel said, "we don't have nothing but a lecture for you today. I know you to be a friend of Jimmy Carr, show some respect."

"Wait a minute," Marty said. "Ike don't mean it like it sounds, Daly. We know you're not up to anything. It's just that today we're on edge. We don't have room to maneuver. Tell Daly you didn't mean it like it came out, Ike. There's no reason to be talking about Jimmy Carr. Bringing up stuff."

"No, hell no," the other cop said. "Daly, I'm working off steam because I don't have nobody but you to talk to—it's Fingers and them hoodlums I was talking to and looking at you. You know what's on the streets now. Fingers and them are pictures in a holy book. There's guys so coked they'd kill their grandmothers. Please, accept my apology. I knew your father by sight and reputation. I had no reason to bring up Jimmy Carr. You old-timers were one for all and all for one."

Daly shook hands with Ike and then Marty and waved at them as he walked away up Forbes.

He stood out on the sidewalk before Number Four. The building was built like a small castle, large stones and a cathedral roof. A block down Oakland, Daly thought, and I'm at the street where the old Ancient Order of Hibernians, Division Nine, used to be; four blocks up on the sidewalk, I'm back at the psychiatric hospital. A block away a kid in a top hat was strangled. Two blocks down Forbes my old neighbor, Mrs. Grain, is on the cash register at the Sun Drugstore.

This fine June morning, he decided to visit old Mrs. Grain.

And there in the Sun Drug, in a booth near the back, was Markie Lisle, the Big Sport, and his cousin, the Little Sport, Bernard Riley, the famous car thief, and Fingers Malloy with the two underage girls, neither of them looking particularly crazier than the young men seated with them. Daly said to Mrs. Grain at the register near the door, "Excuse me, Mrs. Grain, I have to talk to these guys in the booth. I'll be right back."

"Daly, they're not much to talk to."

"They're not giving you any trouble, are they?"

"No, no, perfect gentlemen, but it does make you wonder why coal miners get killed down in mine shafts and God lets that bunch drink chocolate Cokes and eat Oreo cookies in the drugstore all Saturday morning."

At the back booth everyone looked up at Daly, and Fingers said, "Daly Racklin, hey, man."

One of the girls said, "We're the girls just talked to you, went in one door up at the hospital and came out the other while you were talking to the cops."

Daly said, "Fingers, Markie, Little Sport, can I talk to you guys a minute?"

The three men slid out of the booth, the girls watching Daly. Taking Fingers, whom he knew better than the other two, by the elbow, he said, "I got to tell you guys I was just detained by the police."

"You, Daly Racklin, you ain't a criminal."

"It was account of them girls. The police took me as I was walking by the big hospital there—what's it?"

"Western Nut."

"Yeah, Western Nut, and he asked me do I know you guys, and he mentioned you by name. And Grand Larson, he mentioned him by name. Asked if I knew you. I said, Yes, I was acquainted. He said if I see you to tell you it's ten years minimum if someone swears you been tampering with minor girls."

"I'm a minor myself," Little Sport said.

"Guess it'll be five years in that case. Cop told me to tell you, I did it. Does he mean them girls?"

"I don't know what he means," Fingers said. "Them particular girls are each twenty-one."

"Edward, it's not me that needs satisfying on the question of the girls—it's the law. I told you, that's it. The cop put a club in my throat, choking me, thinking I was one of the guys he was looking for."

"Yeah, he got the wrong parties, Daly, top to bottom. We don't know nothing more about it than you."

"Them Italian guys from down in the Hollow," Markie said, "is who he's looking for, not us. My brother is a cop. I wouldn't disgrace his name."

"I told you," Daly said. "I pity them Italian guys; these cops are mean on this. There's no graft, no payoffs, no nothing in it for them. They can pound guys into sardines in a can and nobody cares. It's easy on this; all their brutality toward young guys on the street comes out. You know them, leaving out your brother, the kind of bastards they are when there's nothing in it for them."

"Yeah, thanks, man, these girls are twenty-one."

As Daly turned to leave, one of the girls called to him: "My cousin is turning to stone, Mr. Racklin. Michelle Shortall, the one you said you know her. Hey, did you hear me, I have a cousin turning to stone."

Daly did not turn to look at the group in the booth until he was a safe distance away.

He watched them talking to each other as he stood at the cash register with Mrs. Grain. The woman had veins so bad it was a miracle she could stand, but she did, eight hours a day, six days a week, to support her husband, Bradley, who was in even worse shape. He couldn't walk, had been bedridden for the past five years. Daly decided on the spot to hand her five twenties, all the money he carried.

"I can't take this," she said. "I did nothing to earn it, I haven't worked for it."

"Bradley's not going to tell you, but he lent me two hundred about five years ago. You mention it and you'll send him into depression. I owe you another hundred—I came into a good fee lately—but, remember, not a word to Brad. I'm just not carrying the cash today, but I owe it to you and him."

She looked him directly in the eyes for a long moment but nodded and put the money silently into the pocket of her smock.

When Daly looked over to the booth, Markie held up two fingers in the peace sign, nodding broadly, and smiled at Daly. And given the style of the men in the booth, it could mean Daly, for all his advanced years, was welcome to join them on their caper that afternoon; or perhaps the afternoon was off—for the best of reasons, the police too knowledgeable—or, a friend of yours, Daly, being on the register here, who's the wiser if your young pals filter out the door past her without paying the check?

"There's a lady I used to know turning to stone, Mrs. Grain," Daly said. "I think I'll swing by now to see how she's getting on."

A long time ago, when he was recently married, Daly had committed adultery for the first time. He was twenty-four then, and he knew Michelle, the girl now turning to stone, from that day. He had gone to a wake on Terrace, to one of the houses where friends of his parents had lived, a family named Shortall, the husband, Michael, dead at fifty-eight, leaving his plump, despairing wife of a similar age, and the niece, Michelle.

The house was set back from the street, up a long path that one climbed gradually, an old black stone house, the couple childless. Racklin had sat in the parlor, the room with fringed lamps and ottomans blocking every exit, colors of wallpaper and ceiling too dark to make out maroons from brown. It was mostly neighbors and people from St. Agnes. He washed and dried glasses all night patiently at the sink in an apron and sipped at bourbon and water for hours, helping Mrs. Shortall and the niece, smiling at him and looking up at him from under dark lashes. He cleared tables of ashtrays and set out cookies, a strawberry cake, and potato chips. His wife, as things were falling apart between them, had gone to her family in Cleveland, and the women at the Shortall house found him the hero of the hour, petting him and asking about his marriage. He attended his mother and Uncle Finnerty, his father leaving early to save some institution in the collapsing nation. Daly had been struck by the fancy that most of the company would one day reassemble over at his family home on Coltart, there to sit in wake for his own mother and father, a traveling band of mourners, falling off one by one as time passed. Then he would be the Right Racklin, but what to do with it, having not the energy or the will for too great a portion of goodness or even the contemplation of its burdens.

Soon, he was alone with the niece and Mrs. Shortall, straightening chairs and running a vacuum cleaner until two in the morning, tipsy. He had been brought to visit the Shortalls with his brother and sister twice a year over his youth, and Mrs. Shortall recited to her niece, a thick young woman, stout as one of the oaks in the wide yard outside, reminiscences of Racklin as a boy. Woozy and feeling wanted, he grinned and listened, pleased to be remembered as pious and comical, and he lay on the couch after the niece left and listened to the widow speak of Michael, her late husband, and her tears over the years at not having a child. Somewhere in the night, the widow lay down beside Racklin on the couch in the dark parlor. He held her. She stroked his face and said, "Racklin, you were handsome as an angel even in boyhood." He ran his hands over her as if she were a woman to whom he was making love. "Racklin," she said, "how pretty you are." She pulled up her black widow's dress and lowered her pants and on the brown, homey couch he lay on her and inserted himself and rode her slowly, loving the expanded sense he felt and feeling queer at the same time, the rightness and the wrongness causing his head to feel gripped by a vice. He stayed on her a long time, thinking, She's fifty-four if she's a day and twice my age at least, but it's as good as anything I've ever known: What are we about? There lay no boundaries or a world outside the two of them. They held each other until dawn.

Ashamed by the morning's light, Daly kissed the widow, ate breakfast with her at the kitchen table, and put on his overcoat and walked outside to find snow had fallen. He came back and she gave him a shovel and he cleared the long walk to the street for her.

He visited the woman sometimes twice a week, a familiar figure clearing out leaves from the rain gutters in the house, removing storm windows in the late winter, painting windowsills. People on the street suspected Daly of interest in the thick-as-a-tree niece, the two of them often sitting on the front steps while Maura Shortall sat rocking in a porch swing listening. It lasted seven months and bewildered Racklin. Did the want never stop? The widow took him as a man who knew his way around women: And if she had few qualms, loving him with a festive heartiness, he lay awake at night puzzled about her and himself. In the places where the need should have been quieted after a time Daly still saw it raging brightly in his mother and father's old friend. It was too much to consider. The women, dresses hiked to the knees and flailing away at the Irish Club, or sitting with each other and recounting the antics of children now grown, and grandchildren: The dancing, the swaying to music, the laughter, did it conceal natures as passionate as that of Maura Shortall, who tore at Racklin the moment they were alone? He told her after a time, in the summer, he could not go on with it and she baked him a cake for his birthday, his twenty-fifth, and the two of them had a private celebration in July. He kissed her on the forehead as he should have the night of Michael's funeral; she clung—but only for a moment—and he left to become a good boy from Coltart again. He dodged the niece, Michelle, when he saw her. And he was never the same again with his wife, guilty and hangdog, lost and unfamiliar.

When he told Father Farrell of it a week later, the priest listened quietly, yawned—he had been up all night comforting the mother of two small children who were dying of tuberculosis in Soho—and said, "Serves you right."

Maura Shortall had resumed her marriage and love for the dead Michael on some other level of being twenty-five years ago, and Daly had become the only Right Racklin, and the niece—stumpy as a fireplug and with hair red and brown and gold where she tried to color it to achieve beauty but had succeeded in imposing on her head the chaos in her spirit—was now turning appropriately, in a world long gone mad, to stone. Or so it was said.

At the top of Robinson lay a large vacant field where a veterans' hospital was under construction, mostly a mudhole of cranes and empty wheelbarrows; beyond that lay an abandoned cemetery where no bodies had been buried in Daly's time, and no mourners came. Often, as in this early June evening, a fog lay on the field.

Before he visited the woman turning to stone, he decided on impulse to visit the barren field and perhaps the cemetery where he walked when he was a boy. It once was a place, in its desolation, of romance and comfort. Tonight, he looked for a return of the feeling.

Crossing the construction site, Daly often walked through walls of fog and soot too thick to see more than a foot in front of him. He found the opaqueness frequently a retreat. He could lose himself there. It was a place to go to feel alone. He found the disjointed earth mounds and rearranged rocks in the field a port, no judgment here or even a sense of up or down in the billows of fog.

Perhaps it was the thought of Michelle Shortall in her illness, and death knocking in his chest, that caused his heart to pound suddenly in the peculiar pale ashen fog that lay on him like something personal. He felt as if something was going to be revealed to him: He saw in quick lightning flashes—and he laughed to himself—his uncle on his miraculous streetcar, and prepared to tell Jessie about the wonders of the vacant field. He stopped to listen: Had he heard someone calling his name? He had thought once a crane in this field resembled a dragon, and when he told Jessie she said she wished people saw more than dragons in thick fogs. Today the field and fog glowed with late sunlight. Daly stopped again at a sound. Was he being called in the fog? He had, as he often did, lost his direction.

He saw clearly then, ten feet away the outline of an old car, one from years before the war. There, as sharply as the first photograph his uncle had shown him of the subject himself, stood Pretty Boy Floyd in vest and white shirt, his tie knotted at the collar.

Pretty Boy waved at him. "Hi you, kid!" he called, ducked his head, and ran. He cradled, as he always did, a tommy-gun, and Daly distinctly heard, like a hammer striking hard wood, gunfire.

Daly dropped to one knee, alert and watching. I'm in the last minutes, he thought, in the cornfield where the authorities finally brought Pretty Boy to earth.

Pretty Boy, twisting from side to side, to make a lesser target, dashed off into the fog. Daly crouched. He couldn't see Pretty Boy. More gunfire. He thought, I'm losing my mind and My name is Daly Racklin and I live on Coltart Street and I am going to see—no confirmation of rationality here—a woman turning to stone. And he sighed deeply and said aloud, "Okay, my mind is here," but so is Pretty Boy and those are the sounds of his footsteps and that of the police—I see them, but in a group, not clearly, fog men—and they are all running behind the bright light of the fog. Floyd staggers as the fog momentarily has a gap in it. The gunfire is muted. Daly sees men gathered in a circle around the fallen gangster. Daly starts to run in another direction, but Pretty Boy says in a voice almost gone: "Right, it's me. Charles."

Daly turns. He recognizes the call to friendship. He knows it's Charles Floyd, a man the newspapers call Pretty Boy, and the gangster doesn't like it.

Daly has walked with his uncle Finnerty the very cornfield where it took eight lawmen to kill the gangster. He has gone to the Carnegie Library on Forbes when he was ten and seen pictures of Pretty Boy in old magazines and newspapers, an expert now. Why? His uncle has somehow irrevocably connected his nephew to the Oklahoma outlaw. Floyd, he is sure, is a lesson to him descended on the construction field, a Racklin visitation that can arrive on a 67 Swissvale if need be.

It is a call to him, to something outlaw inside that says burn the jails, let loose the maniacs, we'll never know the difference.

Daly advances. "Charles?"

Floyd looks up at him, then the detective bending over him. "Are you Pretty Boy Floyd?" the detective asks.

"I am Charles Arthur Floyd."

He means, Daly thinks, you can't take my name from me, my life, my breath, okay, not my goddamned name. Charles, he wants to say, It's Daly Right Racklin here—called that because I shoot straight, I honor my friends with love, I try to give more than I get—and proud of it all, like you.

"Right," Charles Floyd says with his last words, "what you ain't and ain't going to be is the best of what you are. Hear me, kid, I died being myself, like I lived, not being what they wanted me to be."

The men dissolve and there's nothing here now except Daly and shining fog. He looks at his hands, real enough; he clicks his teeth. He pinches his ear. He's still scared. He trembles in his knees. He walks in the direction where he thinks there might be the old cemetery and then a narrow street and then Robinson. He can feel the vacant field where a hospital will be built fall away behind and with it the ghostly crew and—the what?—the hallucination brought on by the approaching meeting with Michelle. A fear of death, a call to try danger. He is careful on the leaves of the cemetery. No one tends the place. The leaves are wet and the ground is unsure, although Daly knows it well. He knows from boyhood a path he follows through the battered tombstones, names all but eradicated by rain and sun. He touches them for balance and old times' sake, nodding to the graves of people he has strolled among for years.

He remembered in a rush as he knocked at the door on Terrace the brown parlor, the fringed lamps, and his every passage on the old, worn carpet. He smiled, his lips trembled with the vision of Pretty Boy Floyd and the strangeness of standing at the door to this house now. He knew himself, it was a need out of turpitude that had brought him here once, seeking love more than marriage. Still not being content with one life brought him here today. Charles Arthur Floyd, he explains the mountain of longing in me. He had not thought in years of Maura's old stove, the ottomans blocking easy movement in the rooms.

He waited at the door. "Michelle," he said when the stout woman opened it.

"Daly Racklin."

"Mr. Right Racklin," he said.

"Same as your father. Yes, he was the Right Racklin, too. I knew you'd be coming soon. He told me."

It is the same kitchen that brought back the aroma of cocoa as strong as the heat of the day itself.

"Oh, it's good to see you. It's good of you to think of Aunt Maura and me."

He sat down at a green wooden chair and remembered Maura bustling and the flowerpots on the sills, and Michelle told him Mrs. Shortall had been dead for more than ten years but she had frequently mentioned him up to the end.

She had left her house to Michelle. "I swear she spoke of you as often as she did of Uncle Michael," the woman said. She herself had thickened even more, her face flat as pancakes, her eyes lost in a smooth mask, buried and black.

She wore white gloves. She had a rare disease, it turned out, and its course was to calcify her limbs to a stonelike hardness. She could hardly bend her fingers or her hands at her wrists, and sometimes she stepped on a sharp object and did not feel it. The progress of the disease was slow, but the great dread was that as it moved along from her limbs to her internal organs it would actually cause them to turn to rock, lungs, kidneys, and heart. The time of the disease's progress was uncertain: No one was sure of the movement of the calcification as it hardened and worked its misery on her body. "I wear the gloves because I can't stand to look at it," she said. "My hands are like paws, you know."

Stammering, he said, "You haven't changed much. I'd recognize you anywhere. You're about the same."

"You're handsomer than ever, Daly—no, I mean it."

"I guess I'm lucky, I've never been sick a day in my life."

"And good-looking!" she said emphatically. "People say you're the best-looking fellow there ever was in Oakland. Some used to say Silk Brogan, but I always said you. There was Dennis Joyce who went out to Hollywood, but I said, 'Daly Racklin.' "

"There's a lot of contenders for that crown."

"I say you won it. There's a lot more say you won it."

"They say that?"

He sat at the kitchen table warmed by memories, touched by the thick woman whose eyes followed him as if the two of them shared a joke. She brought him coffee, apologizing there was nothing to drink in the house because she didn't touch it for fear of losing her balance and not being able to crawl for help. A young girl from the government housing projects a block away came in a few times a week to help her clean the house and attend to laundry.

Michelle placed supermarket cupcakes and cookies on the table, and Daly ate three of them, sipping coffee, making elaborate, satisfied sounds over the feast. Outside the church bells rang, the bells at St. Agnes and far off (if one knew how to pick them out) the bells of St. Paul's. There came into the kitchen from somewhere in the government housing project the sound of firecrackers or a car's backfire.

Daly stood, wiped his mouth with a paper napkin, and kissed Michelle on the cheek. "I got to be running now, I was in the neighborhood. I'll see you again soon, sweetheart."

She touched her cheek and said, "It's going to be a good summer."

They stood at the kitchen table both looking down, and she asked, "Daly, do you remember one time on a visit here you fell into a foolish mood and did us a kids' game?"

"I did that? Must have been drunk."

"You jumped all around, boxing imaginary with me and Aunt Maura—and then you did something I never saw the likes of, before or since. You took my jump rope from when I was a kid and you did jump rope on it right here in the kitchen, whack, whack, whack. Aunt Maura and I almost died."

Daly asked, "I did make a fool of myself? It was being young, Michelle, I ain't that anymore."

"Daly, do it now, pretend it's years ago and we're all in the kitchen."

With a slow movement as if she were attached to the chair, Michelle rose and took from a cabinet a jump rope. Her fingers did not close on it. "Do it please, Daly," she said.

He unbuttoned the top button on his shirt, then decided to take it off altogether, standing in a T-shirt. He lay his shirt in a neat bundle on another kitchen chair. "If I injure myself," he said, "you have the number down at Montefiore. Tell them an old fool finally did himself in not growing up." He took a couple of steps, swinging the rope, then a couple more.

FAMOUS MARTYR DIES JUMPING SKIP ROPE FOR AFFLICTED WOMAN

Career of Stunning Mediocrity Ends in Comic Death

He felt lighter than he had before he started. "Holy Mary Mother of God," he chanted. "Excuse me, it's the kind of things ran through my mind from when I was a kid."

The rope felt good, rhythm right, slaps on the kitchen floor precise and quick.

"Susie had a boyfriend," Michelle chanted. "Kissed her on the cheek! How many kisses did she get? One-two, three-four, then he kissed her twice more."

Intent, Daly kept at it, feeling the sweat under his shirt, then his back moist and his face wet with it. "Seventy-two, seventy-three," Michelle continued, and Daly did not miss a beat. When he stopped his heart was pounding and the kitchen seemed far away. He sat down. He waited for his heart to pound itself to oblivion; then he waited for it to stop. He was short of breath, but he did not die.

Michelle laboriously stood. "I used to jump rope for hours," she said. "It doesn't seem possible now that it was me." She walked slowly to the stove. "Let me fill up your cup, please."

"I have to go," Daly said.

COLLAPSES ON SIDEWALK: NOT FOUND FOR FOUR DAYS

"I hope now you found your way here you'll come back soon."

"Sure, I will," he said, pulling on his shirt. "You bring back old times."

Ponderously and breathing hard, Michelle followed him down a long dark hallway to the front door. He knew the smell in the wallpaper and the dark wood. He unlocked the door. "Don't stand too close," he said. "You're not dressed for the heat, it's a killer outside."

"Daly," she said, standing back and hardly visible, "I used to think a nonsensical thing when I was a young girl—I'm forty-one now—and you used to visit Aunt Maura. I used to think mostly you were coming up here, hanging about, putting up the storm windows, fixing the washer one time—we had to call a repairman later anyhow—that you were coming up here because you wanted to see me. That you never said anything to me because you were married and fellows like you didn't say things to girls when they were married. I told Aunt Maura it once and she laughed, and said, 'You never know,' but I could tell she didn't believe it. Was there anything to it? Were you looking in on us so often because you liked me and didn't know any other way to get next to me?"

"What Maura said, I say," Daly said, partially closing the door against the heat.

"I told you she was skeptical, she laughed."

"I tell you the same thing she said, and I do not laugh."

"It kept me awake nights, wondering was the best-looking fellow in Oakland stricken with me."

He took her gloved hand and kissed it. "Don't stay up nights thinking of me," he said. "I'm not worth the loss of ten minutes of sleep."

"You going to come back? I haven't scared you off?"

"Long as skipping rope isn't part of it," he said.

She turned back into the house when she heard Daly Racklin outside on the porch. "See," she said to the ghost of his father, the first Right Racklin, who sat on a maroon couch in the parlor. "I told you he would come, I knew he'd be here again one day. He loves me, no matter what you say."

PART TWO

The Sin Game

Six

Captain Jimmy Carr had placed young Guignan in a nice enough room in East Liberty, but the sight of the boy sitting on the edge of his unrumpled bed made Daly uncomfortable. He had obviously not disturbed the bed. Myself sitting there and afraid to move for alarm that all directions were wrong, he thought, in that one room and counting hours of sobriety on a clock: I'd be drunk within the hour.

He took the boy to a movie theater.

There was considerable gunplay and violence, and Daly was for a moment apprehensive, but it occurred to him it was all the same to young Tommy: It could have been love scenes or rocket ships. He became lost in details. He hardly followed the plot. Coming out of the theater, he blinked his eyes and said, "That was a great movie. But why did the little guy jump out of the window?"

"The other guy was chasing him."

Daly bought him a club sandwich and the boy ate it quickly. He was finished with the sandwich in less than three minutes. Daly walked with him back to the boardinghouse off Highland.

"Well, son, what are you going to do now?"

"Captain Carr said he'd call me tomorrow about a job he found in a restaurant. The lady from social services is going to take me."

"I mean right now—what are you going to do?"

"Go to bed, I guess."

"But it's four in the afternoon."

"I do it all the time."

He called Jessie to tell her about young Guignan. He told her all of it, the toy ax, the movie they'd seen. And he was not surprised when she said, "Of course, he'll live here with me, maybe on weekends at first. I need someone. You can't leave him alone in that room."

It was as if she had told him she was pregnant and he was soon to have a son with her, to raise him, to fall into domesticity—chains clattered just out of earshot.

"No, I don't want you to jump into anything."

"Daly!"

"Well, we'll think about it."

"Church Sunday?"

"Of course."

The eternal *of course*. Daly Racklin is led to his fate, a mighty chorus in the background: OF COURSE!

He had a vodka in Lasek's and listened to a conversation about the Pirates, and, enjoying the lack of immediate problems, none coming down the street at him anyhow, he undertook a pleasant starry-night walk back up Ward, then down to Coltart, brushed his teeth, looked again at the name on the napkin on the table by his bed—Gloria Scone—and fell asleep in his trousers and shirt, to be awakened at nine that night by the phone's ringing.

"Daly Racklin?"

He knew her voice. "Yes."

"This is Gloria. Sydney gave me your number. Did I wake you?"

"No."

"You sound like you were sleeping."

"I sound like that all the time."

"I want you to come up here to Connecticut. You have my number. Do you want it again? Did you lose it? If you don't come up here, I'm coming down there to see you."

When he hung up he lay back and stared at the ceiling: Of course!

On the evening of June 23, Michelle Shortall reported to Father Francis Farrell of St. Agnes Church—who was six months from retirement after thirty-four years there—that she had been visited twice by the ghost of Boyce Racklin, the first Right Racklin. She had remembered him quite well from her girlhood on the Robinson Street hill and it was unmistakably he: From his appearance, which hadn't changed much with his death, and the subject of his conversation with her, it could be no other. Once she said she had seen the handsome Silk Brogan, the former boxer, in church with a strange light over his head, but she did not repeat her story, and he did not pursue her to describe her vision, and heard no more about it.

So different was he than other people that it was accepted that Boyce Racklin, rimless steel glasses, hair wispy, and eyes blue with a childlike innocence, would be able to walk over hot coals perhaps and never know harm. The Racklin family, except for his brother, Finnerty, spoke of him among themselves as if they had been touched by greatness by his presence, as did many other people, and Father Farrell realized they would now, Daly particularly, be offended with their father's alleged visits after death to a comparative stranger.

"Michelle, we've known each other for a long time," Father Farrell said, a pale sunlight falling through a stained-glass window on his right on to his desk and Michelle. "And I know you to be an intelligent woman, bright as buttercups, and I know you to be a woman who has borne with great forbearance a terrible affliction. There's medicine you take, there's books you read that stir your imagination. Is it possible you can pinpoint your vision to a hallucination rather than a visit from Boyce Racklin?"

Watching her in her broad need and the sunlight on her thick arms, Father Farrell thought how beautifully she sat at one with the church itself, the light in the windows. He would miss each moment here, but the Holy Spirit was everywhere, after all—as real here as in Arizona, where after retiring he planned to study rocks and watch sunsets. In the pale blues that fell across his desk and lingered in Michelle's lap ghosts could reside, the miracle of promise and beauty could find its way into anything. We are mystery, by George, he thought.

"No, I know what I saw," Michelle said. "The spirit wasn't wavy at the edges. There wasn't violins, Father, and I didn't see angel wings stirring up my kitchen curtains. I just looked into a certain spot, looked again hard, and I realized, realized, you understand—not like he popped up—I was looking at the Boyce Racklin I knew. It wasn't like a lightbulb going on. He was there, sort of for a while, I guess, and I only just then saw him."

"He spoke to you, you said."

"I spoke first. I said, 'Hello, Boyce! Sorry. I mean Mr. Racklin!' "

"How'd he take that?"

"He ignored it. He didn't say 'Call me Boyce' or 'It's okay, I don't mind.' "

"How'd he respond exactly?"

"He asked me if I say the Rosary every day."

"That's an odd question, isn't it? Boyce was a good Catholic, but I don't remember him being a spokesman. I suppose on the other shore, though, everyone's sort of a cheerleader. He did want to be a missionary at the end. What do you think?"

"I don't know. I said yes."

"Was it the truth?"

"Yes."

"It wouldn't do to lie to a ghost."

"I wouldn't lie to anyone, Father, if you're asking."

The sunlight touched the floor, too, through the stained-glass windows. The scene on the window was of St. Francis and his birds. How would the saint have fared in dry and dusty Arizona?

"Best not to lie," Father Farrell said. "You don't have to spend your time remembering what you said on one occasion or another, leaves the mind free. Did the apparition speak again?"

"Yes, and it's embarrassing," Michelle said.

"Boyce spoke of something personal to you?"

"I'm ashamed to tell you.

"He didn't say anything bad about me, did he?" Father Farrell asked, his face composed and grave.

"Father, you're not taking me seriously."

"I'm sorry. Tell me what he said. I'll look at St. Francis there while you speak and you just tell me and we'll make of it what we can. For all the religious answers we have, they sometimes don't fit the specific questions, you understand? Not exactly, I mean."

"Well, it wasn't religious—not in the exact sense, Father—that the ghost addressed me. He said, 'Michelle, I know what's in your heart. I know you have good feelings and you want nothing for yourself where my son Daly is concerned. The man needs you desperately. He won't say it to you, but he's suffering and it's from women who don't understand him. I think you understand him.' "

Father Farrell looked away from St. Francis to the mosaics that the summer sun cast on his office. The flush to the woman's face was bright and her eyes were shining. She liked reliving her conversation with the ghost. That spectral wanderer said so many things she wanted to hear. Wasn't that the way of most ghosts? When they weren't warning us about our enemies, they were reassuring us of our virtue. Father Farrell had never seen a ghost. Once he had seen a bright light in the sky, but, not given to easy fantasies, he decided he had been reading too long and spots in the shape of crucifixes had come to dance before his eyes.

"Did he give you any instructions?" Father Farrell asked, waiting. Here lay trouble: A ghost's injunctions about people often violated someone else's best interests. Ghosts were most valuable in the long run when they inquired after habits of the Rosary or praying.

"Yes, he told me to tell Daly Racklin of his visit to me and what he said."

"And you're asking me what to do?"

"Well, sort of. I think I have an obligation."

"Then you don't want my advice. You just want me to know Boyce Racklin's up and around on Terrace Street."

"You're making fun of me."

Father Farrell stood and came around to Michelle's side of the desk, walking in the patterns of color falling from the window, his hand blue, his sleeve orange. "Teasing a bit, Michelle," he said, putting his hand on her shoulder. "I don't think this ghost came on an urgent visit. Give his appearance a week or two to sink in, think over what he said, what he meant."

"He said it to me, 'Speak to him of your love. It will save him.' "

"That's clear enough," Father Farrell said, liking the glow of St. Francis enough that he wished he could join him in the window where lonely women had no instructions from the beyond. Official now, he asked in a measured voice, "Were there any witnesses to this appearance?" and to his astonishment, she said, "Yes."

He had been sure the reverse was true, to spare the Racklins and particularly Daly.

"And who might that be?" Father Farrell asked.

"A small girl from the housing project named Kimberly who comes to help me about the house. Eleven years old."

"I'd like to talk to her," Father Farrell said.

The child came the next morning, brought by her mother.

"I don't like it," the mother said. They were not from St. Agnes, probably not Catholic.

"We'll be only a moment," Father Farrell said.

The child had been in the kitchen, saw the spirit, described the glasses, the suit he wore: He stood there talking, she said, clear as Father Farrell was now. She had been puzzled about how he got there, but she thought perhaps he had come down from upstairs, having been there when she arrived. She was a bright child with a vocabulary and a manner of putting her sentences together that indicated to the priest she understood the gravity of her testimony.

Father Farrell watched her. "Did you say anything at the time, to the man, after?"

"No," she said, "but Michelle did. She said, 'Kimberly, we've just seen a ghost.' A ghost, I don't believe it!"

"Did he just disappear?" Father Farrell asked.

"No, he said, 'I'll go now,' and he was just sort of not there."

Father Farrell had asked Central Catholic, where Boyce Racklin had gone to school, for a yearbook with Boyce's picture. He wanted the girl to identify Boyce as best she could from an early picture. He called them not to bother. He was sure that whatever was in Michelle Shortall's mind would be in the child's mind, too. He wished he knew more about transference of images from one mind to another.

Vanish looked into Coyne's in Oakland for wisdom and comfort and on the very first try he found the man he was seeking.

"Daly Racklin, old son," he said.

"Vanish, are you on a fast track?" Racklin asked. "You look like you're taking drugs to accelerate your heart rate."

Vanish's abstinence was a legend.

"I'm fine, Daly, I'm rosy, but I've got a moral problem for you."

"Go ahead."

Vanish wiped his forehead and slid onto an empty stool.

"What if you had some information that would break a dear friend's heart? Would you give it to the friend?"

"Is the friend a man or a woman?"

"A man."

"Is the information about a woman?"

"Yes, you're a quick fellow, Daly."

"Don't tell him."

Vanish stood quickly. "Say no more," he said.

"Don't you want to hear my reasoning?" Racklin asked.

"I don't, no, I trust your hidden logic. The fact you've reasoned it out is good enough for me. Why go over the same grounds my superiors have already trod? You thought it through and that's good enough. No need to chew the cabbage twice. If I was at my best, I'd mull it for six months, and still at my best come to the same conclusion you did. There are very good reasons and you know them. I'll travel with them. God bless you, Daly, you helped me in a dilemma."

"May I ask generally what problem it was affected you? Is this the same problem you discussed a month ago with Rest in Peace?"

"It is. A great soul going to be shattered."

"And you're still mulling?"

"Great problem, great deliberations. The Supreme Court takes years to make a decision on something that's about a humming bird an inch and a half long."

"Vanish, you have to deal with the problem like it's your own and not the Supreme Court's."

"Thinking," Vanish said. "That's my dilemma. Thanks, Daly, you're a cousin."

"Okay, whose great soul is going to be broken? I'm asking you directly. Don't tell me the problem for the moment. Just the name of the person with the fragile soul."

"Silk Brogan," Vanish said, preparing to run from Coyne's as if all the bloodhounds of hell were at his heels. "I never seen a woman happier," he told the killing words to Daly.

"This is Mrs. Silk Brogan we're discussing, not Bette Davis in *The Little Foxes*?"

"Mrs. Armelia Brogan, betraying her husband of eighteen years. And when I tell him, Silk, the murdered party, will say, 'The guy, was he big?' and I'll have to say, 'Yeah, big, you know, like a cop's big. Maybe late forties, fifty, Irish-looking, but he could be Polish, you know. And Silk's going to ask, 'Good-looking?' And I got to say, 'Yeah, not like you, sweetheart, but okay.' "

Daly said, "I see the problem."

"He's going to ask, 'Old? Young?' And I'll say, 'Older than you?' 'Older than me! My wife's running with a man older than me!' "

Vanish caught his breath. "Right, you know," he said, "it's not my business, but it's over between him and his wife. The cop makes her happy. She's not putting it on. I've seen sad women,

Daly, and I've seen happy women, and Silk's wife is one happy woman and it's that cop who's making her happy." Vanish dropped his voice. "Say to him for me: 'Silk, sweetheart, drop her. There's nothing but pain and misery there. She's not worth your time.' "

Pleased that he had said the horrible words aloud that would bust Shane's great soul into pieces, Vanish smiled at Daly. He had been tailing Mrs. Armelia Brogan for three weeks, at Silk's request, a hundred a week and expenses, but it was a favor, not the money.

"Tell me where she goes Wednesdays," Silk had said. "Goes every Wednesday and Wednesday night she's happy, singing around the house."

Well, Silk-o, Vanish told Daly, addressing their imaginary friend, she sees the man Mondays and Thursdays, too, and I think by the look on her face she's happy those nights, too.

"That's the picture, Daly," he said. "You have it all."

"No, there's more."

"No, that's it. What more you want?"

"No, it's something more."

"More! More than a guy's wife meeting a police type in East Liberty three days a week and sometimes two nights?"

"Something's eating Silk and he knows nothing about his wife meeting the guy. There's something else."

"Say it ain't true, Right, this is too much to bear, I mean, for Silk-o and yours truly. My sister and me up there on Darraugh, we're under the guns, too, from the Pitt machine creeping down on us from the top of the hill. There's tennis courts and medical buildings menacing us, and black people advancing on all sides: seige in all but tanks and warfare and now you say there's more treachery about to crawl over Silk and me like a virus. My sister, Dorothy, doesn't care if our home comes to sit in the admitting lobby of one of them University of Pittsburgh hospitals about to devour Darraugh. She says she'll stay until our house falls down on her. She walks to St. Agnes rain or shine every day of her life. But I can't stand no more. There's too much now, Daly."

"Well, these are unusual times, you have to see the big picture," Daly said.

"It's the day to day, the old day to day that's going to kill me," Vanish said.

"The reason I asked you to come by," Father Farrell said to Daly, "is there's trouble I heard about and it bears on you—not directly, of course, but you could help."

"Father, I'm not in your line of work, you know."

"Well, it's Michelle Shortall, she speaks of you. Do people still say smitten? She's smitten with you."

"I appreciate your warning. I'll keep my distance. I looked in on her a week ago and she acted peculiarly."

"No, you miss my meaning. I'm not warning you away. The woman claims she speaks to your father's ghost. He advises her to pursue you."

"You think my father's ghost is giving her good advice? I'd rather she saw James Dean."

"Come on, Racklin, the woman is hallucinating, but it's harmless. She'll be dead quicker than you can say 'Boyce Racklin.' Indulge her for me. It'll be a kindness."

"I'm not Errol Flynn, Father, I'm not going to make love to her."

"Not what she wants. A cup of tea every so often will satisfy her. Do it for me. Don't act like she's something out of a horror movie, that's all I'm asking—that's all she's asking, inventing ghosts to give her a little importance, a little story with a happy ending in her eyes."

"You suppose that's what hallucinations are all about?"

"Never saw one that didn't confirm what the person wanted to hear, good and bad. Devil going to eat you because that's the way you see your story ought to go, angels going to cheer you on and that's the story fits you like a glove."

"I guess we all have our little daydreams."

Father Farrell looked directly into Daly's eyes. "Boy," he said, "I sense something foolish in the air around you. Is there some little daydream you'd be better off leaving to the imagination?"

"Listen, Father, you're not a mind reader. I won't abandon Michelle Shortall, okay? Now stop reading my mind."

It was early on a beautiful afternoon, and the sunlight seemed to Daly to fall purposefully on the houses on Robinson. The old street: Would it be spared in the general carnage waged by Pitt? St. Agnes's entombed under a locker room for visiting golf pros. And even Father Farrell leaving: Would his presence continue to shine like the sunlight on the roofs of his street, the tiny front yards and the ivy on the little wooden columns?

It was an hour for collecting himself, a forgotten memory brought to life in the embrace of a white wine or two.

But in Edward's Bar and Grill, the languorous stretch of the afternoon fell into fragments.

Chomp and Billy both half stood when they saw him walk into the darkened bar. They carried the flush of agitation in their moist faces. "Jesus, Daly," Billy said. "Sit down and hear this. Chomp's up shit creek. He did a dumb thing last week, and he needs to talk to you about legal matters."

Chomp was larger than Daly and broader. They both cast out waves of dissonance in their hands and eyes.

"I'm up shit creek," Chomp said.

"It's not criminal," Billy said.

"Maybe," Chomp said.

Daly turned to look at him, and Chomp said, "You know, Daly, a lot of things can get a person called a criminal."

The beer bottle in Daly's hand felt cold and reassuring.

"I hit a guy," Chomp said.

"Is this a joke? You hit three guys a week."

"No, it was someone I respected."

Daly nodded. "That's complicated," he said.

"It was extenuating circumstances," Chomp said. His broad face had soft brown eyes. His eyes followed Daly's face. "I was minding my own business. I don't like the looks of them on the streets now, they mock religion. You know, they're not Christian."

"Come on, son, you'd bang a brother Catholic, right? A young Catholic boy, you might say, with horn-rimmed glasses and a haircut like somebody put a bowl on his head. You'd shake him to his yellow teeth, wouldn't you?"

"You mean if he was queer?"

"A lot of them up at Pitt look like communists to me," Billy said. He was very pale and his face was thin, his cheeks inward. He had a long neck. He nodded his head. "All of them are voting for communists."

Chomp nodded his head, too. "Sure, I'd rap a Catholic if he was queer or a leftist type," he said.

"Kills you, don't it?" Billy said. "Them bastards fomenting revolution up there at Pitt, professors and them—the Jews and the rest'll be the first ones lined up in front of the Cathedral of Learning and shot the day after the communists take the oath of office."

"Then they start busting into churches like they did in Bulgaria, Yugoslavia, Rumania, and places," Chomp said, "and it's the end of everything dear to people. There's nothing in my heart against Jews, just fairies and commies. Our Lord was Jewish."

Billy said, "I've been puzzling that one since I was a little kid."

"Then it wasn't a Jew you slugged last night?" Daly asked. "That wasn't the dumb thing."

Chomp said sadly, "The wrong Jew. I hit the wrong Jew."

Daly laughed quietly and long and slammed Chomp's shoulder finally. "I'm sorry, Chomp," he said, and wiped his eyes with a broad, white handkerchief. "You threw me. I know this is serious. I'm not laughing at you."

"I don't see anything funny from any direction," Chomp said.

"Daly gets more superior to his friends every day," Billy said.

"Raise my hand to God," Daly said. "I'm not laughing out of superiority. I'm just laughing, truth is, because it's good to be here with you guys. It's a rotten world, but it ain't rotten at this table.

Okay? Life doesn't have to be complicated, just a question of which Jew to slug."

"You don't like talk of Jew-slugging, do you, Daly?"

"No, men, I don't, it makes me feel like my head is in a vise."

"Even if it ain't nothing with Jewish to it, punching someone a matter of some other principle nothing to do with religion."

"Never, talking about slugging anybody anywhere, about anything, makes me feel like I've been slugged. Okay?"

"I went to hit a queer, thinking it was one of them types from Pitt, you know," Chomp said, "acting like they're better than anyone else, and I slugged a doctor. The queer was a doctor."

Daly turned to Billy.

"How'd Chomp know the man was a doctor?" Daly asked. "You tell me, Billy. Don't answer, Chomp. Don't say anything at all, Billy will explain."

"Billy wasn't there, Daly," Chomp said. "I knew it was a doctor because everyone started to holler, 'The hoodlum hit Dr. Sloan. You hit Dr. Sloan!' So I knew it was a doctor, but I don't hit doctors. I never hit a doctor in my life. My cousin Paul is a doctor; old Doc Pierce comes in here twice a week is a doctor. I give him respect. To me a doctor is the same thing as a priest. Daly, it's as bad as if I hit a priest last night."

"There's got to be sin worse than hitting a priest," Billy said. "I don't know it."

"Hitting a bishop," Daly said.

Billy had a priest in the family and was not to be moved. "Bishop has better insurance, better doctors, better hospitals, nuns give him better treatment," he said. "A priest gets hit by a hoodlum like Chomp, he gets no better treatment than the mailman. Worse, it's a doctor don't like Catholics."

Daly, feeling the pleasure in the alcohol, leaned back in his chair.

He said, "Chomp, that fellow you mistakenly popped last night probably wasn't a medical doctor. They have all sorts of doctors up there at Pitt. Everybody is called Dr. This and Dr. That, but don't call on any of them to put your back in place. It's like this is Dr. Jones, Doctor of Egyptology or Philosophy or Skunk Hunting. The man could have been Dr. Sloan of Missing Persons."

Chomp nodded his head in quick happy bursts, laughing. "Daly," he said, "it was Dr. Sloan of Egyptology. I hit him sort of here in the temple, more a slap, you know, not a killer punch, and he falls back and bumps his elbow on a car, and he starts to shout, 'My elbow, I broke my elbow.' A real doctor would have known the extent of his injuries. Daly, I'm clean! I never hit a real doctor in my life and I'm thirty-eight years old."

Daly took out his handkerchief. "Ain't a lot of people can say that and not be lying," Daly said.

"I don't think this is funny," Billy said.

There was never a punch thrown at the Ancient Order of Hibernians, Division Nine, Daly thought, that was not delivered in the name of honor, decency or justice. Not on Forbes either. Streets out there in Oakland under continuous threat while the dark knights stand guard here at the battle's frontier, a barricade against misfits and communists and potential murderers of the living God on Atwood, Oakland Avenue, and at Schenley Park and Forbes Field. To sit with them, Daly thought, was to be among heroes bathed in the dim lights of the bars on Forbes and made fantastic and unreal at their edges by the motion of the overhead fans. Relaxed and filled with knowing for the moment where he belonged, he felt the fading away of troubling things. He stood, with no announcement, and went to the men's room, knowing his footing was not sure and white wine could lift the heart but cause the legs to take on a reckless life of their own.

Daly watched twilight fall outside on Forbes and drank wine and thought it was good to be himself, like smoke to be dissipated through the fingers, no trouble to anyone, invisible, unless he wanted to be there, and then if he was your friend he could be as good as two men at a helping hand. He felt at home. There were things on the coming days, he thought: This is my year at last, done with the rut of the old Right Racklin, like a plow horse on an endless field of others' sorrows.

He yawned. The streets outside were wrapped in a last golden sunlight. He stood unsteadily, swaying.

"Well, you solved the problem," Billy said.

"Usual fee," Daly said. "You hear any more about those girls?"

"Only my aunt says you're a wonderful person."

"Your aunt's wrong."

"Daly, you never slugged anybody at all?"

"Never, nobody."

"Not when you were a kid."

"I talked my way out, and when I couldn't do that, I ran."

"Jesus, Daly, that's nothing to say out loud in most places."

Chomp and Billy walked out with him and solemnly shook hands, almost, Daly thought, reverentially. "Hitting is nothing to do," Chomp said. "Hitting people is nothing to do."

"Chomp's right," Billy said. "It's a habit guys got to break."

Daly called Jessie from the telephone in the Sun Drug on the corner of Atwood and Forbes, and he asked how young Tommy was doing. He was pleased she was there to answer, given the boy's disposition toward unpredictability. He had allowed him to help Jessie around her house from four in the afternoon on his day off from the restaurant where he washed dishes and Saturday mornings. Jessie reported he was a prince of a young fellow, a helper in thousands, devoted to her: in short, covering up for him. But she was alive with him under her roof, and what more could one ask of a rubber-ax murderer?

"It's not him, it's your sister, Daly, I think she's gone around the bend."

"Meet herself coming back I expect. The woman's been on cloud nine for all the time I've known her."

"She called me twice today, said she wants to talk to me about you. I said I was busy. She'll be calling any minute now to see if I'm free to talk—she says I'm only twenty minutes away by trolley. What does she want to talk about?"

"First, the telephone is to her what an oxygen tent is to my uncle Finnerty; without it she becomes a pumpkin at midnight. Number two, what you'll talk about will be what she saw on a soap opera that day or the day before, putting me into the part of the hopeless guy who can't get by in the world."

"What part will I play?"

"A blind woman."

"Hell, no nightgowns?"

"Not in my sister's mind."

"Daly, did you mean it when you said you loved me last month?"

"I did. No soap opera."

"Will you say it again, not for the record, just for me to hear, like I'd be the woman in the nightgowns?"

"I love you."

"You know I love you, too. For the record."

Daly felt himself briefly unable to talk. The afternoon's drink was still with him and he felt teary and became cautious. He said, "I know, it's me who has to grow up."

"Stay twelve."

"I'll go down to Ruth Marie's right now," he said. "And tell her to take you off the list of the fifty people a day she saves from hell. It's still early."

It was more than the afternoon and the drink. Things felt as if they were converging, something important to be said or done.

Daly found Ruth Marie on the telephone when he knocked on her door. She hastily left the party on the other end and said, "Daly, I must talk to you. Jessie is very strange, it's being blind. I have tried to call her—if you're going to be married I think we should be friends. But she tells me she's busy. Now, what could a woman like that be doing all day? I try to catch her at different times. And she's always busy. Isn't that suspicious to you?"

"She's minding her own business."

"Let me get you some lemonade. Or would you like a Pepsi?"

"I'd like you to tend to your own affairs," he said, and then out-raged, beyond anything he thought he contained toward his helpless sister, her mischief and self-adoration a mockery to him of his own bursts of thwarted canonization, he shouted, "Sane people avoid you. Maybe if you had ever known anything about life you'd be like other people; but you know nothing. You're as sheltered as if you'd been raised on a mountaintop and never met a real person."

He knew Ruth Marie would have as soon died a terrible death than tell even her brother, who had observed her boring husband, Mike Drange, in his heyday. Her marriage had certainly been adequate enough as things went before the war in Europe and Japan. But given much that had occurred since and things she witnessed in movies and on television, she knew it was loveless compared to what women could expect these days. She had missed something between man and woman, not exactly ardor, but something else from the late Michael Drange. Daly had seen such looks as he saw in Ruth Marie's eyes in frightened dogs on the streets of Darraugh and Dunseith when he had been a boy: ready to fall fawning on the sidewalk, prepared to run at a sudden motion.

He was instantly filled with regret at her vincibility.

"I'm sorry," he said, "I'm not myself." And indeed he did feel a constriction at his chest, a pressure there of the sort that preceded pain. It had been there all day; he had noticed it only now.

"Daly, am I so bad? Am I that terrible? I'm lonely, Daly. I'm only that, no more, honestly, not a bad person."

She probably, if he knew her in all her posturings, saw herself as a woman who gave off heat like the sun at midday, and had found no mountain slopes to ignite with a lava yellow and orange; hence, like a too-delicate person overwhelmed by the burden of a great passion, as were women in books, never realized in her life, she now, lonely and misunderstood, imagined herself a wavering light leading others in darkness. At her age, light fading, she was truly at a dangerous stage, like himself.

"Ruth Marie, forgive me," he said, and put his arm around her and kissed her forehead. "Forgive me."

A bridge had been crossed: His sister was allowing someone to be kind to her.

"Daly," she said, clutching at him. "I'm so lonely. I'm lonely out of my mind."

"I know," he said. "I know, there, there."

"I'm not strong—I'm not sure, I don't think I'm strong, Daly."

She had certainly been told otherwise by one or another of her friends over the years. Daly had been there to hear it. When Irene's husband of twenty-five years lost his job and then perversely felt no shame or increased responsibility at his situation but chose the occasion of being sacked at Gimbel's Department Store, where he was an assistant to the buyer in hardware, to run off with a woman half his age, Irene told all the intimate details to Ruth Marie. Daly was summoned to see if the man could be sued for alimony or mental distress or criminal negligence, Irene declaring finally in agreement with the sound advice not to let the boy-man ruin her life: "Ruth Marie, you're our beacon, you lead the way always." And when a contractor cheated Caitlin on a roof and then made sexually suggestive remarks when she repeatedly called, Caitlin, hearing she would be doubly damaging herself to let the fraud get to her, said, "You're our pilot and our navigator. Isn't she, Daly?"

Daly knew it wasn't lost on Ruth Marie that in a famous drawing of the Savior He was called Our Pilot. She hesitated at that ancient term; but navigator, there was a word from the bombing crews of the Second World War, dashing, earthly, matter-of-fact, and no blasphemy to it. A navigator for drifting and lost souls: It had a ring. "Navigator," she had said to Daly. "Isn't that a grand name to be called by people who know me best?"

Belle, in her middle thirties, had a child out of wedlock, and Ruth Marie pleaded to raise the boy with her own son. But Belle said it would be too painful; she put the child up for adoption, but Inez, Irene, and Caitlin knew who was the kindest woman on earth. Now, the navigator, he thought, had come full circle and joined the passengers.

He drank a Pepsi, trying to sober up, and they talked of their father and mother and Uncle Finnerty and her late husband, and it was still daylight when he descended the few steps from her house to Ward Street.

A wonderful time of life, that hour of the twenty-four, night near and still almost drunk from his time earlier with Chomp and Billy and promise gathering around him like the shadows lengthening on the streets. He bought three hard-boiled eggs and a bag of pretzels in Coyne's Bar and ate as he walked up Chesterfield and across Terrace to Robinson, choosing an irregular route to avoid discussions, to a hillside behind Terrace Village Two, the Center side of the cemetery. Behind him one of the buildings of the Pitt Medical School sat on a ridge above where he lay on the grass and ate the eggs and pretzels.

He stretched out on the grass, the sun lost in treetops to the west. He dozed, cars far away, distant like the disorder around him for the moment, and then woke slowly, as if he had been cast adrift at sea and had landed on a foreign beach of strange, soothing lights and soft murmurs of night. There was still some day abroad, and he recognized the sky as familiar and himself waking.

At late twilight as Daly sat up on the hillside near the Pitt Medical School, looking down at the city falling into darkness, he heard a sharp sound on the soft evening. He stood and saw on the serpentine drive that wound around the hillside an old car racing in noise and a fury of dangerous speed on the narrow road. It was snorting blue fumes. He did not know the passenger, but he knew the driver, hat down low over his eyes, intent at the wheel. The car stopped only for the briefest of moments. "Charles!" Daly called. "It's me. Right Racklin."

Leaning out the window, Pretty Boy pointed his machine gun up in the air and waved it gaily. "Cops," Pretty Boy shouted. "Two minutes behind me, kid, breathing law and order enough to scare an honest man—and that ain't me!" He put his head down and was gone down the hill toward Center Avenue. The road divided about a hundred feet away, and he could have turned left into Terrace Village; and when the police car, old as the flivver Pretty Boy was driving, came around the turn, Daly was ready.

"There," he shouted, "I saw the criminal go into the Village. Took the turn left."

And he sat down exhausted on the grass. The cars were as real as the night in the trees below, gathering black and deep green swallowing the leaves and branches. He breathed heavily: No need to affirm his name to test his sanity, he had called it out to his friend at twilight, had the wit to misdirect the police, all in all, the actions of a man not only all there but clever. The falling night rang with unseen opportunities, happiness that he couldn't place, and he felt on himself the blessedness of the last of day in the sky. He stood and brushed grass from himself. The approaching night on the roadway below crept into shadows, and a streetlight shone pale and alone against the sky.

He carefully put into a bag the eggshells from his recent meal. He and the scores who drank at the Irish Club had attributed miraculous powers to the hard-boiled eggs sold in a large glass jar at the bar there. With salt and Tabasco sauce, sexual potency was the least of it: There were winning numbers in the daily number of the day, streaks of bad luck in card games that had turned good, women who had abandoned a man and family forever returned contrite to hearth and home after an evening of eating the eggs.

He put the bag with the eggshells into a refuse can before the Pitt Medical School building at the top of the drive.

The Morgan Street Cemetery at the top of the hill was soon to disappear under a field house from the University of Pittsburgh. All that had happened there, the children hiding to frighten each other behind tombstones, the frantic lovemaking on the leafy ground forever gone. The idea of the cemetery itself eradicated when the last person who thought of it no longer remembered the overgrown trees and graves and forgot the touch of white legs and lips and arms: When it was bulldozed and shoved out of the path of tennis courts and buildings of Pitt, dreams of love would be buried, too. Boys dreaded its ghosts but took girls there, having nowhere else to go. The strange lights of their youth, Daly thought, shadows too large for the trees that threw them and tombstones that danced if you watched them too steadily, sounds of sighs and moans no wind made. Exuberance in the dead leaves of the old winter, among the scents of dogwood and wild flowers, whatever truth lay, Daly thought, in naked bodies connecting became known there for the first time.

Still capricious with the outlawry of his hallucinations, he found a public phone and dialed Gloria Scone's number in Connecticut, collect.

"Daly," she said, "I knew it would be you."

"What's going on? It sounds like a party."

"Can you get here tonight? The kids are home from school. That's the noise."

A young man's voice—Daly heard Gloria shout, "Dwight! Give me that!"—came on the phone, and he breathlessly shouted, "One-two-three-four, we don't want your fucking war!"

Laughing, Gloria said, "Hurry, Daly."

In his dreams that night Pretty Boy ran again, luring Daly, summoning him.

Seven

*M*ass with Jessie on Sunday hurt, the ache of his dishonesty in him like a nerve in his face gone wrong with insincere smiles. A fine day, they walked and talked, she holding his arm lightly. And he, loquacious to the stupefaction of strangers, patted her hand silently, chatted over coffee, looked in on Uncle Finnerty, described for her shadows on the bushes, the sunlight off the dome of the Phipps Conservatory, two boys in red pants leaving the Carnegie Library.

No word passed his lips of his coming treachery, his plans as absurd as playing in a rock and roll band or lying on Forbes in a marijuana stupor or soon seeing visions induced by LSD: in truth, doing worse, seeking conquests in Connecticut.

"And Uncle Finnerty?" she asked.

"Uncle Finnerty never did live in the real world," he said. "A coma with all its sweet dreams and soft music was his natural state, for all the throwing fists and cursing."

After he took her home, Daly felt the need of a quiet drink. At Lasek's—hard by the giant Jones and Laughlin Steel Works, which loomed like a large, sleeping whale on Second Avenue, only the rust of the place left in its wake, its dark presence a reminder of toil, not the mill workers pouring out on the sidewalk for their happy first of the day—Daly shook hands with an old man outside the bar.

"Daly," the old man, whose name was Thomas Ryan, said, "a boy young enough to be my grandson or worse walks up to me and, looking me in the face, says, 'Say, mister, you have some spare change?' I say, 'You're damned right I do, you little bastard, and I'm going to spend it on a glass of rye first chance I get.' Panhandling on Forbes. There was millionaires walked there once."

"There was nothing personal in it. They fall over their own feet. One was killed up there on Forbes the other day, throat cut. It's a pitiable condition they're in, too dumb to stay alive. They're like lambs."

The old man made a fist. "And nothing personal in this fist landing in the little lamb's eye," Ryan said, "they don't let an old man walk the streets in peace."

The strange young men and women seemed blank-eyed. And they were rigorously righteous even when laughing—it seemed to Daly their eyes followed him to see whether he approved or disagreed with their merriment or any emotion at all they displayed. Beards now and haircuts put together as if to frighten a pagan enemy over the next hill; but I'm not out there at war with them, I'm here on the sidewalk and their illusions about their hair are a wonder to me, not a fright. Even when they stand together they are apart from one another, he thought, and their laughter is not in their eyes.

Daly made reservations for New York and took a plane to La Guardia the next day. From there Daly took the New Haven Railroad up to Stamford. After the war, he had come to travel more than he cared to, even enjoyed it in part, but it was not a natural occasion to him, suspended between one place and another.

All places not Oakland were not real to him. He had learned from geography that he belonged somewhere more than anywhere else. And, he knew with age, there were people who did not feel they belonged anywhere at all. Or needed to go somewhere else to feel that the place that they had come from was where they really belonged.

When he was away from the streets of Oakland he had only been putting in time till he could return to beloved landmarks of memory. He had driven a Jeep for officers for four months in France, occasionally a courier in the Third Army before Metz. When the war in Europe was over and death was not as pronounced a companion—the bombing of London had brought him to tears for the children in the shattered beams and flames—he realized someone else might draw wisdom from the conversation of a cabdriver or the insights of a headwaiter in Paris, a chambermaid in Berlin, a bus driver in Bangkok, or a mailman in Tokyo, but as far as Daly was concerned, up close they were still the man who lived on the first floor at the Noonans' house on Chesterfield Road when he was twenty-five or the lady with the kid with thick glasses three doors down on Robinson. Daly supposed he never would be able to casually pass like a vague shadow over a foreign street and claim kinship to the place, as irrelevant as the breeze.

He had the same feeling in the small train station in Stamford. Today, to travel was to seem to express freedom, leisure, an ability to choose locales and friends, landmarks, natural wonders and to don added physical presence in food, love and sex, an identity in mobility. Daly felt no more free, no less, no matter where he was.

"Darling!" Gloria said, coming up from behind him. "You look so sad. Let's make you happy."

He would try.

He had discovered that the truth of getting to Metz or Cologne lay not necessarily in following General Patton's orders, funneled down through the chain of command, but simply in getting from one place to another. Turn back, circle, zigzag, find another route, he had choices: It was Metz he was going to, not following orders. And the surest way to get there was by traversable roads: Drivers turned back, plunged forward, and were killed, or wept in frustration at the side of the road. Daly sang such songs as occurred to him and found his way across dry creek beds, mountain trails, and damaged side roads past farmhouses to where he was going. It was a matter of a certain pride: Live with the ruts in the road and not a discussion about them.

From his reading of the honesty of the times, Daly had thought that Gloria and he would soon embrace, and fall into bed, locked in each other's arms. They spoke to each other in an easy manner, comfortably as they drove in her large, open black car; but this was not the woman who had screamed on the phone when he finally reached her in the morning and told her he was coming, "Yes, be here, tonight!"

The flirtations and the world of 1968 and the sexual revolution—Daly felt as if he had traveled a far distance for business as usual. Whatever else was happening, he decided, these were preliminaries, two steps back, as they made talk so inconsequential he became sleepy and bored with it in ten minutes in the convertible as they drove through the Connecticut landscape bright with August on narrow, twisting roads.

He decided that since he appeared steady and dull to her she probably saw him as someone she wanted to marry, a fatal beginning for the wild romance of the sort Daly had expected from reports in the movies, newspapers, and television. She could be on her good behavior: not anything he aspired to observe too closely.

Daly wanted to break with the sobriety of his past. This was altogether too reminiscent of the clumsiness of his early times with women.

He felt the worst of being twelve or perhaps an awkward young man with his wife or doing something taboo. In Connecticut, he did not feel contemporary.

Mrs. Scone talked plenty, mostly of herself, using often the word *love*, defining for the two of them in the warm sunshine the state of their relationship at each stage of its movement to—what? She said provocative things, then dampened them a moment later.

"I am a very passionate woman." Clear enough. Then she said,

"When we've learned our bodies are obstacles—I knew it when I was a kid—we can really experience love. Sex is for plow hands."

It was emotion of a religious cast, but of no faith Daly understood.

She also did and said things that were incomprehensible to him, but since the understanding through her of new purposes and programs was the door by which he was to step fully into 1968, he listened carefully. She drove the car too fast for the turns in the road, seemingly unaware of his uneasiness. It seemed a trivial way to die; not with happiness to leave life as Bobby had, hated for all the right reasons, on the line, and young and forever gallant and an inspiration. The car fought to stay on the narrow road.

He watched the trees on the sides of the road and the hedges that shielded the large houses behind them. Bobby had been dead less than two months, and it seemed to Daly all weather, the August heat, even ordinary rain, formations of clouds and haze too suddenly falling at dusk, was a judgment on a land whose destiny was too well known.

Gloria hardly slowed down at Stop signs, seeming to be alerted only to signals inside herself. If she stopped, she then sped away from the spot at great speed, oblivious to the possibilities of what lay ahead. Daly had ridden in Jeeps and three-quarter-ton trucks, had come ashore in a landing boat two days after D day. He was terrified then, he felt his mouth dry now.

"You're quiet, Daly. We're almost there."

"Thank God."

"Oh, my driving, I've been scolded before. I'll slow down. I feel so much a part of this wonderful day that I'm too exuberant for my own good."

"Mine anyhow. I heard in June I have a bad heart."

She slowed the car, then pulled over into a side road. "Are you joking?" she asked.

"Yes, about the fast driving, I am glad you slowed down. But not about my heart."

"Oh, dear," she said, and reached her hand out to his chest as he sat in the passenger side. "Relax," she said, "there that's it." She pressed the palm of her hand gently to his chest. "Has it stopped racing?"

"You mean with the pressure of your hand?"

She laughed wildly. "No, you goose, I mean overall. I can't do things like that in a second. I mean overall. Stopping the car, relaxing, my hand, has your heart stopped beating too fast?"

"Well, it wasn't beating that fast to begin with."

"Was it beating too fast when I was driving around those turns? Nothing is going to happen to us that's bad, I want you to know that. I should have told you. It's too perfect, you and me, this lovely day—nothing bad will happen, I promise."

"You can read the future?"

"It's as real to me as you are this minute."

"That's quite a gift."

He could feel perspiration gathering at his neck and running down his back. Talking, listening, he felt trapped, but he steeled himself. All the music of the time, the angry streets, the confident walk and stare of people today: He was with Gloria, he decided, in the middle of it. Or was she a garden-variety nut of the sort who wandered Oakland Avenue and Bouquet Street? Mumbling, assertive, no one used to listen. But today no philosophy was without a prophet or two. And, no matter how absurd the rant, someone listened.

"Are you skeptical?" she asked.

He was pleased she started the car again and drove back onto the road at a reasonable speed.

"No, I tend to be a believer," he said.

"I don't mean in the Trinity and all that, I mean what's in front of your eyes, what you actually hear and see."

He did not know how to answer her. But it was 1968: Was everyone in all the houses alongside the road and in expensive convertibles henceforth to be regarded at their most serious as essentially jabberers?

"Daly, don't you know we are all gods and goddesses. We don't need to be told who and how to worship. We make our own rules. You're too intelligent a man to believe in nonsense."

He was warm with the day but the heat in the incantatory power of her certainties was worse; he believed he could feel her palm still pressed against his chest. Had she expected his heart to beat out in Morse code: Thank you, I'm delivered from a bad heart!

"Intelligent men suffer," he said, "intelligent men see other people suffer, intelligent men die, think of dying, see others they love die. They don't find easy answers."

"Oh, my dear, I assure you, I absolutely assure you, I promise you that the life that follows this one has no hell in it. Goodness all started a long time before we were born and goes on a long time after we're gone, us in it, growing in knowledge, fulfilling ourselves as we open our minds to the world around us. Daly, *there is no death.*"

"Well, that is reassuring."

Gloria had three children home for the summer, a young woman going to a New England college, a son about seventeen and another daughter, about twelve. The elder Scone children carried Daly's two suitcases to the house. All shook hands with him with fixed smiles and a rigorous lack of interest in him.

Perhaps it was his imagination: He had never visited a woman with children. He had not known Gloria's children would greet him at their lakefront home in Connecticut. The eldest daughter was blond and very distant; her father had been Gloria's first husband. The two younger children were from her third husband.

The boy did not look at Daly.

Daly himself felt anything he would say would ring wrong. These kids did not like him, for their reasons—he did not like them because there was too practiced an ease in their acting as if he were unimportant. It seemed to cost them nothing; they were good at nodding at him, making it clear they were not really glancing at him long enough to take in details. It was their practiced comfort in causing him to feel unacceptable that bothered him. If their swift absorption in themselves spoke at all to him, it said: You will be gone soon enough.

Daly and Gloria ate a cold salad served by a small Latin woman who did not seem to speak English, but when Daly caught her eye, she smiled broadly and nodded. He spoke with passion to her: "Thank you," he said in relief, "yes, that'll be very nice, more iced tea, certainly." (*Lady, stay!* I have a few card tricks I'd like to show you, some tricks I do with a knotted handkerchief, have you ever been to Pittsburgh? Lady, don't go!)

Gloria spoke of adventures in buying the property, how she had loved it, Nick, this was Nick Scone, industrial real estate, had been hesitant—not entirely fashionable, not much of an investment— and she had prevailed.

"I think you have excellent taste," Daly said. From under an umbrella, he could look down a gentle slope to a small pier with a motor boat and out to a large, broad lake.

"I just go by instinct."

About five, all three of Gloria's children, seemingly dressed for Halloween, came to the table where Daly sat. The eldest blond girl was dressed in a skeleton's costume, carrying the mask of a skull; the boy was dressed in a long monk's robe, and across his chest in large letters was a placard that read: "Death for Innocent People in Vietnam." The younger girl wore a white dress down to her ankles and her face was powdered a chalk white. "Do you think, Mr. Racklin," she asked, "people will know I'm supposed to represent death for innocent children in Vietnam?"

"I don't know that that's the first thing I'd think when I saw you. But maybe if I saw you in the protest parade I'd understand better."

"Mother, do I look okay?"

"They're going to a protest against the war in Vietnam in Manhattan, but I'm worried. You know things happen these days, police, hard hats."

"Mother, we'll be fine. Don't be silly."

"I suppose you're for the war, Mr. Racklin," the eldest girl said. It was not an accusation, just a polite statement on departing.

"No," Daly said, "I'm against the war."

"Really?"

"Yes, I was with Gene McCarthy on it, but I became a Bobby Kennedy supporter later, the war and other reasons."

"Really?"

"Yes, I was in the infantry in the Second World War."

"You were in the real fighting?"

"It was real enough."

"What's it like? Hell?"

No one said anything, and Daly, who felt cornered, said, "Yes, it's like hell, but not just in the fighting. No one sees the whole picture of a war, not even the top officers—they can only guess. Later, maybe historians, but war is complicated, what it does in its peculiar way to ordinary people. Everything that happens even outside the fighting leaves its mark: I don't think anyone denies that. War is like a weird climate, a strange season of different weather and places that get unnatural—where it might seem normal things get pushed to their logical conclusions of savagery and barbarism, but it's not so. Things happen in wars that couldn't happen in any other circumstances, viciousness, heroism, maybe great things, terrors, but mostly it's a season of loss and regret people would never know otherwise. Vietnam will be the same, I guess. We thought we were helping things in the Second World War—we were, don't get me wrong. But we contributed too, in our small ways, to all the general misery that wars bring."

Still, no one spoke.

"We meant well," Daly said, suddenly exasperated. "But once war starts it goes off in a thousand directions and the directions multiply and there's millions of mischiefs and then millions more."

"Where were you in the fighting?" the boy asked.

"Dwight!" the eldest girl said. "We're late now."

"Please, shut up," Dwight said.

"Yes," the youngest daughter said.

"Dwight," Gloria said, "Mr. Racklin may care to keep his thoughts to himself. Please stop asking questions."

"Where were you in the war?" the boy asked.

"England, France, Germany."

"Did you see terrible things?" the boy asked.

"Yes."

"Can you tell us something?"

"I don't want to keep you."

"Please," the youngest daughter said.

Under the fading light of a Connecticut summer the cold winter of a long time ago seemed to have happened beyond the span of years in one man's lifetime.

"I remember," Daly said, "the part of it that seemed to go on forever, that and waking in the morning in London and seeing in the streets what the German bombers had done the night before. The 65th Division, my unit, entered Saarlautern on a cold December day in 1944, Germany, three years to the day from when the Japanese bombed Pearl Harbor. I think of that mostly when I remember the war, although a lot of things run through my mind. All the power lines were down in Saarlautern. The cables crisscrossed in the air, gleaming there in silver webs with white frost when an occasional searchlight or jeep's headlight picked them out of the darkness. It didn't matter that the cables were down. The Germans controlled the electric power plant for the city anyhow.

"German shells from the east fell on the city in periodic bursts, an hour without pause, and then long hours without the screeches and blasts, then sudden panic. In a neighborhood miles from the center of town, by darkness, a squad of us commandeered a quiet house. The man of the house was old enough to evade military service, but it was his limp probably that had disqualified him. The woman, in thin spectacles, somebody's grandmother, looked once at us and fled like a rabbit into the cellar. We weren't Russians, but we were a rough-looking bunch. One of the soldiers laughed, and said, 'Somebody's mother, Daly,' and I laughed, too—I had thought how like my mother the woman with the smooth white hands was. She covered her face with a shawl and ran downstairs. The guy who talked of mothers was named Shorty Briggs, and he meant the German woman had nothing to fear from us. She was safe there with her cuckoo clocks, her worn carpeted living room and the cellar downstairs, the cheap beer steins there, her old radio sitting in an entire corner of the main room like a squat brown person who would see that nothing evil occurred while it watched."

"Where was the rest of the family?" Gloria asked.

"The rest of the family had fled," Daly said. "Two big American soldiers, cold and too tired to remove their clothing, lay down in the parlor over an electric train. With no power to run the engines, they played with the toy train of a kid who maybe had left the place by becoming an adult or maybe the kid had fled the afternoon before; the soldiers made sounds of whistles, of rounding corners, of crashes and train-station farewells and returns. Quiet, you know, like children themselves, a silly, impromptu game, each of the guys talking to himself. They played for more than an hour when the shells started again.

"The house shook. A window suddenly was shattered. But everyone there, except for the two soldiers who played with the trains and me, was asleep on the floor or in the deep beds of the small, clean house or on the couches. I sat shivering in a cold corner, afraid of the closeness of the shells. My squad, like dead men, fully clothed, slept. The two big men hunched, leaning on elbows over the tracks, made these soft gentle train sounds, hardly flinching at the sudden loud bursts nearby. The shells continued while I sat stiffly. I heard Shorty snoring after a while. A half hour later, I stood—trembling from cold and the shells—and crept down to the cellar in the darkness. I was lonely, I ached to see my mother. Downstairs, the two old people sat across the room from each other. Although I couldn't see them in the darkness, I knew they were watching me. I thought of how peculiar it was that having displaced them from the upstairs room of their house, the American army had probably made sure that in the shelling of Saarlautern they'd be the only survivors. The cellar felt safe to me. It didn't shake like the rooms upstairs. I didn't say anything to the two of them. I felt good down there.

"I curled up on the floor, near the feet of the woman. Before I fell asleep I reached over and gently touched the woman's shoe. Then I touched her leg. Touched it for the warm feel of the person there and never knew whether the man sitting stolidly in the chair across the room saw me. I was trying to get the feel of my mother: to remember her. I touched whatever human was close to me. Maybe the old man in the cellar had planned for a night like this for years. Between sleep and waking, I thought I heard him rise in the night and approach the woman, but maybe I never knew when the moment occurred. And, you know, it might have been a thrashing rat among some packing crates in the cellar. I saw it all clear by the dawn's light what had happened. The old man with the limp, you see, he rose sometime in the night and crossed the small space in the cellar and slit with a light sharp razor his wife's throat. She had made no sound that I heard, but maybe in the comfort of the touch of her shoe I had been sleeping too soundly to hear her death cry. The old man then had limped back to his own chair in the darkness and taken some poison, dying with the bloody razor still in his hand. Maybe he'd planned it for years. I found them sitting in their chairs in the cold dawn."

"It wasn't your fault, Mr. Racklin," the son said. "The old people."

"Nothing is anybody's," Daly said. "It turns out nothing done in the dark is anybody's fault."

As the children left to protest the war in Southeast Asia, the youngest girl touched Daly's arm in passing and said, "It's okay, Mr. Racklin."

When they were gone, Gloria said, "They liked you, Daly."

"You see," he said, "talking about it changes things. Anything at all can be said, virtually anything at all can be done. War puts people into straitjackets. There is so little sense to it that roosters give birth to cows and people who would ordinarily spend their lives fixing carburetors in car dealerships drop flaming bombs on people they've never met—and get bullets from strangers they meet in the dark as part of the regular business of walking around at night."

"Oh, you have been hurt," she said.

"No, please, don't work me into an idea you have about things."

"I understand, I do understand, you'll see."

Under a large oak, its live roots bending and twisting virtually down to the lake where her property sat—she had an apartment in Manhattan, too, and Mr. Scone, very rich indeed, had left her a third place in Palm Beach—she said, as darkness fell, that if people understood themselves better they could make the oak tree bear apples.

"We don't know our powers because we never try to use them. Just knowing what can be done is steps toward making things happen."

"Why would the tree change natural law just to accommodate us?" Daly asked, sipping a gin and tonic. "It has its function. What would make it change?"

"Because it understands it doesn't have to have only acorns. It can bear apples. It doesn't know anything about natural law, and, Daly, it has a mind as sound as your own. It's different than ours but a mind all the same. When you were a child you heard the thunder and you knew it was speaking and you tried to hear what it was saying. Today you'd say it was only thunder rumbling, but when you were a child you had more sense than now. You knew the thunder was talking. Same with the tree, you know apples would look lovely on it and the tree might think so, too."

"But what will make it change to apples? It's been acorns for centuries."

"Our will. We'll help it along—if that's what it wants. We must never impose our will on nature. Everything is free, men, women, trees, grass, stars."

"Have you ever seen such a thing?"

"I'm afraid I caused an airplane to fall from the sky once. Fortunately, it was a small craft. Thank God, I hadn't willed an airliner out of the sky."

"How many people lost their lives in the small plane?"

"People who didn't understand thought it was a miracle no lives were lost. There was only one person in the plane, the pilot, and he walked away. They called the crash a miracle; they meant the pilot's escape. But of course I hadn't wanted him to be hurt, only, foolishly, to see if I could bring the plane down, certainly not to damage anything on the ground. Once you've mastered this kind of thing you have to be very, very careful."

"I'd say so."

"Curing diseases is comparatively easy."

"Compared to causing apples to grow on oak trees, a piece of cake. May I mix us another drink? Metaphysics always makes me thirsty."

She wore shorts, pleased with her firm, long legs. She knew he was aware of them too. Her graceful bending and leaning as she talked, her slender hands and long, tapered fingers with no nail polish were waving with an elaboration not necessary to any purpose but performance.

"Daly, are you making fun of me?"

"A little. But I don't want you to cause me to vanish. I came a long distance from Pittsburgh not to just vanish in Connecticut."

"Do you really call this far?"

"Going up to Gus Miller's on Oakland Avenue and Forbes for a late *Post-Gazette* is a long distance for me. I live on Coltart, you know, and that's six blocks away."

"You could be Owney's twin. He used to think a trip was racing in his Cadillac seventy-five miles an hour down to Harrisburg, then racing back to Pittsburgh."

Daly laughed. "Yes, that was Owney."

"Do you know he liked me to do a sex act on him while he drove? On the way to Harrisburg, then another while he drove back to Pittsburgh."

"Now, how would I know that?"

"Well, he did. Does it shock you I used to go down on him on the Pennsylvania Turnpike? He liked that. Is it a surprise?"

"Not like the oak bearing apples would be."

She laughed, but said, "I'm sorry I brought up the oak tree and airplanes. People who don't understand the principles make so much of those things."

Owney in his white gloves at the wheel of his car, his little cap at the right slant: Perhaps he had died with happy memories just as he remembered himself at his most fulfilled. When people smiled at him in his costume he smiled back. Knowing what people are really smiling at, Daly thought, can be as dangerous as willing airplanes out of the sky, and he realized he was smiling.

"What's funny?"

"Gin and tonic."

"Did you think I wanted you here for sex?"

"It crossed my mind."

"Why would I want you? I can get almost any man I want."

"A lot of women with a lot less can do just as well."

"Do you think men are easy?"

"Compared to airplanes brought down out of the sky, getting a man for sex is a trick a dull child can learn."

"So getting you is no accomplishment."

"No, it's not an accomplishment."

She stood and walked down to the water, her arms crossed, deep in thought, not entirely angry, but not pleased either. She did not look back at him. She faced the water resolutely.

CONNECTICUT LAKE MYSTERIOUSLY RISES FROM ITS BED TO ENGULF TOWN OF STAMFORD

Supernatural Force Suspected

Daly mixed himself another drink while Gloria studied the water. Then he mixed himself yet another drink. The sun was behind clouds. But its light reflected around the clouds, and in part through them colored the lake with a broad stripe of phantom, flowing sunshine, making the lake as bright as the late light in the sky overhead. As darkness descended, she still sat by the bank of the lake.

Uneasy but nicely drunk, he thought he should join her, and he stood. Stiff-legged, he walked toward where she sat, not having looked at him once in the past hour. Slowly, inexorably, he thought, she causes me to stand, goddess of night and power, resources to cause the sun to orbit the earth and the moon to dance the Charleston—why not?—while she sits and broods on the fate of nations and her responsibilities and her gifts.

"Oh," she said, turning up to him with a faint, amused smile, "excuse me, Daly, I was lost. I forgot you were here. You'll see a light soon come on across the lake. In rain or shine a man there, feeling me, turns on the lantern in front of his cottage hoping I see it."

"Have you ever met him?"

"No, why should I? It's better for him that we don't ever meet."

"But you cause him to turn on his light?"

She said sadly, "Not willingly. I wouldn't for the world do that to a stranger—this is very, very dangerous stuff. He may think himself happily married, he may be old and sick. I simply sit here, watching the sun set, and he turns on the light, knowing without words I'm here. That's all there is to it."

She came later to the room where he slept down the hall from her, and crept into bed with him.

"I knew it would be like this," she said, searching his body with her tongue.

He said, "Yes."

"It must be sacred between us, or it's nothing."

"Yes, I think I understand."

She slowly tumbled over him, then moved more quickly, kissing him everywhere, massaging his arms and pressing her lips to his fingers.

There was a moon off the lake, from a shore a good distance away, and its reflections fell through the thin curtains in the room. He could see her long, sinuous arms as she held him and his own hands in her hair. He kissed her and her skin was fresh and smelled of lemons and almonds; she had prepared to come to his room. While things were undoubtably fated, ointments, perfumes, and lotions might be in the cards too. They held each other, drew apart, and then once more she sighed.

"I knew it would be like this," she whispered.

"I hoped."

"I saw you a few years ago, but you didn't see me. I go back to Pittsburgh sometimes just to remember things. Things were small and good there; it's like no place else."

"You should have spoken to me then."

"No, it wasn't the right time."

In the morning before the full light of dawn he dressed for departure, repacking his suitcase. Gloria had left for her room sometime during the night. The people in the house behind him slept. Daly went downstairs and sat on the pier looking out at the lake. In the light haze over the water he saw a small boat with a man in it. The man wore a straw hat. The boat was too far from shore for Daly to recognize the face, but he knew who the sturdy man out there leaning on the oars was.

Daly waved, not calling out. He wanted to wake no one with his hallucinations of death. One day Pretty Boy would be there beckoning to him, joking with him over the false authority the world claimed over a man's soul, and the next minute he'd be dead? Floyd, his particular messenger, come to call him to the beyond.

This morning he did not die. Pretty Boy waved back at him. Then he stood up in the boat and stretched his arms out to the sky, welcoming it, basking in the approaching dawn, and quite clearly even at that distance, shook his head with the wonder of it. Turning to his oars, Pretty Boy rowed away into distance.

"So long," Daly said softly. "It is a beautiful day."

Gloria kissed him gently on the cheek an hour later and said,

"Goodness, I thought you'd fled when I went to your room this morning, but your suitcase was still there. I might have thought it was all a dream, such perfection of our destinies rolling out with such precision."

"No, I'm here and hungry."

Gloria gave the cook orders and they sat indoors in a room overlooking the lake.

"It's perfect," she said. "Everything's in place—you, me, the children, us at Owney's wake, all beautifully written in a hand with every *t* crossed, all the *i*'s dotted."

He asked her, "Did it have to begin at Owney's funeral? Was that the right time?"

"I didn't know until I was there that it was the right time. I didn't know almost until the very minute I spoke to you if it was the right time for things to happen between us."

"Do you cure people—knowing when it's the right time?"

"I can."

"But you've never really tried?"

"No, what if I failed? I'm not a fool. I don't want to inspire false hope in anyone. You ask so many questions. What I'm describing to you is perfectly natural. There aren't any priests here, no mumbo jumbo. This is the natural world and it's here to be understood by us. What if Einstein had not decided to look at the natural world?"

"And what would Einstein, a great scientist, a very great scientist, tell Bobby Kennedy's children the morning after their father was killed?"

PLANE FALLS FROM SKY OVER CONNECTICUT

Lout from Pittsburgh Angers Goddess

As he finished his eggs, he did not know how to begin, but she asked, "When are you leaving? I saw your suitcase was packed. I want to take you somewhere tonight."

He said boldly, "I plan to leave this afternoon." He had plane reservations for two days later, but it had come to him that he would either die or go insane if he heard any more. She believed every word, saw no contradictions, in anything she said. He trusted that in her need to seem composed she would not quarrel with his abrupt departure.

"You can't stay longer? Must you really go?"

"I'll be back soon, if you want me."

"You know I do. Daly, I understand. I understand things. You feel you have to go, and if that's what you want that's what I want, too."

"Good."

She said, "Last night had an aura about it. I felt things, I know new things. Daly, I knew you would be very good for me."

"You felt it then, too."

"Oh, who could not understand what you and I meant to each other last night?"

"Yes."

"You understand what last night meant?"

"It was magical."

"More."

She continued setting the scene. "We must be absolutely honest with each other," she said on the ride back to the train. "We must never lie to each other."

"Never," he said, reciting. "It would destroy the magic."

"Oh, at last," she said, "someone who understands. I wish you'd stay."

In the mood of the mystical sense of destiny that pervaded every thought of his hostess, Daly said, "I wish I could, too."

Why couldn't she ask: *Well, why the hell don't you stay, then?*

Instead, she nodded gravely as if Daly had said something correct. He nodded too.

Before they left the convertible, she placed her hand against his chest, palm flat against him. "No harm will come to you now," she said. "I promise, darling."

"Well, I feel better already."

"This is not a joke. Remember there is no god or goddess except you or me."

"Not me. I'm vain and shallow and vengeful and generally aspiring to stay drunk and forgetful and—did I say vain to the point of people pointing me out on the street?"

"Yes, and cute, but not very funny."

"And, yes, not very funny and troubled by bad dreams."

"None of it means anything, that's the human part of you. All in all, you're divine."

"Okay."

While they stood in the train station, she said, "I'm really rich, Daly, and I want you all the time. We don't have to get married—but if you want to, I want to. I want to do everything to make you happy? Did I make you happy last night?"

"It was enchanted."

She kissed him gently and whispered in his ear, "Till then."

Traveling had frightened him again. There was too much strange and unsteady terrain under his feet away from his home. He had learned in Europe only that he could survive horrors by holding on to thoughts of familiar music, shadows on streets he knew, the shape of silhouettes of beloved rooftops against the late gleam of a Pittsburgh twilight. His time with Mrs. Scone had been less enchanted than when Donald Duck pursued Goofy with a broom on the screen at the old Strand Theater on Forbes; but true wonder lay in the mind's ability to find comfort in the good, routine things that lay curled asleep there.

The rest was quicksand.

He remembered on the train to New York from Stamford his terror in London at the sight of great cathedrals lying in ruins. And the daily runs of the *Luftwaffe*. People said the Nazi bombers had good taste: They destroyed only the best castles of the human spirit by Wren and the rest. Still, he had drawn comfort as he walked the morning after the bombings in the rain and mist: St. Agnes stood as always at that awful moment at the foot of Robinson. It was a rare building he would dream about in all sorts of places, at all times, like now, when he had come from a beautiful home on a lake with a woman dying of abundance. The disease of our time: too easy an excess and its advanced stage of illness, boredom, and silliness in its grasp for the impossible. A cathedral is a cathedral, he thought, amused with himself at his ability to act the ignoramus, but a church like my old place is a rare pearl in gray waters.

In the taxi home from the airport in Pittsburgh, Daly was confounded as he had been for decades in the enigma of the varieties that the search for lost innocence took. He had seen others suffering with the same dilemma as Gloria. But long before he knew her, seemingly from birth, the question had plagued him of why men and women seemed armless and legless and sightless and subject to terrors in the night when they first touched the place in themselves where innocence had once been and discovered, as Gloria had, nothing there at all.

Alone in his house on Coltart, the emptiness of Connecticut made the world seem as tight as a coffin to him. He decided to walk outdoors, to feel home, up toward Fifth and St. Agnes. He was thinking at the foot of the long hill up Robinson of the long years of laughter on the good streets, when two young men in leather jackets moved toward him.

Daly had never been coldcocked. It was a matter of principle, sensing anger in his vicinity like storm clouds forming and preparing for it. Life's most terrible blows, he had decided, came when at least one party thought negotiations were still under way. He could feel the menace in the warm August air from the approaching boys.

From a few feet away, the shorter boy asked, "You have a cigarette, buddy?"

There was no answer to avoid the impending assault. Say no, and it's looking for fast trouble; say yes, and then it's a request for a match next, and after that for two dollars, and next, Lend me your shirt, faggot, I think I'll go to the fairy's ball tonight. Daly smiled as openly as if he had not been born and raised in Oakland and did not know all the street crushers' games.

"Well . . ." Daly started to say in anticipation of conversation or flight when the taller boy said, "Jesus, Mr. Racklin, I didn't see it was you. Honest to God, Mr. Racklin, the moon was in my eyes and I was thinking about something else. Mr. Racklin, Mikey was very mistaken; he's Greek and a new pal to me. He don't want no trouble either. I'm R.J., Norm Buncher's son from Wadsworth Street and a really good friend of Terrence Carney. You know Carney from the family. You're like their inspiration and they love you like a father."

"Sure," Daly said, "sure," young Carney an unlikely reference.

"Mr. Racklin who?" the short boy asked.

"Mikey," the taller boy said, "forget it, there ain't nothing to talk about."

The shorter boy flexed his shoulder muscles and made fists of his hands. "I asked the man for a cigarette," he said. "Where's the crime? Who the hell is he someone can't ask for a cigarette?"

"R.J.," Daly said to the taller, paler boy, "explain to Mikey there's no hard feelings, and just to keep walking. I have things on my mind or I'd be happy to talk to you and Mikey, but there's things on my mind. Make him understand that so far there's been no harm done, okay? Please make him understand situations get out of hand and there's a lot of trouble for everybody."

R.J. Buncher took Mikey's arm and said something into his ear. "Yeah," Mikey said, "let him try to put me in jail. A lawyer ain't a cop."

But he let R.J. move him away.

"Mr. Racklin," R.J. said, "I'll buy you a drink, Saturday. Straight, man, Mikey is Greek, he don't know his way around Oakland yet. No trouble, good guy, same as us."

"No trouble," Daly said, and quickly crossed the street.

"I'll tell Terrence I seen you," R.J. called. "You're a good guy for good people, Mr. Racklin. Keep up the good work!"

It was all home in Oakland, and right and wrong as ever.

But a boy named R.J. with red, scaled hands and a brother named Head because he was notoriously stupid and the other brother called Crash because his main method of assault in a fight was to lower his large head and charge brought back feelings of home to Daly. To Daly tonight there was a quality about the two boys—the familiarity and warmth he felt in the reassurance in the symmetry of certain memories, people, streets, and sounds and scents. In R.J.'s broad face he read his own; and in his expression he saw all that he had once not known, a self on these home streets with beliefs uncommitted to too much awareness.

Daly felt he had left something with Gloria. Home, he had not recaptured his feelings that good times lay ahead; he had been wounded in Connecticut when he had felt himself prey to a woman and the rush of new beats to old drums.

He asked Jesse to walk with him in the park, and she met him in the dark before the Carnegie Library. He had chosen the park to bring back youth inside himself, to forget the days on an invisible calendar being crossed off. But he was not the same boy who had once come to Schenley Park. They walked under trees dark in their trunks and bright where streetlights shined in the upper branches. Other people walked there, too. Daly's gloom lifted as they talked.

As he walked with her toward her door later, both silent, he warmed toward the night without Gloria Scone in it and the pall of outsiderness that had fallen on him while traveling. He relished the goodness Jessie had wanted for him, running to meet him at his late phone call. Hadn't Jesse come through and made *something* of the sad night? He held her hand hard.

At her house he put her hand to his lips, and said, "I'll take you somewhere now. It's too early for sleep."

She looked at him full in the face. No, he thought, we aren't going to drive down to Maryland and get a marriage license. I'm no answer to your problems, Jessie; I'm not an answer to my own.

"There's a place that's a secret of mine, I want you to go there with me tonight."

"Can I ask where?"

"A cemetery I love."

"You've told me about it. Yes, I want to go there."

But the phone rang and she went to it, and spoke swiftly, and he heard her say, "No, not now. Call me in ten minutes."

"Who's that?" he asked.

"Someone."

"That's no answer."

"I have a life outside you, Daly. You know where you stand with me."

"Is this a man?"

"Do I have to draw you a picture?"

"I have a rival?"

"It is a man calling me."

"Okay, I have no right to ask. But be careful."

"Go to hell. Good night."

"Who's someone?"

"Just someone."

It was an idea of mixed emotions that had often occurred to him: Someone else waited, an opportunity for Jessie. With her hair pulled back, dark but reddish in glow at its fringes, her face in perfect symmetry of features, strong nose, forehead swept from her eyebrows long and prominent, her lips full and broad, she was more than handsome. Tonight, hearing her voice in his mind, her laughter and appreciation of him—and comfortable with him, knowing that for all his reticence, she was at the core of things for him—he missed her as if she were already kidnapped by a lurking stranger, never to be seen again.

He called her house from a drugstore, but the line was busy. He made himself place the phone back in its cradle gingerly: Thank God, he thought, one outlives some part of the passionate past, at least the smashing hapless telephone rages of youth.

At the top of Center, he walked toward the half-decimated cemetery. Boys used to try to get girls to come up there in the dead of night. The dark cemetery settled in around him, the drooping branches of trees, the sense of being enclosed, a tomblike closeness above ground. He felt safe. No one could see him in all his shyness and sense of loss at impending failures; there was no one to hear him. The air held all secrets in the presence of the graves and the still lack of light.

"Excuse me," Daly said, walking in the dark on graves.

Once he came here often, and he had settled that with himself a long time ago. Everyone had forgotten the people buried under his feet, and they might enjoy a little company. Some had been buried almost a hundred years.

He patted a tombstone.

"Ready or not," he said. "Tonight I'd like to start off with a medley of requests from the audience."

He sang, as loudly as he could, taking on the refrain by the Andrews Sisters in one voice, then adopting another for the Bing Crosby parts in "Don't Fence Me In." Then he sang "White Christmas" with depth and sincerity, stumbling over the low notes where his voice vanished altogether.

His voice rang out fearlessly the length of the cemetery, going nowhere except into darkness, no judgment here where things were surely beyond weighing and measuring.

He sang next for Owney O'Doherty, "Moonlight Becomes You."

Taking a deep breath, and enunciating every word, he sang "That's My Desire" as he remembered the late Chickie Muldoon used to do it, in imitation of Frankie Laine.

Still diffident before his lack of ability to sing well, he patted again the closest tombstone.

Since "March Tenth, 1878," the name on the tombstone illegible, the person here has been dead, Daly thought, and he said aloud, "He or she never heard anything that bad in all these years."

Once young, he and other young lovers had tested themselves against the eternal dead. It was in the shadows of tombstones decaying with the seasons, names not legible, that the genesis of life's desires bloomed, needs bursting into nights of cemetery love with neighborhood girls as it was only once and never again:

nights kindled to flames over the corpses of nameless strangers. He was an old lover now. There was little to be tested. He shook his head with the wonder of it, Chickie Muldoon, bold and in no great voice, challenging nightly the respect of his listeners at the Irish Club and dead early of the presumption in one bad song too many.

He turned at a sound in the darkness under a tree. "Charles?" he asked softly. "Mr. Floyd?" Tonight there was no invitation to the gallop. The branches on the tree were silent. The twig that had fallen was another call, autumn and winter waited, not Pretty Boy Floyd and wildness. And himself in dried leafs and seasons of frost, a singer only in the darkest of night, cemeteries his arena of contest, where nothing but the wind and old trees were alive, and Jessie, vibrant and somewhere else, was receiving an offer other than his own.

He could not sleep.

In the morning, he took a trolley down to Jessie's, and said to her when she answered the door, "Who is it?"

She asked him to come in.

A man sat on a couch in the living room.

"Daly," she said, "this is Bruce Lowry, my first husband."

Daly shook hands with the small dark man. His eyebrows grew across the space over his nose, but of course Jessie would not note the simian appearance it gave him. His suit was well worn, the pants too short in length. His grip was callused and his hands were large.

"Daly's a friend of mine," she said.

"Yeah?" the man said, drawing it out.

Daly sat in a chair across the room from Lowry. No one spoke.

"Does anyone want tea?" Jessie asked.

"No," Daly said. "I think I'm interrupting."

He stood and went to the door. "I'll talk to you later," he said to Jessie.

"What about?" Lowry said, standing.

"Bruce, please!"

"Pardon," Daly said.

"I don't like lawyers," Lowry said.

"Fact is, neither do I."

"That's what I mean," Lowry said. "How would you like a punch in the mouth?"

"Not much."

"Well, you'll get one you don't leave Jessie alone."

"Bruce, please leave."

"You choosing, Jessie?"

"Please go."

Lowry went to the door and asked, "How did it happen he was leaving and it's me who's out the door."

"Please go."

When Lowry had departed, Jessie sat in a chair and wept. "It was like happy days are here again seeing him like that," she said. "He used to want to fight with waiters he said were looking at me wrong."

"I do bring out the worst in people," Daly said, relieved. "This was the man who called last night? I'm a little relieved at the competition."

She stopped crying. "It's complicated," she said, "but I don't own this house entirely. He owns half of it. He says he wants to sell it, but maybe before he does, he and I can get married again and I can continue to live here with him."

Daly laughed. "That's a resistible deal."

She was quiet.

"It is, isn't it?" he asked. "You wouldn't do something like that for half a house?"

When she was silent, he realized he should no longer feel relieved. Another moment between them had arrived, and in this moment, sudden and strange, he had no words for her.

"Do you really love me?" she asked, reaching for him to take her hand.

"Yes," he said, "and I suppose we ought to get this straight now:

I want to marry you."

Again, she was silent.

"Jessie, what's on your mind?"

"I know Bruce loves me in his funny way. Daly, I don't understand you."

"Simple enough, let's get married," Daly said.

"No," she said. "You're saving me. That's not love."

At Lasek's, before he visited the Carneys, to at least count them and be assured none had been apprehended hijacking an airplane, Daly found Rest in Peace. Sitting alone, Dr. Pierce was reasonably disturbed.

"Where've you been, you reactionary bastard?" he asked Daly. "Who's around for me to complain to when you're not here? I thought, He went and died without telling me."

"You know I wouldn't do that."

Daly's wine was smooth and he waved to the bartender for another.

"I been trapped by these youth in Oakland," Doc said. "They're coming at me from everywhere. They scare me they're so dumb about themselves."

"Only seems like it."

"Imagine," Doc said, "an enemy put a gun to their heads and said, 'Now, young men, uncertain as young men have always been, we want you to look ugly, menace your parents, wear hair sideways like porcupines, out, ferocious, comical.' And they do that, they choose to do it to themselves, a marvel, Daly, a delight, and an interest. I think of other boys who used to walk these streets. I ask myself: Why had Corny Ryan, who hadn't yet shaved, been chosen to die in a blazing tank in North Africa? Why had poor little Mel Walls, who was deathly afraid of the water, gone to drown in a Higgins boat off Sicily? Now on these streets, who are these replacements for dead boys we knew? The Oakland boys, too, didn't know either where they would fit in the order of things, but they didn't need to scare us that they were going to hold their breaths till they burst."

"Doc, I'm off on an errand today. In fact, there's more than one. I've been out of town for a couple of days. I think if I ever stopped running, I'd fall over dead. Hurrying through like this, I still feel like I'm not making contact."

Doc punched him gently on the arm. "Okay, you here now?" he asked.

"Not that easy, soak. It's no contact with life in general, my former wife, my father, my sister, Ruth Marie, my brother Al left home and never came back, other people, the times. I'm sailing by all of it like a kid on ice."

"You didn't skate by me, son."

"No, I maneuvered too fast past myself. It was myself I never caught a clear picture of—I saw the rest, they saw me, but it was all happening somewhere else while I was flying here, jumping there, never getting a clear picture of what exactly I'm doing in the blur. It's dreams, too. I feel like I'm here during the day mostly, but at night I wear disguises that cause my soul to grow cold. Behind my eyes in the day, I see the trees after the troops pass coming back into bloom in the spring in Europe, and I wonder how they grow and prosper over where so much terrible happened. I dream I'm a tree and wake up in a sweat, but happy, not feeling frightened, just in my mind leaves and sunlight in the branches."

"The subconscious has things going on there like a masked ball, dancers coming and going, men dressed as women, women dressed as bears, you get my meaning? Trees, hills, sense and no sense to it. It's no more real than all this." Doc pointed out Lasek's Bar and Grill, which looked real enough to Daly Racklin.

"Doc, I never had that much to drink that bars didn't seem real to me. Only what happened and where I've been, not where I am. You ought to see a doctor."

"So you really left town? My sense you were dead was accurate. Being out of Pittsburgh for some of us is like being in purgatory.

Don't leave town again, it disorients you. You talk strangely. You connected to Silk Brogan yet? You have that horse-at-the-paddock look about you, going to gallop even if it's into a stone wall."

"Silk is still the calamity around the corner," Daly said. "Every street has its own catastrophe. I'm running to put out the fire up the block on this street." He said good-bye and hurried up Ward to the Carneys, feeling something was wrong there—but he slowed his pace in the summer heat: He always felt something was wrong there. Intuition was no resource around Mark Carney's family, something of imminent disaster always lay on the air.

Outside the apartment house, in a shirt too large, no great favorite of Daly's but nevertheless his shirt, a gift from Jessie with the initials *R.R.* on the pocket, Terrence Carney prepared to rush by Daly. Daly caught him by the elbow.

"Terrence, it's old Daly," he said.

"Uncle Daly, there's big trouble. I don't know how you feel it, draws you like a magnet. You been sent."

"What's up?"

"That pregnancy, the one I committed."

"Terrence, that was weeks ago."

"Well, it's on the griddle."

"Slow, very slow."

"The girl's going for an abortion. Terrible!"

"This is news to you? You know it's illegal."

"It's my kid is what it is."

"You wanted money for an abortion from me, remember?"

"No. Hell, no, I wanted it for sending the girl away to have the baby. I'm religious, Uncle Daly, I don't go for abortions."

"Just tell the girl that, honestly like you're telling me. Is she Catholic?"

"Catholic and from Tacoma, Washington. Raised by the Sisters of Mercy out there."

"Do you want me to talk to her?"

"It'll do no good. There's another man involved."

"What's another man have to do with it?"

"He's the one everyone will think did it."

"Does the girl think that?"

"Uncle Daly, she was raised by nuns to tell the truth. She knows it was me, and she told me the facts."

"What's the other man have to do with it?"

"His situation ain't good with his wife to begin with—and the girl's begging him to take her somewhere to get an abortion. And it gets him off the hook of suspicion and mistrust and people going to look at him out of the side of their eyes and twisting their mouths up like they're going to spit, and he does her a favor. There'll be no kid, nobody will blame him, even though the man never touched her. Everybody's happy, everybody's dandy—killing my kid!"

"Where are you going now?"

"To see Colleen, to beg her, you know. I can't see the guy. She's staying at his house, and that's where the innuendos started about him and her. It ain't sure his wife heard the innuendos about it yet."

"Who is the guy? Do I know him?"

"Silk Brogan, the guy was a great boxer, the guy will knock my head into Rice Krispies. He fought three guys coming at him with cue sticks in the Diamond Billiard Parlor, middleweight, used to fight light heavies, nobody'd come near him, guys from the pool hall still walking with canes, twenty-five years ago."

"Silk Brogan?"

"Silk Brogan, like I tried to tell you. His fists were lethal instruments when he was twelve years old, Uncle Daly. He's the accused party in this. He's going to take her to get rid of my kid. Leaving out my personal feelings about him and her doing homicide on my kid, you know what kind of sin they'll be committing. I know you, Uncle Daly. You know your sins, you know what this one is. None worse and under our noses."

Out of a sadness so grim as to make the approaching night the last blackness ever to fall on Ward Street, Daly said: "I'll talk to him."

*   *   *

Daly in a ceremony elaborate with thoughtful glances at each of them, somber reflections on his part at each exchange, took back the keys to his house from the Carneys. He asked each person, the sisters, Terrence, and the mother, if they had had any others made. Assured they had not, he nodded as if the matter were closed.

"Uncle Daly," one of the girls asked, "haven't we been doing a good job with the cleaning and things?"

"Excellent, excellent, I'm just changing my work habits. I'm going to be keeping different hours. When I have it worked out I'll be giving these back to you."

Why not change the locks? Because, the truth is, he thinks the Carneys will come through the windows or down the chimney if need be—no lock built has ever kept their types from the brandy in the desk drawer or the coveted tie in the rack. He smiled at them, thankful he had nothing of value to steal and what was there had little meaning to him. He would not need a television set where he was soon going: Consider his dismal furnishings part of his legacy to the awful bunch.

The young woman in trouble was not at the Isaly's Dairy on Forbes, where Terrence and Daly waited an hour for her.

A thick gathering at his chest reminded Daly that he might keel over at Isaly's, falling into the excellent chipped-ham sandwich and milk shake, spilling the liquid on his clothes, hardly a heroic end. He took his pill and it gave him a headache briefly, good news, it meant the medicine was working.

"Where do you suppose she is?" Daly asked.

"She talked the slugger into taking her down to West Virginia for an operation."

"Silk wouldn't be that dumb, he knows it's an illegal act and the girl is a minor."

"Better than his family busting up about making a seventeen-year-old girl pregnant."

"You'll tell the truth."

"You know," Terrence said, "I think I'll stick with my own truth on this, Uncle Daly. I see no evil, hear no evil, speak no evil. I don't know nothing. I'm in no position to currently raise a kid."

"Nice shirt," Daly said, standing and wiping his hands on a napkin.

"Well, she ain't here. That lets me off the hook. You're a witness I did my best."

Leaving, Daly saw Inez and Caitlin, each walking stiffly down Forbes—toward Ward, he assumed, and further audiences with his sister.

"Ladies," he said. "Good day, a very good day."

They continued walking, but Daly, who had come to mistrust even his hearing as his attention dwelt too long on his dying heart, thought he had heard Caitlin distinctly say, "Your sister has a lover!"

He laughed at the whimsies of his imagination and did not pursue them. Possibly Caitlin had called, "It's tough all over."

Oh, Silk, Silk, don't do it.

Daly raced for the phone when it rang at nine.

"What I spoke to you about," Silk Brogan said, "was a matter cleared itself up, Daly. I appreciate your interest. It's good to know there's a friend there without questions."

Given the constellation of abominations that had fallen on the head of Silk Brogan, which matter had mysteriously evaporated, leaving only ten more homicidal possibilities?

"That's good, things have a way of smoothing out with time."

"Misunderstanding. To tell you the truth, you probably spotted it was Armelia on my mind, right? I asked her straight out: Honey, we been at this too long, you have something on your mind? Daly, she looked me in the eye, and said, 'I love you as much as the day we married.' I feel good I put it to her, and I feel good she answered honestly. Daly, I even asked a guy to follow her a couple of times—he swore to me the woman went to church in East Liberty. In the afternoons, I was distrustful, but she was meditating, probably in there trying to figure out how to hold our marriage together."

"There's nothing else bothering you?"

"No, hell, no. My wife's been honest with me. What more can I want?"

"Well, there it is, like so many things we worry about at midnight, gone with the sun in the morning."

"How are you and that widow—or what? What's her name?"

"Jessie, she's been divorced twice. We're fine."

"She's blind? Really blind, no sight at all."

"From girlhood."

"Has to be strange."

"All of it is."

"Put that to music and sing it," Silk said. "Here I was a couple of days ago, rich, you know, new Lincoln every year, beautiful, two boys almost raised, raising a young girl like she's my own, orphan from the convent, wife built like a movie star—and crying in my beer. A few hours later the world looks right again. It's all in the—the—what do you call it?"

"Angle of vision?"

"Yeah, that's good enough. Now, you can do one more thing for me. I told Armelia I saw you at Owney O'Doherty's wake, not saying of course I was troubled out of my mind, and she says, 'I remember him. Why don't we all go to church at St. Paul's this Wednesday, Feast of the Assumption?' "

"She really said that?"

"She says you're a gentleman, she says you always are so witty, you talk like a book sometimes. You know she went to college, Daly? I said you'd probably be going with Jessie, a woman you see a lot—and she says, 'Bring her, too. Let's make a day of it. We'll make a day of it.' What do you say?"

"Sure, good, it's better than good."

"We'll be there with the kid we've been looking after, Colleen McManus, young girl from the state of Washington, sweet, really a sweet kid. I worked out a certain problem for her, and everything's fine. Armelia says her and me ought to be doing more things together. She misses me, always working. Too much time on her hands."

When Daly called Jessie to talk to her about that Wednesday, she asked who would be there.

"The devil," he said. "The Prince of Lies, the Father of Mischief, the Arch-deceiver. Dressed up like one of us."

"What's he want with church on a holy day?"

Ascending the steps of St. Paul's Cathedral on August 15, the Feast of the Assumption—a celebration of the Virgin's assumption bodily into heaven—the day dry and sunny with summer fatigue, the joy in the rightness of things dimmed by assassinations and calamity and the promise of more to come, with Daly and Jessie a few steps down, Silk walked between Armelia and Colleen. It was a fine day of crowds and fresh clothing, Daly thought, of people making the best of bad news on the sidewalks, bright cheeks and steps gleaming in sunlight and old friends shaking hands. Bobby dead called for greetings a little louder than usual, elbow grabs harder, handshakes firmer.

At the top of the steps, like a line of policemen guarding the entrance to the cathedral, stood a band of strangers. They formed a human barricade to Armelia, Silk and Colleen, Daly and Jessie. They glared at Silk Brogan.

"Careful, Silk," Daly said. "You have no argument with anyone here today."

The strangers gazed down, not prepared to move. They stood their ground as Daly tried to pick out faces in the group. "Who are they?" Daly quietly asked Silk.

"We're Colleen's cousins, uncles, and aunts," a tall, ruddy boy called out to the four people climbing the few steps. For a great cathedral it had no imposing sweep of broad steps leading to the entrance lobby.

"I'm Jane Donlon, Mr. and Mrs. Brogan," a stout woman as tall as Silk's shoulder said. "And this is Chester Beale, my brother."

Silk seized the hand of a cleanly barbered man in his sixties. "My sons, Desmond, Toddy, Bobby, and Gerald, my daughters, Mrs. Bryce, Mrs. Hurley, Mrs. Shostak, Barbara, the youngest, and my sons' wives, Katherine and Frances—her husband died a year ago. And Karen, Joyce, Ellen, and these gentlemen are my daughters' husbands, Edward, Robert, and Kevin. And this gentleman"—she motioned to another man hurrying to climb the steps, hot in a stiff white collar—"is my other brother, Maurice Beale. We're all gathered together in Pittsburgh for a family occasion, the wedding of our youngest daughter on Tuesday night. They came from all over, and, seeing you Brogans, I thought we'd wish you well, Mr. and Mrs. Brogan, and say good morning to Colleen, my niece, and invite her to our good times."

Silk said, "This is my pal, Daly Racklin," but before Daly could smile and introduce Jessie, the assembled guests began to shake hands with Daly and Silk. Armelia left them all and walked away.

Silk and Daly shook hands frantically with everyone who put out a hand.

Silk turned to say to Armelia, "Isn't it a fine day?" but she was gone. He turned to Daly, introducing him to various people, names not connected to anyone. Daly smiled, and nodded. "How grand to share a happy occasion," he said, shaking hands, mumbling names.

"May we take our niece for a minute?" Mrs. Donlon asked, and Daly, uneasy with Armelia's departure, nodded, watching Colleen marched off and soon lost in the circle of Beales, Donlons, Hurleys, Bryces, and Shostaks.

"Is everything all right?" Jessie asked.

Daly whispered in her ear. "No, it's Silk's wife, Armelia. I smell trouble like smoke in dry leaves."

In a pew, Armelia sat silently through the service, speaking only once to anyone. "They can have her," she said to Silk, loudly enough for her voice to carry to Daly and Jessie four rows back.

Jessie nodded and said to Daly before he explained, "I heard her. I know who spoke."

"Little tramp!" Armelia said.

"I heard," Jessie said.

Daly said, "I'm praying Armelia ends this between her and Silk. They brought this on themselves somehow. They have to end it."

And soon Armelia did.

Standing outside St. Paul's on the third step down, Armelia braced herself as the combined crowd of Donlons, Beales, and the rest left the church. Where people greeted each other, smiling and shaking hands, Armelia pointed Silk out and then Colleen.

"That one committed adultery," she announced to the world, "my husband, a peach of a man, under his own roof with a girl young enough to be his daughter. The other's the prostitute, the one I sent for to raise, the deceiver, the one in the purple dress I bought her. The two of them ran a brothel around me. I'm not like them. My father is Conn Daugherty, the man who gives more to this parish than any ten, and with friends in New York and Rome my husband has disgraced. My husband comes to church with the blue-eyed face of St. Patrick and he knows what he did and I tell you all now. Whore! Whore! Blasphemer! Don't touch me."

She spoke to a priest who had come to take her arm. Her voice rang the length of Fifth in front of the church, caused people on Dithridge to look back to the cathedral, halted everyone on the steps momentarily as if a tiger had burst a cage.

"Do you see that crowd of criminals there?" Armelia asked, pointing to Mrs. Donlon and her family. "They knew what we had on our hands. They refused her. They knew the whore book that family wrote in Tacoma, Washington. They're one with her. They're all prostitutes, leaving the trash on my doorstep and running away like thieves in the night. The girl's name is Colleen McManus, Colleen McManus, and their name is Donlon, Donlon, the girl is one of them and they're one with her, thieves and swindlers."

She seemed calm. "You all have a good Feast of the Assumption day," Armelia said. "But I want you to know who was with you today in church, every one of them thinking they're fooling God.

Well, they're not. My husband made her pregnant and it was done in a room under my roof. And, he says to me, the girl is pregnant, father unknown. We'll adopt the kid!"

"Armelia," Silk called, chasing her down a step. "She was going for an abortion. I couldn't let her kill a kid."

She looked at him once before she turned. "You killed me, Silk," she said, and she strode away down Fifth toward Webster Hall.

Daly looked about for Colleen and saw her surrounded by her cousins and aunt and propelled toward the further reaches of Dithridge where they had parked their cars. In the direction where Armelia confidently strode, Daly thought, lay the seemingly Protestant domains, the broad, rich streets of the country of rich people, even if they were Catholic.

Armelia did not look back. Daly took Silk's arm, the conciliator and make-peace artist in him taking over. "I'll go with you whever you're going," he said. "We're together on this. Hey! Holy hell! Watch out!"

Which of the Donlons or Shostaks or Beales, Bryces, or Hurleys, man or woman or child, threw the first punch was uncertain. It certainly was not one of the priests who had come to break up the warring factions, and it was not Daly who hit anyone first. It was, in fact, Daly thought, in his long life the first time he had ever been punched. He fell back to protect Jessie. As he did, he took one of his nitroglycerin pills and felt the instant headache that came with it but was pleased, the capsule was working. "What is it?" Jessie asked. "What's happening?"

"There's men and women hitting Silk Brogan!"

"Are there many? Will they kill him?"

"That's not the problem."

Silk's predicament was that in protecting himself he did not land a solid punch on any of the people assaulting him. Jumping about, feinting and pushing, not punching, he sidestepped any blows coming at him, but several men cornered him and Daly dived into the center of things. How better to go than in defense of an old boy from Robinson? Even if the defense was calculated to save him from murdering one of his adversaries.

Daly, as peacemaker, was punched several times, but it was not like he thought it would be. Punches were nothing compared to worrying about them. He hit no one himself, tugging at the arms of men and women seeking to land a blow on Silk, stepping between Silk and the mob after him. Occasionally, he grunted to Silk: "Doing great, doing great, don't hit them, please don't hit them."

Under the weight of Donlons, Shostaks, and Beales, Silk finally stumbled backward on the few steps of the cathedral and fell to the sidewalk.

Daly shouted, "My God, he hit his head! He struck his head. He may be dead."

Silk pushed someone off himself: He had not struck his head on the pavement, but he writhed for a moment in pain.

The priests pushed back the crowd on the steps. "Please, disperse," one said. "Please, disperse." Several parishioners, obviously policemen, burly and efficient, moved in to shepherd away the angry combatants. There had never been a fight on the steps leading to St. Paul's Cathedral, but, Daly thought, these are peculiar times: No one can deny that. Silk, clutching his ankle, sat up, alone on the sidewalk. He waved away people trying to aid him, two of them physicians.

"Daly," he said, looking for him.

Daly helped him to his feet. "It's my ankle," Silk said. "It's broken. I know it's broken."

"They fell on you like a pack of demons."

"Not like my own true wife. She did it, Daly. Not one of them relatives of Colleen landed near the punch she did. But I'm here standing upright, son, one leg short, but standing."

"You sure you're okay? You took a tumble, it was a fall."

"Daly, there was a guy from Kentucky, a middleweight like me, hit me once in the first round, second or third punch in the fight, and I ain't recovered yet. What this was here is love taps. I've been hit!"

Daly assured Jessie Silk was fine and that he would accompany him to the hospital and then visit Uncle Finnerty. "You'll be okay? You'll take a cab home, okay?"

"I'll be fine. But why can't we all take a cab to the Montefiore. I'll wait."

But Silk said, "No, I'll walk."

Jessie kissed Daly on the cheek, but she seemed too withdrawn for the occasion. He tried to press her hand before he left with Silk, but she removed it, not angrily, but with firmness. Together with Silk, Daly began the long walk down Fifth to the hospital, Silk hopping and leaning on Daly. Daly thought he understood: His man Brogan wanted to travel, after the circus at the cathedral, under his own steam.

Silk had not brought his car, proud to be living on Fifth within walking distance of St. Paul's. "It's only hitting me now, Right. If Armelia leaves the marriage, her old man isn't going to give me the time of day in the warehouses I run for him. I'm on my way to hell, inevitable. He closes down the trade to the warehouse, I'm cooked. I knew it before, but I never saw it like on a television screen the minute she said what she said and walked away. Daly, I never touched that kid, she was like a daughter. Colleen knows it." He closed his eyes against the long night of being a guy who never made it and had the facts unravel on church steps. He winced as his sound foot struck the pavement. Daly felt him writhe with each hop as he tightened his grip on Daly's shoulder. "I'm a mess, Daly," he said, sweat running down his face.

"You're doing fine. Slow, slow, the hospital will wait."

"Daly, one of her relatives kicked me in the face."

How Colleen died, ten days later, was clear enough after a while, but the reasons for her descent lay with her in the district known as the Hollow, down below the Panther Hollow Bridge.

The cast assembled to testify to the last hours of Colleen McManus, according to Captain Jimmy Carr of the Number Four, as he related it to Daly, was broad in its survey of Oakland Street characters and respectable citizens wandering in solid places and able to bear witness. The girl had spoken to Silk Brogan's sister, Brenda, the younger one who had gone once to be a nun, and had been asked to stay at the Brogans' but had fled the house on Robinson when there had been some difficulty in locating Silk.

Next Colleen was seen in the company of the Little Sport and Fingers Malloy, who seemed, according to a woman passing the Pitt Tavern at the time, to be urging her to go into the saloon with them.

Next, she was observed on Forbes about twenty-five minutes later walking with a young man named Mouse Murphy, who told Captain Carr that he was very apprehensive about young women like Colleen McManus, although she had told him her name was Lois Swift: "There's a lot of crazy people in the world, Captain, and a lot of them are women and among the women, you know, a lot of them are young. I don't want on my record that I have anything to do now or in the past with crazy young women. Truth is, it's on my record I associate with a lot of crazy young guys and that's bad enough. Sometimes it's the bad company a person keeps that gets an honest person convicted. You know that to be the truth, Captain."

"I know that to be the truth," Captain Carr assured him.

The man and the girl were walking about three long blocks away from the Pitt Tavern, so it was probably true that she had not gone into the saloon with Fingers and the Little Sport, as they both testified, but the identification of her body was impeded when no purse was found—neither Fingers nor the Little Sport was ever absolved of the crime of lifting the bewildered young woman's purse. But they were apparently several miles away from where she died.

Mouse was seen in the Carnegie Library by himself at about the time Colleen was walking into Schenley Park. There had been a rash of briefcases snatched from every floor of the library and Mouse had been under suspicion for some of those crimes, but no one pursued that matter in the investigation of Colleen's death.

"Mouse, we see you within five blocks of the Carnegie Library it's going to be a long six months you're going to do in the workhouse," Captain Carr said.

"Jesus, Captain," he said, "a person ain't allowed to go into the library no more? I been going there from a kid. Reading is one of my main recreations. And what if it's not the books I'm going there for but the bathroom? It's not illegal to go to a public toilet anymore, is it?"

Mouse had been working the venerable Oakland trade of boosting homosexuals he picked up in the men's rooms of the Carnegie Library, the University of Pittsburgh, and bars the length of Forbes, descending down into Soho as his trade drove him. The captain studied him.

"Mouse, do you think I'm a fool?"

"No, sir, I'm a fool. Out of public toilets the rest of my life, out of the library, out of Pittsburgh, you say so, Captain. The state. The United States. I'll go to the toilet in Mexico, you say, only don't put no involvement between me and that dead girl. I spoke to her total in my life three minutes. I said, 'Say, sugar, you lost or what?' and she gave me this blank stare and says, 'My name is Lois Swift, and I have the wings of an angel,' and I said, 'Bye-bye, I have a reputation to think of'—to myself, you know."

She was then seen at the Panther Hollow Bridge by a retired city fireman. "You remember Charlie Shields?" Captain Carr said to Daly.

"Eddie Shields?"

"Younger brother, this was Charlie, a fireman for twenty-two years and he was taking his two granddaughters to the Phipps Conservatory. And it was about twenty after two, and Charlie says she walked out about a quarter of the way onto the bridge—he was with the kids across the bridge—and before he could run to stop her, she jumps. Dead when she hit the ground, Charlie hollering, 'Stop! Don't do it! Lady, stop!' He ran through traffic, leaving the little girls. But what he saw when he looked over the railing was her body, a good leap, has to be two hundred feet."

"Jesus," Daly said.

"She wasn't pregnant. She wasn't a virgin, but she wasn't pregnant."

"Thanks, Jimmy Valentine."

"Anytime."

Eight

*C*alvary Cemetery on a hot day in September 1968 was ashen in earth and sky, brown leaves curled into themselves and part of the dry grass. Colleen's spirit, in its confusion and earthly completion, lay six feet in the slate ground, Daly thought, and he trembled under his nylon cord coat with the prospect of the convent girl's ever returning as a ghost, broken and mutilated from her fall, angry with all of them over what had happened to her.

Daly watched Brogan. Silk wiped at the tears at his eyes, not looking at the assembly of Donlons, Bryces, and Beales contriving even on this somber day at Calvary to look like an army platoon arranged to advance on him. He had come alone, meeting Daly at the cemetery. All warmth was absent on the hillside where the Latin words fell into clumps of rock and mud and the young girl's body was made part of the ground. The sky was knotted overhead with blue-black clouds hurrying to some destination.

Daly wiped his moist brow with a handkerchief, rubbing against death and the day and further harm to Colleen. "I wish the girl were here," Silk whispered to Daly. "Death is like a bone in the throat when a man is alone out here at a cemetery."

"Not alone, things are always crowding in," Daly said.

"I guess Colleen has all the answers now," Silk said, as he and Daly started their descent down a path to his Lincoln; and when

Daly didn't answer, Silk said: "I'm going to sell the business, Daly, I'm on to better things. Armelia's father is choking me off, it's a matter of days."

Daly said, "Last act, but sometimes they're a long time coming."

There was a small wind, a blessing in the turgid day, and Silk seemed tired, morbid as a shadow at the ceremony, hard now. He asked, "What's the matter with me, Daly? What do I do wrong from when we were boys? Criminals went to their fate better served than me. I was everybody's darling, I know that, Daly."

Silk leaned on his car. "My old man used to come to watch me fight, by profession a man hanging from bridges, painting against the wind. Where's the people going to come to replace him, your old man?"

"Nowhere," Daly said. "No replacements."

Daly thought Silk had the family look, hair black and long, black lashes, thin face and blue eyes with a jaw pushed forward with a cleft chin. Around them, other mourners left in their cars, and Daly bent to scrape mud from his shoe with a twig. Silk Brogan used to dance with a lateral movement that confounded the fast and cunning and iron-chinned and long-armed guys. Now he groped in the dark for something misplaced like a pair of glasses he needed to read the notice on a medicine bottle. Daly knew the feeling.

"Hey, Brogan," one of the young men with the Donlons called, "you ain't going to be on them crutches forever—and when you're better, watch out, cowboy!"

Daly and Silk drove slowly down toward Wilkinsburg, through the business section on Penn, past Silk's apartment on Fifth, then St. Paul's Cathedral and into Oakland. At the stately, columned Pittsburgh Athletic Association, Silk said, "I never thought when I was a kid I'd see the inside of the place, Daly. Married to Armelia I used to have dinner there once a week. Now I can hardly remember how it felt to be a welcome guest there."

"I've never been inside," Daly said. "And you know, Silk, I lived in Oakland all my life, born here, and I've never been inside Pitt. Going down to Duquesne with the other Catholics from our neighborhood I never had a call to go inside Pitt."

Without asking, Silk drove with Daly to Robinson Street and turned up the hill past St. Agnes. Again, Daly remembered the lost gray afternoons in the Pittsburgh of his boyhood, streetlights often lit at noon, even then failing to penetrate the haze of smoke and dust and fumes and sulphur on the air; streets too dark in Oakland to see a dog from three feet away, a person until he or she spoke into one's ear, houses blending into each other as he trudged again up Robinson from St. Agnes's Church on the corner of Robinson and Fifth to the Morgan Street Cemetery, desolate and broken-backed with untended tombstones at the top of the hill. It was a land of illusions and certainty in belief. But it was us, on the streets and in all the houses, in all our foolish glory, the merging of us in the sunlight the same as fog, Daly thought, that was the beauty of it, and the mystery was why we came to separate.

It was not the houses or truths spoken on the street, but ourselves in our entirety that made these long hills in Oakland sigh with the endlessness of our way of life.

"Same feelings every time I come here," Silk said.

"Yeah," Daly said, "being here is like being yourself. Recovering something you lost."

"I see my sister once a week. We eat the same food every time I come, from when I was a kid. My aunt tells the same stories. My sister, Brenda, corrects her—you know, the two of them will never sign a paper Silk Brogan lost his punch. I sell the Lincoln and buy a Ford. I become a well-known character in the bars on Forbes. There goes what's-his-name. My sister, my aunt, I'm Mr. Silk to them win or lose—only there's no lose with women like my sister and my aunt."

"I'll tell you what," Daly said, "promise me, when I die you hold a wake for me at Brenda's house on Robinson, nowhere else. Tell

Ruth Marie it was my last request. I don't want the last talk of me to be in sunshine and flowers and polished linoleum and little brown things on crackers."

"You'll see me gone first."

"You gave me a promise."

"Okay, I did."

"I'll hear you served people shredded goose from trays when I'm gone," Daly said, "I'll know it."

"Daly, we'll hold the wake in back of a bar I know between Soho and Uptown. I promise you four fights among old friends, two among strangers, all the main events before the third round of Pio wine. Okay?"

"I'm serious."

"I know you're serious. I'm serious, too. But I want one promise from you to me, too."

"Anything."

"Promise you ain't going to die, ever."

"Easy. I promise."

They left the car at the top of Robinson and walked down the hill to Brenda's house. She had never married and had kept the place for twenty-five years for herself and an old woman called Aunt Flora, solitary the two of them with only Silk's brothers and sisters occasionally visiting. It was not a time of free-spirited return for Daly; each walk down Robinson for him held a thousand low Irish voices from his past, sitting on their porches, murmuring in his ears of lost worlds before their eyes, and now themselves fading shadows in the streets of the unremembered.

"Well, Daly Racklin," Silk's sister said, "come in, stranger."

Thus had sounded the sweet triangles of welcome on our streets since the earth emerged from water and swamp, he thought, ready to compliment the old aunt, who was only eighty but had looked a hundred and eighty for the past twenty years, and Silk's sister, who had prominent teeth but smiled as warmly as if the Brogan family had patronized the finest dentists in the years when they used to sleep three to a bed: greetings and iced tea and the old stories and tapestries gray with age and sofas under plastic and a large fan, a scene seemingly cast forever.

Listening to the radio, one of the first on the street, in this house, the father of the family had come into the room and asked Daly and Silk who it was singing so boldly on the radio. Silk said, "It's Bing Crosby."

"That's a good old name," the father had said proudly. "I'll bet that Irishman has himself set up where he makes twenty dollars a week doing nothing but singing."

"Your house has memories for me," Daly said now. "Memories I wouldn't trade for a million dollars."

"I'll start you with half a million, Daly," Brenda said. "Give me a memory for a half million. What do you say?"

"Well, in small bills maybe."

The old woman, whom everyone called Aunt Flora—Daly thought vaguely she was Silk's late mother's sister, but she could have been someone else's sister, the specific relationship lost in time and discreetly never discussed—said, "I remember you, Daly, you used to slip up and try to give me a kiss when I wasn't looking."

"I remember it was you used to slip up on me and try to kiss me."

"He's lying!" Aunt Flora said. "I remember him, the worst of the lot, with that angel look he carries around even today to disguise what's in that heart. He used to have hands fast as fish, that one, too. Brenda, keep your distance. I know this one."

"We all know his reputation, Aunt Flora."

"You brought it out in men, Aunt Flora. I fancied you myself," Silk said, "but I was afraid of your right arm and the fist on the end of it."

"You were! And you could knock out colored fellows with one blow."

Before he left to walk home, Daly asked, "Do you forgive me, Aunt Flora, for my youthful indiscretions? I was carried away. Boys used to argue and bet which you liked best."

Old Aunt Flora had never married, a fixture among the Brogans for decades.

"Of course, I forgive you, doing what I did to men I'd have to have gone live in a cave crazy as you all acted when I came into a room."

Daly kissed her on the cheek, then Brenda.

"I'm restored," he said. "I'm made eleven again."

When he left the house on Robinson, Silk staying on, he called Silk to him and said firmly into his ear, "Silk, it is not a joke, my wake is to be here, in this house. I have nowhere else, and I must be remembered on Robinson even if I'm forgotten in palaces."

"It's a vow."

Daly called Jessie and dozed before his television on the second floor of his house on Coltart until he was awakened by a pounding at his front door. His heart raced, and he lay back in a chair, trying to quiet it. It would not be still. He took a small pill, nitroglycerin, and the headache was sudden, but the approaching pain in his chest stopped its progress. He stood weakly, sweat on him from the back of his neck running down his arms and his forehead wet with it. The alarms at his front door continued—not an ordinary experience, most of his clients prepared by habit to shout their agonies over the phone as if they were in an uninterrupted conversation with him. He walked downstairs slowly. He knew whoever it was would not leave, his venerable Chevy outside an announcement he was probably home.

His first floor had no furniture but a battered old couch. He believed he would rent the place one day. A plumber had been there after the hypnotist, a foot doctor, two young women, a newspaper briefly run by Pitt graduate students. Then he thought he would not rent the place, just die peacefully probably years before he found a suitable tenant, no interviews, no ads, no strangers at his door and using his first floor for their purposes. He had no carpet there. The students had absconded with it.

Outside his door in the night stood Inez, Caitlin, Belle, and

Irene, four muffled figures large enough to occupy his porch and wooden steps.

"I'd ask you to come in, ladies, but the truth is I'm ready for bed. Is it something that can wait till morning?"

OAKLAND MAN DIES IN NIGHT

Smile of Triumph on His Face

"Is your sister something that can wait till morning, Daly Racklin?"

"Has she had a seizure?"

"Worse."

"Ah, her telephone is out of order."

In the old days before prices rose on everything and Daly was younger in heart, he used to send each of Ruth Marie's eternal four friends and Ruth Marie herself a dozen roses on Valentine's Day; but the cost of the roses went up to fifty dollars or more and Daly stopped the practice. He reasoned that with the fifty dollars he could buy the two Carney girls shoes and that while in the long run he knew they would walk with them into unseemly adventures, they might at the same time go somewhere edifying in his purchases. Optimism was always the main tune with the Carneys, the total of their lives too resonant anyhow with the daily disgrace that dogged their footsteps—maybe fool the devil by believing good could come of the bunch. His sister and her friends were reduced to exchanging flowers with each other on Valentine's Day, whatever romance each of Ruth Marie's friends had with a man generally evaporating around holidays requiring gifts as testimonials of undying love.

Annually, they each spoke of the loneliness in being betrayed at Christmas and New Year's Eve, degraded on Valentine's Day and St. Patrick's Day, reviled and humiliated on Easter, birthdays, and Thanksgiving.

"She has a man!" Caitlin said.

"Living with her," Irene said.

"Coming and going with him like you and me," Inez said.

"Racklin, don't leave us on the porch," Belle said.

"I'm sorry," Daly said, closing the door on the four of them. "I'm waiting for an important call. Yes, a most important call."

"Who?"

"My uncle Finnerty," Daly said. "It's life and death."

"He's been in a coma for months. There's no important call coming about him."

"Investments. New York. Check the stock market."

"You gone crazy?"

"Police are out checking the neighborhood. You all must go to your rooms, they're beating up women in front of houses. Go home, I'll be in touch with you all in the morning." Inez—he knew it was she—pounded on his door three times more, and then they all departed. Daly thought it was a simple choice really. If the feeling in his chest returned he would drive up to the emergency room at Montefiore; if it did not he would make an appointment with Dr. Cobble as soon as he could—and of course if he died in the night the decision would be out of his hands altogether. He staggered upstairs, tired, but strangely exhilarated: This was breaking news. Perhaps he would have time for one last good-bye. Jessie, I love you. He took a capsule and lay back in bed.

But two hours later when the phone rang the heaviness and the anxiety had passed, the sweating gone, a sleepiness in it as if he had labored and was weary but sound.

It was Silk. "Daly, I just got home. She cleaned me out. Took everything, didn't leave me a can opener. I'm telling you she shredded up my suits. Ripped up my shirts, must have hired a van—there ain't a chair, not a table. Left a note: So long, lover boy. I guess that's how it's done when they have money."

"I'm sorry, Silk."

"No, it's right like this, it ain't like death. I'll call another lady I know in Squirrel Hill, and she'll say, 'How could anyone do that to a fine man like you, Silk Brogan?' "

"Well, that's the thing to do. Call that lady. Go on with life."

"Tomorrow's another day," Silk said.

Maybe yes, maybe no to that proposition, now that you mention it, Daly thought as he hung up, and was asleep in minutes, dreamless, dark, long, and easy. He knew, even as he heard clocks ticking and the old boards of the house creaking, that he was there in familiarity, and it was to be an ordinary night and then a day with sun or showers. The dawn will break and after that might come in sanctity of breath and promise the moon of another night.

PART THREE

Soul and Stone

Nine

Daly, pulling up in his car before Ruth Marie's house, was astounded to discover at nine in the morning a man boldly leaving. The man was burly in a thick sweatshirt and fairly dirty with oil stains on his cap and paint spatters on his pants. He was big and bent forward with long arms, and if he had a neck he had acquired a turtlish trick of concealing it by drawing his head into his shoulders. In his furtive movements, head unmoving, eyes darting, Daly thought him a burglar surprised in a coincidence of timing, and said to him, "Say, where you think you're going?"

The man—not an easy customer, broken nose, face lumpy but with steady dark eyes—said with a thick accent, "My house, I live here, buddy." He pronounced it "boddy."

Daly let him pass to an old car parked at the curb.

He rang his sister's bell, believing as he tried to put together the man's description that he would soon need a full account for the police of Ruth Marie's murder. But she came to the door, dressed for the day.

When she was not guiding her friends through the dangerous journeys life could become, sensitive as she was to the breezes of the moment, Ruth Marie made friends all day long. At the Giant Eagle on Forbes it was a woman in the checkout line who had the face of someone desperate for understanding. She never missed:

Later at her dining room table hurt people unburdened themselves to her. "If there's a saint in Oakland, it's you, Mrs. Drange," she heard innumerable times, as she weighed and considered the awful ache of a suffering man or woman abandoned by everyone but her.

At church, too, after Mass at St. Agnes, as her small circle of friends sometimes found a lull in the struggles that gripped their lives, she had room in her heart, and when she saw a certain stranger, man or woman, she approached them, shook hands, told them who she was and pointed toward Ward Street to where she lived. And before night fell on another Sunday she had made another friend, navigated another soul over enemy waters to a safe return at a loving air base.

In church was where she met Robert Botkar.

Botkar, it developed, had been standing on the steps at the Fifth Avenue entrance, a recent immigrant from communist oppression in Europe and the tyrannies of the middle sixties, in borrowed clothes too large for him, needing a shave, vacant-eyed. Ruth Marie told him who she was and on the spot invited him to dinner that night. Father Farrell had spoken on communism that morning and asked a few people who had fled the dictatorships to stand, and when he did, Ruth Marie told each of her friends she knew here was a man who needed her. He came to her house promptly at six.

He had been shown friendship by other members of the congregation. They had clothed him, found him a job—he was a housepainter by trade—found him lodgings, and the Knights of Columbus financed a small Chevrolet. Still, that lost look hovered about him. Ruth Marie said she saw a mighty hand in the direction he had been swept in, to arrive today at her house. He could not laugh yet. She would teach him.

Ruth Marie told Irene, who had been married three times, she knew she would one day marry Botkar and in his large workingman's arms find the passion she had missed the first time. Before her dessert of apple pie and ice cream she invited him to live in her third-floor rooms that once had been occupied by her son.

He ate three pieces of pie and a gallon of ice cream and accepted her offer of shelter, of course, even though Belle, Inez, Irene, and Caitlin objected, telling her it wasn't right; but what did they know of the fires of love in the heart of a person like herself? she asked each of them, knowing they would repeat her words to her brother.

In a day's time, he moved in his meager belongings to her third floor. She heard the meaning of life in his footsteps on the stairs, the smell of paint and turpentine in his passage through her halls. He joined for her a mysterious communion with the sidewalks outside, the weeds in the cracks, trolleys clanging somewhere on Fifth. There was a fresh excitement in her days. Daly put his head into his hands as he listened. It was a time of new beginnings, a casting off of old quandaries, she said.

"Can you understand me?" she asked. "There's something going on, Daly."

The vision of their fathers in Oakland was for their sons to become accountants, dentists, pharmacists, policemen, firemen, schoolteachers, or to hold a steady position with the state, city, or county, the girls only that they marry well, a few rare ones to become nurses, bookkeepers, or teach public school and retire with a pension.

He spoke to himself as surely as to her, advancing on the unscalable cliff of another person's impregnable, false assumptions. "Only our lives are in the air," he said. "Our own prospects. There's nothing new or good here for you or me."

"Daly, I'll marry again if he wants me."

He nodded—it could happen—but if we left our young men from St. Agnes unprepared for the fact that while God's road was true it was also tortuous, what had we planted in the minds of women like my sister? Marriage was the key, marriage was the door, marriage was the burnished path to success in the bedroom, good for the digestion, an insurance policy for old age when a woman's children loved them as no woman without children was ever loved. It had been an accurate workable summation of a plot for millions of our mothers and sisters, but should there be a tiny, almost invisible crack in the concrete walls of husband and marriage and children, the world trembled with the panic abroad, the fright, the rumble of earthquake on our streets.

"No, live with him instead. Don't marry, Ruth Marie, he has nothing, he'll take whatever you have of anything of your own. Marriage is not in these cards. You're fifty-five, a good age, but not nineteen. Don't jump, there's not enough time to make your way back at our age."

"What do you think I am?"

"Think of your mother and father. Ask them in your heart what they would have you do."

"Thank you, no. I know more than the two of them combined about life and suffering. If I was not a strong person the human race would disgust me. How sick I am of him and your precious Uncle Finnerty, claiming resurrection. The experience didn't make him stop drinking, or fighting with strangers. I have no interest in him or your father."

"Is that why you don't go to the hospital to see him?"

"They have nurses to take care of old drunks and lechers."

"You're saying this to annoy me, and you're succeeding."

"It's the truth and I'm better than the whole bunch of you—and I don't walk around with people calling me Mrs. Right Racklin. No, I'm a simple, humble woman. But I know my rights, and with Robert Botkar I may be on my own rocket to the moon at last."

"Don't marry him!"

"My intention was not to shock you, but I was seventeen when our father committed suicide and I went to my high school graduation two months later, suffering the burden in silence. And you were eleven, and it was all 'Protect the child.' Well, I was a child, too, and no one protected me. I have my own life to live, starting with Robert Botkar. Have some coffee, you're pale. I'll fix you eggs and juice. Really, I don't like your look."

"No, I'm leaving. Your talk of father committing suicide is crazy. I heard the stories too. There are always stories. He dove into the water after he heard children calling for help."

"Well, that's the story was peddled with the fish. But I never bought it. Your father was a coward, and he committed a mortal sin. Racklin the First, and Racklin the Second! And what was left for me but artificial flowers. Please, Daly, sit down."

"Ruth Marie, you're not a saint."

"And neither are you, and neither was your father. Leaving all the money to you, excuse me!"

"Ruth Marie, it was four hundred dollars. Do you want half? Do you want me to divide it up into thirds, you, Al, and me?"

"Keep it all and the rest you're going to collect at fifty."

"Ruth Marie, that's some kind of joke. It's going to be forty-six dollars. I'll give you half. I'll give Al my share. Don't marry this guy."

"Live in sin, Mr. Racklin! What do you think I am? I respect the sanctity of my marriage to Michael Drange."

Daly became desperate for the feel of morning away from the suffocating atmosphere of his sister's confidence. The queer innuendos about the manner of his father's death did not shock him. The stories about what happened on the water would never be resolved; only the first Right Racklin knew how he died, and who was he to judge, given particularly the exemplary life the man had lived?

He believed he knew all there was to know about his father.

He turned over the motor to his old Chevy. He had bought Jessie a set of wind chimes and not remembered to take them when he left his house. Back on Coltart, he went indoors for the chimes; he had placed them on a table near the door, and lifting them the pain in his chest returned.

At the kitchen sink on the first floor, he took nitroglycerin and water; and, with the quick headache, a pain moved up his shoulders and into his neck. The night's sweat fell on him evenly, down his legs, into his eyes. He called Jessie and told her he was going to drive up to the emergency at Montefiore, a distance of ten minutes, no great alarm, just checking his heartbeat with a doctor at the hospital.

She read his tone of voice.

"I'll be there," she said.

"Don't be silly," he said.

She hung up.

He went out to the Chevy and turned the key in the ignition, and the motor would not turn over. In its long, noisy history—he had bought it when Eisenhower was president—the car had never failed to start. He sat back; well, die here at the curb before my house on Coltart, the Chevy and me, soldiers with batteries down, the pain intense, the car silent and old.

He staggered from the car and went inside again and called Silk Brogan, no answer; and then he called Father Farrell at St. Agnes, again no answer. He called Number Four for Jimmy Carr, and the desk officer said he was out and, before Daly could tell him he had something of an emergency on his hands, the cop hung up. He then called Sydney and a woman answered; this time Daly hung up and he found a card of Doc Pierce's and dialed the number and no one answered the phone. That left four different bars in Oakland and the reading room at the Carnegie Library where he might be. He could call Ruth Marie, but he supposed death would be a kinder finish than listening to her in his last minutes.

Soaked in sweat, Daly began the long walk to the Montefiore. He walked up Coltart, trying not to attract attention; but for all the interest he created in his stumbling lurch, his hands clenched, shuffling at best, he might have been dead for fifty years or an unremarked refuse can. People he passed did not turn to look at him.

He leaned on a pole on Forbes. The pole became a great friend. He reluctantly left it in the morning sunlight.

A grand moment it would be to have an assassin spring from behind a shopping cart at the Giant Eagle and empty bullets into the staggering man! Rather that, Daly thought, than death by his heart's betrayal and the ordinary grasp of gravity on the sidewalk. He crossed Forbes. And he almost made the emergency room, crossing Fifth safely at the Shanahan warehouse, on to the sidewalk across the street when he collapsed in front of the iron gates at the main entrance. He said, "Help," feebly, before darkness closed in.

The world was dim at its edges while Daly lay in quiet comfort, no great pain anywhere, only his throat dry. After a while, he realized he had a tube in his nose and mouth. He closed his eyes. For a certainty there were no tubes at the final destination of the race; and he felt good inwardly, living on borrowed time, but perhaps this was a last hour and there might not be much more of the putting one over on eternity. He felt gripped as always by an implacable world of distance and the terrors in the loneliness of being not with people. If only, he thought, as he fought to wake himself from the presence of a nature that cared not for children, him, or the whole procession of human weakness in the presence of such majesty and uncaring, if only the trees could reassure us by dancing like little kids: But the forest in his fever stood remorseless without song, a beautiful sky perhaps and the rest awe-inspiring, but finally nothing but still trees and dank, leafy ground without mercy.

Sometime in the night he was visited by a nurse; he saw her fair hair and pale blue eyes as she looked into his and smiled.

"Mary Muldoon," she said.

"Not Chickie Muldoon's daughter?"

"Yes."

"I never had a real quarrel with him, you know? It was a misunderstanding."

"No harm done, Mr. Racklin."

"He sang beautifully."

"Liar. He had no voice. This is a voice."

And somehow there was no strangeness to it: She stepped back and sang, "Ah, Sweet Mystery of Life." Daly watched her every move, thinking Chickie's daughter had turned out to be a handsome woman. He had hoped she'd sing more, but she was gone in his clouds of sleep. He closed his eyes, aware that in the room's one chair with arms against the wall sat Pretty Boy Floyd, either alternating turns in the chair with his father or the two of them becoming one then the other. Daly looked away from the chair and was pleased that after a while mostly no one at all sat there and Mary Muldoon seemed gone for good.

He became aware vaguely Father Farrell was in the room, but sensed him a friendly visitor, not a phantom, talking to other people, and not here on official business, and Jessie was there and once—bent over him in concern as real and palpable as a hot breath, closing out all light with his anguished face—young Guignan. And was it Gloria Scone? No, she was an apparition out of the illusions of a ridiculous man seeking gold in far-off Connecticut. In the room's shadows, receding and advancing, Ruth Marie occurred real and ghostly, but there surely, coming to raise him from the dead if Gloria Scone could not. People coming and going, the rustle of nurses, people standing in the doorway to observe him, the merging of dream people and real ones in the room, and then a terrible pain in his neck, and when he moved his head slightly it became less, and he knew he was closer to life than death.

He slept and when he woke after a time he became aware that Doc Pierce was speaking to him; and he had apparently given Doc the impression that he had been following a conversation. Doc was in the middle of saying something, sitting at the bedside, and standing over him, behind Doc, was Dr. Cobble.

"Well, your man Eric here, was one of the best," Doc said, and Daly remembered Dr. Cobble's first name was Eric.

"Best teacher we had at Pitt Med School," Dr. Cobble said, speaking now of Doc. "Ethics and Principles of Medical Practice, none of us who heard him were ever shooting for anything but being Richard Pierces the rest of our lives."

"You're hearing all this, Right, you're noting it, I'm charging for this visit."

"Doc, how did you find me?"

Dr. Cobble said, "Excuse me, I'll see you later, Mr. Racklin. Good seeing you, Dr. Pierce. Great man, Mr. Racklin."

Doc said, "I came on the last rites for a friend of yours when I was up here a week ago to see Spots Gallegher, you remember him? Not a friend in the world, hopeless even if he were among hyenas. Gasping along in the last stages, next room, was Vanish Hagen, himself, and Father Farrell was there with his sister, crying, and I was in the next room commiserating with Spots. And, seeing it was Father Farrell and he was here for Vanish, I tried to terminate my conversation with Gallegher. But, you know Spots, holds on to you like a fat leech.

" 'It's Farrell,' Spots says, 'I see him pass,' turning paler than the pillow his head was on. 'He's come to shepherd me to purgatory.' When I heard Gallegher was up here I knew there wasn't a person in the world wouldn't wish him a slow, miserable trip, friendless. So I came, knowing he hadn't anything in his lousy life but people he wronged, but the bastard had me counting the minutes till I could slip away from him. He'll never die though, rotten, lying bastard. I say, 'Spots, I swear to you your prognosis is all good. You'll be up in two days. I'll go right out into the hall and find out Father Farrell's business.' "

"Old Gallegher, most hated man in Oakland, worse than John Crumpton, who threw his mother and old aunt down the stairs," Daly said.

"Curse of drink in that case," Doc said, "no excuse for Gallegher except he's been a hundred pounds overweight from a kid. But plenty of fat guys are princes, genuine princes, but not Spots. Outside in the corridor, Vanish's sister is about to head in the direction of the great divide herself and Father Farrell has his arm around her. She's staggering. 'He's gone,' his sister says. 'The University of Pittsburgh killed him, and now he's breathing his last.' Putting a little poetry to it since Vanish was hit by a car and not by an institution of higher learning, inevitable, you know, for a man himself claiming the powers of invisibility. Father Farrell nods to me, and says, 'It's nice to see you, Doc, although I don't see much of you through the year at St. Agnes. How long has such rectitude flourished in our parish? Old Mary Gannon, ninety-two, comes to confession once a week, and we have someone blameless like you doesn't come once a season.' I don't say, 'Rash of high fevers, sweating palms, chills, very busy these days, Father.' I dodge the question of my soul on the line, and say, 'Can I go in and see Vanish for a minute?' Well, Vanish's eyes are closed and I pat his hand, and I say, 'Take heart, old boy,' and he opens his eyes, and asks, 'Do you run into the Right Racklin?' And I say, 'Lately I have, yes.' 'Tell him,' Vanish says, 'all this happened because I lied to a friend. Pray for me that God forgives me what I did to Silk Brogan. I could have prevented his life in ruins like the lava was flowing down from the volcano in the movie about the old Italian city. Daly will know what I mean.'"

"Poor Vanish," Daly said. "All our problems are too big for us, much less a fellow that weighed a hundred and thirty pounds. I've been so under these tubes I never heard Vanish died. And right under the same roof with me at the last. Repulsive Gallegher, and Uncle Finnerty too. A fine collection, some here to joke, Spots to whine, and some to draw a last breath."

"Vanish didn't die. Last rites and all, he recovered: As far as I know he's back home this morning, sitting in their kitchen! drinking a cup of tea, rejoicing over his good fortune, and discussing miracles with his sister—she'd find one in the mail being delivered on time. The car hit him was a taxicab bringing someone out of town to Pitt, and his sister sees a plot there, banged him up good, lung punctured, but he'll be fine. Last words his sister says to me when Vanish starts home: 'Pitt will get us yet!'"

"I'll see him if I get out of here," Daly said. "I'll send him a basket of flowers. It doesn't look like it's up for him and me both."

"Spots, too," Doc said. "He recovered, digestion problem, small wonder, eats a whole ox for breakfast every morning, then goes to

Scotty's Diner and has some ham and eggs, double order of rye toast, sound as a dollar this minute."

"And my uncle Finnerty, he's still here? Nobody is going to die anymore, considering all the senseless deaths in this year, miraculous." Daly talked slower, not as much air there as when he'd started. "Not a day goes by kids in Vietnam don't leave by the big trapdoor; and Oakland is still filled with dancing men like me. How are you feeling, Doc?" Daly caught his breath and happily stopped talking.

"Truth is, I may break the string soon, son—I can't climb two steps without grabbing for a railing."

"You saying it, or is it the truth?"

"A little of both. There's no happy ending at my age, Right."

"Any ending that doesn't say 'This way quick to the exit' is fake, Doc."

Daly caught his breath. He felt a wave of fatigue sweep over him, numbing and complete.

"One or two slip through," Doc said.

"Rumors with no substance, you know that."

Doc said, "Don't talk anymore."

"Doc, how'd I do? If I was to go tonight, how would you score me?"

"Two on a ten."

"No, I mean it."

"Why ask me? I'm a zero in any given nine innings."

"There's only us for a score on ourselves: No one knows us, no one knew us."

Maybe things counted somewhere else; but what was said about a person born to the long hills of Oakland began on the narrow porches and meant nothing if it was not part of the common history of how he was regarded by his neighbors. The truth was in the church at the foot of the hill on Robinson, and there might sometimes be painting outside the lines, but what there was stated there was the final word for judgment of each other.

"I never knew none better than you," Doc said.

"You mean it?"

"A bigger bastard Oakland never raised."

"Thanks, Doc."

At the first visiting hour, Jessie came with Tommy and the boy began to weep after a few minutes and had to leave the room. He had brought roses and thrust them awkwardly at Daly. Unable to move, Daly had twisted away. "He's not taking the flowers, Aunt Jessie," the boy said.

"There's thorns," Daly whispered. "The roses are beautiful, but they have thorns."

Jessie came to the bed and Daly gave her the flowers.

"He's broken up to see you in here," she said. "The flowers were his idea. He's crying because he thought you didn't want the flowers and he can't stand you in bed like this."

"Call him in before you leave, I'll tell him I love the flowers."

"Daly, do you feel like you're going to die?" she asked, sitting on the edge of the bed, holding his hand.

"Why do you ask?"

"I want to marry you."

"I may recover. Then you'll be stuck with me."

"I'm expecting you to recover."

"Then why ask what I think about things?"

"I want to go to Ireland with you. That's my real question. It's this: Are you thinking you'll be well enough soon so we can go to Ireland?"

"I don't think it's what I think that matters. Up to me, and we leave tomorrow."

"Come on, Tommy," he said to the boy when he came in the room to stand with Jessie. "You take care of Jessie now—"

"Daly!" she said.

"See she doesn't drink too much."

"Aw, she doesn't drink, Mr. Racklin. Me neither."

She kissed him good-bye, and Daly clutched the boy's hand, and the boy began to cry again before he left.

It's like being a guest at my own funeral, Daly thought.

And it was not twenty-five minutes after Jessie and Tommy left that Gloria Scone came into the room, silent, profound, assessing the situation, evaluating her role in this particular contest between life and death. She stood observing him in the doorway, sending vibrations by the carload. Good ones, he hoped. Should she decide to have him evaporate at this moment it would have been a piece of cake. He felt half dissolved now, tired, weak, not quite disembodied but certainly not there.

After she kissed him, she asked, "Are they giving you medicine?"

"Yes."

"You must put a stop to it. Their medicine kills."

"I'll tell the doctor."

"What kind of medicine?"

"Blood thinner to get the blood into my veins around the closed arteries and into my heart."

"My God, it's witchcraft. What else?"

"I don't know. Maybe something to relax me."

"Oh, Jesus, it's a conspiracy. Somebody wants you dead."

Courage: He leaned back and closed his eyes, but he felt no warrior bold; she terrified him with her certainty.

"I don't know that sleep's the best thing for you," she said.

"I'm not sleeping."

"May I touch your chest. Place my hand there ever so gently, let the life from me—I have more than enough for both of us—flow from me to you, my darling. Please. I've done it before."

"No, don't touch me."

"Poor darling, they've frightened you, haven't they?"

"Yes, I want to sleep now."

"Daly, our time in Connecticut was sacred. You do understand that?"

"Yes, come again, visit me, but for now I want to sleep."

"They've drugged you. It's their tactic, take away your will so they can meet their quotas with the pharmaceutical companies."

She kissed him on the forehead, and he tried not to flinch. Ah, bravery, it departs before a heart skipping beats and sluggish blood. He would never tell her now: "Jump out the window without a parachute and tell me how you landed on a cloud because you chose to be light as feathers."

He felt something at his foot. Mother of mercy! The woman had taken his bare foot, held her hand to it, enclosing it, and now as he watched she kissed the sole of his foot. "You'll sleep now," she whispered. "We will win over their medicine."

When Doc came in the morning, before visiting hours, Daly said, "Doc, I'm having visions. They didn't start in here. I was hallucinating from the minute I heard my heart was going to stop. Is it the medicine?"

"It could be," Doc said, "but it's a phenomenon not much has been written about. The shapes and shadows our mind casts up when our body's immune system tells us a battle is underway for the soul, light and dark, here or there, living here, trip to there."

"I've been seeing Pretty Boy Floyd, the gangster; Uncle Finnerty took me to see where he was killed, the cornfield outside East Liverpool, and I read a lot about him over the years—now I see him."

"Is he here now?"

"No, only you."

"He say anything special?"

"No, nothing you wouldn't expect. I feel funny about things like that. Up on the hill Michelle Shortall says she sees my father."

"Good example. Her system knows what her mind's only hinting at."

"You put no stock in the visions, they're not telling us anything?"

"I didn't say that. They're telling us plenty—the best conversation, us to us, on the deepest level."

"And what?"

"I told you, a masked ball. It could be this, like psychoanalysis says, and then again it could be the opposite, what the psychiatrist next door says. Choose your poet."

"So it's a well-known thing happening to me?"

"I knew a guy, about twenty-five years ago, the clock in his hospital room used to bust into song, leap around in the dark, and sing in three voices, like the old cartoons, 'Three little fishes in an iddy-biddy pool.' And he says to me, 'Doc, what's it mean?' "

"What did you tell him?"

"Well, he was a retired railroad man, you know the family, but forget it, it's private, serious guy, trains on time, big railroad watch. I says, 'You know the early apostles called themselves the fishers of men, maybe it's the call to come to the big pond in the sky,' and he says, this sensible guy, 'Really, Doc? So it's fishes going to come for me. I see them clear as you.' "

"How long did he believe?"

"He may believe it to this day, even though I told him straight out, after the joking, it's lights and shadows and nerves. He's walking around somewhere down in Florida thinking the Lord had a plan for him once loud and clear and with singing fishes, and he beat the summons. Now, you rest and concentrate on the all too real. The good news is if you're getting your notice it doesn't mostly come with a melody we can hear. I'm on my way down to look in on Gallegher. Ugly bastard."

When Doc left Daly dozed, and checked his watch. Visiting hours were over. He closed his eyes again, pleased he had survived the world washing into his room like an ocean tide, regular, insistent, always present.

But there within the hour, in a bathrobe large enough to house Ringling Brothers and Barnum and Bailey's Greatest Show on Earth, was Spots Gallegher at Daly's bedside.

"A last punishment on me brought you here," Daly said to his visitor. "Doc told me you were cured; I was hoping you were safely home. I'd rather hear a choir singing, 'Three Little Fishies.' Visiting hours are over."

"Hell, I'm a patient, too, Daly. I thought I'd stay on a day or two. My health isn't what it ought to be. God gave me this body, but He didn't tell me what to do with it."

"Bother us is what you done," Chomp said from the door to the room. "How the man read us chapter and verse about his goddamned body, every hour something with his ass or his plumbing. I come to visit you, Daly, Billy's out there looking for your room now, but I found it first, and here you be talking to Spots Gallegher. He's the worst human being in the Fourth Ward, counting Schenley Park."

"Chomp! Good to see you."

"You leave me alone, Farnsworth," Gallegher said.

"Chomp," Daly said, "Spots was just telling me his health isn't tops."

Gallegher's sexual lies were of the nature of uncanny events never to be known by other people, often related to things about his body and always in terms calculated to draw attention to its broad abnormality. His body, his health: a continuing story.

"When the bastard had eczema," Chomp said, "he pulled up his pants legs three times a day to show the scaly and red scales on his legs to all of us."

Daly said, "There was no audience too small; and when he had bandages removed from his back where he fell through a piece of plywood covering an open sewer he pulled up his shirt to show boys and girls in the schoolyard of St. Agnes his scars, sutures, and stitches."

Chomp said, "It ain't a nice thing to say, Spots, but some guys at the Irish Club used to swear they could *smell* the fat on you."

"Nobody has to believe me on what I seen and done," Spots said. "I know in my heart what happened."

Daly said, "I can't tell you it's been a pleasure to see you, but

Chomp's here now, and Billy can't be far behind. Let me just say: Those lies, you were too much."

"It was the truth," Spots said. "No one believed me because I was a size-forty waist in fifth grade."

"It was because it was lies, that's why. You never did anything with Lois Shrapp."

"It was the truth."

"Please, go away, before you tell us the other one almost got you killed in grade school."

"You're talking about Sister Celestina!" Billy Curran said from the doorway. "Daly, how are you? Looking good, man; but why are you letting Spots Gallegher tell them stories to a man sick in bed? It's going to give me a heart attack I have to listen."

Daly shook hands with Billy, and Billy said, "I almost died myself when I heard you hit the pavement with a ticker seized you. 'Not Daly,' I says to Chomp. 'Daly's going to die in bed with the radio playing good music. Classy music.'"

"He did," Chomp said. "It was what Billy told me about you dropping over in the street with a bad heart, and he says exactly what he said he said."

"I couldn't pull myself together for an hour," Billy said. "And then I come up here today and there's Spots hovering over you and fouling the air. Gallegher, you suck up the oxygen Daly needs to catch his breath."

Daly said, "Time to leave, Spots, you're upsetting these two gentlemen of delicate character."

Billy said, "I guess you're laughing at your friends again, Right, but I don't mind. It's just you, it's yourself, a bad quality, you know. But it's yourself and that's good enough for me. Did I say it right, Chomp?"

"You're no better than the rest of them, Daly," Spots said.

"Chomp, Billy, excuse me for a minute," Daly said. "I want a last word with Spots."

The two men left the room, and Daly asked, "What makes a guy like you go on, Spots? Give me a clue. Good people drown themselves for an imperfection here or there in themselves, and you go on without a care in the world. Tell a man near on his deathbed what keeps the old motor going. Give me a hint."

Gallegher sobbed in wild audible gasps. "My mother told me a long time ago," he said, "nobody was going to understand me."

Daly nodded and said, "Okay, is that it? No more than that: early training, nothing mysterious you heard somewhere."

"Ma said God died for everyone, but more for me."

Gallegher had no friends: From the children at St. Agnes's on it was all loss, children growing up remembering him with distaste and the imposition on them of his thick legs, his beefy neck with the huge chin already forming under the first. Somewhere in adolescence he had acquired a synthetic, explosive laugh, thought himself famous for it, then dropped it in manhood for the distorted face and tears of remorse. A long life of performances too exhausting for most people, Daly thought, but given the comfort in his special elevation as misunderstood and unloved, however mistakenly, it was cause enough for joy in a world without much deliverance in the common air. Billy and Chomp came back and Spots left.

Chomp had taken a job in a Chinese restaurant where the cook had an argument with a diner about how many kumquats were to be served for dessert; and he had asked Chomp, who was working in the kitchen, to explain forcefully in English to the customer that only three kumquats came with the duck dish. And Chomp had gone out boldly to the dining room to discuss the kumquats, but not ever having seen a kumquat before that night had thought the customer was poking fun at him when he held out the fruits to him in a tiny dish for his inspection. "You call that kumquats for dessert?" the customer asked.

Unsure, Chomp said, "Yeah, sure."

"Count them!"

Chomp said, "There's three, same as always. How many did you want?"

"Two more is what they serve at the Bamboo Gardens."

Chomp dumped the little dish of kumquats on the man's head, thinking the man was insulting him.

"Put them little things right up in my face," Chomp said, "and I'm thinking, Give him three more of whatever he wants and it's still nothing makes sense to me. I never saw one of them things before. I thought he ate what was the dessert and was shoving the pits at me." Daly felt the laughter tearing at his chest and tears in his eyes, and knew he would die if he continued to listen to Billy and Chomp. He asked the two of them to leave.

"I call them little oily slippery things nothing for dessert," Chomp said of the evening. "I give the complainer a shampoo. Kumquat Brylcreem, I say it right?"

Billy said, "You have to work on that superiority complex, Right. It's okay tonight you're half dead, but it's generally offensive to Chomp and me. Laughing all the time, you know? You're holding back that laughter right now—for your information, I never heard of kumquats either. Never saw one, wouldn't know one if it bit me in the ass."

Daly swore he would call one of them, or both, the day he was going home; and they, in state, a cab at the entrance, would accompany him back to Oakland from the hospital.

The young man who came to his bedside an hour later could be none other than Tommy Guignan's twin brother, Louis. The resemblance was marked; but this twin was poised, sure of himself, looking directly at Daly and extending his hand. Daly did not take his hand.

"I want you to know I appreciate what you've done for my brother," Louis said. He wore a shirt and tie. "I'm getting married," he said, "up in Toronto. I'm going to send for Tommy as soon as we get settled."

"Tommy's fine where he is."

"No, he's my responsibility."

"Are you ashamed that I know you've abandoned him?"

"I haven't abandoned him: nothing to be ashamed of."

"You could have fooled me."

"He's a lot of problems."

"What isn't?"

"I mean, I'm his age."

"Do you see him going down with rainwater when you look in the mirror every morning? He could have been you. He could have been me and I'm not his twin brother."

"Mr. Racklin, I came to thank you, not to argue with you. I appreciate what you've done for him."

"Is that why you hang up on him when he calls and never call him?"

"He's a lot of problems, and you can take care of him better than I can now—I'm in no position, you understand? I'm his age. Later, I'll do right by him. I'm sending him an invitation to the wedding."

"Being young gives you a long time to dodge, Louis. Good luck. I don't think he'll be joining you soon in Toronto."

"You have to understand my position."

"I do. I'm not placing blame."

Daly closed his eyes, knowing Louis was trying to think of something to say. Give him time, Daly thought. And he'll have an answer satisfying to himself anyhow. When he opened his eyes the room was empty, and he slept.

The next day Daly was attached to a heart monitor, a small black box, carried around with him wherever he walked, there when he slept. It was a series of wires in the box connected to parts of his chest and recorded the beats in his heart. He was cautioned not to leave the area of the station on his floor where the monitor was being received on a screen. The electrical impulses were sustained over about fifty feet, no more. Under no circumstances was he to walk where the electrical impulses from the box could not locate him.

Losing electrical contact with him, the nurses attending the machines that monitored the patients' heartbeats would not know whether their rhythms had become irregular—or, the unstated reason, whether they had died and that was the reason for the failed signal.

In his bathrobe and paper slippers, he took the elevator two floors up to see Uncle Finnerty, who lay in his coma. He knew he had dropped from all electrical contact with his monitors on the floor below. Daly stood over his uncle for a time and then went to a window at the end of a corridor and looked out over Robinson Street, the bright green land of his youth.

It was always return when he saw that street; it was always acceptance. If the houses below had toppled with fatigue at that moment, Daly would not have been astonished, but if, in the nature of things, after the last hydrogen bomb had destroyed the last peasant's hut in Vietnam or outhouse in Kentucky, Daly would have expected at least those Pittsburgh houses to be there, clinging to their place while the scarred and ashy dead planet whirled through meaningless space.

He patted Uncle Finnerty's white hand.

"It won't be long now for me," he said softly. "Maybe it'll be me who greets you. Can't know from minute to minute, can we, really?"

"Mr. Racklin," a nurse said when he returned to his floor, "you were off the screen for twenty minutes. We didn't know what to think. You could have died for all we knew."

"I didn't," he said. "Check the screen, you'll see."

Ten

Not wishing to make a stir, he occupied himself all day in the hospital, calling Billy in the afternoon. After dark, the day he was discharged, he walked grandly down to the Atwood Cafe with Chomp and Billy. They each carried a small bag for him.

"Right Racklin's home," Billy shouted to the crowded bar.

Daly drank three beers, but insisted he'd walk the few blocks back down to Coltart by himself.

His friends walked with him up to Forbes and once more shook hands formally. "I never knew how I missed you till I seen you up there in the hospital," Billy said.

"I have a certain problem, Right," Chomp said, "it ain't pressing, but you know? Work in a few minutes for me."

"Call me. But not tonight. Okay?"

"Jesus, Daly, you act like we're morons."

"I'm sorry," Daly said. "Call me anytime—you're going to do it anyhow. Why confuse things?"

"Explain again why you don't want us walking you to your door."

"Because I need five minutes to think my own thoughts."

"Maybe you can talk things over with us. You ever think of that?"

"It's a thought."

"You laughing, Daly?"

"A little."

He carried the two small bags Jessie had brought him for a change of clothes and toiletries. He had told no one but Billy and Chomp he was coming home, looking forward to general surprise when he announced he was back on Coltart sound as a dollar. Entering his house, he was struck first by the sound of emptiness rather than the sight. The house felt hollow; and it was, like a shell.

Whoever had looted it took everything but the plumbing fixtures. They still were in place; but all the electric light bulbs had been taken with his lamps. None of it, except the light bulbs, was less than twenty-five years old, all plain junk, a house furnished by someone who hardly cared what it looked like. Daly did his entertaining at Frankie Gustine's or Lasek's, never at home. Since his wife had left the house on Coltart, he had never brought a woman into the house: Ruth Marie had never been there, nor had Jessie. He was not ashamed of the furnishings, but he did not care to display them. He thought once if he ever remarried he would put fresh furniture in, new drapes and carpets, but lately he had occasionally thought, listening at night to his heart, that with a new wife, a breakaway romance, he would sell the house and live somewhere else.

But his thumping heart these days often caused him to smile at that unlikely program; he would be found here in the rubble of his life, in striped pajamas, dead on a bed he had occupied for thirty years.

His television set was a black-and-white and small and now stolen: To hire someone to strip the house and leave with his junk would have been a task. Upstairs, he discovered his law-school books had been hurled to the floor—in a search for cash on the shelves—but otherwise his books were there, kicked across the room, perhaps insulting to the thieves but scattered about in disheveled glory. Pictures had been removed from the walls; the thief or thieves had taken pictures from the nightstands with the tables themselves, the frames worth perhaps a quarter if one found a foolish middleman—he had paid fifty-nine cents new for each of them. The pictures were without meaning to him: Ruth Marie had a complete collection of everything Racklin, the package to be submitted in the year 2069 in her sure bid for canonization. In the kitchen he found that the refrigerator had been stolen and with it the milk and butter, stove gone, ironing board, mops, brooms, fittings from cabinets in the walls unscrewed.

He had a sense that the thieves were on to something: It was him quite appropriately they were removing from a place. But the place was in their minds. It was not anywhere that he belonged anymore; he belonged nowhere.

He went to the telephone to notify the police—a formality, he did not want the junk back—and found the phone gone.

Well, I'll just go up to the Giant Eagle and use the outside telephone or drop in on them at Number Four personally, he thought, have a beer at Gustine's and book myself into a hotel for the night, maybe Jessie's, until I can put a mattress on the floor.

Who do you think did this Mr. Racklin? he would be asked. Any suspicious characters lurking around your house?

Sure, first myself, the most suspicious character I know. Second, the Carneys, the ones I tried to help the most. Good candidates that bunch, chicanery and thievery, by nature, being equal in response to the amount of the victim's concern and unearned malice, on balance an excellent equation, gentlemen. It was to be said in their favor, though, that while they cleaned out the house, they left me my teeth.

He would probably go now to live with Jessie: Oakland had been shot out from under him. Robinson and Dunseith and Darraugh, Terrace and Forbes would stay fresh and glowing in his mind, the Irish Club and its visionary drinkers, a child's city on the hill. He slept on the floor and rose at dawn with the first light.

He dressed quickly, putting on a thin leather jacket. He tried his Chevy. It still would not start.

Daly started up past the small porches where the old-timers

used to sit on summer evenings staring into their pasts instead of the identical houses across Robinson, like cats with eyes open moodily dreaming of lizards and mice. Did the old-timers see in August their childhood cottages across the ocean with thatched roofs in the haze of late twilight? Was it Mother in her shawl in the streetlights' circle on the cobblestoned alien pavement before them and Father's silhouette in cap and scarf against porch railings of a Pittsburgh neighbor's house? Even sitting on their porches, he had been lost to them in the scent of their pipes. He might have been a trail of old heather blowing down from barely remembered fields in Cork so little was he observed, a boy who came and went like their own moods.

He called Jessie from the phone at the Giant Eagle and said, "Jessie, I'd like to move in with you."

"Where have you been? Ruth Marie says the hospital told her you checked out yesterday and when she went to your house no one answered and she looked in the window and saw all the furniture was gone. She said she thinks you committed suicide. Sold the furniture and jumped into the river like your father. She says she knows what she's talking about."

"Her concern for me revives my faith in human nature."

"Your whereabouts was only partly it. She says some man—did she say a communist?—wants to kill her."

It was Ruth Marie who climbed the stairs to his bedroom a month after the Hungarian came to live in her house; and there she discovered—"I am a realist," she told Daly, "no more, no less"—that Botkar was not the gallant, liberating knight of her fantasies but more like the late Michael Drange, preoccupied, not sensing or caring at how she burned. It was all, once more, too ordinary. Well, she was fifty-five, as Daly had so pointedly told her, and perhaps the lesson she learned was that particular truth: Age, no matter the buoyancy of the spirit, could not be denied, even though for his part he was forty-one, he said. Perhaps he lied about that, too, and was ten, even twenty-five years, older.

She looked from Daly to Jessie as she sat in Jessie's parlor. Without preliminaries she had thundered and bolted like chain lightning into the house the day of Daly's arrival and began reciting in bursts and fragments the account of her fall, wild-eyed and striking herself on the chest with emotion.

She did not care, she said, for anyone's opinions of good conduct as it applied to her; she who swam in sweet cycles of love and endearment beyond even her own understanding. No, Botkar was wrong in many ways, as she soon realized, and she knew all about him, as much as one could with such a man, but persisted anyhow with her trip to his room, recognizing full well from a letter addressed to him from Hungary, which, she admitted she had opened two days earlier, that he was married, had seven children, and a very unhappy wife in Budapest. Mrs. Budny, who was a seamstress on Forbes and translated the letter for Ruth Marie, said, "She says he is a bandit and a loafer and does not care that his children might starve."

He had lied about himself. Even knowing so well what lay in every human heart, she had let herself be deceived into betraying herself. It was not in her mind a condemnation of Robert Botkar. He was a heavenly gift to help her understand herself better. What did he really matter, except as another suffering soul with his lies and distortions about his life in Europe and here? This disaster was about a woman fated to be of service to the human race generally about to be brought down by a housepainter: not a noble fall, or a graceful one, but one marked by the same crude panics of Inez kicking apart a birthday cake or Belle sending used condoms through the U.S. mail to the man who had made her pregnant. Ruth Marie Drange was better than that and would not tumble into the man's snares and be leveled with him. But, she asked, as she prayed in church, what was she to do exactly? Her kindness had not stopped her son from departing at an early age; and she had not persuaded Michael Drange to awaken the sexual woman in her.

"I freely confess this to you," she said to Daly and Jessie. "I am a woman first, whatever else I am."

"Whatever else would you be?" Daly asked.

"Daly, you know I am not an ordinary person: I think it's time I dropped the mask." There was no answer to the question of the fate of an extraordinary woman in the sunlight falling in dappled shadows on the sidewalks of Oakland, the scent of dry grass in the wind blowing in from Schenley Park. All the sights and sounds of her affinity to nature still spoke to her of her connection to everything in the universe, binding, uncanny and unique; but the way to grappling with the here and now eluded her. She found herself one day, she said, walking alone in the park, talking to herself, and had a stranger turn to look at her in surprise, and pulled herself together enough to smile pleasantly at the passing woman.

She had been in her mind asking the late, dull, and unpassionate Michael Drange what he would do in her present situation. "I was calling on that man," she cried. "The one who betrayed me first!"

She turned to look at Daly. The day was hot, and he remembered his heart. Did he hear it because he listened for it? There was, considering the inexhaustibility of Ruth Marie's demands, a very fine chance that he would indeed die listening to her, simply slump forward onto Jessie's carpet and forever sail off, his sister's insistent themes in his ears, to join all the Racklins in history. She would not know it until twenty minutes after it happened, finishing off at some landmark where her lament wore down momentarily.

"Next, Botkar will kill me," she said, "the one I gave shelter under my roof. He has a murderer's eyes and a murderer's heart."

She stood, and, running to the door, shouted, "And no one cares!"

"What happened?" Jessie asked, alarmed, at the suddeness of Ruth Marie's departure.

"I survived," Daly said.

* * *

Botkar probably stole things from her house and sold them. She could not keep count on everything in the house, candlesticks, picture frames, silverware. She would not know for months what was missing.

"I am a stranger in my own house," she said to Daly on the telephone. "He rearranges things so I never know what's been moved or taken from one day to the next. These are your family treasures, too, Daly. I would not take my problems with this man lightly."

Daly looked at the telephone. "Why do you think I take this lightly?"

"I sense things, I know things."

"What would you have me do?"

"There's enough you do for strangers. Why not your own sister?"

"I'll think of something—but I think the man isn't the problem. Ruth Marie, you don't know what to want. And Botkar is not the problem."

For the third time that week she hung up on him.

Jessie came to sit in his lap. They had begun a long interlude of lovemaking and initial agreements of emotion in their marriage. They slept together almost as if they had been accustomed to it in each other. It had been years: They talked now, still things she had read, places she had once seen, and Daly was very happy. Had he known, he told himself, they would remain the same friends after lying without clothes all night long and late into the morning he would have asked her sooner to marry him. "No," she said when he asked her the first night they kissed and held closely the newly discovered feel to their bodies, "I asked you first."

"Well, yes," he said. "Of course. I accept your offer. But I may die before it happens."

"Then let's marry soon."

"Tonight."

"Next Tuesday."

"The cathedral?"

"No, St. Agnes."

"All right, St. Agnes."

"You must do something about Ruth Marie."

"Oh, no, that's why there's an afterlife, for special cases like Ruth Marie."

Botkar had never told Ruth Marie he was married, but he obviously was not interested in her coming to his room. Still, she went three times more, she told Jessie, each time thinking it was a test of herself, him, what had there been between them to bring her to climb the stairs. Had he led her on at all? Was it all a dream of hers born in the coldness of her late husband? She would never with taciturn Botkar know: He fumbled through the act with her twice and the third time said, "I go sleep now, okay? Big warehouse in Bloomfield tomorrow."

She said to Belle, "Hearing this from you, I would have said, 'Once is enough for that kind of talk from a housepainter, my dear woman. If you see that man again cross the street. He's a beast, he's laughing at you. Sleep! And he claims to love you.'"

Belle called Daly that night. "Your sister is of unsound mind," she said.

"I know," Daly said.

But, of course, Robert Botkar never made such a claim of love to her: Self-deluded, foolish, she was too old for such stunts, now humiliated—while the man stole her possessions and sold them to send money to his wife, to see him at his best, Daly thought. He could possibly be giving the money to a younger woman; he could be paying prostitutes.

Nights, Ruth Marie reached for her red wine on her night table, weeping softly at first for herself, then, rising as the noble spirit she knew she was, including in her tears Belle and Inez and Caitlin, but not Irene. Irene had lately become mysterious about her visits to a certain dentist. Ruth Marie told Daly she suspected they did things in his office—Irene said she did not care to discuss the dentist, and Ruth Marie forced no one to confide in her. But where would they all have been if that attitude of holding back details were general?

"Then," she screamed one morning to Belle, who called Daly immediately on the strange conduct, "I made the mistake of going to another man about one of their kind. I tried to talk to Father Farrell."

He was no help at all when she went to him to warn him that his precious victim of communist oppression had turned out to be no better than a godless hoodlum himself. Father Farrell thought she was warning him about having the congregation give him gifts, a bigger car, or sending sums to his undeclared wife and children in Budapest, or hiring him to do work around St. Agnes.

"I am telling you the man is a bloodsucker!" she said, standing one step below Father Farrell as he stood on an outside landing at St. Agnes. "This is not a warning about co-signing loans for him. Don't, of course, but my intention is to tell you he is a savage. Nothing more, nothing less. There . . . is . . . nothing . . . to . . . be . . . done . . . with . . . him. He is a fiend from hell."

"Of course," Father Farrell said, "that's not our belief. We don't think there's anyone that we can't see some improvement made."

"Father Farrell, those are words. You know there are incorrigible people, monsters."

"No, I don't know that, and it's not my final judgment to be made, or yours."

"Let them eat us alive, suck our blood."

"No, but don't make pronouncements on them."

"I'm merely saying—"

"You've been wounded, avoid the man—but find forgiveness in your heart."

"Why, that's my motto. I tell people to do that all the time."

"Then practice your motto."

"Well, I don't exactly say forgive, I say forget."

"Not the same thing, of course."

Exasperated at the man's self-sufficiency, oh, those ready answers, she said, "Next it's hate the sin and forgive the sinner, love him, right, Father?"

"Yes, as a matter of fact, I was thinking that very thought."

"Easy to say."

"Yes, very easy to say, sometimes impossible for most people to do."

They stood on the Robinson Street side of St. Agnes, Father Farrell with a small, ecclesiastical bag in his hand. She had caught him on the stairs. He stood patiently waiting for her to speak, holding over her head that he was about to attend a person dying or someone in pain or someone lost—but it was his job, his vocation: She served the same God with no one but herself to know what peace she created where there had been only loss or sorrow.

"Father," she cried, "I'm good! Don't treat me any other way."

He shook his head slowly. "I don't want to treat you badly—but, Ruth Marie, it's not my good opinion you finally want."

"God? What will that get me? I won't know until I die."

"Maybe yes, maybe no."

"Sometimes," she said as he started down the stairs, "I don't think the church would know a holy person if she were standing out here on Robinson in rags and sick and burning with fever begging for the poor."

He stopped and said, "Of course, you're right, we often miss, very often, we wouldn't make any team in the National League with our percentage of failures in recognizing saints. But we try, we play catch-up, you know. There's hope, not for me, of course: I renounce sainthood, gave it up for Lent in 1936 and never picked up the habit again. And now please laugh, Ruth Marie, I'm trying my hand at some very feeble jokes—and it is not what I do best."

She wanted to call him unfeeling, but checked herself. "Goodbye, Father," she said. "Thank you. I know you're busy."

After she told Daly about Ruth Marie, Belle said, "She's heading for the padded cell, Daly."

"Has been for years."

"She always said you were a cold bastard."

"Confirmed," he said, and Jessie came to him at the phone, where he sat and touched his cheek.

She said, "Daly, you shouldn't—tears for anyone but yourself are dangerous these days."

"I am crying for myself: Ruth Marie, the fool, is like myself to me."

Ruth Marie rushed home to call her friends and report Father Farrell's smugness. But the entire day conspired against her, a priest who would not help her, see things her way, none of her friends at their telephones except Caitlin. In a time of emergency, like the present moment, she would not have chosen her, the most dim-witted of her circle. To try to explain to a woman who occasionally had sex in a taxicab or on a stairwell about her dilemma with Botkar, even omitting certain facts—and Father Farrell too tired to know a refined spirituality when he saw one—would not be easy. Caitlin always agreed, with tears and moans, her own conduct had been deplorable, blaming it on drink or a confusion in her mind with some other great love of her own past.

But today even ever-agreeing Caitlin Corrigan, hair dyed several shades of red and blond, face sticky with makeup from her heated rush to come visit, seams erratic and each freckle in her chest and upper bosom showing like dots to be connected for an answer to the problem of the woman's being, was as crippling as the rest of the day. After Ruth Marie had explained carefully what a liar and cheat Botkar was, the wife, the children, probably a criminal past in Europe, and her kindness trampled under his feet as if it were a serpent—delicately avoiding the details of her good heart that had mistakenly yielded to a sexual wrong turn in the road through generosity of spirit—the listening woman still seemed bereft of common sense.

"Well, why did you invite him in the first place you didn't expect some trouble?" Caitlin asked.

"I expected no trouble!"

"There's always trouble when it's a man involved."

They sat on the back porch and Ruth Marie made a motion with her hand to indicate that Caitlin should drop her voice: The fiend could hear.

Caitlin shouted, "I'm tired of being shushed for speaking in a normal tone of voice, do you hear? It's always me who's a stepchild around here generally."

"Please, they'll hear you at Forbes Field."

"I don't care who hears me. There's lots on my chest and it's not for bottling tonight. I think it's time you saw close-up what the rest of us have been doing with our lousy lives while you played grand dame."

"What are you talking about?"

"A happy marriage, a man regular as a coffeepot and gone to heaven, where you'll probably meet him and go on like always in eternity, plenty of money, lots of it, yes, left well off and here's the bottom of my shoe, kiss it."

"What are you talking about? Have you lost your mind?"

"No, just speaking it like the rest of them would if they were me and sixty-three and nothing but two rooms to show for it in my sister's house."

"What do you know about my money?"

"There's plenty. When you ever worked?"

"You leave now."

"And your husband?"

"Lower your voice, you've been drinking."

Caitlin shouted to the approaching night, heat heavy under the promise of August and summer on Ruth Marie's garden, "I'm telling you, don't quiet me. I have feelings, Ruth Marie."

Still a little vaporous from the wine she had been drinking, Caitlin took a taxicab to Jessie's house, and, still filled with the wrongness of the world's treatment of her, particularly that of Daly's sister, shouted when he opened the door: "I have feelings, Right Racklin, do you hear me?"

"Of course you do, dear woman, probably more refined than

most, but surely as real as this day is hot. Come in and tell us the occasion for your need to state the obvious."

Not a happy occasion, Daly thought, but one that must be lived through.

He called Ruth Marie to tell her he planned to marry Jessie soon.

"Daly, she's blind," she said, "and I'm sorry, I have troubles of my own. I won't be able to save you. You are all on your own now."

When he hung up, Daly made a sound like a lion roaring.

Jessie turned to him. "What is it? What did she say? Is something wrong?"

"No more than usual."

Mrs. Ruth Marie Drange did a thing very strange the next day, not clear in reason even to herself, but necessary. Daly marked future events from that day, as important in Ruth Marie's sad narrative as the moment she had impetuously invited Botkar into her house. She bought a large woman's pocketbook at the Woolworth near the Strand Theater and walked up to the Mellon Bank on Fifth Avenue where she kept her savings and withdrew two thousand dollars and placed the money in her pocketbook in twenties and fifties.

She took a streetcar out to Wilkinsburg and got out on Penn Avenue. She walked up Penn and into a five-and-ten, a barbershop, a newsstand, and at each place where she saw someone whose face she liked, man, woman, or child she handed them a twenty or a fifty. She had chosen Wilkinsburg because she occasionally played bingo in a church there with one or another of her friends. She gave away three hundred dollars in a half hour, and boarded, unfollowed, a trolley back to Oakland. She did not want to be arrested as a lunatic, perhaps jailed. Caitlin's assertions of her well-being in the face of her friends' deplorable lives had touched the final chord in her movement toward immortality. She wanted the world now to know who she really was.

The next day there was nothing in the newspapers about her giving money away, and she felt the better for that.

When the phone rang she did not answer it. She did not answer the door when Daly knocked; he walked with a cane slowly. He leaned on it occasionally. She watched him from a second-story window. She felt as if now she had nothing to say to Daly or any of her friends or anyone else.

Leaving the house, Botkar spoke to her. She listened and walked away. She had nothing to say to him.

She revealed later she had for a long time been mistaken in her conduct. Love for all things did not require her to make judgments that needed to be shared with anyone; her attempts to create harmony had been proof of the opposite of who she really was. She would learn soon with practice, in silence, to let the love in the universe speak, through her if need be, but not urged on by her as if she were ordinary.

Judgments to be traded were for Caitlin, Daly, and the rest.

She took the trolley across the high-level bridge on a clear morning out to Homestead. There she distributed money in a saloon, to people on the street, to mill workers congregated on a corner, to women she was sure were prostitutes; and then she quickly boarded the streetcar back to Oakland again. This time she had given away two hundred and sixty dollars, and the *Pittsburgh Press* had a story about it and the next day Bill Burns had it on the noon news. The stories were all told in a comical way, people who were interviewed hoping the mystery woman would give them money, too.

The newscasters treated Ruth Marie's charity as a weird story, one involving an eccentric, another thing that was happening in Pittsburgh in an August that was as peculiar as the rest of 1968. They called her the Money Lady.

Ruth Marie called one station and shouted, "Is nothing holy to the people on television?" and slammed down the phone.

She had not expected to be mocked and wondered, only for brief moments, whether she was acting in a manner susceptible to misunderstandings of her intentions. She decided people would see her conduct through their own values, not to be controlled by her. Derision was nothing: Sometimes the blessed were burned alive. Let them laugh on television.

Ruth Marie, praying various devotions, calm and collected, did not answer her phone all week, but leaving her house one day after dark she was accosted in the street by a woman tall and slender, fashionable, even in the gloom notably tanned and poised.

"Mrs. Drange?"

"I don't know you."

"My name is Gloria Scone," the woman said.

The night of the Democratic Convention, while two television sets over the counter played the events in Chicago, Ruth Marie Drange and Gloria Scone sat huddled in a booth at Cantor's Restaurant, looking into each other's eyes, both amazed and soaring with hope in the presence of promise the other offered.

Neither had known there could be a person like the other.

Ruth Marie felt faint several times.

"You knew he would marry?" she asked again.

"Not the woman, not the time, of course, this isn't astrology," Gloria said, "but yes, it was clear to me from the aura around him that something imminent was going to occur, occasioned by him, a choice made—there were vibrations there in the hospital. As soon as I was sure he was going to live, I knew the next battle would be to prevent him from making this step. You see, he's doing it to avoid what his heart's telling him to do, that is, listen to his inner being, come live with me."

"How did you know he was going to live?"

At that moment it seemed to Ruth Marie that this beautiful woman, poised, fingers long at the end of arms slender and actually bright with a glow of sun, her neck delicate as a swan's and with eyes alive with green and golden and blue glints had come to her to answer prayers. She would know what to do to stop Daly in his unfortunate choice of a wife; she would help her with

Botkar. Nothing was impossible to this woman of steel and purpose.

"Ruth Marie, at this moment you have a reflexive aura around you, light, energy, positive forces that are life signs as surely as I watch you draw breath—you're personally on the threshold of something important, if that's what you're curious about. Your glow is golden, that's the best way to describe it although it really isn't a color, and Daly had the same aura, not as bright, to be sure, but much life there."

"Like a halo?"

"More like light emanating from the whole body. You know when you take a picture with infrared film of a place where a person was, even an automobile where it sat, the camera records the outline of something not there but visible on the film. You can train yourself, as I have, to see the outline—except in a kind of color—when the person is still there in my company. I'm sure it's a life force we give off. In the truly sick or dying the aura is very dim or not there at all. In Daly it wasn't strong the first time I saw him in the hospital, but when I touched him it became momentarily as bright as yours."

"Mine's bright?"

"Like the morning star."

"Like the morning star."

"Yes."

"And you have the power to heighten this force, to make it stronger?"

"So do you, we all have it."

"Mrs. Scone, Gloria, I don't know what to say. I knew such things were possible, but I never thought I would meet someone like you. You give me hope."

"I can tell you this," Gloria said, "you are doing what you should, even as Daly is not."

"I am?"

"My woman, the air around you is bursting like firecrackers. Don't tell me about it. You are on to something. You sense it and I feel it."

She reached across the table and touched Ruth Marie's cheek. Ruth Marie trembled. And Gloria held her hand pressed to her cheek. After a while, Ruth Marie reached up toward her face and touched Gloria's hand resting on her cheek. "Gloria," she said, "I feel something."

"It is the power of love," Gloria said softly.

"Yes," Ruth Marie said, "the power of love. It's there, in your hand, in your eyes."

"Now, it's to rescue Daly."

"What must we do?"

"Why, what our natures tell us to do."

"We must think."

"And feel, above all, feel, thinking is a trap."

"Of course."

They agreed to meet in two days' time at Ruth Marie's, each to concern themselves with their own feelings in the interim, to find inside themselves the right course of conduct. Ruth Marie had a direction, she would pursue it. And Gloria had a son and daughter at the Democratic Convention, protesting the Vietnam War.

"I'd worry," Ruth Marie said. "There could be violence."

"I worry as a mother, but"—Gloria tapped her chest—"I know there will be no violence there."

"You know it?"

"Yes, there are people there, friends of mine, absolutely dedicated to preventing violence. They have their ways. All the nightsticks and guns and even tanks can't prevent the power of this force. Not airplanes. Airplanes will fall from the sky."

"Oh, that's so good to hear."

Even when the news the following day had been of nightsticks and tear gas it had been clear to Ruth Marie that there was a sensible explanation somehow confirming the truth of what Gloria meant by her prophecy. Before Gloria told her, Ruth Marie knew that a far greater harm had been prevented by Gloria and her friends: No one had died. In all the terror of policemen and shotguns and knifes and rage, no one had been shot and killed. What had happened, as television clearly demonstrated, was that a bloody war had been fought in Chicago but with astonishingly little permanent damage to either policemen or protesters. "Does no one question," Gloria asked her when they met again, "why it happened that the forces were gathered for a massive loss of life, fifty people, a hundred, a thousand, and not one person died? I think sensible people might conclude something remarkable happened at the Democratic Convention. My own children were, of course, as safe as if they had been in their beds. They were spectators and my daughter—she's a very clever young woman—said to me on the phone last night, 'Mother, I felt your hand in this.' "

Ruth Marie said, "I did, too."

"Did you? Did you truly?"

"Yes, truly, with all my heart. I feel something like I've never felt before, as if I understand not just love, but *truth*."

"Yes, I've heard that. I've heard the emotion described like that, but I've lived with my own feelings on things so long I can't begin to guess exactly what other people feel around me. I do know your brother loves me; he is fighting the feeling in himself, it's like a tiger jumping at the bars of its cage, raw love seeking to escape a man who has hardly known it in his life."

"Oh, you know him so well. He has gone out of his way to avoid loving anyone, not even himself."

"I know that. I know all that."

"I know, how could it be otherwise?"

"Now," Gloria said, "we must free Daly from himself, let loose inside him the creature roaring to be released, not the tiger, of course, I'm not young anymore, and I don't think given his physical condition it would be entirely safe—and we can do something about that, too—but enough for even that stubborn man to see what his true feelings are."

"You have an idea about it then, a plan?"

"I can't make promises. I never do, I try."

"Then you must help me, too. After Daly."

"I'll tell you everything this time next week," Gloria said. "I must meet my children in Connecticut, but I'll return here to complete our business. Rest assured, your brother will not stumble into a bad marriage—may I suggest it?—as you did."

"How could you know that?"

"With your life force there's an edge, another color, not gray, oh, no, but a dimming, occasionally the pulse is not steady. It is not unusual in women; men do not have this uncertain light. It is something else, not a wavering over a woman. It comes through in them as a different light altogether. I can't even truthfully say I can read it at all, it is in its tones so different than women. I'm not sure at all that they have feelings like we do."

"It would explain a good deal."

"I have been married more than once, I know them well enough. They have feelings but not like ours."

"And what shall I do now?"

"Follow your heart. This is not a casual thing; this is as real as a pill victims of the pharmaceutical companies take, this following your heart, listening to it. Sit quietly, undisturbed, and think of yourself, then visualize yourself. See yourself as if you were in a moving picture. Then do what the picture tells you, follow the script in the movie being played out. That is your heart speaking to you."

Ruth Marie gave away money the next day in Squirrel Hill, the north side and East Liberty. By the hour there were stories about her on television and in the newspapers. She could only give away money for ten minutes at a time before she felt uneasy. She boarded buses and trolleys to avoid being questioned by policemen. She did not want to be locked away for being insane at a moment when she had finally lost all delusions. She decided after three hours that giving away money in various sections of Pittsburgh was not practical anymore. And she had not distributed more than twelve hundred dollars.

In Oakland, walking home, she saw a woman whose face she liked.

She walked directly up to the woman who was carrying a shopping bag and handed her two one-hundred-dollar bills. "This is for you, sweetheart," she said. "May you never know want."

The woman reached inside her shopping bag and took out an orange and shoved it into Ruth Marie's face. "Did I ask for your charity?" she said. She crumpled up the bills and threw them to the sidewalk. "You go to hell, hear?"

When Ruth Marie bent to pick up the bills the woman kicked her, hard, in the ribs. "Go somewhere else with your charity, witch!" she said. "I can take care of myself. I don't need crazy people to seek me out in the street. Do I look crazy to you?"

Ruth Marie, sobbing, ran home, hurt but not daunted.

She withdrew another thousand dollars the next day. She planned to go up to Botkar's room and to show him she forgave him by placing twenty-five hundred dollars in an envelope on his pillow. After all, it was only money he wanted from her.

She had not, in the larger picture, understood why the disorder around her over the years had not been quieted despite her own uncanny gifts, modest before Gloria Scone's but real enough, and now she realized it had been only a misunderstanding about money, not really her or the wisdom she conveyed. They thought, all of them, not just Botkar, that she spoke to them from a position of safety, but they did not know that she suffered not only her own problems, unknown to them, but theirs, too, and the world's, the dead of all wars and burned churches in Bulgaria, the hateful terrors of communism, the sickness in the faces of strangers. And they had thought her poor money insulated her from the heartbreak of the world.

She was troubled by the events at the Democratic Convention. The scenes on television had not been what she expected. The protesters had been beaten bloody, there was tear gas and people hurt. But she imagined Gloria Scone could be wrong on some accounts; in the larger picture, she had understood to an astonishing degree the proportions of what the world was like. She decided that it was probably the presence of the television cameras that had caused the chaos in the streets. Even the prophetic and peaceful auras of Gloria and her friends could not stop the power of cameras to incite people to their worst.

Entering the third-floor room of the man, Ruth Marie realized in a flash, as such things often came to her, this was not the thing to do: The monster would regard the cash as her payment for sex. He would demand more, and she wanted to do nothing but demonstrate to him that he had been forgiven. Would he ever know or understand? It did not matter. That forgiveness lay in her soul was the reason for the money to him, money being all he understood, perhaps even some of it to find its way to his wife and children. But it would not do to give him a gift: She had tried once, she thought now, and it had been misunderstood. She had come to him out of her goodness, and he had mistaken her for a woman with longings—and why not? She had ridiculously thought herself that too at the time.

She placed twenty-five hundred dollars in an envelope and put it in a copy of *Valley of Decision* she had read over the years. She allowed an inch of the envelope to show, as if she intended to hide it, but enough protruded that a thief on the prowl might spot it. Returning to the book over the next few nights was like checking to see if rats had eaten cheese left for them.

Botkar took three hundred, then more assured that she had not remembered the money was there, four days later took seven hundred more.

Botkar came into the kitchen where she sat drinking tea and stood over her.

She looked up and said, "Yes?"

He said, "Something here I don't like."

"Perhaps you can find another place to live."

He wore an undershirt and his arms were thick with hair. He swung them at his sides when he walked as if they had no connection to the rest of his body, in a fashion she thought European, not controlled like an American man. And when he was not walking, he fell into a crouch, like now when he bent his head to look into her face. His teeth were bad.

He peered into her face, and she asked, "Why are you looking at me like that? Stop staring at me."

"I don't like you in this place."

"Me? This is my house."

"You keep your house."

"Thank you, I intend to. I spent many happy years here with my husband Michael Drange."

"Then why you come upstairs to see boarder? Michael Drange!"

"Don't you say his name."

"I say to him, 'Mr. Michael Drange, I fuck your wife down here. How you feel up there in heaven now?' "

"You leave this house now. You take your things and get out. I'll call my brother and he'll bring his friends and they'll put you out."

"I tell Michael, 'Say, Michael, your wife was not so good. I do better with a chicken.' "

"Get out!"

He spit in her direction and in his crouch, arms swinging, he strode from the kitchen.

Fearing him, she stayed with Belle in East Liberty that night. When she returned the next day he had moved out, vanishing from her house. Botkar took the last of the money and the book itself. When she saw the book was gone, she ran to his room and found it empty: missing towels, bedclothes, a mirror, a locust's descent on her property, but welcome to it, anyone, anywhere.

While Ruth Marie prayed and walked in the beautiful summer, her every footstep resonated with her belonging to sidewalks and sky and a vast love that lay on the earth like a second blanket of life-giving air itself. She knew where safety lay, in herself, in herself in places where no false longing could overcome her, a costly, horrible lesson, but one done being learned now.

She met Gloria at the entrance to Schenley Park on Forbes two days later, and they walked together into the park, across the Panther Hollow Bridge, the air bright as a polished wineglass, their feet silent on the concrete walk. Outside the Phipps Conservatory, the domed glass building behind them, they sat on a bench. Talk was not necessary.

To bring Daly to himself, to save him, redeem him as she would help the rest if she could, now seemed the summation of everything she desired. In Daly's elevation, his escape from the blind woman—it wasn't the woman herself, Jessie was only a symptom of what was wrong with Daly, his lack of appreciation for himself—she would make a move toward righting a good many old wrongs.

Gloria said, "We must not hurt anyone, no one at all, not Jessie."

"No, this is best for her. Daly is not for her. He'll tire of her, he can be very shallow. She'll be alone again and bitter. He'll cause her bitterness. She'll think herself married and happy and she'll see it was an illusion."

"You can be very wise, Ruth Marie."

"Experience has taught me important lessons."

"Daly needs a strong woman."

"He's a child."

"I love him, Ruth Marie."

"I knew it; but is he good enough for you?"

"With me he can reach his potential."

"Well, I don't see much there, but perhaps you know him better than I do."

"Oh, yes."

"How are you going to save the two of them from each other?"

"Obviously, reasoning with them won't do it."

"Talk to a wall. She's as difficult as he is."

"No, we have to resort to our wills."

"Gloria, please let me interrupt you—at this moment you are very beautiful. I almost think I can see that light around you. Is it what we're talking about that does this to you?"

"I don't know: I draw people to me. You probably draw people to you, too. We must use all of our powers, yours and mine—there's plenty I sense in you. Of myself, I know what I can do."

"What? Tell me what? I understand what you're saying."

"First," Gloria said, "I must do this." She reached with her long slender hand toward Ruth Marie's face. She touched her cheek gently. Ruth Marie sat perfectly still on the hot, summer day, insects in the grass, a cloudless sky overhead. Gloria's palm against her cheek was cool and then it was very warm and she felt a quiet moment of rest and contentment as from her cheek to places all through her the comfort spread.

Later, Ruth Marie described herself as having been filled with a light that seemed to give her moments where her already extraordinary sense of belonging to a connection that included everything within her range of sight and sound now included things inside the very appearances of things. She felt as if she knew what inanimate objects felt, a tree, wheels on automobiles; the walls of houses had a language that hovered over the street where she walked. "The Shanahan warehouse stood there where I walked a thousand times," she told Irene, "but now I knew it was listening."

"You mean like a person listens?"

"No, like a dog or cat, head tilted, not able to talk—like a dumb animal—but understanding in its way things being said around it. But not in the language of humans, not understanding any more than cats or dogs can understand human language." Around her things made sense that never made sense before. *The wall of the building was hearing the language of telephone poles and the roof of the Montefiore Hospital.* "Maybe more, much more than I couldn't begin to describe to you."

"Maybe the woman put something into your lemonade, like LSD. They do that today, you know?"

"I can't deny it. Maybe it was so. But I think it came from looking at her and listening to her."

Then Irene asked, "What else happened there in Schenley Park? Something else magical?"

" 'No,' I said, 'Gloria, I feel something. You do have powers. I can't describe it. Tell me now, where do we start with Daly?' "

" 'Logically,' she said, 'it has to begin with St. Agnes and Father Farrell. He'll be our instrument for saving Jessie and Daly.' "

Daly felt pressed enough by his approaching birthday and perhaps a marriage in the offing that he phoned the law firm of Syms and Hardy. Both Syms and Hardy had been dead since the days of the Korean War, and the person who normally handled old estates had become too ill to work regularly. But two days later, a young woman from their office phoned to tell him that the trustee for the estate, a man named Phillip Lynn, an old friend of his father's, was alive and what he could not handle his son, known as Junior Lynn or Juney, was doing his best over the years to resolve.

Boyce Racklin had insisted the elder Lynn deal with his estate, no bank, no lawyers, but a trusted friend from the old days. Daly had never heard anything about Lynn except that he was a shark, a carnivore, bloodthirsty and unreliable but capable enough at business matters. He asked the young woman to arrange for him to meet with Phillip Lynn, but he had no office anywhere. She gave Daly his home address in Squirrel Hill.

"I guess I'd be uneasy if this was about anything," he told Jessie. "But it's something to be done."

Daly took the bus out to Squirrel Hill and transferred to a trolley, then walked down Penn toward Mellon Park and turned into the section of Pittsburgh called Point Breeze. There were single- and double-storied houses there, some with attics, an old part of town. But it was known as a good neighborhood. There were large old mansions surrounding it. Henry Clay Frick, for whom the huge park on the other side of Point Breeze was named, that old pirate and millionaire art collector, had lived there in a huge columned home, along with the owners of the names on steel mills, prosperous and famous physicians. At the top of Hastings Street where it met Beechwood Boulevard were more palatial homes, and, a house to rival the largest in the neighborhood was under construction. It was next door to the address Daly was seeking. Surely, it was not a house for the old man: Juney Lynn was building a big house. The construction seemed to embrace two lots.

He briskly walked up to Juney Lynn's door, envelope in hand, and rang the front doorbell.

"Who'd you say?"

"Daly Racklin."

"Yeah, oh, sure, I knew your father. Boyce is your father? He and my father were great pals."

"That's right."

"Come in. It's always good to see a guy from the old days."

Lynn was himself a hard late sixties or seventies. His face had fallen away into a loose jowl and was red, and his blue eyes were small and thick with age. He was enormously heavy but wore a loose, summer sweater several sizes too large; it hung down almost to his knees. It had a brown reindeer in the center and smaller reindeer in a pattern running across his big chest. "I knew your father, I did," he said, indicating a chair in the living room. "Great privilege of my life knowing the Right Racklin. Sit down, I can't join you in a drink, diabetes, but it'll do me good to watch you have one. What'll it be?"

"Nothing," Daly said. "I'm here on business. Small business, I guess, but business. They called you from Syms and Hardy?"

"Well, they called the old man—technically speaking—I'm the son. The old man is in no shape, you know what I mean?" He leaned forward. "Don't recognize any of us when we come to see him. But I looked it up when they passed it to me. You're right it's very small business. Tough, you know what I mean?"

"It's an inheritance," Daly said. "It was dewdrops in 1948 when I collected the first part when I was thirty. Going through the motions, picking up what there might be now that I'm fifty."

"Why do you suppose the Right Racklin set it up that way?"

"Mystery to me."

"Well, it could have done well by you, but I guess it's our fates to die poor, not that I'm not holding my own, but my old man wasn't much of an investor. You wanted to lose money you picked my old man."

"People said he had a lot."

"Stories, you know? Money went through his fingers, give it away, missions in Borneo, Africa, built a chapel in Yugoslavia, sick, little kids. He set up a blood bank at the Mercy Hospital, open to anybody regardless of religion, race or nationality. That kind of guy—like your father, you understand. Not that he gave away your old man's money. Just lost it fair and square. I got a box in the cellar for you with bills and things, you, a couple of others he handled the money for when they died. He'd buy a building hearing the county was going to put up a courthouse, and they'd change it to cross town. Things like that. He lost a million dollars on an air-conditioning patent for cars, going to put it on the roof of the car in a separate unit so as not to screw up the car motor. It went wrong. When he wasn't being cheated, he was being—you'll excuse me saying so—he was stupid."

"How much of my father's money did he lose?" Daly said, his chest tight. He would not under any circumstances die in this living room, talking about money with Juney Lynn. It was obvious to him that the house on Hastings Street and the one next door was somehow, probably in very small part, an extension of his father's ridiculous legacy.

"Well, at its best it come to three hundred and sixty thousand dollars, give or take."

The chill that swept him, Daly knew, was from the past.

This was not about his inheritance. Under discussion was nothing less than the life and times and ultimately the fate in eternity of the Right Racklin.

"Where do you suppose the money came from?" Daly asked quietly. Nothing accusatory in his voice; he knew the box in the cellar was going to cover any tracks of theft that the elder, or the younger Lynn, for that matter, might have left.

"The money? The money your father left?"

"It's a little larger than I thought."

"Yes, a good sum for those days, but you know, even with a man as fine as your father was—I'd put my right hand into a fire rather than say a word against him—there was ways of doing business in the old days, things, you know, that helped people in the long run, but today might look bad if people were placing judgment. Not me, you understand. You can only live in one world at a time; and my father always taught me: Live in this one. Who's to say some of those strikes in the old days, your father there at the table negotiating the rights of the workingman, would have been settled fairly, equitably, best interests of all parties, if your father hadn't been given an incentive to get closer to the middle? To work it out."

"You're saying he took money from the company owners to see it their way?"

"Jesus, Racklin, it was common practice. Some of your inheritance come from union people, too—look down the middle, was the message. Don't be swiveling your head looking for trouble under rocks. Union people trying to protect the long-range interests of the union, maybe holding on to something for themselves, who knows? It's all history. Company trying to save jobs and profits and misery. Your father was like the doctor there, choosing the medicine, being compensated for his skill."

"He sold out the union!"

"Hold on. Benefits running out, no jobs, hardheads ready to see the company set on fire, no jobs for anyone. Your father was a savior of the workingman. I'm not the one saying he took a dime that didn't rightly belong to him."

"And it come to more than three hundred thousand you and your father cheated out of his estate."

"Listen, Racklin, I'll send someone down to the cellar to get that box. The truth is, you're liable to owe my old man maybe a thousand or two, but I see your disappointment, so I'll say nothing for now. But don't start throwing accusations around, not about my father or me, or not about your father either. Who the hell are you to be so pure? You could live to be nine hundred years and you wouldn't have done the good your father done in his short life. And, by the way, get the hell out of here before I call the cops. Coming in here and making accusations."

Lynn had white hair, thick as a bear's, shining white and his bright blue eyes were fierce. He did not appear to pay much attention to Daly now, waiting. He said, "Too bad about your father. Lot of potential. He could have done a lot more the Lord hadn't taken him early."

Daly stood easily. He made no move to leave.

Lynn did not change expression. He looked up and asked, "Logic beats me. Do you know why he held off the money till you were fifty? Not knowing, of course, there wasn't going to be anything there."

"I know my father's attitude about money. Bad, real bad, Mr. Lynn."

"Well, we can't blame him for that. Money is the root of all evil. Protecting you from it might have been his last good work."

"I wouldn't screw around, Mr. Lynn."

"How screw around? This don't have nothing to do with me, except an old friend of my father has been colored a little human. Son's nose a little out of joint about reality. Fuck around, how?"

"Maybe I'll look into your father's business, maybe yours."

"Yeah, I heard that before. It's nothing new you invented. Go home and take a cold shower. You came in expecting nothing and that's what it is. Now what do you want? The old days are nothing to do with me. I get stories from the graveyard like this three times a week from the old boys. Sometimes I can put in a word their kids need work, a donation to a good cause, sometimes I'm just a voice on the telephone the people I call. 'Who? Juney Lynn? You got the wrong number.' I try, you understand? I get a hernia trying, but in some situations there's nobody listening. Now, I'll put myself in your hands, I'll tell you something confidential. I killed myself for your father. I did. I tried to turn the investments into something, leave you with something! Maybe it was a criminal enterprise I was abetting for the sake of friendship. Went way past what I should have done, but to no avail. Now you know. Killed myself in pieces, honest to God. Went to the mat, put my reputation on the line to save his good name. And I did. Nobody heard a word about the size of the estate. Who knows this ancient history except a few of us? Your father's reputation is like a lamb's. This stuff would have come out about him he'd have been in disgrace by people didn't understand that was the way things were done back then. He lost the money fair and square, make it, lose it, that's business."

"You didn't try hard enough. I'm the one never should have known the facts. Your father is the one known for putting too much sand in the concrete for hospital buildings. Nothing to lose that you'd understand; but no matter what he did, my father might have been a good person."

"Okay, you wore out your welcome. Next time we meet, I'll lie if it'll make you feel good. It was your old man was the hustler, not me telling you about it."

Lynn walked to the door, his face red, his eyes lidded. He opened the door.

"You don't listen," Lynn said. "It's a bad quality in a man. I see a lot of Boyce Racklin in you."

"My hearing's good," Daly said. "And so is my eyesight. I can spot a thief a hundred yards away."

"What are you going to do to me? Think the worst: Make me old? Make me sick? Give me diabetes and hard arteries? Excuse me, Racklin, there's no punishment ain't already been visited you can dream up."

"What about your ratty reputation? A trial?"

"Now, there's an idea. You'll remind people my old man and me ain't in hell yet."

Lynn slammed the door on Daly, but Daly walked slowly to the construction site next door. He ducked under a wooden barricade. He picked up a two-by-four, knowing he was watched. He kicked at a pipe on the ground. He leaned on a wall.

Lynn opened the door. "Hey," he called. "Get the hell out of there. That's private property. You're trespassing."

Daly said, "Nice place. For everybody you and your father fucked, I wish you long life here."

"You're a couple of sweet pieces, you and your old man. No, it's not the money, sweet Jesus—hypocrites!"

Daly visited Uncle Finnerty and spoke softly to him. "I come three times a week, Uncle Finnerty," he said. "I don't see much hope for you, but truth to tell, I don't see much hope for myself either. So soon enough you and I will have a real conversation elsewhere. There's lots left unsaid, that's for sure." Later, walking up the stairs to the front entrance of St. Agnes on the way to visit Father Farrell, Daly was certain he saw Gloria Scone and his sister driving down Robinson in a long, blue car. He stopped to watch them round the corner to Fifth; he would have thought them an apparition except that no visions in recorded history simultaneously bent both their heads at scrutiny, trying to avoid being observed. The two of them, he thought, standing on the steps to St. Agnes, were an unholy sight. Their proximity to each other on a day he had come to work out details of his marriage to Jessie was disturbing.

"Father," he asked Farrell, "you did not happen to see my sister with another woman somewhere around the church today?"

"I did. The woman's name is Gloria Scone, she says she was once married to Owney. She says she's thinking of becoming a Catholic. A lie."

"You spoke to them?"

"Only after Sister Mary Margaret told me there were two women, one of whom she recognized as Ruth Marie, loitering around the church all week—observing me, following me, she said—and I went out to ask Ruth Marie what in the hell she thought she was doing."

"And what did she say?"

"The other woman interrupted and said she was thinking of converting to Catholicism. Well, it's a peculiar route to the true faith, you know, tracking a priest as if the two of them were the F.B.I. and I was on the ten-most-wanted list with my picture in the post office."

Daly laughed. "You know, Father, you have a criminal way about you."

"Daly, I think your sister isn't playing with a full deck."

"I've heard that before."

"After Sister Mary Margaret told me the two women were sitting out in a car studying the church and me as if it was a bank to be robbed, I realized I've been seeing Ruth Marie in strange places for a while now, her ducking behind the cabbages at the Giant Eagle, leaping into doorways on Forbes when I look at her, the other woman too. I didn't know I was worthy of being shadowed. You suppose there's any sense to it at all?"

"Gloria Scone thinks she can bring down airplanes from the sky with her thoughts and cause men to feel her presence across a broad lake."

"Really? Do you suppose she's working an exorcism on me before she commits to our belief?"

"I don't know, I can't begin to know."

Father Farrell paused. "Daly, it's good to see you. I'm sad today. Too many thoughts about leaving St. Agnes, Oakland, Pittsburgh, all of you. I'm retiring in a month."

"But you'll marry Jessie and me before you go?"

Farrell laughed.

"I'm sorry," Daly said. "You tell me your heart is heavy and I say, Well, lend me a fiver before you cry too loud to hear my request."

"Same as always. Come in by that door, go out the same. A priest is never quite a man to his parish. Why should I be any different? I'm a man, Daly, a man all day long and a priest."

Daly knew his man, the right music and he could turn the priest dancing.

"Father, more than one commentator has noted your resemblance to John Dillinger. I think you ought to know that before you leave Pittsburgh."

"I see the resemblance between you and Darwin's monkeys. I know where he conceived the idea, watching a bunch like you staggering home from the Ancient Order."

Father Farrell said, he hardly knew whether he wanted to fool with Jessie and Daly, she marrying two Protestants and he marrying his first wife in a civil ceremony. "Were the two of you trying to be sure your marriages didn't count?" Father Farrell asked.

"I guess it was the way the cards were dealt," Daly said.

Farrell's rectory was ordered like the man himself: a globe of the world in a corner although he never traveled, on the wall a map of the planets, a picture of a young man on his desk, his brother who had died young, and on a corner of his desk a small, shiny stone brought to him by a parishioner, it was said, many years ago from the Red Sea. Over the room fell the colors in the stained-glass window etching of St. Francis standing among white doves and dark sparrows.

"The two of you are like a couple of cave children coming out of the wilds to civilization," Father Farrell said, "but I don't suppose there's any reason for me to draw judgment on you, pleased as you are with yourselves."

"Then there's no reason not to marry us?"

"None except good taste."

"And soon, Father, given the state of my health."

"Your spiritual health has been teetering a lot longer than that heart you're lately parading around like a badge requesting charity, and Daly, your spiritual health is going to have far more serious consequences than that threadbare organ in your chest. St. Dennis walked for six miles without his head," Father Farrell said, smiling, "carrying the head under his arm and bidding strangers good morning. He didn't let a little inconvenience slow him down from his moral obligations."

"It was rare, Father," Daly said, "and it was probably why they made him a saint. Confusion's in me, I'd be better off carrying my head in my hand. I know what you're saying is true, that's why I'm here."

"The Lord rejoices: Daly Racklin came to save the day."

Daly laughed. "I'm a disaster to the end," he said.

"It's not the end, that's the bad news. Tell them out there in

Oakland they only think it's the end they see. The end isn't when you close your eyes the last time."

"You're hard today, Father," Daly said.

"My own retirement, the end of me at St. Agnes. I'm taking stock."

He had not ever burdened the congregation with his own dilemmas; enough to say that they were there without drawing anyone road maps. Today, he thought, he would console poor, suffering Racklin. The prognosis Daly had down at the Montefiore was not good, and no reason Daly would not know it as well as the doctors. "Damn it," Father Farrell started out, "the more there is to us, Daly, the more there exists to suffer spiritually. I guess the wish ought to be that there were less to suffer. But what it is in us that suffers for ourselves and the outrages that life visits on other people is as much part of us as our hair. And maybe one day, given science and all its cures, we'll be able to go to something like a barber and he'll cut away, if that's our choice, our capacity to suffer."

"I guess I'd be first in line not to have my hair cut," Daly said. "I'd put grease on to keep it standing on end and my suffering thick around me."

"Me too, I guess. It makes us more human, or, anyway, able to read more of what's human out on the streets. I'm not holding up suffering as a cure, just a way to look at things, you understand?" He thought for a moment, and he said, "You know, Daly, it's that thin line between whether you fall over dead with grief at what life offers or bust out laughing at the craziness of it that makes the difference in how you face the last mystery. Chesterton tells us a story about how the priests gave Jesus a last chance to announce himself as something less than the Lord and He turned aside and His shoulders were shaking and they thought He was theirs, giving in to their way of looking at things, maybe crying, you know. But then they looked again and they saw the Lord was quaking with mirth, holding in from laughing out loud."

"No other way," Daly said, "looking about and listening to what goes on."

Francis Farrell said, "That boy in the picture there, smiling, you know he was the brother I had who died young, certifiably mad from his eleventh year on when he took a trumpet, Daly, lovingly wrapped it in tinsel and tissue paper, and threw it through the window. He went on from that time to live out weird punishments and entrapments; we watched him deteriorate, the family able to hide him for a time. Perhaps with the drugs for schizophrenia these days, he could have lived a somewhat productive life. But no matter. He was called away early, stealing a car and blessedly smashing it to pieces against a tree with only himself in it and no one else brought to grief except the owner of the tree, who was circling it at the boy's death, wringing his hands over the shattered bark in his yard while the police and ambulance drivers bore away my brother. Even crazy and prone to violent demonstrations, always a dread in our every day, our family still deeply regretted his death—I think of it twice a day. But who knows what mischief he might have brought on himself and others with his tests? A dignified car crash, a brake which had failed, a final chapter for my brother as if a playwright was tidying up odds and ends and making things come out plumb level."

"How long ago was it?"

"Forty years since he threw the trumpet through the window, thirty-two years since he damaged the man's tree so grievously. I saw the death as an instance of the mercy of God, and I changed my course. (Nothing serious: I had planned at first to be a librarian.) I took Holy Orders. I felt that the hand of God had allowed itself to be observed—at least by me—for some purpose, and I became a Franciscan, ordained in Thurles Cathedral in Tipperary. It was my one time away from America, a seminary education, St. Patrick's Seminary in Thurles. 'Thou art a priest forever,' became part of my cells and being. What a blessing!"

"I always thought you were a very fortunate man, Father. I'm sorry it came in the beginning out of suffering."

Father Farrell waved away the commiseration. "I'm not going to tell you being a priest, serving God, balanced out what I saw in my mother's face when she found my brother cutting off slices of his fingers and ripping open his eyes in crazy ecstacies. My father died by a year every time we took my brother to the hospital." He breathed deeply. "Well, I understand suffering a little, did a little. It comes in all shapes and sizes, to me in the shape of a boy with his eyes rolling around in his head and talking to God, sometimes the devil, in his head.

"I was never much for the wilds of scholarship. I couldn't go far in examining myself with philosophy or my brother—the facts were known to me, Daly, I needed no embroidery."

He had gone for a time to Catholic University of America in Washington, while others traveled the length of America and old Europe, enjoyed recognition and elevations. "I grew gray at St. Agnes, baptizing babies, marrying them, counseling them on death, as solid as rock, knowing I wasn't stone, but human. I buried them, loving them: spare, little houses on Robinson, Terrace, Darraugh, and the projects which rose over and around St. Agnes. Reliable all of us, each to each," he said, "as the hills, the ground, the weeds, the wind, the craggy abutments on which the houses stood. But we're not talking about your marriage, a happy occasion, a time for high spirits. Forgive me for my hard-luck story."

Daly sighed. He stood from where he had been sitting. He said, "I'll call you tomorrow, Father. The streets will be here after we're gone anyhow." But that was probably not true either, he thought. Maybe parking lots will be here where we grieve and linger over our lost selves, or a tennis court will blanket the stones and people will walk here with no memory of us.

At any rate, Francis Farrell was not listening. He had picked up the picture of his brother and by the light St. Francis and his doves and sparrows cast from the window stared into the youthful face there, as if he expected the photograph would give him a reasonable answer for sorrow and old aches of life with no remedy but the passage of years to mislead the soul with forgetfulness.

Eleven

*I*n the rented car on Robinson ten days before Daly and Jessie's wedding, Ruth Marie finally turned to Gloria and asked, "Were we expressing our deepest, most honest feelings, about Daly and Jessie on anything specific? I'm not sure I'm using my life force right."

Gloria said, "It can only be used on what's right. The life force is a good force. If it's not used properly, we will fail. That's the trick to it. It requires responsibility. If we're selfish, we are talking to ourselves. It must be right for the two of them."

"Well, what if it's right that they should marry?"

"Are you kidding?"

"You're certain they shouldn't marry?"

"As sure as you're sitting there. Can I see you? Yes, I can see you. Can I see the two of them married, no. It's not going to happen, Ruth Marie. I can assure you of that. Let's go now and stretch ourselves and then we'll go down to the Isaly's on Forbes and have a hot fudge sundae. It's a beautiful day, I'm tired of sitting in this car."

"I am, too, but won't someone from St. Agnes see us?"

"Oh, sure, but this isn't arrogance on my part. If someone sees us, then they'll become part of Daly's and Jessie's destiny. Whoever sees us becomes part of the larger plan. Frankly, I don't see them marrying even if I hadn't used my will against it. And your help to me, feeling your goodness beside me this past week, was a great service to Daly. It's just not rational, the two of them married. You told me yourself your marriage was not happy—imagine if someone had cared enough to see that it was averted."

They walked up the street from where they had been parked on Robinson across from St. Agnes, and at an empty house with a "For Sale" sign in front they climbed the steep stone stairs and sat at the top on the landing.

"Shall we still concentrate?" Ruth Marie asked, settling herself on the hard concrete.

"I think you can relax now. The things I've expressed in my heart are about us indelibly now, on this street forever. It's as if a giant flower opened its petals and put out on the air a sweet perfume of the rarest scent. My thoughts will probably linger here after all this is gone. I couldn't change what we've done this past week if I wanted to. I'm only outdoors this minute with you because I was cramped in the car. Our work is done. I've looked into Father Farrell's soul, I've thought about this church. Last night I stood and deliberated in front of St. Paul's; I'm leaving nothing to chance."

"I was cramped, too, Gloria, and I'm new to this. All I thought about when you said, 'Think this is not going to happen,' was that Daly was very foolish and he always had been. And I thought Jessie shouldn't want to marry him. She knows she'd be a burden. She's been married twice already; marriage isn't for her."

"Very good."

Gloria stood and yawned and stretched, putting out her graceful arms to her side, slender like a dancer at the top of the stairs. From where she sat, Ruth Marie thought Gloria was as beautiful as a statue that someone had placed on Robinson, like a child's angel on a Christmas tree. Turning slowly to look down at Ruth Marie, Gloria smiled and said, "Oh, this has been a good morning. Over these past seven days I think our business is done. It won't happen."

Ruth Marie smiled and stood, too, feeling good about their efforts and close to Gloria.

"Do you suppose Jessie will come to her senses, or Daly?" she asked. "Were we making St. Agnes an impossible place for them to marry, even St. Paul's?"

"We certainly were. We closed all entrances for the two of them, slammed shut the door."

As she looked down at the street from the high perch where she and Gloria stood triumphantly like two queens reigning over the stale brick and cobblestones, the ground below clear in its outlines, charged with the truth of its being and real, each summer shadow a point of ending and beginning, Ruth Marie felt a chill through the moisture on her skin from the hot day. She felt good no longer. In the sudden starkness of the afternoon a terrible realization had touched her, icy and forlorn.

"Gloria, were we casting something bad on St. Agnes? Were we hoping something awful might happen to Father Farrell or one of the nuns? Gloria, I know what I was thinking. But what were you thinking about St. Agnes that would prevent Daly and Jessie from marrying? Why did you go out at night to St. Paul's?"

"You silly goose," Gloria said, taking her by the arm as they walked down the steps, "do you think I was wishing harm to that lovely church? What must you think of me? The well-known Racklin silliness has rubbed off on you, I see. No, I was visualizing them not getting married, no more, no less."

Ruth Marie pulled away her arm.

"But if a tragedy occurred, if the steeple there fell, if the ceiling at St. Paul's Cathedral collapsed, that could happen with your visualization?"

"Well, I would hope their adolescent hearts wouldn't need something like that to stir them. I take them for reasonably sensible adults. But I don't want to deceive you about how vast and wonderful the world is. Yes, once these forces are set into existence—you see, I make no claim for the absolute control of my powers, or yours for that matter, when you understand how extraordinary we are as goddesses—a roof here or there might collapse. Heavens, a plane fell from the sky once on a foolish whim of mine. I regretted it, but I learned. This is no kindergarten we're in now. Cosmic, Ruth Marie. Beyond death, before birth, enterprises involving the whole continuum of being. And we are a small part of it."

"Father Farrell could die!"

"He is an old man. We'd never know for sure. Still, it could happen, yes—but not in malice, not in selfishness. Our intention is to save your brother from a wasted life, no crime there, no desire to hurt anyone. But I can not guarantee that once our will is unleashed our aspirations don't find strange destinies. I've come not to question it. There's so much I don't know; I learn more every day."

"Father Farrell dead! That's what we've been working at?"

"No, no, but yes, it could happen—and then we'd know that that was the fate we'd written, not had thrust on us as if we were sheep."

Ruth Marie began to run down Robinson silently, restraining a sob, remorse clutching at her feet as she fled down the familiar street, looking into the face of what her antagonism to her brother's marriage had brought her—a party to what?

"Ruth Marie! Where are you going? We promised ourselves sundaes."

Ruth Marie ran as if the devil from somewhere behind called to her of ice cream and normal things, obscuring his indecent intentions by the most ordinary of suggestions.

"Darling," Gloria called, "isn't this what we wanted? We're going to get our wish. No one will be hurt."

Ruth Marie did not turn to hear more, but the last words were clear enough: "It's only that I can't promise anything—this is the way the world is to the brave!" She turned on the fan in her living room and sat with the shades drawn. The noise of the fan spelled out a message to her in the hum of the motor, but she could not make out the words. Perhaps the roof of St. Paul's would not fall and all the other mischief that taunted her in its specific terrors would not happen. But how Daly and Jessie might come not to be married lay heavily on her. She had not meant to call down the cosmos on her inept brother.

She boldly called Daly where he lived now with Jessie and said, "Both of you put your ears to the phone," and when they had, she said, "Your loving sister wishes you the best, long life, peace, and harmony. I greet you as my brother, Daly, and, Jessie, I welcome you as my sister. May you know eternal happiness."

"It's going to be very, very small," Daly said. "Please come."

"I have wronged you both," she said and hung up.

She sat with the shades drawn for a week, hardly breathing, until the day of the wedding came and passed. There was nothing on the radio about a catastrophe in Oakland; she crept out after dark to discover St. Agnes still stood and then she took a cab to the cathedral and in the moonlight it shone as sturdily as ever. She went to Mass the next morning, conducted by a very real Father Farrell, and afterward Robinson Street lay in its quiet summer somnolence as if Gloria Scone had never sat in a car with her and projected her reckless will on the shapeless cobblestones and ivy-covered church.

"You know," Daly said to Jessie on their wedding night, "I was thinking, maybe it's right for us to go to Ireland. Call it a honeymoon. I'm never going to be any better of heart than now."

She took his hand. "What changed your mind?"

"I think it's a good life," Daly said.

"It never was me who wouldn't travel with you," she said.

Outside Jessie's house, as Daly looked out a window later that night, unable to sleep, the trolleys had stopped running. The lights were out in office buildings, restaurants, and stores. The city was dark and broad and empty around him; he still thought he was himself at his best at such a time when everything closed down, nothing to be said, no one to be rescued. He could not help, he could not, for quiet was in him and not injustice raging to be cured, hurt anyone. He pulled the bedclothes around Jessie and himself.

Brenda Brogan woke two nights after the wedding of Jessie and Daly Racklin from a deep dream of when the house had been filled with brothers and sisters and thought that one of them, perhaps Silk, was in some trouble. Something had pursued her in a dream; waking, she feared, as she had many times, that there was a menace to one of them somewhere and she thought in panic of the family, and remembered they were gone from Robinson now, and then of the old aunt in the next room, and worried it may have been she who cried out for help. She tried to sit up in bed to slide on her slippers, but the waves of physical desolation that held her were too complete, and, before she died, she was only able to utter, "Aunt Flora."

The aunt did not find her until morning and was more baffled than terrified that it had been young Brenda who had died and not she; Flora dialed the number at the Montefiore and sat to wait for an ambulance. When the medics came to take the body, the old lady touched one's arm as he carried the stretcher, wanting someone to know, and said, "It should have been me. This mistake took the wrong person."

A light rain fell, and Aunt Flora, who followed the stretcher and had planned to go in the ambulance wherever the medics were taking Brenda, was gently accompanied back into the house by a young man who held an umbrella over here. She let herself be led in the house.

"But what will I do here without Brenda?" she asked.

At her wake in the old Brogan house the lamentations were sincere, Daly thought, an old-fashioned loving daughter, sister, friend, neighbor, reflections of her form in an old drape, a beloved family couch cushion stating "Niagara Falls" with us now where there had once been a woman. Particularly stricken was Aunt Flora, the closest connection to the departed woman, who could not comprehend the grim silence that hung over things where Brenda had been.

"But where will I go?" she asked virtual strangers.

No one could answer her. She asked the same question of the next person who fell to her vision, wandering from room to room—looking, it might be supposed, for Brenda Brogan, who had held answers for most of her dilemmas for years past. The sad thought lay on the assembly, even those who did not speak to each other from feuds that extended back decades, that while there many fine places, sound Catholic institutions of compassion and generosity, the gathering on Robinson had the feel of a funeral for old Aunt Flora, too. Many in the rooms, say the best about the well-kept Catholic old-age home as one might, considered sending one of their own there a defeat.

"She was the sister closest in age to me," Silk said, putting his arm around Daly. "Part of me, the best part, goes with her, never to see sunlight again."

"She touched us all," Daly said, "the last Brogan on Robinson, the last in Oakland."

"I thought she'd be the last of us to go," Silk said. "She was the one held what we were together. We're gone now, feathers on the wind. The house ain't nothing but brick and stone, eight of us born under this roof, a mother and father died here. It's nothing but a house, might as well let Pitt put up portable outhouses for the football team."

"Not while one of us lives will the memory of the place die," Daly said.

"Look at them," Silk said, pointing out his brothers and sisters, cousins, nephews, and nieces, "scared all of them that someone will foist Aunt Flora on them like an old pile of laundry on their doorstep. Weeping for Brenda and dodging looking me in the eye for worry about the old lady."

Jessie said, "We'll take her. We have plenty of room and she'll keep me company through the day while Daly is out doing good deeds."

"Don't let your good heart overwhelm you, Jessie," Silk said. "In my state I'm hearing your words and I'm not listening for sense. What will you do with an old lady, you and Daly freshly married?"

"We can do it, can't we, Daly?"

Daly said, "Jessie."

"Daly," Silk said, "it's your common sense I admire. Restrain your wife's kindness. She'll be giving away her wedding ring next."

Youth lasted a long time in those years on Robinson Street. It was here now with him, Daly thought, at the end—while he was here in this familiar place. Daly felt as he walked home with Jessie, his failing heart pumping vodka and dying memories, that the golden time of summers ripe and green and winters white with stark shadow on the snow would be his last good memory in the final minutes when the doctor's diagnosis fell true. Nothing more had been said that evening, the soft summer night falling on the people leaving the house on Robinson, and Jessie did not speak to Daly about Aunt Flora, but Silk called the next night.

"Daly, I take you to be a man of your word, and I'm a man who keeps a promise," Silk said. "And I intend to honor your whimsy, even though it was probably no more than a passing thought."

"What whimsy was that? I'm ankle-deep in funny ideas."

"A wake in the Brogan house on Robinson when Right Rack-lin ascends the golden stairs."

"I'll die tomorrow if I thought you meant it."

"What if I was to say to you the Brogan family wanted to give you a wedding gift? What if I was to say it was our old shanty of a house on Robinson?"

"I'd say, Silk, it was one head blow too many from the days you used to knock out guys thirty pounds heavier than you."

Silk had called all his brothers and sisters, each of whom by will owned a portion of the house on Robinson—some not speaking to each other for a very long time. None of them really wanted the house and the paltry sum it might bring divided seven ways.

"You could sell Jessie's house," Silk said, "and move yourself back to Robinson if that's your fancy or burn the place down for kindling. It's yours, you want it. My brothers and sisters say the cash involved ain't worth the torture of talking to each other, even through a lawyer. It's not all of them, of course, only Ben and Margaret, and it's mostly the husbands and wives. They want done with it."

Daly said, "Excuse me."

He put his hand over the receiver and said to Jessie, "Silk wants us to take the Brogan house, a wedding gift. Can I tell him—it's the least we can do—we'll let Aunt Flora live with us."

"I don't want to tend no old lady!" she said. "I'm old myself. I need someone to tend me. I wasn't born to be a nursemaid to a crotchety old lady." She nodded, laughing, clapping her hands once. "Say yes, Daly, say yes! or I'll burn this house down."

Silk and Daly shook hands the next day and Daly drew up the papers; it was agreed he and Jessie would take possession of the old house as soon as possible and Aunt Flora, too.

"You remember what Aunt Flora said?" Daly asked as they saluted each other at the Metropole. "I always did fancy her."

"It's not the best deal you ever made, Right," Silk said, "my brothers and sisters would have kicked in a thousand dollars more apiece to be rid of Aunt Flora with the house. But a deal's a deal. Say, O'Malley, you still purveying better drinks here?"

The bartender said, "Have one on me, gentlemen. I'm holding open house tonight for celebrities. Looking to the future, I'm building a better-class clientele."

He put out two white wines.

Eventually, when it was observed Ruth Marie was not responding to the telephone, her friends came unannounced in singles or pairs, to inquire about what had happened, Caitlin to apologize, the others to ask what had they done. Only after repeated ringing of her front doorbell did she answer, seemingly solitary—but really lost in wonders they would never know—emerging to sit on the back porch, lost in her thoughts. She made no pretense she was listening to them, to anything but the sound of the annual roses growing in her yard, the electricity overhead humming in the telephone wires between the poles on Robinson. To feign interest in what they said would deceive them, and then not to answer would be rude or might appear indifferent. She was neither. She cared, but only now had she allowed them to join the general misery of the world she felt in every cell in her soul and body.

They came in a group one Saturday night as if nothing had changed, jovial and joking, pretending the old days were not gone forever. They surrounded her on the back porch, blocking her from leaving, and they talked about themselves and remembered the departed and teachers they had shared and times past. She looked up at the stars—it was a fair night—and they talked until well past ten, she traveling to distant places.

Finally, Inez turned to her. "There isn't something, it isn't something, is it something we did to make you change, Ruth Marie?"

She stood and she might as well have been speaking to one bright, remote star overhead, so foreign her voice: "I have nothing further to say."

She entered her house, and they heard her lock from inside the kitchen the door to the back porch. They sat for a few minutes more, then filed through the yard around the house back out to the street and home, knowing they would never return.

Sitting on her porches on Ward, Ruth Marie thought, her sense of humor as keen as ever, They will soon send painters to my porches, and they will paint over me, too, like the trellis or the flooring or these false old pillars or the porch swing. She laughed hard to herself, thinking, That's a good one.

But Botkar came to her in dreams.

He bent and lifted her and held her with his hands under her armpits above him. His arms were stiff and unwavering. She looked down at him in terror. "What are you doing?" she asked. "Stop it, I'll call the police. You can't do this to me."

He shook her gently, then harder. He shook her until her head rolled.

" 'See, Michael,' " he said, breathing hard. " 'See your wife.' "

"I'll call the police—I'll scream."

"Scream."

He pushed the tea and sugar pot on the floor, spoons clattering, the cup breaking, and, still holding her with one hand, this time clutching her at the neck of her bathrobe, he tore off the robe with his other hand. He ripped down the front of the nightgown and caught it and threw it on the floor. She wore underpants and he tore them off.

"Please," she sobbed.

"This is what you want, I give you it."

He pushed her back on the kitchen table and mounted her. As he entered her, he said, "So I give you what you want. I say to Michael, 'She want this, but she ask for something else, Michael. Okay, I give her what she don't ask.' "

"Dear God," she said, "stop. Make him stop."

He imitated her voice: " 'God, you listen!' "

He finished quickly, and she slid from the table and lay hurt on the floor. Something had cut her face and it bled slightly. He went to the kitchen sink and poured Palmolive soap on his hands and washed them, talking softly to himself. "Michael, you better off now than down here, she come up to a man's room. I kill a woman like that, Michael."

When she woke from the dream, Ruth Marie found she lay on the floor of her bedroom.

She lay for an hour on the floor covered with her robe, then she slowly stood and showered and came downstairs and took the clothes she had been wearing that day and carried them down to the cellar. She burned them all in her furnace, and she returned to the kitchen and began to scrub the table, but after a while she knew it would never be clean enough. She took a pliers and dismantled the metal legs. She put the red formica tabletop and the legs into a pile in front of the house. In time, she did not know if it was a dream of Botkar, any of it, or whether none of it had happened. But she waited nights, trembling in bed, for him to return.

Lost, she thought, as all the truly great immortal souls were, hurt and neglected, deceived and buried in their own time by the traffic of inconsequential people, the woman who asked only to be a servant to the poor of spirit, rocked on her porch, forgotten by all except future historians who would examine her remarkable life.

They would know.

Father Farrell told Daly he would say good-bye to the parish in a sermon on Sunday at St. Agnes, then slip away on Monday. Was Daly's old Chevy in any condition to take him out to the airport?

"The car will rise to the occasion, Father."

Daly waited outside for the priest on Monday. Inside the school tears and murmurs, sighs and more tears. The curtain falls, Daly thought. While two nuns stood on the steps of the school, Daly went for Father's suitcase on the landing. He could barely lift it. One nun called, "We'll pray," as Daly and Father Farrell walked toward the car.

"God be with you," Father Farrell said, and seated himself in the Chevy. "You see, Right, I'm a humble man," he said, "stooping to ride in this rattletrap. I'm hardy, Daly, but I should warn you, these springs coming up in the front seat would kill an ordinary man."

The Chevy sent sounds of tin cascading into the afternoon, bolts loose, hubcaps jiggling, bumper askew, doors not quite closing.

"Excuse me," Daly asked. "Father, what do you have in that suitcase? Are you taking burglar tools to Arizona?"

"Some rocks," Father Farrell said. "A brick from the school building. Another chip from the gymnasium downstairs. Our church is founded on a rock, St. Peter assures us. Beautiful and holy things with us, rocks. They fell into bad reputation about the time people started to mark the age of the earth by the etchings on rocks. Rocks became the measurement of what looked like our misconceptions about the world. Rocks proved us wrong, it was said, the earth was older than we thought. But excuse me, I'm falling into an occupational hazard, Daly. I talk too much. What's on your mind?"

"I'm wondering about my father."

"You know there's another opinion that's going to count more than yours or mine and that one takes all the evidence into account. There are people disposed to hear bad about him and everyone else, and fortunately they don't do the final judging."

"I think I know what you mean."

"People say vile things about St. Augustine. The question is, on total—accounts we don't know written in his ledger—was his passage good or bad?"

"I heard some bad things about my father, a number of bad things."

"I heard good things myself. I think there are people who knew him, don't give a damn about his weaknesses. Maybe he wasn't perfect."

"My sister, Ruth Marie, is the saint, she told me so. What if my father was a thief and a cheat?"

"I'm not the person to ask questions about the Racklin family, or anybody else for that matter, I'm not one of your original thinkers. But if your sister would like it I'll think of her as saintly. As for your father, I'll assume your question is hypothetical, preparing yourself for your graduation from seminary, but if it's a question about a real man, a substantial difference, my answer is easy: Let him rest. This is not a brilliant observation, but I'm only a priest from St. Agnes on the corner of Fifth and Robinson Street."

At the airport Daly carried one suitcase and the cabdriver another heavy suitcase into the lobby where a porter took it. The porter looked up. "What's in here, Father?" he asked.

"Rocks."

Daly and the priest shook hands and stood looking at each other.

"Father, I swear I hate to see you go. This leaves me the ugliest man in Oakland."

"You're a good lad, Daly," the priest said, and, because it knew it would please Daly, Father Farrell said, "You're a credit to your father," and turned and walked into the terminal.

Once aloft, the clouds comforted him, the sunshine on them. It's inadequate to think, he thought, that God is merely in the atoms of sun and the clouds: He's there in what looks like the meaningless space between the clouds and the sun millions of miles away, in me as delicate as the host. And remembered with a start Michelle Shortall, her spirit calling for a release to some easier form: after the torment, wings of fire and gauze forever. Now a disease crept through Michelle's fingers, into her arms, past her toes into her legs: It turned her thighs to stone and her shoulders and her neck, reaching in its granitelike turbulence toward her heart. But—it was a consolation to him—it would be all its inexorable passage in her body never touch her soul. Father Farrell put on his seat belt at the landing sign. Hardness, bitter with cruelty, as tenacious as concrete, was always eating at the soul of the world through all of human history but it was destined never to reach it, and that was no news.

Terrence Carney came in to the Number Four Station to give himself up. He had heard that a certain friend of his had confessed to robbing a house on Coltart Street, and, as Terrence knew the owner of the house, Daly Racklin, he had assumed he would be implicated. Captain Jimmy Carr of the Number Four knew on sight Terrence had conceived the robbery. He could not swear it, of course, but the boy seemed to be wearing a belt of Daly's he remembered.

"Terrence, if this is a confession, you might want a lawyer present."

"How about my uncle Daly?"

"The one whose house you robbed?"

"It wasn't me. My confession is it was Eddie Larson, not me."

"Then, as a citizen, you want to swear out an information on Larson?"

"Did he confess on me?"

"I'm not familiar with the case."

Daly was called, and Jimmy Carr said there was no doubt in his mind Terrence Carney and probably Larson had looted Daly's house.

"Jimmy, I'm gone from there," Daly said. "Saved me the trouble of carting away the old junk. Find some way to let him go. The Carney family's about to go into collective nervous breakdown, all of them on the edge."

"He says if the other guy turned him in he wants you to represent him."

"Tell him it's against the law, conflict of interest."

It was found that there was an outstanding warrant on young Carney. He had been arrested for assault on the north side. In selling certain watches he claimed were stolen he had become angry when a man in a bar hadn't bought one for seven dollars that had the original sixty-dollar price sticker on it. Terrence himself believed the dollar watches sold somewhere for sixty dollars; he became enraged that the man did not trust him. He hit the man with the bottle from a display of Pabst Blue Ribbon beer. He had not made his court appearance and a bench warrant had been issued.

Terrence called his mother to tell her to get Uncle Daly fast to get him out of jail one more time. But in his haste to explain the complicated reason he had come up to Number Four in the first place he intertwined his north-side crime with the looting of Daly Racklin's house. His mother, who had it in for Daly anyhow, considering him acting arrogant to her and the family's problems, not at all a loyal friend of her late husband's, said this was the last straw from Mr. Daly Racklin and his insults.

Mrs. Alice Carney revealed her plans to her brother Ernie, retired from years of selling fine business stationery in Cleveland and visiting the family in Pittsburgh, when she received the news of what seemed to be Daly Racklin's treachery at the Number Four Police Station. She had called back there and spoken to Terrence himself. She danced away from the phone. "Ernie," she said, "that

Racklin will defame us no further: The man is on a train out of town after this slander."

Ernie McIlroy had retired from the selling line a year earlier. He found life in his sister's house, even on short acquaintance, not all perfume. He seldom saw her not knowing her rights: As a student of character, a stationery salesman does learn certain things; he thought the alleged attack on the family name at Number Four had left her more purposeful than he had seen her for years. There was a quickness to her walk, a tilt to her head.

Ernie listened to her for hours. She saw unfairness to herself when it rained in Oakland and she heard there had been no showers in East Liberty.

"I know just the man to handle this for us," Mrs. Carney said. "Do you remember hearing one Easter the lawyer was pushed into a fountain and held there by a man who said he had ruined his life? It was a divorce case. The papers said it was the third attempt on the lawyer's life by a client. This certain person also tried to shoot the lawyer in court. The man hates lawyers, and Daly Racklin is a lawyer or I'm a gorilla. This man is Beverly Nolan's cousin, Beverly, the real-estate lady, and she said to me, in passing, 'You ever need a rat terrier, Alice, there's always my cousin, Mole Caldecott,' and I think the moment has come.

"I asked, 'What would I ever need a person like him for?' But today my son has been infringed on, Ern, and I see my duty."

"Alice, you want to do this?" Ernie asked. "Lawsuits, such?"

"As God is my witness," Mrs. Carney said. "I want to see justice done. I'm not going to have Caldecott kill Racklin, just tell him to respect other people's rights. Scare him."

She gave Caldecott three hundred dollars, a gift from Terrence for a deal he had brought off in selling the contents of an estate down in Oakland entrusted to him; and Caldecott, who had once looked like a mole, his head deep in his shoulders, but growing older looked like a bear as his head became smaller and his face receded behind his nose, went to find Daly. The truth was, as even Mrs. Carney knew, Mole Caldecott's ferocious conduct was long in the past. Her hired enforcer, it turned out, was close to seventy-five years old.

She and her brother, Ernie, both feared he might do himself harm in trying to frighten Daly.

But it did not come to that. When Caldecott took the trolley down to Coltart Street, confusing Daly's address in the telephone book, he found the house empty. He decided Terrence, in jail waiting for Daly to bond him, would know where he could find Racklin.

It happened that at the time Caldecott arrived at the jail Daly Racklin was entering the old stone building on Forbes, once more to save young Carney. But Racklin stopped to talk to Jimmy Carr on the sidewalk, accept congratulations on his wedding, talk over places to go in Ireland, to work in some compassion for Terrence. Seeing them, and not too accurately either, given his advanced years, Mole Caldecott convinced himself that Captain Carr was Daly Racklin. He growled in his throat. He remembered how the strongest men would retreat at his appearance; and he did hate lawyers.

Daly entered the building, and Mole walked up to Captain Carr, who was in civilian clothes, and said, "You're not much, are you, without the law to back up all your lies?"

Jimmy Carr said, "Is there something you want, old-timer?"

Mole wore a heavy black turtleneck sweater, and he took Jimmy Carr's arm. "How'd you like to fight fair and square, shyster? This ain't an innocent boy you're railroading."

Carr took the old man's arm, not too forcefully, and pushed it up behind his back. He motioned to a cop in the doorway. "Will you please see what this gentleman wants?" he said. "Not out here, for God's sake, he may die on the sidewalk in front of witnesses who will say we killed him."

Recognizing his error, Caldecott moaned, "It was an error, an honest mistake."

"Well, who the hell did you think you were threatening on the sidewalk?"

"I thought this tall gent here on the sidewalk was my brother. It's a family way we have of talking to each other. No serious harm intended. Check it out, you'll see I have a tall brother."

Terrence was released on Daly's recognizance and Caldecott spent the night in jail.

Daly called Mrs. Carney to give her the good news, her boy was free, and was delighted and puzzled when she cried, "Thank God you're alive, Daly, thank God. You don't know how good it is to hear your voice. Who says there ain't no God—here you are among us, the finest man I ever knew."

Daly was touched. Not hearing from any of the Carneys in his recent hospital stay, he had expected no more from them except they, one or two of them anyhow, rob his house in his absence. But here was Mrs. Carney herself, expressing herself in simple love for him, a testimonial to how little we understand other people.

As Daly, Jessie, and Tommy packed for Ireland, the phone rang and it was Gloria Scone.

"Where are you?" Daly asked, not knowing whether to be pleased or anxious.

"Connecticut, but there with you."

"Well," he said. The distance was sufficient.

"Daly, there's trouble."

"In the world generally or something specific?"

"The world, of course, but you're in trouble. And Ruth Marie."

"Nothing new in either case."

"She won't answer the phone."

"She will one day, it's her life's blood."

"Do you understand that you're part of an on-going battle, that this trouble you're in began before you were born? Can you imagine giant spaceships fighting over whether you'll be a person fulfilled or a person lost? That's what happens. I think your pattern is becoming apparent."

"Why?"

"Why what?"

"Why are spaceships fighting over me before I was born?"

"They fight over everybody, Daly, not just you. And they are not spaceships—it's just the closest words I can use to describe these armadas out there battling over our destiny."

"I feel the same way I always did, no more, no less troubled."

"It's Jessie. She's a symbol of your problems. Daly, you must believe in symbols, they're our guides."

"I'm packing now, Gloria, may I say good-bye."

"Where are you going?"

"Ireland."

"Daly, that's a mistake. I don't feel it's right."

"Good-bye."

"Wait! Daly, I forgive you marrying Jessie. It won't last. Remember, I'm here for you."

"Good-bye."

Downstairs in the kitchen, making breakfast, Tommy Guignan faced a problem.

"I didn't mean to buy cracked eggs last week," he said. "Uncle Daly, they were just there."

"It's nothing big, forget the little things."

"It's big," the boy said. "I let you and Aunt Jessie down."

"You see, Tom, when you go to the supermarket to buy eggs you have to open up the carton like this, to see if any of the eggs are cracked. You can't eat them if they're cracked."

"Why would they put cracked eggs in there if people can't eat them?"

"It could be an accident," Jessie said. "Maybe the store didn't mean it, they don't want to sell people cracked eggs."

"But maybe they do," Daly said, "and that's why you have to check. Whether they mean it or not you can't eat cracked eggs."

Tom nodded his head vigorously. "It makes a lot of sense to me, Mr. Racklin," he said.

Daly went upstairs to finish packing. From the landing he looked down to the first floor and saw Jessie in an apron with large apples sewn on, and Tommy was wearing an apron, too, that read "Kiss Me I'm Irish." The rooms were lit with lamp light, and Jessie and Tommy moved into the light and then shadows. They talked to each other, but he could not hear what they were saying. A radio played softly downstairs. He leaned on a small railing on the landing observing them both as they walked around Jessie's first floor, in the house that would soon be sold to accommodate Daly's return to Oakland. There had been little discussion on the subject. They were a family, each in place. He sighed with the monumental rightness of the accidents that had brought the three of them together.

This minute downstairs, in relaxed certainty, comfort lay his cracked-egg facsimile of a family: blind Jessie worth any pains to comfort and restore, and unhatched Tom Guignan. He breathed in deeply, enjoying the waiting for their traveling across an ocean together.

Arriving in Ireland, at the customs office the man there, checking his passport, had said, "Well, Racklin, coming over to see a few cousins and aunts?"

Not sure how direct the man meant to be, Daly said, "No, there are none of us left. A brother abroad in America and a sister in Pittsburgh, and that's the Racklins in the world."

"There's plenty here will adopt you, poor orphan," the man said.

A phenomenon not easy to describe: Everywhere people looked like people on Forbes or in New York, Irish surely, but not exactly the real thing to Daly even though a man could hardly be more Irish than one who strolled Dublin's streets. Still, the customs man looked like Vanish Hagen, and the doorman at the hotel said, "God bless you," to Daly and Jessie, looking like old Doyle who had once been a part-time bartender at the Ancient Order of Hibernians in its loft on Oakland Avenue. Everywhere there were replicas of the giants left behind in Pittsburgh, some now of blessed memory, some as drunk as skunks this very moment in Lasek's, Edward's, or Gustine's, others, men and women walking out of St. Agnes's after Mass, faces lit with the eternal truth, women who could have been twin to Inez, Ruth Marie, Silk or the late Brenda Brogan. It was this once again: The truth of himself lay in those ragged streets of fading delights and regrets. There were no substitutes anywhere, even in the home country that had spawned them all.

Listening on a tour of an old castle to the guide tell of the history under their feet, Daly was gripped by the tapestries, embraced in a long warm afternoon by carpets of unique and bold configurations, and amazed by the presentness of the pictures on the wall. There stood a family picture of men and women, assembled in confidence by the portrait painter, representing them strong as they stood, to perhaps die one day, reluctantly, this moment capturing their sense of worth and continuity.

"All killed by Oliver Cromwell," the guide said, and Daly felt tears in his eyes at the lost young men and women in the portrait. And subdued.

Talk here and talk there is what kept us afloat in bad seas. Talk was all that mattered, Daly thought, a refuge and a redemption. It was us with our talk against all the facts that gave us our dreams of heroism and then the truth of it beyond talk, from the cops at the Number Four Police Station on Forbes to the gates of heaven open only to any brave or capable enough to present our side of the case. We were an island of voices rising even in Pittsburgh, Daly thought, as green as the home base thousands of miles away but here verdant with our memory and green with not knowing the odds against us.

All true, their history and his, their sorrow and his: but not the part of his mind owned by the Oakland streets, by snowfalls over his knees and plowing through it drunkenly home with Silk and the late Owney and stumbling, all having been trapped a long night in the Irish Club and drinking away youth and screaming pleasure at the snow. Ireland's terrible history was his, but days on the streets of his youth were in the blood, and history was not only a long-ago recitation of great sorrows and joys and accomplishments, but his mother's face lit on her Robinson Street porch by the late sun in spring.

In a month, as the leaves were turning brown on the few last trees on the hill where he'd been born and where now he knew he'd die happily, Daly and Jessie returned from Ireland and moved with Tommy into the old Brogan house on Robinson Street.

Silk's old aunt was quiet, unobtrusive: With the passing of Brenda, her favorite niece, perhaps finally the whole long line of Brogans who had slipped their mortal coils became more real to her, and with that the realization of her own precarious position. Not that she feared joining them; it was not knowing what to plan for dinner for Mr. and Mrs. Racklin and the boy and herself or who exactly to think of from her past lovingly, as each lengthy memory might be her last—Brenda, Margaret, Richard, Billy, Ben, or Mary. To which one would she be bidding farewell at the moment the sword fell? In shoes made silent by thought, she walked around the house, cheerful, but moody with obligation.

Uncle Finnerty died, and the day of his funeral was quick with yellow and soft browns in the soil of the Cavalry Cemetery. There were few people in attendance. He was an old man and he had outlived almost everyone who remembered him. The sky was very blue and the trees still had enough leaves to make sharp, rustling sounds. Not a man given to attentiveness to his surroundings, Uncle Finnerty would find no great discomfort were he alive in the wideness of the sky over him: bustle, bombast, and dreams of talk being all for him, and then more talk for dessert. What fantasies in unspoken words had entertained him as he lay months in a coma, the genetic spokesman for everything that passed from his brain down to his tongue? But unable to talk, perhaps Finnerty had one last good long monologue before his breath faltered and ran down like the fine voice he had once been to permanent quiet and then there was only death remaining. No tears here. It had been a long life and finished, sanded at its edges and complete.

After the burial, Daly walked alone over to where Colleen lay buried. Father Farrell had once said, in speaking of tombs and gravestones and burial sites: "Wherever our people are, Daly, their souls or whatever exists after their bodies, I can assure you they're not under the ground in that spot."

Still, the grave evoked the dead girl for him. And how death always, no matter how complete in its finality, always ended in misunderstanding: no voice without at least one more song to sing, another apple to eat, a door to open for something bright that might lie on the other side.

"Good-bye," he said to Colleen. "There's a lot I don't understand."

Silk came to visit Aunt Flora twice a week. His romance in Squirrel Hill had slowed to inconsequentiality, and he did not seem unhappy. He confessed he still loved Armelia for all her shenanigans, from running with men to outrageous displays of wild, public conduct. Never to live with her again: but the greater part of wisdom here, he said, was to welcome the good when it came in memories, and let slip the bad like an escaped child's balloon into the clouds when the real Armelia with all her faults intruded on kind thoughts of her. She had left him and another woman had dissipated into ordinariness and now there was before him the drawing up of the chair to the fireplace for whatever warmth there still might be in the life remaining.

"It ain't so bad, is it, Daly?" he asked one day. "Once you know how bad it really is."

"Not so bad."

One day Daly and Silk took a walk around the grounds at Pitt and on impulse walked through the revolving glass doors on the ground floor, strolling inside the cathedral of learning to sit on the benches and watch the students and faculty in the section called Commons Room. Daly knew the place from outside. As boys they had hung around the courtyards hoping to attract sex-crazed young women with no morals who had come here to do degenerate things with local boys. Alas, these women, too, seemed soldiers in the cause of virginity that hung on the air in Daly's youth. A good education, free thinking, being non-Catholic in looseness of behavior, was no cause for the women acting any less removed from the great need and longing that consumed us all, Daly thought. There were lies and exaggerations and famous encounters, but, on the whole, Pitt might as well have been the Mt. Mercy Academy for all the unbridled lust showered on us by immoral, overeducated women with atheistical tendencies in their lovemaking. "Why are you laughing?" Silk asked.

"I'm thinking how this place used to represent money and sex and freedom to us," Daly said, "and never a damned thing about education."

"Never could get anything going over here," Silk said. "I'd get something under way and we'd walk in Schenley Park and talk, me pretending I was studying engineering here—bad right there, I should have said theater, put some glamour to me—and they'd start talking about their things. It wasn't that I didn't know what to say, it was I couldn't stand listening to them talking about nothing."

"It was over your head. You didn't get the fine points."

"It made no sense."

Daly laughed. "Don't say that too loud, they'll put us out. You'll be closing down a racket going for centuries, them what thinks they have the superiority handed to them by paying tuition, and them what believes the propaganda and accepts the crumbs from the table."

"They're dumb as I am most of them around here, and I can't think worse to say of them."

"Now you got the secret, only you not knowing that is what keeps them in place."

With its vaulted effects inside, the place did look like a religious building; and the students, harmless enough in their self-confidence, seemed to Daly beyond his grasp of comfort in oneself.

"Jesus," Silk said, as Daly was thinking the same thoughts, "look at them fucking parade like they own the stars and space."

"We hated them," Daly said. "Grew up thinking they were invaders."

"I never went to college, Daly. I still do."

"They're scared, too. Putting it on."

"They could fool me. I get the old feeling: Hey, shrimp, who died and left you foreman?"

They drank a cup of coffee in the Tuck Shop on the ground floor, and, standing, Silk said, "Well, I'll be a son of a bitch, it tastes just like coffee at the Sun Drugstore."

"Scared, Silk, same as you and me. Down at Duquesne they were a mystery to us. College felt like an extension of St. Agnes, priests, brothers, classes in religion, an extension of being good and virtuous—and good ain't easy, as we have come to know, right? Up here at Pitt, in our own neighborhood, we saw every day in Oakland what looked like an easy life passing us by. They came, they went here, and it was like money was no problem for anybody but us. But they were some of them mill worker's sons and daughters and bus drivers, some big-money types, too, but no matter, scared as us looking at them like kids with their noses pressed to the glass of the window in the candy store."

In the corridors young men in sunglasses and hair in cascades down their back and swept high in ringlets on their heads did not move to allow them to pass; young women in flowing garments to their ankles swept by them, lost to thought, every moment a pose and provocation. Some of their stares were glassy. Many wore dirty shirts. "Stop the war," a young man said to Daly.

Daly said, "Okay."

As they were leaving, a uniformed security guard, with a tall young man, large and beefy, probably a football player, stopped them at the revolving doors and asked, "Say there, you two have some identification?"

Daly, sensing Silk's posture, immediately took out his attorney-at-law card and handed it to the guard.

"Oh, sorry, Mr. Racklin, we have to be careful lately. There's an undesirable element drifts through here these days, and we don't know what's next."

"And what element might that be? These drug addicts in there asleep in the booths of the Tuck Shop?" Silk asked.

"Sure, them," the football player said, "but local hoodlums slipping in and stealing books and things."

"Stealing books!" Silk said.

"Sure, they sell them a tenth of the price. People leave books around carelessly and these vultures descend."

"You had me quaking," Silk said, "the thought of them locals stealing books to read."

"Have a good day, gentlemen," Daly said, pulling Silk though the glass doors.

Outside, Silk said, "Bad ankle and all I'd have chanced it. How'd you know I was this close?"

"I was that close. Well, Silk, we took a tour of the University of Pittsburgh and a forty-dollar-a-week guard and a football player on scholarship knew we were undesirables on sight. If the president of the school saw us, being of a more intellectual turn, he'd have dropped a bucket of water from the tenth floor down on us before we made it inside."

"I'll be by in a few days, Daly, to see Aunt Flora ain't disruptive."

"Another undesirable element. I'm keeping my eye on her."

As the weather became crisp to cold at the end of autumn, Daly took Jessie to the top of Robinson one late afternoon when the sky was streaked in silver and gray. Leaves were fragile under their feet at the cemetery, and Jessie raised her head to catch the scent of old vegetation and trees turning bare in the new wind. Daly, with the collar of his leather jacket turned up, took her elbow to ensure that she did not stumble over the exposed tree roots on the spare ground. "Some boys brought girls here in the old days. It never seemed right to me for those purposes. The place meant too much to me. I mean, there's got to be some souls of the dead hanging about. Do you think that's possible?"

"I promise not to shame the dead by making love to you," she said, holding him by the arm. "But why didn't you ever bring me here if it meant so much to you?"

"I thought it just a foolish place and myself foolish in it."

The fall lay thin in the air. Branches rattled sharply in a light wind. Each place now, Daly thought, renewed and revisited, was a triumph: It might as well all be the first time if you're able to be there and know that it was probably a precious last time.

Gently, he guided her to a mound of earth under a tree, putting down the blanket he had brought for her to sit on. The late light stayed in her auburn hair.

"I'm standing near a tombstone," he said. "And I'm going to throw my arms out and stick my chin in the air for the high Cs."

"The tenor's last aria, Act Three, *Don Giovanni.*"

"Close enough. Studied with the masters many a four in the morning at the Ancient Order of Hibernians, Division Nine."

She had never heard him sing full blast. "Will you shake the twigs on the trees?" she asked. "Are you going to cause the dead to wake?"

"Maybe roll over at the racket."

While she followed with her hand the melody, he sang to her and the cemetery "Ghost Riders in the Sky" and then "Prisoner of Love."

Jessie clapped her small, delicate hands when he was through, standing and shouting: "Bravissimo! Bravissimo! Encore. Encore."

"It was great? Great then? Good as Chickie Muldoon?"

"Better. Who is Chickie Muldoon?"

"One of the famous men of our time. So it's him and me finally great."

"Not great really, Daly, I don't want to give you false encouragement and then have you misled about your talent. Loud and flat at the same time and you could give a person a toothache listening too close. But bravo, darling, bravo. I loved every note."

"I'm a wonder, that's true: knowing in my soul how badly I maim the art, and still I sing? My next number is one I've never tried before—listen carefully. Here's my own version of 'Because of You.' "

Daly made his rounds, Mrs. Grain, Michelle, down to Ruth Marie's, where she would not open the door to him and discussed her with Irene, Belle, Inez, and Caitlin in the street when he could not hide from them.

He went to St. Agnes weekly for Mass and with Jessie to the Carnegie International Art Gallery on Forbes and described the paintings to her. They walked in the presence of the Manets and he stood with her before the water lilies and sought words to make real for her the immensity of the artist's vision, only flowers on a pond after all. He kept his voice low. He felt people listened as he talked, and he and she were not a show. She listened intently, nodding. She remembered the paintings. Explaining them, choosing the tone of voice, inflections, and exact phrases, he had never been closer to paint and brush and canvas as he bent low to murmur into Jessie's ear the lines and colors of genius. The paintings achieved an importance and he with them a size as he translated them into images in her mind. He kissed her often. She had moved him, as always, in their being together, into somehow feeling more important than he was without her.

She herself told him of paintings she had once seen, musicians she had heard. Afterward, they walked back down Forbes, the sun on the streetcar tracks and their faces. "I'm squinting now," he said. "The sunlight is bright on the streetcar tracks."

She said, "I remember such afternoons. I never thought I'd live them as happily again."

"You're happy in Oakland, with me?"

"Daly, you're a fool."

"This is not an original conception."

"Am I pretty?"

"Yes."

"Better than pretty?"

"Yes."

"You know, the last thing I miss is how I look."

"You are very beautiful."

"So are you."

Terrence Carney, despite Daly's efforts was sentenced for ninety days to Blaw Knox, the state prison across the river in Sharpsburg. The Carney family could take the bus there but insisted that Daly drive them on certain Sundays. Daly had a sense there was something to be said to Terrence, the words being close, but he could never form them. He supposed they were not there because there was nothing to say to Terrence Carney to persuade him that jail, now that he was of the right age, was inevitable given his view of the general stupidity of the world.

Daly persuaded Rest in Peace to drive out with him one Tuesday morning to Blaw Knox.

"There ought to be something to say to him, Doc," Daly said.

"Sure, here's rat poison. Mix it with 7-Up."

On a lazy autumn afternoon, the slow movements of the prisoners caused Daly to think he was witnessing a collection of employees on a public payroll; unhurried, the men walked about in their pale uniforms like men working on hourly salary. Give or take a couple of hours on the clock and no one the wiser, the foreman someone's brother-in-law. Jail was like things outside, only with high stone walls. There were rows of peonies planted around the main buildings and mounds of dirt where prisoners loaded wheelbarrows and took the dirt to another part of the yard. Prisoners openly stared at visitors, some smiling faintly as if they shared a joke with each other the visitors would never understand. It was Daly who looked away.

If Daly had not thought about it before being inside the walls at Blaw Knox, it came to him as he waited for Terrence. These were not in their expressions or evasive glances the tough guys out of the movies. Although they seemed like people off any sidewalk, on the whole these were runts and weasels, Terrence Carney redone many times, slipping around, sly, one up on strangers who hardly noticed them as they worked out their sure-to-fail plots.

The strutting bully in a tailor-made shirt and fitted pants seemed like someone from the outside momentarily transplanted here, normal. The prisoners Daly saw were mostly like the vague and dispirited half-mad drifters on Forbes, men who cleaned up saloons for drinks. But there were clean-handed men, too, averting their eyes, men once trusted and now found out, like Boyce Racklin in his prime but these men apprehended, with dossiers and court dockets to prove their fraud and deceit.

One man in rimless glasses, of the sort the first Right Racklin wore, walked past Doc and Daly where they stood waiting outside a dayroom. The man wore a blue-gray prison uniform but was small-boned, stooped, and carried a briefcase. He could have been a visiting attorney.

"Does that man look at all to you like my father?" Daly asked Doc.

"You get stranger the older you get. That man has con written all over him."

"You see nothing of the old man there?"

"Nothing at all. Con, that's all, carrying a briefcase. Your father's been gone ages."

Daly was thinking, No one ever told me prison was one step away from the crazy house in its putting together of schemers of unworkable daydreams and those who get caught, when Terrence appeared. Mary and Joseph, Daly thought, the boy belongs here, right at home with his phony smiles among all these guys smarter than everyone else.

"Terrence, you—you're not very smart, getting in here isn't easy. People have to work at it."

"You bet, Uncle Daly. I learned my lesson."

Daly and Doc left the boy with quick, awkward handshakes and walked down a narrow sidewalk back to the main gate. As he observed some of the men in the courtyard, Daly felt the presence of someone else there, hovering around the prisoners, glimpses of the non-prisoner in their foreheads, their eyes and mouths. It was the shadow of who they might have been, another person there, not a jailbird walking by restriction tightly two feet from the corridor walls inside the jail by order, bars their setting, eyes downcast and then the ferocious look upward to catch the observer unaware, an advantage. He sighed. Next, he would see the mark of the prisoner on the free men outside the massive stone walls of Blaw Knox.

Driving home, Daly said to Doc, "But Terrence didn't learn, he's conning me. He's lying. He has schemes and devices. He's like the rest of them, so brilliant they'll hang him one day."

Daly started to speak of his father—then stopped. The statute of limitations had long since run out for sorrow in the heart about misdeeds decades old. Yet, it persisted, always there, like a small cat mewing in an undiscovered place.

"Daly, unless you're planning to bring charges on your old man, drop the inquiries, okay?" Doc said, and Daly nodded and said, "He's gone."

Daly in his routines of keeping up with calamities called on Vanish Hagen and his sister; and Vanish's prognosis was good after his accident, but his sister had taken to talking to herself, sighing and waving her hands in gestures as if another person were there. It was a long discussion, interrupted when Daly came to their house to include him; the University of Pittsburgh in all its wicked forms pursued her. Daly agreed with everything she said, occasionally writing down on an envelope specific charges and claims, promising to look into legalities for her.

Every afternoon, he took a memorial stroll on the street where he'd been born, savoring a certain bush, the sunlight on one of the old pillars, now unpainted on the small porch of a family now cherished in remembrance. "Salvator Mundi" read the engraving over the entrance to St. Agnes. He drew some comfort from the three-petaled paper clovers pasted in the window of the grade school attached to the church, white paper Crayolaed green, drawn and traced and cut out with tiny scissors by hands as small as his had been when he had decorated the windows. But the entrance doors to the church needed painting. The red paint at the foot of the door had blistered and was peeling; no surer sign of Father Farrell's absence could come from the heavens. Big things had once seemed possible on these streets.

It had once been a dream to take a forgotten person and lift them from their sorrows, and the awful things in wait would be called to wait even longer. And I personally outright failed, he thought, a matter now of unpainted churches and people no more important than dust to each other.

Across from St. Agnes on Robinson there still stood on the hillside a looming four-storied house of terrible, black stone, and for generations children in the elementary school at St. Agnes were sure they knew where resided the evil they heard about from their priests and nuns. It waited. And, unhappily, there stood a funeral home directly next door to the school at St. Agnes's. The devil's house and a place of coffins and weeping mourners, a beloved church, and people walking up the hill as if they were not in a long play with all the elements complete within a child's stone throw, Daly thought, all of it was enough to send the mind into morbidities and portents of disaster unknown on streets not five minutes away.

Yet, he thought, there must be such omens of a bad end on every street where people congregate; but why credit the harbingers of bad tidings? They will hunt us down soon enough with their dark promise.

Arriving at the corner of DeSoto and Fifth one afternoon, the sun already falling in autumnal patterns through certain well-known trees on his route, Daly paused and thought about the Pitt Tavern across the street. It was a temptation: a cold beer as in the old days, each drink, every day now a tribute to itself and his new happiness, a well-loved porch on Robinson, a direction of a soft summer wind, sand soft to his feet even though the streets were still of concrete.

He remembered, like the memory of a friend he had never known well, the man who wanted something else than this. Forgive me, he said to himself, I did not know the second Right Racklin well, scarcely better than I did the first.

"Daly?"

He knew who it was before he turned, and when Gloria touched his arm he involuntarily pulled away. She was handsome in a colorful, sun-backed dress, young, her mouth full and her features composed. "Gloria, what brings you here?"

She smiled, her teeth white in the sunlight. "You called," she said.

"More mirrors!" he said, courageous. "I did not send for you. I do not intend to bring you to Pittsburgh. I have nothing to say to you. I am not single."

"Do you think things like that matter between people like us?"

"They do to me now."

"Can we go over to the bar on the corner for a few minutes? I want to talk to you."

"No."

"No?"

"I don't want to talk to you. I don't want to remember you in that bar. It's called the Pitt Tavern. I drank my first beer in there when I was sixteen. I smoked my first cigarette in there. I sat in there with my Uncle Finnerty. He bought me my first beer, an Iron City. Gloria, I am as big a fool as any of your people levitating and bringing down airplanes. Strange memories are precious to me. Perhaps it is stupid. I do not want to knock over the building blocks I've assembled since childhood."

"I understand perfectly."

"You don't. It's not for me a world of change, where everything is possible. With me it's maybe yes, maybe no. Maybe change, but mostly it's not to be devoutly prayed over. Okay, it comes, but nothing to be pursued all on its own. There's too many good things that go in the rush for something else. Sorry, I'm flawed. Goodbye. I'm not saying what I mean."

"Oh. And I love you for all of it, what you say so well and what you think you say badly. Really, can't we sit somewhere? Somewhere where you have no memories precious to you."

"No, there is no such place."

"Daly, I was called because you're in trouble."

"Thank you, good-bye."

"No, this is a last call."

"Then good-bye forever."

"Daly, this is good-bye forever. You are near your end."

"So are we are all."

"It was a cry in the night. 'Save him!' "

"I'm not worried about the future."

"That's it!" she said. "There is no future for you. Not on this plane of existence."

"I'll take my chances on what waits beyond this plane."

"It's not what you think it will be."

He turned and walked up DeSoto. He knew that if he turned he would find her standing watching him, perhaps offering him one more poignant wave. No future? When here he walked once more as he had a thousand times, his footsteps from the past trudging the hill, and on Saturday afternoons, this very street, thousands gathered to see football games at the Pitt Stadium, and Oakland boys, wondering at such cake and candy and colorful scarves and polished shoes, puzzled at the strangers descending from all over America on the very hill where they lived. Uninvited guests, but who would not feel, growing up here and ignored, that the sun still rose and fell on their importance in the scheme of things? He circled the block and strolled down Fifth again and had his cold beer in the Pitt Tavern, buying a beer for a man named Reilly who never left the bar while it was open.

"Always good seeing you, Right."

"Same, Reilly."

When postcards came from Father Farrell in Arizona, they were about rocks and occasionally a thoughtful quotation from St. Thomas or St. Augustine or a sober passage in the New Testament. And that was a point of sometime melancholy to Daly, a meditative spell that plagued him for days after the card with its profoundities. What was happening to the man and his research in geology out there in Arizona? He would write him about the recent logicality of his postcards.

Taking a customary small walk before breakfast, Daly looked up Robinson and there strode a man named Troubles he had thought long departed from Oakland, if not the earth generally.

He was called that because when he drank too much he told long, rambling stories about his mistreatment in Ireland at the hands of the mercenary police the English authorities had sent to keep order. He shook hands with the man elaborately.

"Daly, my son, stay indoors in this Indian summer, you'll die of heat out here on Robinson. It's the dehydration that does it every time."

"How old are you, Edgar? You look the same for decades."

"Eighty-two, and I swear, Daly, I feel thirty-nine most days, eighty-one anyhow."

"It's not dehydration is going to get me," Daly said.

"You ain't heard anything, have you, son?"

"Nothing I wasn't expecting."

They shook hands again, and the old man said, "Every morning I wake up I think of all the bastards I knew are six feet under and it gives me a lift better than my vitamins at breakfast. I drink a shot every morning with my eggs, Daly, and toast them bastards in hell, all gone and me prepared to start one step better than them, living yet, bowels good, eyesight same, liver chugging along like a little steamboat running white wine through the carburetor."

"Always a pleasure to see you," Daly said. "A man needs a little uplift."

"Watch yourself out here," Troubles said. "The streets is running with lunatics, more than usual, far greater percentage than I seen in my whole life."

"Where you going this morning in these precarious times?"

The old man pulled out a folded newspaper from his back pocket. "It says here," he said, "there's a restaurant opened on the north side and it's big and it don't say, but a place like that is going to need waiters and it's my estimate I take the streetcar downtown and get a transfer I can get there about eight o'clock, look the place over, and if I like what I see I'll give them the opportunity to put me on the payroll. I'll last two days until they notice I'm falling down as often as I'm standing up and they'll sack me, but it'll be two days' pay I wouldn't have otherwise."

"You're thinking all the time, you don't stop thinking."

"I didn't get to where I am in life without thinking, Right, it's my major strength. Watch out for the pimps, they'll turn you in fast as you can say 'Jack Frost.'"

"You raise my spirits."

"To tell you the truth, things ain't perfect with me, Right, but who cares to hear complaints? Bruises is the natural element of mankind."

Daly said, "A point well taken, Edgar."

"Smile, chin up, the bastards will never know you're sore and aching and crying and thinking three times a day you're done for and finished. But it ain't their business, right?"

A subject for discussion with Father Francis Farrell: Had he forgotten among his geological finds in Arizona that the first line of defense against the defeat by old age and impending catastrophe and the termination of all things lovable in being here was the laugh that came from the lungs and erupted in the throat and barked into the air with a glee at the same time innocently animal and free human spirit? Where lately was the cheering word from him, strong as midnight, bright as sun?

A young man has been studying Michelle from across the pew at St. Agnes. She is aware of his golden eyes on her as she receives the host. On this Sunday the interior of the church in its sea-green shadows and faces white as ghosts is able to charm her, to quiet and assure her that even as the stone eating her arms and legs and working its way to her heart with calculated evil is magic so is there good magic possible. The young man is dressed in white tennis shorts and a white T-shirt and his hair is as white-golden as his eyes. He is not from St. Agnes, not, Michelle knows, from this world. She looks away from him as she makes her way up the aisle, helped by an altar boy, moving side to side as much as making headway forward. It is known now she cannot walk as people understand the term. "Good morning, sweetheart," people say as she passes. "How nice to see you, Michelle." She makes her profound and grisly procession through them, nodding, saying a name here and there. She does not glance at the young man shining beneath a picture of Jesus at one of the stations of the cross for fear he will vanish, or think her rude, or, God knows, poke his tongue out at her in derision.

She is sure he is an angel, a healthy and wholesome angel, one fit for St. Agnes, a building where even as a child—before the bad times set in on her—there was a fairy quality, almost the miraculous in the elfin pillars and the pale beige walls with their curious, almost Oriental designs. She stumbles along; let the angel do what he will, she has a taxicab to catch. The cab comes for her every Sunday, takes her, leaves her on the sidewalk at St. Agnes—to be led inside—and comes for her later.

It is not a long distance she travels, a matter of a few blocks, but she cannot now make it from her front door to the sidewalk unaided. Once led inside her house by the taxi driver, she bumps her way to the kitchen for her Sunday tea; and there the young man is again in a self-contained glow that does not reflect on the kitchen cabinet, the floor, or the table and chairs. He is smiling and his golden eyes dance. He sits and clutches his shin, his knees bent up.

"I saw a fellow like you in the movies once," Michelle says. "I don't remember his name. He wasn't the star of the picture, you understand. He was a fellow that came on and I remembered him."

"I'm that fellow," he says, laughing as if Michelle is a great wit.

"I'm scared," she says. "Am I going to die? Is that your purpose here?"

He laughs again, harder than the first time. "You're a character,

Michelle," he says, just the way boys said it when she was young.

Bolder, she says, "Then what's your business here?"

"Came to see you."

"Come on, it's not a usual thing?"

"No, just came to see you."

"In the moving picture you were somebody's brother."

"I was if you say I was, I don't remember."

"Would you like some tea?"

This time he laughs until he is holding his sides.

"Tea?" he asks. "Michelle, you should have been on the stage. You have a way of saying things that makes me laugh. Don't do it. You have a gift, funny woman, funny, funny woman."

"My father said the same thing," Michelle says, "but after he died, no one said it."

"I could run circles around you," the young man says. His hair is combed straight back from his forehead and is piled high on his head; as it falls down the back of his head it curls in golden corkscrews, but pale. His eyes are blue to white and he smiles at her mischievously now, liking his own joke.

"I suppose you could," she says. "I'm a telephone pole these days. I don't move ten feet a day in any direction. You know, like a fireplug, but I'm not painted red."

"I could snap my fingers and jump four feet in the air, land on the floor and do a split," he says.

"Why'd do you want to do that?"

"To show off and make myself laugh."

"What's your name?"

"Tim."

"Tim?"

"I was kidding. Andrew."

"Andrew?"

"Don't believe that. Mark."

Michelle bumps her way down a dark corridor to the front door at the sound of a knock. Unless her eyes have gone mad as her brain, it is Daly Racklin, dressed in a leather jacket, the collar up against the wind. She blinks her eyes at him. "Is it the Right Rack-lin?" she asks.

He breathes hard. "I walked up from down below," he says. "Can I come in? It's cool out, we came back from a little vacation two weeks ago, and I've been thinking of you and the old days."

It takes her ten minutes to return to the kitchen. He walks with her slowly. "You know I'm married now, Jessie O'Brien," he says. "We're living in the Brogan house. You have to come visit us."

"I heard, I was happy for you. It's good you're on the street again. I think good things are going to happen for all of us. I'll make us tea. Kimberly is still in church. She's a great help to me, Daly."

They sit at the kitchen table, and he asks, "How are you feeling?"

"Not good," she says. "It's like I'm turning to ground."

He nods. There is something unsaid. "The ghost of my father," he starts.

"Father Farrell thought it was a hallucination, so I shut up about it."

"You don't believe it was a hallucination?" he asks.

"We'll never know," she says slyly. "I haven't seen him in a long while."

He drinks a cup of tea with her, and she asks him to jump rope for her again. He takes off his suit coat and loosens his tie. "I'll be a little slow getting started," he says. "Foolishness with my heart, I pay it no attention." The rope feels like silver in his hands; its sounds on the kitchen floor ring into the corners of the room, causing Michelle's face to start with each joyous slap-slap. He wants to tell her: Forget my father, he's not a ghost worth seeing. You're better than he is. But, seeing her good, pained face, he knows she'll outdo any ghost, glorious, sinful, proud, or taunting, who may come to her.

He sits at the kitchen table, worn with the jumping but exhilarated.

"Daly," she says, "I have to tell you something. I'm not as good as some people think I am. Aunt Maura used to call me an angel. Can I tell you something?"

Daly says, "If you want. You're a fine person."

"I'm almost not a virgin, Daly. Do you remember Shea Dinan's brother, Alfred? I almost let him. We were in the grass out there back of Mount Mercy, about fourteen, Daly, and I wanted to. I almost wasn't a virgin. Alfred didn't know what to do, and I couldn't help him. Do you remember him?"

Daly does. "Tall guy, thin."

"I wanted to," Michelle says, "that's the point. Fourteen years old. Do you promise you won't speak of it if I tell you something else? Maybe I'm being punished for it."

"Michelle," Daly says, "I'm not a priest."

"Okay, you promise. There was a little statue of a black missionary child in our fourth-grade class, and you had to put a penny into it and it'd nod and nod with every penny we pushed in. Well, the whole box, the little boy and the money was stolen, all the money going to go to African missionaries with it. Gerald Durgin was blamed and he confessed. Sister hit him on the knuckles with her ruler, hard, twenty times, but the statue and the little box with the boy were never found. You know why? Gerald Durgin didn't take it, I did. I took it and I never told anyone. It's been on my conscience all this time. I'm being punished. Do you think it's the devil? People used to say the devil lived in the old house on Robinson, across from St. Agnes, and we were picked out to be his favorites. He hid out here on our street, we kids said it. Do you think he's in me? Do you think he jumped down my throat when I yawned one day and that made me as bad as I am? I'm surely being punished, Daly."

"No," Daly says, "I know you're not being punished."

A dead cat on the doorsteps, ghostly howls about the sentinel house at the foot of Robinson place on Halloween—but the devil didn't show himself. It was just the Polish fellow who came out to shout something in his language to the boys hiding on the hillside. Daly knows now that goodness like Michelle's is the punishment.

She will suffer in this world because goodness is a magnet that draws all the accounting of sins in the hapless victim's imagination into itself.

He rises slowly from the table; he feels his rope-jumping in his knees but thus far, not that he hasn't earned it, no assault from his heart. He asks God to grant mercy to fools and knaves, too, calling down kindness for his father with the rest. At last, having seen the old man whole, there is nowhere to hide from his father in his many sides, loving the first Right Racklin as he did the rest of the sorry parade, now part of the crowd.

He ran over their faces in his mind: He expected to see them again at their best one day in eternity. He supposed all of them together might be a composite drawing of the face of God, perhaps his eyes. He would finally look without subtlety directly into the face, if all went well. He put his arm around her shoulder. He felt close to her. She'll never think I hold myself superior to her, he thought. It's her and me climbing the stairway to the stars. Being here and amusing her by jumping rope made him feel as if something had been accomplished. She occupied moments and territories that were part of much larger things: Any star removed from its constellation and the galaxies move inexorably to collapse.

"Stay longer next time," Michelle says. "Say hello to Jessie."

"Don't have funny ideas," he says. "We're all doing fine."

"I'm not really doing that well, Daly, honest."

"But you're here, we're talking."

"I guess."

"You guess? Do I look like a ghost to you? Of course, we're here."

"To tell you the truth, Daly, I'm not sure I'm here. This is all so bad."

He nods and takes her hand. "No one but you can understand what's going on," he says. "But I'll try, okay?"

She tries to speak but cannot. Her lips move, but there are no words. "I don't know myself, Daly," she says. "I don't know myself what's going on."

Within minutes after he left, she resumes her conversation with the apparition in tennis clothes. "Clark is my name," the spirit says. "Don't believe that."

Boldly, seizing her chance, Michelle asks, "Can you cure me, cause me to be well? Can you see to it I can jump rope and run— maybe less than that. Fix it so I can walk out to the porch, twirl around, and skip back into the parlor like once."

"You want *that?*" he asks.

He stares at her as if to discover the joke in it, and when she doesn't answer, he shakes his golden head in mock, comical disbelief, and puts his thumbs in his ears and wiggles his fingers.

"Stop that," she says, but he continues with his childish prankishness.

She stands with great effort and says, "If that's the way you're going to act, I'll call Daly Racklin right now and he'll put you out on the street," floundering in the direction of the telephone and realizing, after a long, few minutes, she was not moving at all, shaking and trapped. "Daly, I need you," she wailed.

Night had fallen outdoors. The skies overhead were clear and each star was bright and separate. Daly stopped. He thought he heard his name sounded in the dark. "Next it'll be a ghostly tapping on my shoulder to summon me to rectify the wrongs of the past, too," he thought. He did not move, listening. He heard only the creaking of tree branches. He heard 1968 passing and felt himself alive. The sidewalk reflected white in the pale moonlight as Daly walked to his home.

Evil and outrage and the sinister is so simple when you're young, he thought: There it was, or there it wasn't. Daly felt in every bone, his blood singing with it, that something of the good and simple from his moments with Michelle traveled with him and was spread like waves of sunlight in a cathedral window around his steps when he walked this sidewalk. Three cheers for the devil! Better to see him coming down the chimney or under the bed than looking in the mirror and beholding his familiar face. The closer you peered into the heart of things the more you saw it was our own fat, lonely Michelle who was the Ripley's Believe It or Not Girl Turning to Stone, call her evil or possessed, at the least a threat to the general tranquility and a tool of the devil. But who believed that after what the world had seen in its recent century?

He stopped again at the sound. Damn it! he thought. Someone's calling my name.

So there it lay. Given a choice of where to ply his trade, the devil had as many crafty hands to aid him these days as he ever had. He could put together more promising quarters, more wildly steaming with pride and far from Robinson. Why spend his time twisting up Michelle Shortall's stubby fingers until she couldn't hold a coconut-and-chocolate Giant Eagle cookie in them?

Daly caught his breath once and heard and saw nothing further.

When death came to him in the moonlight on the sidewalk, Daly felt no pain or turmoil, nothing of a preparation in it, thinking at that moment of Michelle Shortall and then oblivion fell on him. A child the next morning approaching the steps on Robinson leading to the school in St. Agnes saw him first and ran screaming into a classroom. "There's a man on the sidewalk." A maintenance man ran out to see what caused the uproar and nuns and a priest and a doctor were called, but no one thought the man on the sidewalk was alive. Later, there was a wake for him in the old Brogan home where he had lived for a short time; and many old people were there, his wife bewildered that Daly had actually died, but everyone, people who had known him for decades, assured her he had lived a good life and would have loved the wake, small, hot, crowded and the day tear-stained. Mrs. Grain brought a noodle casserole and her husband, in his wheelchair, sat quietly drinking a beer and accepting paper plates with potato salad on them. Syd Mahon, Silk Brogan, and Jack Longley, who had come up from Asheville, stood on the back porch drinking from a flask of Jack Daniels. No word spoken that night not heavy with remorse over the irreplaceable loss felt in the house.

Daly's sister fainted several times and his brother, Al, did not make it back to Pittsburgh for the funeral. Father Deane, the new priest at St. Agnes, offered the apologies of Father Farrell from Arizona, where he had stumbled down a small canyon and thrown out a hip very badly. Father Deane read a telegram from Father Farrell to the group, people on the fringes of the crowd in the living room asking others to be quiet for three minutes so they could hear the priest's words.

Doc, thinking he knew Daly fairly well, sipped a white wine, mostly pleased for his friend who had believed to a celebrated degree in the fraternity of all present and a few ghosts for good measure. All was in place here as best it could be, given the uncertainty of keeping count. No one from their island of concern and connection in Oakland, even absent, was left out of the imaginations of the unhappy company.

Later after the wake, as night settled in, Silk, Jimmy Carr, Syd, and Doc strolled down Fifth toward Oakland, someone suggesting a quiet toast to Daly might be in order.

Syd said, "Daly would have been proud of Tommy's son, Tom, there, wearing that 'Kiss Me I'm Irish' apron, running drinks like a pro to the thirsty."

"The truth is," Jimmy, in uniform, said, "Jessie says the minute he heard Daly was dead the boy ran out of the house like the hunters were after a creature in the forest. She found him hiding behind a tombstone on top of the hill, said with Daly gone he was dead himself. She told him that's no kind of talk. People go on for other people even when there's not much here for them."

"Can't argue with that," Doc said. "The sight of all you types ruining your lives with drink and women, when you find one drunk and unstable enough to want you, keeps me going. It's like the circus when I was a kid."

Silk said, 'I didn't see Michelle Shortall, the woman with the sickness in her bones. I guess I'll look in later tonight. I stopped up there before the funeral to see if I could give her a ride to church, but she was talking to somebody in the house, arguing, you know, loud like she was mad. I didn't catch none of it, but boy, she was mad. Maybe it was the kid who comes to clean was with her. I can't think of her missing Daly's funeral and wake. But she was shouting in good lungs up there this morning."

"You know that Bradley Grain, in the wheelchair," Syd said, "he drinks more than five times what an ordinary man can put away. And can't walk a step to get himself a drink, poor bastard! Every time somebody comes by to say hello, he says, 'Say, can you fetch me a beer?' He had young Tommy breaking records." He paused, then said, "Something on my mind . . . What did you make of Owney's wife showing up at the house like she come to haunt the place, white powder, a black dress, fingernails like a dragon lady? Daly's sister ran out the house when she saw her. I would have myself. She liked Daly, I know she did. Asked me for his number, when he was single of course."

"Lot of women admired Daly," Silk said.

"A small café, mamselle," Syd sang, "a rendezvous, mamselle."

Doc Pierce looked at the sky as he walked down Fifth toward Gustine's with Jimmy, Silk, and Syd and said, "It looks like rain, but I guess that's not going to mean a lot to Daly."